MAFIOSA PRINCESS REDEMPTION

LIZA MALLOY

CHAPTER 1

Giada

I jolted upright at the sound of my name, blinking as I struggled to orient myself. Somehow, I'd managed to fall asleep. I was in the great room of my own house, seated on the oversized, cream sectional. Beyond the windows, the world was pitch black. A fire glowed in the gas fireplace, offering serene lighting, but little to no heat.

Someone shifted beside me. I turned, hoping against the odds to see Luca, but it was Thomas. He offered a tight smile, and I realized I'd trapped him there for god-knows how long, probably drooling all over his shoulder.

"Sorry," I mumbled, rubbing my eyes. How had I fallen asleep? A handful of people still filled the house—all men, of course. They weren't exactly loud, but they were talking.

Alessio crouched down in front of me, gripping my hands like I was a child. "Come on, princess, let's get you to bed."

The idea of bed was appealing, but I'd already slept through too much. If Alessio was back, Luca must be, too. "Where's Luca?" I croaked.

"He's with his mom. I think he'll stay there tonight."

I shifted to stand. "I'll get some things packed. I should be with him."

"Camilla wants just Luca for now, okay? I'm sorry. She's—"

I shook my head. Camilla had to be in shock. She'd just lost her husband. Of course she wanted to mourn him alone with her son.

"Why aren't you with him?" I asked Alessio. Luca needed one of us. If Camilla didn't want me there, at least Alessio should be by Luca's side.

Alessio tugged me to my feet. "Camilla just wants Luca," he repeated. "And Luca wanted me to make sure you were taken care of."

I yawned, then noticed my phone on the couch where I'd been sitting. Thomas stood and handed the device to me. I blinked at the screen, surprised to see it was nearly three a.m. I had only one unread message, and it was from Luca.

"Get some sleep. I'll see you tomorrow," was all he said.

I clutched my hand to my chest, biting back tears. It wasn't just the thought of how much pain Luca must be in now that bothered me. More so, it was the awareness that there was nothing I could do to make him feel better.

The last several hours had been a blur. I'd spent a few minutes alone with Luca once I learned the news of Salvatore's sudden death, then Camilla had asked for Luca, and he'd been swept away to his dad's house. Well, his mom's house now, I supposed. Alessio had gone with Luca initially, leaving Giovanni and Thomas to babysit me. A half a dozen of Luca's other guys had come back to the house with us, though, and I'd fielded calls and texts from my own family as they learned the news.

I had a niggling sensation that I should've been prepared for this day. I'd been born into the mafia, although I'd spent the first two decades of my life blissfully unaware that my father was a mob boss. I'd then married Luca, fully aware that his dad, too, was a boss in the mafia. I'd also known that someday, Luca would follow in his father's footsteps and take over the Marino family criminal enterprise, whether he wanted to or not.

I just never dreamed that day would come so soon.

I let Alessio help me up the stairs, but didn't expect him to follow me into the bedroom.

"I'm planning to stay awake tonight, but if I do end up needing to lie down, I'll just go to the guest room next door," he said. "So I won't be far if you need me."

"Thank you," I said. "Should I set an alarm?"

Alessio shook his head. "No. And turn off your notifications so you don't wake up every time someone texts you." He sat on the foot of the bed, his back to the bathroom, so I left the door cracked as I brushed my teeth and changed into my pajamas.

"We've got a long stretch of days ahead of us, Giada. You really should get some sleep. Luca is going to need you."

"He'll need you too," I pointed out.

I rubbed a makeup remover wipe around my eyes, then dabbed on some undereye gel and concealer before returning to the bedroom. Alessio stood when I returned, giving me space to pull down the comforter.

"Do you know what happened?" I asked, crawling under my covers.

Alessio walked towards the door as if confirming no one stood outside the bedroom eavesdropping. He sat on the edge of the bed again, and spoke quietly.

"There was an explosion. A car bomb."

A fresh wave of nausea rolled over me, along with a hundred different thoughts. I parted my lips to speak any one of my questions, but only a squeak came out.

Alessio handed me the glass of water from my nightstand. "He died instantly, Giada. No suffering. And no, it could never happen to Luca or you. We check."

"Then how…"

"My guess is that Elio, the guy he trusted to check for him, was the one who set up the explosives. He was supposed to drive Sal home, so it looks like he took himself out, too. And Daniele." Alessio paused, then added, "Luca and I already had suspicions about the guy. Sal wouldn't hear it."

I listened with a cold disconnect. None of what he said sounded real. This was like the crap we saw in that Godfather movie. It wasn't real life. I waited for more tears to come, waited for some crippling sorrow to overtake me at this realization that, not only had my father-in-law died, but so had his bodyguard Daniele and some other guy. I knew Daniele, or at least I had seen him hundreds of times. I couldn't actually remember ever speaking with him. I didn't know if he was married, if he had kids, or what he did with his free time.

But still, he was a person, and now he was gone. Just. Like. That.

I inhaled slowly, confirming I still felt nothing.

"Do you know what happens next?" I asked a minute later.

"We can talk tomorrow, Giada. You should sleep."

"I'll sleep better when I know what to expect," I insisted. "I assume Luca will help Camilla plan the funeral, but do we know when it'll be? Or what country?"

"I don't know," he admitted.

Alessio switched off the bedside lamp, but didn't leave. I wondered if he planned to watch me sleep. I could picture him doing something like that if Luca asked, but it wasn't necessary. I didn't feel unsafe, just unsettled.

And besides, it wasn't myself I worried about.

I waited so long to ask my next question that Alessio had probably thought I'd fallen asleep. But really, I'd just been debating whether I really wanted to hear the answer.

"Is Luca the boss now?" I asked, my voice echoing through the dark room. I already knew Alessio's answer based on how long it took him to answer.

"Yeah," he said, swallowing nervously.

"Good night," I whispered, turning onto my side so he wouldn't hear me crying into my pillowcase. A minute later, I heard the bedroom door shut with a click.

Luca

The day passed in a blur. At first, I'd been too busy comforting my mother to process any of my own feelings. Then, when she promptly passed out after taking a handful of pills, I spent the next hour panicking about her safety. She'd gone from inconsolable to unwakeable in a matter of minutes. Surely that couldn't be good.

"What did you give her?" I asked Tomasso, one of my papà's top men. I tore my eyes from my mother just long enough to register the look in his own eyes—a mixture of concern and compassion that I suspected matched my own.

"She'll be fine. Just some nerve pills and something to help her sleep," he said. Then he glanced around the room. "She can't sleep here. Help me carry her up to her bed."

"I'll do it," I insisted, stepping in front of him. I gathered my mother in my arms, surprised at how light she felt. Tomasso led the way, not that I didn't already know the house like the back of my hand. He tugged back the covers, waited for me to place her gently on the bed, and then he tucked the sheets and duvet over my mother.

I stared at her, watching the rise and fall of her chest as if expecting her to stop breathing at any moment. Maybe this was how it happened. I'd just lost one parent; clearly, there were no guarantees in life.

Suddenly, darkness flooded the room. I cast an accusatory glare at Tomasso, whose hand still rest on the light switch.

"You need your sleep too, Luca. The next week won't be easy."

He was right, but I couldn't have slept then if I tried.

As if reading my mind, Tomasso reached into his pocket. He offered me a tawny prescription bottle. "Two or three should do the trick."

I hesitated, then grabbed the bottle and made my way to my old room.

I didn't remember turning out the lights or climbing into bed, but when I opened my eyes, sun streamed through the wooden slats covering the window, and a thin gray sheet covered my lower body. I rubbed my eyes, instantly orienting myself to my old bedroom, but taking a moment longer to recall why I was there.

The second I remembered, my chest spasmed painfully. But a soft knock at the door distracted me before I could panic about my impending heart attack. I rubbed my eyes and reached for a bottle of water, swishing a sip in my mouth before swallowing, then addressing the knocker.

"I'm up," I said. I waited for the door to open, then realized I'd locked it. Groaning, I swung my legs out of bed and stepped into the pants I'd worn the previous night. I stifled another yawn as I opened the door.

Tomasso stood in the hallway, a steaming mug of coffee in his hand.

"Grazie," I said, accepting the coffee and sipping without a second thought. "Is she up yet?"

He shook his head. "I thought I'd speak with you first, then wake her."

I dropped onto the bed and traded the mug for my phone on the nightstand. It was barely eight am, and I'd been awake well past three. No wonder I felt like I'd been hit by a truck.

"I need a shower before I talk with anyone," I said, skimming my texts then clicking on the most recent from Alessio. He confirmed that Giada was asleep in bed, then asked me to text when I woke so he could bring me some clothes. I considered what I'd need for the day, then sent a reply. I hated taking him away from Giada, but as my second-in-command, Alessio's presence was essential for everything that would happen over the next few days.

I considered the options, then texted Lorenzo Alfonsi. The guy worked for Giada's father, and had basically been her driver and bodyguard when she was younger. I'd had my qualms about him over the years, but Giada felt safe with him.

I tapped my fingers along the back of my phone while debating what to say, then began typing. "Giada shouldn't be alone. Can you pick her up and see if she can stay at the Conti house for a couple days?"

Tomasso cleared his throat and I jerked to attention, having completely forgotten he was there.

"Sorry. I'm…" I stopped talking and shook my head. There were so many ways I could've completed that sentence, and all of them would've been sorely inadequate to describe the sleep-deprived, stressed out, angry, sad, confused, and completely overwhelmed mess that I was at the moment.

"You don't need to apologize, Luca. No one expects you to be okay right now. You're allowed to grieve."

I downed another swig of the coffee. Yes, I had just suffered a life-changing loss. But I wasn't just a son trying to process the abrupt death of his father. I was also the newly crowned boss of a very serious, and very deadly business.

And I couldn't sit on my obligations.

My phone rang before I could answer Tomasso. I held up a finger, then answered the call. The familiar tenor of Alessio's voice soothed me more than I would've expected, even though he sounded just as exhausted as I was.

"I've got your clothes. Enzo called me, but Giada's still asleep. Do you want me to wake her?" He skipped all formalities, and I appreciated that.

"No! Let her sleep. See if Enzo can just wait. Maybe Thomas or—"

"I'll make sure one of the guys stays with him until Giada's up and ready to go," he promised, reading my thoughts. "She's not going to agree to stay away from you for more than one night, though. Last night was a stretch."

I sighed. I didn't want to be away from my wife either, but I didn't imagine everything would be resolved that quickly. "Just for tonight then. If it's okay with Marco." Giada's dad had old-fashioned views about his married daughter returning home without me for any reason, but I assumed he'd make an exception this time.

"Yeah. Enzo said it was fine, and um, he said to tell you he was sorry for your loss."

I snorted. Lorenzo fucking hated my papà. To be fair, though, literally everyone not currently in the house detested the man. Probably, many of the home's current inhabitants did too. My papà had been a violent narcissist. But apparently, now that he was gone, we'd all have to pretend he was a fucking saint.

"Bring your own stuff to stay the night, okay?" I asked.

Alessio agreed, promised to arrive as soon as he could, then disconnected the call. I finished my cup of coffee, then turned to Tomasso.

"I'll meet with Tony as soon as I'm done showering. But interrupt me the moment my mamma wakes."

Tomasso nodded. "Her sisters are flying in from Italy, along with a few of the guys. Maximo and Lodovico were going to finalize the funeral plans and then run it all by you and your mom later today."

"No one's fired Maximo yet?" That news surprised me. As my papà's primary bodyguard, it seemed the events of the past thirty-six hours more than justified his termination.

Tomasso sighed, his calm face devoid of emotion. "You can do what you think is appropriate, Luca, but if you want my opinion,

I'd wait till the dust settles before making any major changes. We don't even have the full story yet."

I drew in a shaky breath, relieved that I was seated. I hadn't yet processed the full implications of the fact that the scariest and most powerful man I knew had just been murdered. Presumably, I'd now inherited all of his enemies, yet I lacked the numbers of loyal soldiers he'd had.

"I need to meet with my guys, and then…"

"We'll make it official after the funeral, Luca. You don't need to rush things."

I wished he'd stop saying my name. The word felt like a death sentence now, suffocating me with each breath. I pushed to my feet.

"I'm not the one rushing things," I said. "I thought I had another decade before this day." I made my way to the bathroom, shutting and locking the door behind me. I twisted the shower faucet all the way to hot, hoping the water could scald away my fear.

I'd been training for this job since the day I was born. And yet, I knew without a doubt that I still wasn't ready.

CHAPTER 2

Giada

"I'm not going to my parents' house," I repeated for what felt like the tenth time. I'd barely slept, my head was throbbing, and I hadn't even spoken with Luca since the day before. What I needed was to be with my husband, not shipped off to stay with my parents.

Thomas grimaced and turned to Enzo, a look of complete helplessness on his face. I rolled my eyes and stormed into the kitchen. I needed more coffee to be able to think straight. Then, I could figure out my next step.

Alessio had already left for the Marino house, without waking me or offering to bring me with him, a fact that would permanently mark him as a traitor in my mind.

"Giada," Thomas's voice reminded me of a whiny toddler. "Luca said you—"

I whipped around to face him. "If Luca wants to talk to me, he can tell me to my face. I don't need his B-list henchmen ordering me around like a child."

Thomas flung his hands in the air, but before I could celebrate my victory, Enzo grabbed my arm.

"Giada, come on. I know you're stressed out and worried about Luca, but he has a lot going on, too. I'm sure he's doing the best he can right now. What he needs is—"

"Me," I interrupted, tears brimming my eyes. I'd tried to focus on the anger, but all of the other emotions were teetering too close to the surface now. I couldn't hold off any longer. I sniffled. "He's going through the most traumatic thing of his life, and I should be there, by his side."

Enzo's expression softened, and he tugged me against his broad chest, wrapping his arms around me in an embrace that felt equally parts comforting and restraining. "And you will be, Giada," he said, squeezing so that I couldn't have moved if I tried. "But you know how he is. If you're there, you will be the only thing on his mind. He won't be able to concentrate on anything else."

I squeezed my eyes shut, but more tears escaped. Enzo wasn't wrong, but that was why I needed to be with Luca. I could distract him from his pain. I could relax him.

"He just needs some time to get everything in order. He needs to take care of his mom and figure out a plan for the guys. He doesn't need to be worrying about you," Enzo's tone changed at the end of his sentence. "This is how you support him now, by giving him the day to handle things, without the distraction. He's the one who asked me to take you to your parents, not Alessio."

The steady rhythm of Enzo's heartbeat calmed my nerves, but the firmness of his grip on me reminded me that I wasn't going anywhere. I didn't move for another minute, until my own breathing had slowed to match Enzo's. Then I relented.

He must have sensed the moment I accepted defeat, since he released me from the embrace, gazing silently at me as I wiped my eyes on my sleeve.

"One night," I said. "No more. I'll be ready in five minutes. Get me coffee in a travel mug." I flipped Thomas the finger as I stomped up to my bedroom. I'd already packed a bag, thinking I'd join Luca at his parents' for the night, so I just needed to swap out a few things.

Thomas watched Enzo like a hawk until he'd climbed into the car beside me. As Thomas started to head back inside, presumably to go meet my husband, I rolled down the window and called after him. "I want to talk with Luca on the phone today, and voice mail doesn't count."

Thomas nodded, then Enzo drove off.

I stared out the window for several minutes, then decided the silence was too depressing. "I don't like how he watches me. Like, if he doesn't trust me enough to leave me alone with you for five minutes, why let you drive me in the first place? We could just as easily start our illicit affair now."

Enzo snorted loudly, then turned to me, biting back a grin. "He was not worried about that. You're not even the one he was watching. He just had to make sure I didn't steal any top-secret papers or plant a wire or anything."

"Why would you do that?"

"I wouldn't, but I work for your father, not Luca. And at times like this, they can't be too cautious."

I considered that. "What do you mean, at times like this?"

Enzo took his time answering, delaying long enough to let me know the situation was more dire than he was about to make it seem. "Only that with the transition, there's more uncertainty."

"What kind of uncertainty?"

He sighed, frowning at the traffic and checking his blind spot before changing lanes. "The head of the family business died suddenly. They need to find a replacement and figure out how everything is going to run, going forward."

"Luca is the replacement," I said. "I mean, unless...does someone else want the job?"

"Not that I know of, but I'm not privy to the inner workings of the Marino family."

I considered the possibilities. "That would be a dream come true, if someone else wanted the job."

"No," he said, his voice more serious now. "I know you don't want Luca following in his father's footsteps, but it's better than the alternative."

"How so?"

I could tell Enzo was choosing his words carefully, and his hesitation only served to multiply my anxiety.

"If people within the family challenge him, it could force everyone to choose sides. People outside the family will jump when they see the weak spot. Luca could end up fighting two wars at once."

My pulse raced at the implication of Enzo's words. "Luca's not safe," I said, bolting upright in my seat. "You need to take me to him."

Enzo pressed his palm into my thigh as if he worried I'd leap from the car. "He's fine, Giada. No one will come after him in his home. And not now. It's all so fresh."

"You literally just told me people in his own family might try to kill him to usurp his position. It makes the most sense for them to act now, when he's not focused."

"That is not what I said."

"What if someone inside the family murdered Salvatore, and Luca's their next target?"

The hand on my thigh squeezed. "Luca is safe, Giada. Alessio is with him, and they won't leave the house."

I sucked in a ragged breath then turned to peer out my window, trying not to think about the fact that he hadn't actually said I was wrong. Until we knew who killed Salvatore, and why, we couldn't possibly know whether Luca was safe. My stomach churned, and I dug my teeth into my bottom lip, letting the zing of pain distract me from my worries.

Luca

$\mathcal{I}$'d spent the day jumping from one stressful conversation to another, pausing only enough to down more coffee. By late afternoon, the caffeine had left me tapping my foot faster than a dog wagged its tail. I figured I came off as impatient, or perhaps annoyed, but that was better than the alternative, looking scared shitless.

I wanted to harness all my anxious energy and shoot out the front door of the house, running until I reached Manhattan, or possibly further. I wanted to run right into a different reality, one where my papà was still alive, and I wasn't left holding the very heavy bag.

I'd met with my mom, hammered out the funeral plans, then chatted with Tony briefly until Alessio came. I'd hoped for a few minutes alone with my friend, but the second I stepped out to change into the fresh clothes he'd brought me, Tony had dragged Alessio into a conversation.

Finally, Tony said he needed to check in with his wife, so I took the opportunity to retreat to the kitchen. I was about to brew another pot of coffee when Alessio stepped in front of me, blocking my access to the carafe.

"No more coffee, Luca. You look like a meth-head detoxing."

I rolled my eyes, but grabbed a bottle of water instead. Then I started back to my bedroom. Alessio followed. I sank onto the bed the second he shut the door, hunching over my knees and thrusting my head into my hands like I was about to be sick. My friend sat beside me, patted my back twice as if burping a baby, then sighed.

"I'd ask how you're holding up, but..." he said.

"I just need time to think. Then I'll figure it all out."

"You don't have to figure it all out now."

I gazed up at him, hoping he could read the skepticism in my eyes.

"You just lost your dad, Luca."

"No shit."

"I only mean that people will understand if you need some time to grieve."

"Will they?" I exhaled slowly. "Would you?"

Alessio sighed. "You had a complicated relationship. Just because you spent most of your life hating him, doesn't mean you wanted him dead. You're still allowed to be sad."

I considered that for a moment, then let a wry grin pass my lips. "He would be so disappointed with how I'm handling all of this. If he were still here, he'd tell me I should've figured out who ordered the hit, how they carried it out, and I should've already punished the perps and everyone they'd ever met. I should've already assigned new job titles, and hammered out organizational details, and confirmed everyone's loyalty. And I should be taking better care of my mother."

Alessio shrugged. "Tomasso seems to be doting on her enough for everyone."

He wasn't wrong. I supposed that made sense. If I died, I liked to think that my guys would look after Giada. *God.* My chest spasmed at the thought of her. Thomas had told me to call her, said she was a bit of a mess. But I didn't even have the nerve to do that yet.

"He was proud of you when he died," Alessio said, cutting into my guilt over Giada. "I know that feels like forever ago, but it was this week that he told you he was proud."

I nodded. "I guess I should be glad he went out on a high note. If he'd stuck around another day, I was sure to disappoint him again."

Alessio patted my back again, then we were both silent. After a moment, he spoke again, this time his voice softer. "I don't think Tony wants the job. Lodovico and Iacopo aren't leaders, and Tomasso seems too gentle. What's your read on your uncles?"

I shrugged. "I can't imagine they'd be willing to take me out. They always seemed to like me."

Alessio wrinkled his nose. "I don't know about that, but they definitely seem to like Italy. Too much to move here part-time." He rose to his feet, walking over to the window and peering at the drive below. "What about Maximo?"

He was a wildcard for sure. My papà's bodyguards had never liked me, and the feeling was mutual. But I wasn't ready to condemn anyone if they weren't truly to blame for his death. And if I was willing to pardon Maximo for his lapse in guard duty, surely, he'd be willing to accept my leadership. "Xavier hates me too," I said. I'd only been seventeen when my papà had forced me and Xavier to fight, but I'd done some serious damage to the guy, and he'd clearly never forgotten about it.

"He isn't going to challenge you as head of the family."

"No, but I also don't see him ever being loyal to me, no matter what he says."

"Maybe, but you can deal with that down the road."

"How? How am I supposed to lead these guys if I can't trust them?" My mind reeled. "They were all loyal to my papà and he still couldn't survive, so what makes me cocky enough to think I stand a chance of…" I let my voice trail off before expressing my true fears out loud. I wasn't naïve enough to think I could protect myself, let alone Giada, not in a world where my would-be opponents didn't have the wrath of my papà to fear.

"We will figure out something, Luca. You can buy out the guys you don't trust or kill 'em off. You don't have to worry about that today. Besides, you're safer than you think."

I quirked a brow, certain he'd never come up with anything comforting to say. To my surprise, he did.

"You have me, Luca."

"My papà had Tony."

Alessio shook his head. "Yeah, Tony can be scary as fuck, but it's different and you know it. More importantly, everyone else knows it." He paused. "Tony will avenge your father because he's expected to. I would take out anyone who crossed you because I wanted to."

I cracked a smile at his words. Alessio and I did have a different bond than my papà and Tony. We weren't just friends or partners, we were brothers in every way that mattered. And Alessio was right. People did know that.

"You also have Giada."

I chortled at the thought of my petite, God-fearing wife taking vengeance on anyone. "I know she can be terrifying, but—"

"She's a Conti, Luca. And if they want to keep her safe, they'll need to keep you safe." Alessio lifted my phone off the bed and thrust it towards me. "Call Marco. Tell him you need backup. He's not going to say no."

I hesitated. Alessio was right. Our best protection for now might be to join forces with the Contis. A united front should ward off any threats from inside or outside the family.

But no part of me wanted to call my father-in-law and beg.

"Get it over with, then call your wife. We'll meet with our guys, and then after dinner we can all chat with all your dad's captains."

I opened my mouth to protest, but Alessio shook his head. He tapped something on my phone, then held it out to me again, this time showing me that he'd called Marco Conti.

I snatched the phone from his hand, and he sauntered out of the room before I could snap at him.

"I wondered if we'd hear from you today," Mr. Conti said, his deep voice booming through the phone as confidently as if he were in the room beside me. "I want to express my condolences again. You've suffered a great loss. We all have, truly. The community won't be the same without him. Your father was an incredible man."

I considered his wording and decided that was accurate. My papà hadn't been a great man, or even a good man. He certainly wasn't magnanimous or kindhearted, but he was pretty fucking incredible at times.

"I appreciate that, sir," I said, clearing my throat. "And I appreciate you taking care of Giada tonight. There's just so much I needed to handle, and—"

"Of course, son. It's not an imposition. I know how she can be." His chuckle at that sentiment annoyed me, and it took me a moment to regain my train of thought.

"I know you're busy, but I wanted to call to, well, I guess ask a favor. As I'm sure you can imagine, we…uh, my family, are facing some big transitions now. Especially since we don't know exactly what happened with my papà, there's a lot of uncertainty about who I can trust. I don't have time to deal with challenges to my authority from inside the family now, and I'm worried we might come off as weak to any of my papà's enemies while we're…restructuring."

Mr. Conti took his time answering. "I can see how those would be concerns. How can I help?"

"I want to reassure your daughter that she's safe, but I can't protect her if I'm not safe." I paused. "I was wondering if you'd be interested in helping us present a more united front."

"I'm not sure I understand."

"I think it would help if you could make a statement, letting people know you support the Marino family."

"A statement…where?"

I blew out a breath, wishing Alessio had given me a minute to figure all this out in advance. Of course, then I probably wouldn't have called at all.

"I'm not sure," I admitted. "Maybe a recording?"

When he didn't answer, I continued, "I understand if you're

not comfortable with that, but with your daughter involved, I suspect that you would consider any threat to my family a threat to your family as well. I just don't know if other people realize that."

"I think I follow what you're saying," he said after another pause. "Let me see what I can do and get back to you."

"Okay, thank you."

"Please give your mother our best. And take care of yourselves."

"Will do. Thanks."

Mr. Conti disconnected the call before I could stammer away any longer. I wasn't sure what exactly he'd interpreted from my request or whether his solution would help any, but I'd stuck my tail between my legs and asked for his help at least. Now I just needed to knock out one more stressful call.

I dialed Giada before I lost my nerve, cringing in anticipation of her yelling at me for not coming home the night before or for banishing her to her parents' for the day.

Instead, her voice was sweet as sugar, her tone as kind as could be. I squeezed my eyes shut and sank into the bed, soaking up all of the comfort. She sounded concerned, not angry, and when I declined her offer to join me for the night, Giada didn't protest. Instead, she said she understood and that she missed me.

"Call me if you need me, okay? No matter what the hour," she said.

I agreed, though nothing could make me call her when I thought she'd be sleeping. I had just started to try to end the call, telling her I needed to meet with the guys in a minute, when she interrupted.

"Sorry, but my dad said he was sending over a care package. I know my mom already sent some flowers to your mom, but I guess this is something else for you."

Instantly, I felt more alert, and my heart began pitter

pattering faster. I hadn't expected Marco to come through this quickly, but definitely wasn't going to complain.

Giada paused as if listening to someone else in the background, then I heard movement and the background noise disappeared, making me assume she'd shut herself in her room again. "Nevermind, apparently he sent one of those edible arrangements or something. Hopefully fruit and not cookies, but who knows. He's got this new sugar addiction, and I'm sure with his cholesterol—"

"Baby," I interrupted. "I love hearing you talk, but I really do have to go." At the realization that her dad interpreted my request as seeking snacks, all hope I'd harbored sank straight to my stomach, where a lump of dread was weighing me down. The last thing I needed was to start bawling while still on the phone with her.

Giada's sigh was wistful. "I wish I could hug you right now."

"Me too," I said. "I love you."

I disconnected, then rubbed my forehead. I went to the bathroom, splashed cold water on my face, and was patting it dry as my phone buzzed with an incoming text.

The message came from Angelo Conti. It read, "This ok? If so, will forward to contacts."

I clicked on the video accompanying the message just as Alessio poked his head in the door. I motioned for him to join me as Marco Conti appeared on the screen. He was seated at his desk, with the camera zoomed close enough to him so as to obscure the background.

Looking straight into the camera, Marco spoke. "I'm sure you've all heard by now of the tragic passing of the respected Salvatore Marino. While Sal and I didn't always see eye to eye on everything, I considered him a friend. Moreover, since my daughter's marriage to his son, Luca, I've regarded the Marinos as family. If anyone were to threaten or harm Luca Marino or anyone else in the Marino family, I would interpret that action the same as a direct threat to the Conti family." He stared into the camera, his eyes serious, for a full ten seconds before finally blinking, then ending the recording.

"Damn," Alessio mumbled. "Guess your call went well. He works fast."

I nodded, still unsure if the fruit basket was also coming. I replied to Angelo, "thanks for the support."

I took a breath, then turned to Alessio. "Alright, let's do this."

We rose together, ready to meet with the rest of the Marino men.

Giada

Speaking with Luca had calmed my nerves for a bit, but by evening, I grew restless again. Angelo attempted to comfort me by reminding me that Luca hadn't even liked his dad, but Enzo stuck around to keep me company. I flipped through an interior design magazine, but I couldn't even concentrate on the images I liked.

I sighed and tossed down the magazine, then rose to pour myself a glass of wine.

Enzo eyed me warily. "Should you be drinking with those pills your mom gave you?"

I rolled my eyes. I did not need someone to monitor my alcohol intake. "I'm saving them for the funeral, if I need them." My mom had made a big deal about how the last thing Luca needed was an overly emotional wife embarrassing him when he was trying to impress new business associates. The whole lecture was incredibly demeaning. *As if* I couldn't be trusted to act appropriately on a formal occasion.

Still, I did think I'd benefit from some form of aid in the relaxation department. I was more tightly wound than a Jack-in-the-box ready to spring. No matter how hard I tried to distract myself, my intrusive thoughts would flood my brain with images of Luca bursting into flames as a car bomb exploded in his car.

"Your brothers aren't worried about him," Enzo said, in a tone I suspected he intended to be reassuring.

"My brothers don't like him."

Enzo shrugged, acknowledging the point. "Matteo doesn't mind him."

I supposed that was true. "Where is Matteo anyway? I haven't seen him."

"He's almost never here lately." Enzo leaned forward conspiratorially. "I think he's got a girlfriend."

I pondered that possibility for a minute, trying to focus on the potential gossip about my brother and not the impending doom threatening my family. I stared at my phone for the eight millionth time, as if a text from Luca could have silently appeared on my phone.

"How'd he sound when you talked to him?" Enzo asked.

"Stressed. Tired."

His eyes narrowed as if debating telling me something. "I'm sure he's feeling better now. Your dad made a statement of solidarity."

"Huh?"

"He basically said if anyone messed with Luca, they were messing with the whole Conti family."

I must have looked confused, because he continued.

"Everyone now knows the Conti family has Luca's back. So he's still got everyone he had before—"

"Minus his dad."

Enzo cringed. "Okay, but everyone else, plus your entire family. He's the safest he's ever been. The safest he'll ever be. So finish your wine and get some sleep. He'll need you to be supportive when you get back. And mentally stable. Not a sleep-deprived, emotional mess."

I glared, then made my way upstairs. I'd just watch TV until I fell asleep. As I lounged in my bed, in my childhood room, I tried to picture Luca doing the same. A smile widened across my face as I thought back to our high school days. On school breaks, when we were both at home, we spent hours talking or texting from our respective beds. As confident as I'd been back then that we'd end up together, I hadn't ever pictured this scenario…both of us grown up, and married, but still sleeping separate in our childhood beds.

I snapped a picture of myself in bed and sent it to Luca with a message about how I pictured him doing the same and how I was reminded of our boarding school time. I waited a few minutes, but when he didn't reply, I switched off the light and, somehow, eventually I fell asleep.

CHAPTER 3

Adrian

*L*ess than a week after learning a car bomb had taken out Salvatore Marino, I found myself at his funeral. I wasn't sure what to expect, it being my first mafia funeral and all. I was a bit surprised to have even been invited, since I'd only spoken to the deceased once, at the wedding of his son to my ex-girlfriend, Giada. But much like that event, my invitation wasn't so much a request for my presence as a summons. And from the looks of the crowd, a lot of people got the same summons.

I'd seen the video Marco made and knew that, at least for the time being, the Conti family was supporting the Marino family. I wasn't surprised that Marco would do such a thing, but I had expected Angelo to be more pissed about it. Instead, he was fairly chill. He actually made a comment about how he'd have wanted the same support from the Marinos if it had been his dad to die, which was quite possibly the most mature sentiment Angelo had ever spoken aloud.

The thought had crossed my mind that perhaps the Conti family had something to do with Salvatore's untimely demise, but that didn't make sense. I'd also wondered if it wasn't real, if maybe Sal had faked his own death, much like Luca had years before. I scoured the news reports for any hint of that possibility and even raised the question with my boss at the law firm, Gino Russo, and a couple of other guys in the know with the Contis. They all seemed legitimately convinced that this was real. Salvatore Marino was truly gone from this world.

At the end of the day, we were all better off without him, and I didn't doubt that anyone—even his closest family or friends—would truly disagree. The guy was a monster, from everything I had heard and seen. Despite that, today we were all putting on our sad faces and pretending we'd lost a beloved father, friend, and business owner.

Whatever. I could fake it for an afternoon. Actually, since beginning to work as a lawyer for the mob, I'd found my capacity for faking a lot of things had grown.

The church was packed, with immediate "family" taking up the front three quarters of the rows. I sat near the back of the sanctuary, with the other Contis. Giada was the only woman other than Salvatore's wife seated in the front row. Even when the full mass finally ended and the guests seated in the front filed out first, I couldn't really get a good look at her because she was flanked on all sides by large men. I recognized those from Luca's inner circle, but many of the others I suspected were mere bodyguards.

I rode with Lorenzo and Matteo to the cemetery, where finally I got a good look at Giada.

For years, I'd heard Giada referred to as the Princess, or la principessa in their native tongue. Today, she played the role flawlessly.

Her long hair had been pulled into a tight bun atop her head, accented by diamond-crusted combs on the sides. Her black gown fell just above her knees and dipped into a modest V-neck just below her collarbone. Her heels were stylish, but a modest two inches at most. Her jewelry looked expensive yet tame and well-coordinated. She looked sophisticated and gorgeous, but above all, proper.

Giada's appearance didn't offer the slightest hint of her sass, independence, or any other aspect of her personality. She was the picture of a generic, dutiful daughter-in-law, mourning some dude she never really liked.

Giada walked gracefully, with a serene expression on her face that matched her poised posture. She kept her eyes straight ahead and her fingers wrapped tightly around her small black clutch. She stayed beside Luca, but showed no expression as man after man shook Luca's hand or did that European air-kiss on the cheek move. When it was time to walk, Luca pressed a hand against her back, nudging her forward. When he left her to walk with his mother, two of his guys flanked her on both sides and kept her moving forward. Maybe she was more robot than princess.

I planned to leave without speaking to Luca, certain my presence wouldn't perk him up. But before we could sneak out, Giada spotted Enzo, Matteo, and me in the distance by a tree.

She started towards us, only to be stopped by two of Luca's cronies. Her brother Matteo breached the distance between us, nodded to the men with Giada, then escorted her across the cemetery, as though she were a child flying alone and in need of tight supervision.

"Thank you all for coming," she said, her voice oddly void of emotion. "I know your presence means a lot to Luca and Camilla. This has been a challenging week for everyone."

"Are you okay?" I blurted out.

Enzo flashed me a look, but I didn't regret asking. Giada seemed…off. Much more so than I had guessed from afar.

"Thank you," she said, a slight nod of her head.

Her answer was more concerning than silence. At the risk of being shot by any of Luca's bodyguards, I ushered her off to the side. Fortunately, Matteo and Enzo seemed to understand what I was doing and let us move a few feet away.

"You don't seem like yourself, Giada. Are you okay?" I repeated. I leaned closer to try to get a view of her eyes, but her thick black sunglasses offered full anonymity.

"I'm fine, Adrian. My husband's father was unexpectedly murdered, so it's been a rough week. Nothing you need to worry about."

Her words lacked their usual emotional tenor, though, so I was still worried.

"Are you scared of someone here?"

She turned and gazed around the crowd. "No, I suppose not. These people are all either my family or Luca's."

I regretted the precision of my initial question. "Are you scared of someone else? Or something?"

Her shoulders rose as she drew in a slow, shaky breath. "As I said, my father-in-law was murdered. My husband will now be filling his former job, so..." Her voice trailed off, and her eyes locked on two men leaning against a blue sedan parked at the edge of the cemetery. I instantly registered them as plain-clothes officers, but I wondered if Giada realized that.

"You're scared for Luca, not yourself?" I confirmed.

She nodded, just as a man popped around the tree. He looked even less Italian than I did, which sent alarm bells off in my head. Luckily, Enzo dove in between Giada and the man before he could even speak. That didn't stop him from trying, though.

"Giada, can you confirm that your father-in-law was killed in a mob hit? Are you aware of claims that he was the head of a large organized crime family? Do you..."

I turned as he abruptly shushed, only to see that Lorenzo had removed him from the area. Still, it was discerning that Giada didn't even flinch at the man's sudden appearance or pressing questions.

"No one is getting within a hundred feet of Luca," I said. "He's fine. I'm worried about you. Not your safety, but your... emotions. You seem like a robot."

"That's preferable."

"To what?"

"To being myself. You know I'd say or do something to embarrass Luca or offend Camilla if I weren't."

"If you weren't what?"

"I took some pills. Muscle relaxants, I think. And maybe mood stabilizers. I don't know. My mom gave me some."

I was relieved to hear her mom had supplied the drugs, but still concerned. I remembered what Giada was like after she thought Luca had died. I wondered if she was having flashbacks to then. She glanced away from me and gazed over to him just then, confirming my suspicions.

"I'm really sorry, Giada. If you need a friend, I'm here."

She blinked several times, then turned and glanced at Enzo. "Thank you for coming. You should say hi to Luca before you leave."

"I...don't think that's a good idea."

"Both of you," she said, her tone firm.

Enzo and I exchanged a look then followed her over to Luca. His hoard of guards parted to let Giada through, then reluctantly let us pass, as well.

Luca was deep in conversation with a man I didn't know by name but had recognized as he walked Luca's mom down the aisle at the church. After a moment, Luca turned and acknowledged Giada.

"Adrian and Lorenzo wanted to express their condolences," she said.

Luca eyed me, but Enzo stepped forward first. He said something in Italian, then turned to me.

"I'm sorry for your loss," I said, my sentiment sounding unauthentic and awkward.

Luca nodded politely in acknowledgement of our words,

then turned to Giada. I wondered if he realized she was medicated, if he knew how terrified she was. Did he even know she hadn't liked his father? Did he care? Narcissist that he was, Luca probably didn't realize the day was hard for anyone but him.

But then, before Enzo and I could disappear back into the crowd, Luca bent forward, dipping his head against his wife's.

"I'm perfectly safe, Giada. I'm right here, tesoro." He spoke softly, but in a way that made me suspect he'd been uttering those same words to her over and over.

Giada's body swayed towards his, and it was as if watching her relax instantly.

My stomach clenched. I *should* be happy for Giada. She'd clearly chosen the right man. Luca was, despite the odds, good to her.

But instead, it was entirely unsettling. I watched as Luca squeezed her fingers, whispered something in her ear, then walked away.

Giada gazed at me, then turned. "Is Mom still here?" she asked.

I followed her gaze to see her oldest brother, Angelo, beside me.

"She and Dad just left," he said. "We're heading out now, too."

Giada frowned. "I thought I'd ride with them."

Angelo shook his head. "We're not going back to the Marino house. That's just for your family."

Giada opened her mouth as if to protest, then shut it, likely realizing what Angelo meant. Giada was now a Marino, not a Conti.

Alessio, her husband's best friend and second-in-command, pressed a hand onto her shoulder. She jumped, then relaxed when she saw it was him. "Lincoln will drive us. Luca's riding with Camila."

"Call if you need anything," I said, walking off with Angelo.

Giada

Somehow, I'd survived the day of the funeral. There'd been a full mass and church service shortly after lunch, then another ceremony at the cemetery. After that, we headed to the Marino mansion for a dinner that ran well into the early hours of the morning.

Luca had insisted Lincoln drive me home at some point after midnight, and I'd relented, but only because I was falling asleep on my feet. My mom's cocktail of anxiety meds and muscle relaxants had gotten me through the funeral, but compounded my fatigue to the point that I literally couldn't stay awake.

Luca promised he'd be home soon after me, but when I awoke that morning, he was already gone. The only sign that he'd ever even been in our home was his funeral suit draped over a dresser in our closet. He'd changed into a different suit and likely returned to his parents' house.

Today was the day I'd been dreading since I first learned of Salvatore's death. Today, the entire Marino family was supposed to pledge their loyalty to Luca. Today, he would become the boss.

I wasn't supposed to know the details of what went on in that ceremony, and to be honest, I didn't. I also probably wasn't supposed to know that it was even occurring, but I'd never be the type of wife who could tolerate remaining that oblivious.

I showered, then wrapped myself in a robe and went downstairs to make coffee. I doubted Luca had left me home alone, but I figured he'd probably asked whoever was babysitting me to stay outside. Still, I was surprised to hear the doorbell chime right as I reached the bottom of the stairs. I made my way to the door to check who it was. Assuming the visitor was my driver, Lincoln, or whoever was watching the house, I could let him in. He probably just needed to use the bathroom.

As I rounded the corner, I nearly smacked into a shirtless Alessio. Judging from the slight glaze to his skin, he'd just finished a workout.

He yanked out his earbuds and turned to me. "Sorry, didn't hear you coming. I'll deal with the door."

Alessio flashed me a look that I recognized as an order to go away, but I was curious who was at the door. So, I pretended to head towards the kitchen, then turned back right as he opened the door.

A man I didn't recognize lifted a giant camera and snapped a series of photos while yelling questions about Salvatore. In the two seconds it took Alessio to shove the guy outside, he'd probably gotten a handful of photos. I watched through the window as Alessio spoke with the guy. He gestured wildly with his hands, but much to my surprise, he didn't punch the guy. Or break his camera.

I scurried to the kitchen and focused on the coffee maker right as Alessio returned to the house. He joined me in the kitchen and gave me a once-over.

"Care to explain why you were going to answer the door dressed like that?" he asked.

"I figured it was Lincoln babysitting me today and that he needed to use the bathroom or something."

Alessio sighed. "He had a conflict today, so you're stuck with me. But now, some reporter has a photograph of the two of us in the house, half-naked." He retrieved his t-shirt from the back of a barstool and tugged it over his head. "Luca will be thrilled."

I couldn't help but smile at the thought of anyone assuming I was having an affair with Alessio, of all people. "Thank you. I think that's the first time I've smiled all week."

Alessio chuckled, then rubbed my shoulder. "It'll get easier. He just needs to get through today, then—"

"I should've married you," I said, thinking aloud.

"Excuse me?"

"Yeah. Then you could've been with whoever you wanted and no one would suspect anything."

Alessio frowned. "And Luca?"

"Well, he's the boss, so no one would bat an eyelash if he kept me on the side."

"Luca could never keep you on the side. Nor could he ever share you with anyone else, even just on paper," Alessio said.

He grabbed my freshly-brewed cup of coffee and slid it across the counter to me. "And I think maybe you're still a bit sleep deprived. Or loopy from your mom's meds. I'm supposed to drive you over to the Marino's for the day, but it's probably best if you just don't talk. I'd hate for you to accidentally tell a stranger you regret not marrying me, especially now that the paparazzi has incriminating photos of us."

I sipped the coffee then rolled my eyes. "Why is the paparazzi here anyway?"

"Sal was infamous before he died, and then the way he died… Well, car bombs don't explode every day. But the fascination will pass. Everything will go back to normal soon," Alessio promised.

I sighed, certain he was wrong, but I wasn't in the mood to debate it further.

I dressed and styled my hair, then Alessio drove me to the Marino house for another day of making small talk with people claiming to have loved Salvatore. Shortly after dinner, Lincoln drove me home. He promised to stay in the car until Luca or Alessio returned, and he instructed me not to open the door for anyone.

I debated going to bed, but quickly dismissed the idea. I was too tense to sleep, and I was worried if I did fall asleep, I'd miss seeing Luca entirely. Again. So instead, I kept busy.

Exhaustion riddled my bones as I tried to pen one last thank you note before rewarding myself with a break to refill my mug of tea.

It had been dark for hours by the time I heard Luca's car pull into the garage. I gazed down at my outfit to see if I was decent for visitors, only to realize I was still in the modest dress I'd worn all day. Playing the role of dutiful wife was exhausting and struck me as pointless. Luca and I would never eat all the casseroles people were bringing us, and listening to all of the feigned sorrow was exhausting.

I'd managed to sneak away from the Marinos' for an hour to see Father Ryan, and that had helped immensely. I had needed to confess that I never liked Salvatore, that my grief now was solely over the fact that Luca now had to fill his father's shoes. I'd shared my fears over Luca becoming like his father. I'd even mentioned the shitty timing, as we'd just decided to start trying for a baby and now that plan was surely on the backburner for at least another year.

I gazed up as the door opened, surprised when only Luca entered the room. He froze by the door, his face as void of emotion as I felt after days and days of worrying. I held my breath as though expecting some miracle, but he simply dipped his head in a nod and shucked off his shoes.

"It's done," he said. "It's official."

I stared at him, searching for clues as to how I should react. I couldn't tell if he was relieved or anxious, excited or sad. To him, I supposed, this had always been inevitable. I was the only one dumb enough to have held out hope that things would change. Or rather, that they wouldn't. That Luca could somehow never become the boss.

Maybe nothing had changed. Outwardly, Luca looked the same. Actually, he looked hot even. He draped his suit jacket over the edge of a barstool and dragged his hand through his dark hair. Wearing just his black pinstripe suit pants and the matching vest over a crisp white shirt and a black tie, he still had the sexy professional look, but now it was more casual. He'd loosened the tie, rolled up his shirt sleeves, and ditched the jacket. He was barefoot too, which I also loved for some reason. I supposed that since Luca was always so meticulously pulled together, seeing him comfortable always had that effect on me.

Luca broke our gaze as he turned to wash his hands. I swallowed the lump in my throat, willing the inexplicable desire I felt to simmer down, certain it was inappropriate to even think about that now.

Luca crossed the room, stepping behind me too quickly for me to turn. I expected him to wrap his arms around my waist, but he didn't. He simply rest his chin on my shoulder. Neither of us spoke, but I heard his breathing speed up in tune with my own, and I felt him pressing against my backside, multiplying my inappropriate thoughts.

He brushed my hair over to the opposite shoulder, inhaling deeply just behind my ear. "You smell like jasmine," he said. "Are you writing thank you notes?"

It was a pointless question, as he clearly could see that was exactly what I was doing. "There's a lot," I said, sounding equally stupid.

Without warning, Luca tugged the zipper on my dress down to my bra-line, then quit, apparently realizing the dress was intended to be lifted over my head to remove. His lips closed around the tip of my ear, sucking gently there before moving to my neck. He nipped my shoulder then hiked the hem of my dress up towards my waist. My heart thudded erratically at the promise of what he'd do next.

I gazed to the side, realizing I could see our reflections in the window just beyond the table. I briefly considered whether anyone outside could see what we were doing, then dismissed the thought as I saw Luca's hand work at the top of his pants. He yanked my panties down and licked his fingers before using them to dampen both of our bodies. I held my breath as he drove into me, then stilled.

I flattened my palms against the cool marble countertop and closed my eyes so I could better focus on the sensations I was feeling. Luca rolled my dress higher and pressed his hand into the small of my back, guiding my chest down to the counter. When he finally did begin to thrust his hips, his movements were faster and rougher than I anticipated. Something about it all was jarring and unsettling rather than the deeper connection I so desperately craved.

It seemed like only a few minutes had passed when he groaned abruptly and pulled out of me. I felt him against the top of my buttocks as the warm liquid spilled out of him. His head dropped down towards mine again, his breathing still ragged.

Luca mumbled an apology, and I realized it was the first time since college that he hadn't insisted I come first.

Luca backed away from me, grabbing the first thing he saw, I supposed, and using it to wipe off my lower back. He then dropped it on the counter beside me, and I saw that it was a tea towel—a gift from one of the church ladies.

"I should shower," he said, his voice gravelly. "You could join me."

Luca disappeared from the room before I could answer, confirming my hunch that it wasn't a real invitation. I sighed, reaching my fingers behind me to confirm he'd thoroughly cleaned my backside before I rolled my dress back down. I stacked up the notes I'd finished, leaving the others for the next day. I switched off the light to head back to the bedroom, then paused.

The kitchen was eerily dark now, and oddly soothing. The cool air hit my upper back where my dress was unzipped, and for a moment, I felt like I was freer somehow. I ran my hands along the countertop, relishing the coolness there, too. And then I simply stared around the dark room, breathing.

I didn't feel like I'd been standing there in the dark for long when I heard a click at the door. My body stiffened, right as Alessio popped in. I dropped down and grabbed my panties off the floor and wadded them inside the tea towel, clutching both in my hand as he peered at me, a deer-in-headlights expression in his eyes.

"Sorry. I saw the lights off and figured you'd gone to bed," he said. "Luca didn't set the alarm, though, so I wanted to check that everything was okay."

"He's showering," I said, though as the words left my mouth, I realized the water was no longer running.

Alessio nodded, but even in the darkness I could see the worry on his face. "Are you okay?"

I wasn't sure how to answer that. I certainly wasn't going to tell him my husband just came home and fucked me like some hooker then took off again. I couldn't admit I was terrified of Luca becoming his father, and I definitely couldn't say how exhausting it was to pretend I was sad to see Salvatore dead. So instead, I just didn't answer.

After a minute, Alessio quit waiting for a response. "Everything went well tonight. No hiccups. He just needs some time to settle into the role, and then everything will go back to normal."

I nodded, as though there were any chance of us ever finding normal.

"It's just a really hard time for him now, you know?" Alessio continued. "He doesn't talk to me about this stuff. He needs you."

I stared ahead at him for a minute, but still had no response.

"Sleep well," he finally said. "I'll lock up."

I turned and shuffled out of my kitchen, pausing to drop the items from my hand into the laundry room. Luca was still in the bathroom when I reached our room, so I took off my jewelry and moved all the pillows off the bed.

Luca

I scrubbed my skin in the shower, desperate to wash away the sins of the day, perhaps of the lifetime. On paper, the day had been seamless. All of my papà's men, even those I'd questioned, pledged their loyalty to me. All of my guys reiterated it. Tony, my papà's second-in-command, even gave a speech, proclaiming his support for me. No one behaved in a way that made me question their loyalties, and literally nothing happened that should've worried me.

And yet, a plethora of worries flooded my brain. There were the obvious concerns, like how I was ever going to follow in my papà's footsteps without actually becoming like my papà. But there were also the other fears, like what would happen if I couldn't track down my papà's killer? Or, worse yet, what if I did?

We'd finally answered the basic questions. We'd combed through all of the security footage from nearby businesses and determined that Elio was not in the car when the bomb detonated. He'd climbed into the backseat after shutting the door for my papà on the passenger side, and then a moment later he'd stepped out, jogging back towards a building. More than a minute passed, but none of the cameras showed Elio returning to the car before the explosion, which witnesses said happened the moment Daniele started the ignition.

Had Elio told Daniele and Papà that he'd left something inside? I supposed we'd never know, but that was my best guess. He and Daniele both had been alone with the car prior to the explosion, but Elio's fast departure from the car just in the nick of time cemented his fate as the guilty party in my mind. The police presumably had the same footage we did, plus they claimed crime scene investigators would confirm how many people had been in the car based on dental records.

But that process could take months. If Elio truly escaped the explosion, he'd be long gone before the police concluded as much. Alessio and I had both harbored suspicions about Elio long before this, but my papà never listened to our concerns. Although, we'd believed Elio was an undercover cop, which didn't make sense. Cops didn't usually kill the bad guys, not unless they, too, were crooked. So was Elio a bad cop? Or had he actually been working for someone else, and not an undercover cop at all?

I wanted justice as much as the next guy, or so I told myself. But I also couldn't handle thinking about what would happen if and when we did find Elio.

The water ran cold before I began to feel even reasonably clean, but I knew I needed to head out and face reality.

Sex with Giada had released some of the tension that had been building up over the past week, but also created all new stress. I hadn't meant to use her for a quick release, but I had. Worse, she clearly knew it.

Giada had been a saint the past week, too. Even my mom couldn't find fault with Giada's behavior since the explosion.

God, I felt like shit. Giada was playing the role of the perfect wife, and I was…what, turning into my papà already? No. I wouldn't let that happen.

I wrapped my towel around my waist and went into the bedroom, surprised to see Giada already wearing her short, silky blue nightgown. Her eyes met mine only briefly, and she flashed me a smile so obviously fake that I cringed. She scooted past me to brush her teeth. I could've taken the time to talk to her, but I didn't know what to say. I knew she was scared, and I was too. I didn't have the words to make her feel better, and pleading with her to just give me a year or two to figure it all out didn't seem like a great idea.

I switched off the lights and climbed under the covers, waiting for her so I could apologize without speaking, the way I did best. Giada took her time, then when she did join me in bed, she stayed all the way on her side. She was mad, even if she'd never say it. I inched closer.

"I'm sorry," I whispered through the dark.

"Luca, it's fine."

The way she said my name made me wince.

She rolled onto her stomach, clearly intending to avoid me that way, but I was an opportunist. I crouched beside her and began massaging her shoulders, working my way down her back. When she didn't slap away my hands, I stretched out beside her, hooking my leg around hers and peppering her arm and shoulder blades in soft kisses. When I had kissed every inch of her skin within reach, I shifted to cover her other arm, then ducked under the covers.

"Flip over," I said. I half expected her to ignore me, but she complied. I rubbed each of her feet for a minute, then kissed her toes and worked my way up her legs, alternating between the right and the left. As I neared the v at the top of her legs, I reached my hands up her slip, quickly finding her breasts. I rolled her nipples between my fingers, relishing the sensation of them hardening beneath my touch. I kissed her between her legs, chastely at first, until she bent her knees to the side granting me full permission to proceed.

I could've made her come that way, almost did, actually, but she stopped me. She tugged on my hair, then pulled me up her body. She shifted her hips, positioning me right at her entrance.

"No baby, this is about you," I told her.

"I want to look at you," she said. "I need to see you." Giada reached her hand between us, and I had no desire to resist again. We slid together like two pieces of a puzzle. Hovering over my beautiful wife, I couldn't help but smile for the first time in a week. Feeling that good when I should be mourning was surely a sin of some sort, but, at the moment, I didn't care.

I pressed to my knees, slipping my hand beneath Giada's

lower back to raise her hips to meet mine. Her lips parted in an erotic O, but her eyes stayed locked on mine, as promised.

"I love you," I whispered, and that was all it took.

Her body tightened around me, and her hips thrashed wildly. Her fingers clenched around my wrists, her nails piercing my skin. "Yes, Luca! God, yes. Just like that!"

Nothing was more arousing to me than her frantic cries and drawn-out moans, but I managed to restrain myself for another minute before my own release overtook me.

I stayed inside of her as we both waited for our breathing to even out. I rest my head on her chest, trying to decide if I was forgiven or if I'd need to do something else to make up for my selfishness earlier. By the time I finally pulled out, her eyes had drifted shut.

"I'll grab a washcloth," I offered.

"I'm just going to sleep," she said, curling against my bare chest.

I didn't mind if she didn't, so I held her tight to me and listened as her breathing slowed to a level, sleepy pace. It wasn't until she was sound asleep that I remembered.

Giada had stopped taking her birth control.

Shit.

CHAPTER 4

Giada

I couldn't believe my eyes when I rolled over in bed the next morning and saw Luca asleep beside me. I wasn't sure if he'd overslept, or if he truly had the morning off, but I wasn't about to wake him. I didn't dare breathe too loud, let alone shift to release the pressure on my numb arm.

Within a few minutes, though, Luca inhaled a sharp breath and jerked upright. He peered around, eyes wide, then sighed and relaxed against the pillow.

"Did I wake you?" he asked, his voice heavy with sleep.

"No." I snuggled against his chest, pressing my ear over his heart. To my surprise, his pulse was racing like he was running laps. "Did you have a nightmare?"

"Something like that." He smoothed my hair back and pressed a kiss to the crown of my head. A moment later, he shifted out from under me. "I wish I could stay here with you today, but I can't."

"Seems like being the boss means you set the hours."

"Maybe someday." Luca looked miserable as he made his way to the bathroom.

I waited a minute, then followed him. I brushed my teeth next to him then watched admiringly as he dressed. "I hate seeing you look so unhappy. What can I do to help?"

He lifted me onto the counter beside my sink and stepped between my thighs, kissing me languidly. When he pulled back, I reached to his chest and finished buttoning his shirt for him.

"We'll be here most of the day," he finally said. "But I'd like it if you could get out of the house, maybe head into the office for a bit? Or visit with Gabriella?"

I quirked a brow. "So you're trying to get rid of me? I already told work I was taking two weeks off. They understood. And I don't want to hang out with Gabriella while everything is so…volatile."

He appeared to consider that, then suggested I go to a movie. "Alone?"

Luca thought for a moment, then tapped the counter as the solution came to him. "Matteo. You've hardly seen him lately."

I considered the idea, then texted my brother. I assumed he'd say no. He'd been unusually busy lately, although I wasn't sure exactly what he was doing with his time. But within a matter of minutes, he agreed.

Lincoln dropped me off at Matteo's apartment less than two hours later. He physically walked me to the door, not leaving until I was safely inside the building with my brother.

"Apparently, the paparazzi is hung up on Luca," I explained.

Matteo grimaced, but nodded. "So what movie are we seeing?"

"I don't care. Anything that'll distract me from…well, you know." I gazed around the room. "Also, I'm starving. I didn't eat breakfast, so we either need to go to that theater that has good food, or we're going to need a lot of popcorn."

Matteo checked his watch. "Giada, it's after noon. You need to eat. Can I cook you something while you figure out what movie we're going to see?"

I considered that option and nodded. Matteo was no Julia Child, but he was a better chef than I was. Not that *that* was saying much.

He opened his fridge and stared inside. "I have eggs and bacon, so we could do breakfast, or..." he glanced around the room. "There's bread too. French toast? Or a sandwich?"

"French toast, please," I said. Then I shivered. "Why do you keep the place so frickin cold. Do you have a rotting corpse somewhere that you're trying to preserve?"

Matteo rolled his eyes. "There's a sweatshirt on my dresser."

I made my way into his room. Matteo was relatively tidy, but today, his bed wasn't made, and there was a gum wrapper on the rug by his dresser. I bent to pick up the gum wrapper and dropped it into the trash can. As I did, I caught a glimpse of the other contents of his trash. There was not one, but two, condom wrappers.

I jerked my head away, terrified I'd see any other evidence of my brother's recent activities. I grabbed the sweatshirt and pulled it over my head, sniffing for any hint of another girl. Luckily, it bore only the scent of fresh detergent. I resisted the urge to check the trash one last time and instead went out to interrogate my brother.

He was apparently aiming for some speed cooking record or something, as he had already mixed the batter and was preparing to drop the bread onto the hot skillet. A sizzle emerged from the skillet, and I inhaled the sweet aromas.

"So, what did you do last night?" I asked, trying to appear casual.

"Nothing much. Had a friend over. Went to bed early."

"Which friend?"

"Hmm?"

"Which friend did you have over?" I repeated.

"Uh, no one you know," he said.

I quirked a brow, but dropped the interrogation.

Later though, as we walked back to his apartment after the movie, Matteo reached into his jacket pocket for his car keys, and a tube of cherry red lip gloss fell onto the ground. I bent and picked up the item, staring straight at my brother's now rosy face as I handed it back to him.

"Not exactly your color, but a quality brand," I said pointedly.

"It's, umm, not mine. I loaned the jacket to a friend."

"The same friend who was over last night?"

"No. So should I drop you off at your place after the movie, or..."

"Matteo, come on," I said, stopping abruptly. "I know you're dating someone. I saw...what was in your trash can."

He scowled at me. "You were snooping through my trash?"

"I wasn't snooping. I just glanced down, and—"

"It's none of your business whether I'm dating someone or not, Giada," Matteo interrupted. "You know, I cancelled everything I had planned for today so I could keep you company. I was trying to do something nice, and now you're interrogating me like I've done something wrong."

I took a deep breath instead of replying. I'd heard this story before, from practically everyone in my life. Clearly, I was supposed to be grateful my brother was willing to babysit me for free. Instead, I just felt renewed pain at the realization that when I thought we were both hanging out for fun, he was simply fulfilling an obligation.

I was about to tell him I could just call Lincoln for a ride home, when I noticed a familiar car idling in the street in front of Matteo's apartment.

Adrian climbed out when he noticed us approaching. He held a large manila envelope in his hand. He eyed me like a poisonous snake, then turned to my brother.

"Angelo wanted me to give this to you. Apparently, I'm now his courier on my day off," Adrian said.

Matteo accepted the envelope. "No such thing as a day off in our line of work. Do you want to come inside? I need to drive Giada home in a bit, but…"

"I'm sure Adrian could take me. I'm not that far out of the way. Then I won't have to burden you any longer," I said, glaring at my brother.

Adrian opened his mouth, his expression leaving no doubt that he was about to protest. But then, he appeared to sense my desperation and simply nodded instead. "Yeah, I could drop you off at your house, if that's where you're headed."

"Yep," I said, moving towards his Jaguar. "Thanks for the movie and lunch, Matteo. Sorry I ruined your day."

"You didn't ruin—" my brother began, but I slammed the car door before I could hear the rest of his lies. I watched as he and Adrian spoke for a minute, then Adrian joined me in the car.

He waited until he'd pulled into traffic before speaking. "Care to share what that was about?"

I offered the short version, then asked, "Do you know who he's dating?"

Adrian raised an eyebrow and turned to me. "No idea. I didn't even realize he was dating someone."

I eyed him warily, then determined he appeared to be telling the truth. We made awkward small talk for the duration of the drive. When he pulled up to the gate, he pressed the intercom button.

I was about to just tell him the code, but a crackly voice answered.

"It's Adrian Patras. I have Giada."

A loud beeping sounded, then the gate swung open. "Thanks for the ride," I said, unfastening my belt. "Do you want to come in for a bit?"

Adrian stared at the excess of cars filling the driveway and shook his head. "No, I'd rather not die today. Thanks."

I rolled my eyes then went up to the door. To my surprise, Luca was the one who answered.

I smiled and leaned in to wrap my arms around his neck for a kiss, but he pulled back.

"Seriously, Giada? You brought Adrian to our house?" Luca kept his voice low as he lectured me through gritted teeth. "I thought you were going to the movies with your brother, not your ex-boyfriend."

"I did. Adrian just gave me a ride home. It's not a big deal." I started to push past him, but he stepped in front of me.

"Just like it was no big deal for you to answer the door half naked with Alessio?"

For a moment, all I could focus on was whether Alessio told him that or he saw the pictures. Then I realized it didn't matter. "Yes, silly me. I thought I was allowed to live my life in my own house. Guess I know better now."

I stormed past him to the stairs, glaring at the two dozen men filling the first floor of my house. If this was how life was going to be from now on, I'd need to adjust the design of the second floor so I never again had to go downstairs.

Luca

The slam of the bedroom door reverberated through the living room, where all of my papà's former captains began to chuckle. I offered a placating smile to the group while inwardly stifling a groan. I hadn't meant to piss off Giada, but after listening to a handful of jokes about my lack of control over her thanks to those fucking pictures of her with Alessio, I already looked like a complete pansy.

These guys were old school and didn't understand my relationship with Giada. Their wives were possessions, figureheads who hosted dinner parties and birthed their children. They didn't know the first thing about love. And I couldn't fathom how to gain their respect as long as they thought my wife walked all over me.

I was still struggling to regain my concentration and remember what we'd been discussing when my phone rang. The caller ID had been blocked, so I would've rejected the call in any other scenario. But right then, I needed the break.

I signaled to the men to give me a minute, then answered the call, making my way to my office where I'd have a little more privacy.

"Mr. Marino?" The caller was male, with a distinct Italian accent.

"Who's asking?"

"This is Franco Gambino. I assume you've heard of me?"

My stomach clenched, and I motioned for Alessio, who had been loitering in the hall just outside my office, to join me. I mouthed the name to him, not daring to switch to speaker phone in case the caller was, in fact, Franco Gambino. The infamous mob boss controlled much of New Jersey and was likely savvy enough to notice any changes in the connection now.

"How did you get this number?" I asked, careful not to give away any information before confirming his identity.

The man chuckled. "I told my men I wanted it, and they made it happen. I'm sure you understand."

I wasn't sure how to respond to that.

"Listen, your father wasn't my favorite person, so I'm not going to pretend I'm sorry he's gone. But my problems with him were of a personal nature. I have no bias against you or your business. I'm actually calling as a show of good faith, in hopes that we could perhaps build a different type of relationship than the one between your father and me."

"And why would you do that? Surely you don't need my help."

He chuckled again. "No. But I also don't need the Conti family and the Marino family as enemies, and I'd hate for you to catch wind of some gossip and misunderstand."

I inhaled slowly, trying to calm my racing heart. If Mr. Gambino was calling because of Marco's video, that made sense. He wouldn't want to piss off two families if he could avoid it. But I didn't understand what he meant about the gossip or a misunderstanding.

"I'm afraid you'll have to spell it out for me, Mr. Gambino. I don't know what gossip you're referencing."

He sighed. "Well, you're a smart man, so I suspect the news will make its way to you sooner rather than later. I'm glad I called before, though, so you don't jump to any conclusions."

I peered at Alessio, eyebrow raised, but he shook his head, apparently as confused as I was.

"I have something you want, Mr. Marino. But I'm not going to divulge any more than that over the phone. I'd like to meet with you tomorrow, if you can spare a few minutes."

"Sure. You can stop by the house whenever it's convenient."

The man chuckled again. "You certainly do have your father's gumption. I was thinking my house might be a more appropriate location, or perhaps my office? I could even send a car to pick you up if you like."

"That's very thoughtful of you, but I have my own transportation, and maybe we should wait until we get to know each other better before we start visiting each other's homes and offices." I paused. "How about a church? You bring whatever guys you want to stand outdoors, but only you and I will meet inside the sanctuary."

Alessio glared, clearly disagreeing with my assessment that I could handle the meeting solo.

When Mr. Gambino didn't protest, I rattled off the address to

Giada's favorite church, confirmed the time, then disconnected the call.

Alessio and I filled in the other men, then they spent the next several hours filling me in on my papà's full history with the Gambino family and trying to guess what intel or other "gift" Franco could possibly want to share.

Giada ignored me all through dinner, and then when I started to lie down in bed beside her, she made a big show of picking up her pillow as if she were moving to the guestroom. I groaned, then went to the guestroom by myself. I didn't want to sleep in our bed without her, and I was too tired and exhausted to formulate a decent apology until morning.

CHAPTER 5

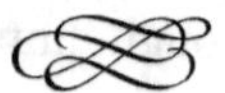

Giada

The clock read 9:30 when I awoke, but I was still so sleepy that I assumed it was wrong, until I noticed Luca's dirty gym clothes in a pile outside our bathroom door. I heard the shower start, and decided it wasn't too early for a call with Gabriella.

Aside from a supportive text, she hadn't really contacted me since Salvatore's death. I didn't blame her, and I wasn't about to push her. But I really needed to hear a comforting voice this morning.

I wrapped my robe around me and made my way to the balcony overlooking the garden, quietly shutting the door behind me before dialing Gabriella. She answered on the first ring. I planned to keep the call casual, just to catch up with her and distract myself from reality for a few minutes, but the moment she asked how I was doing, I burst into tears. Over the next several minutes, the whole story came out.

"I'm so sorry Giada. That's…a lot," Gabby agreed.

"I'm just so worried he's going to turn into his dad," I admitted. "I mean, it's been less than two weeks, and already he's changed."

Gabriella took her time answering. I didn't expect much from her, since she wasn't Luca's biggest fan. But what she said surprised me.

"He's under a lot of pressure now. I don't think what you're seeing in him now is necessarily representative of the man he'll be when the dust settles." She paused. "For your sake, I hope not anyway."

"Me too."

"And you guys always have problems when you're apart for too long," she continued.

"We haven't been apart except for two nights over a week ago."

"Right, but you're not exactly talking much either, from the sound of things. If you want my advice, get him out of the house or go anywhere that the two of you can be alone for a while. Tell him what's worrying you, listen to what's bothering him, and work your magic."

"My magic?"

Gabriella sighed. "You make him a better person, Giada. You know that. He knows that. We all know that. So do it. Before it's too late."

Luca appeared just outside the balcony doors, naked aside from a small towel wrapped around his waist. I turned away abruptly, refusing to be aroused by someone who'd treated me so horribly the night before. But when I glanced back, he was picking up his dirty laundry and making his way to the closet.

A small pang of guilt hit me. Could a man truly be that bad if he picked up his own laundry and looked that hot in a towel?

I stared out at the garden, remembering the pure joy I'd felt when we'd first completed construction on the home. I'd been so excited about the future Luca and I would share, and I'd entertained countless fantasies about what we'd do on this very balcony. So far, we'd only managed to use it a handful of times. I wasn't ready for all of my hopes and dreams about the house to be crushed so soon. I needed to fight to fix things with Luca, before it was too late.

I started to stand from my chair right as the door swung open. Luca now wore dark suit pants and a white sleeveless undershirt that clung to the ridges of his abdominals and did nothing to hide the muscles of his chest or arms. Even sexier, though, was the fact that he offered a steaming mug of coffee to me before even opening his mouth.

"Thank you," I said.

"Can I sit?"

I nodded, then gestured to my phone. "I was talking to Gabriella. She said to tell you hello."

His mouth twitched as he tried not to smile. "No, she didn't."

I sipped my coffee in lieu of answering since, of course, he wasn't wrong.

"I'm sorry for snapping at you yesterday. You can wear whatever you want in the house, and you can hang out with Adrian if that's what you really want. It's not you that I'm mad at. I'm... mad at my papà, I think. And myself. And the whole fucking world."

Luca gazed up at the sky, as if the gray clouds would hold some solution to his problems.

"I don't know what I'm doing, and it's only a matter of time before everyone figures that out. I'm used to disappointing my papà, but now I'm letting down the entire family and you, and I'm not sure I'll be able to handle the consequences."

I swallowed another swig of coffee and then, once it was apparent that he had nothing else to say, I turned to him. "I didn't hang out with Adrian. I went to the movie with Matteo, but then he was being a jerk and we got in a fight. Adrian showed up then with some delivery from Angelo, so I got a ride home from him. That's all."

Luca nodded, then pressed his fingertips into his brows as if warding off a migraine.

"When I'm overwhelmed and scared and looking for answers, I go to church. Nothing else relaxes me as quickly as simply sitting in the sanctuary, alone with my thoughts."

"I wish that worked for me, but it doesn't."

"You don't know that until you try. I'm just asking for you to give it an hour. For me?"

Luca started to shake his head and then frowned. He rose to his feet, stroked his chin, then nodded. "Actually, yeah. Let's do it. Can you be ready in a half hour? I have some business near the church after lunch, but we could go sooner and then Lincoln could drive you home."

I was tempted to protest since I didn't want to be stuck with another unwitting babysitter, but I stopped myself. Luca just agreed to go to church with me. I needed to accept the win.

"Yeah. I'll hurry," I promised.

⁂

Luca

I hadn't slept well, thanks to my unease about the meeting with Franco and my guilt over the fight with Giada. So when she suggested I go to church with her before lunch, I agreed before I realized it was a terrible idea.

Alessio cringed when I told him the plan, but then he reasoned it might be a good time to scope out the place before Franco arrived.

"You sure you don't want to just head out for lunch instead?" I suggested as Giada and I drove to the church. "We could talk there."

"No. You need this as much as I do. Nothing calms my brain like sitting in church," she said.

"We are different people, Giada. I don't think it'll relax me."

"Just wait and see," she said, shaking her head.

When we arrived, she headed towards the confessional. She asked if I had anything I wanted to share in confidence with the Father. I nearly laughed out loud, imagining how that conversation would go.

"Nope, I'm good. Can I just sit wherever and wait on you?"

She nodded, then disappeared into the tiny booth. I strolled around the sanctuary, getting a feel for the space and any hiding spots it might offer. When I ignored the whole religious aspect, I could appreciate why Giada liked it there so much. The cavernous room was gorgeous, dimly lit, and quiet. It felt like an entirely different space than during Sunday mass, when the scent of two hundred different perfumes clogged the aisles and chatter made it impossible to concentrate.

I heard Giada's familiar laugh, then she left the confessional, loudly thanking Father Ryan.

"I thought it was supposed to be anonymous," I said, following her to a pew near the front of the sanctuary.

"Yeah, I mean, it can be. But it doesn't really matter if they know who you are anyway, since it's all confidential."

I was tempted to point out that there were, in fact, exceptions to that confidentiality rule, as I'd researched it years before. But instead I kept quiet. Giada retrieved her rosary from her pocket, then turned to me.

"Usually, when I have a lot on my mind, I start by thinking about all the things stressing me out. Not trying to solve anything, just acknowledging in my brain each item that worries me."

Giada paused and watched me, as if this step alone may have been too much for me. When I didn't protest, she continued.

"Then I pray the rosary. By the time I'm done, I always give myself a few minutes to just sit in silence, and the answers just come to me."

"What answers?"

"The answers to my prayers," she snapped, as though it were obvious. "Sometimes, real solutions to my problems come to me, and other times, there isn't an actual solution in my head, but I feel comforted and less anxious about the situation."

I frowned. "I could just swallow some anxiety pills if that was all I wanted."

Giada squeezed my hand. "Just trust the process, okay? What do you have to lose?"

"An hour of my day that could be spent working on actual solutions," I replied.

My wife's responding glare was icy. I quickly turned away, folded my hands, and tucked my head down as if in prayer.

"I'll give you a few minutes to think, then I'll say the rosary out loud so you can follow along, okay?"

I bobbed my head up and down but didn't dare open my eyes. I decided to give it a try and think about my problems. Unsure of how long she'd give me before she launched into the prayer, I mentally listed each of my current stressors. There was the death of my papà and the complex feelings with that, the stress of leading an entire fucking crime family and multiple semi-legitimate businesses, and there was the uncertainty of what had happened with my papà.

I was also stressed about the state of my marriage, my mom's future, and whatever Franco Gambino was about to share. Oh, and I was really fucking anxious about the possibility that I'd never be able to keep myself and Giada—let alone my entire family—safe.

"Our Father, who art in Heaven..." Giada began, her voice soft but steady.

I quietly listened as she moved through the Lord's prayer, which I did actually know despite my hedonistic upbringing, to a series of prayers I wasn't familiar with. After a few minutes, I opened an eye to peek at Giada, relieved to see that her eyes were closed.

Giada was always beautiful, but she looked more serene when she was deep in prayer. Her full lips moved seamlessly from one line to the next, and her fingers delicately worked along the beads in her hands. Sitting this close, I could feel the warmth radiating off her soft skin, and I could smell the sweet scent of her vanilla lotion.

I watched Giada as she flowed through the prayers, wondering how anyone so pure and so good could ever love someone like me. I thought about how stupid I was to let any of my current stressors come between us, and how if anything was going to save me, it wasn't some all-mighty God I didn't even know if I believed in. No, my only hope for salvation was Giada.

As if sensing my gaze on her, Giada paused. Her eyes flitted open and she offered the slightest hint of a smile before resuming her quiet prayer. She placed her hand over mine, guiding me to the beads and then releasing them into my fingers once I responded. Without a doubt, I now knew I was going to hell, since the close proximity of Giada's hand to my groin was affecting me in the most predictable and unholy of ways.

"You're still staring at me," she said, her eyes opening again.

"Can't help it. You're gorgeous."

"What are you thinking about?"

I drew a blank. "God. And um all his, uh, glory?"

She breathed a laugh. "What were you actually thinking?"

"I was thinking that you're gorgeous and kind and perfect. I don't deserve you, and I can't believe what a dick I've been lately." I cringed the moment I realized I'd just sworn in a church.

"You've had some things on your mind. I don't expect you to be okay right now, but I do want you to talk with me. Stop shutting me out, Luca."

I didn't have an answer for that, but Giada didn't seem to care.

She squeezed my hand again, then let both of our hands drop to my lap.

This time, when her eyes opened, they were wide with surprise and dropped immediately to my obvious erection, which was now jabbing her hand.

"Okay, maybe I was thinking about how much better the world seems after we've made love."

Giada inhaled slowly, crossed herself, then peered around the sanctuary. Aside from one elderly man near the back, we were alone. Giada tugged my hand and led me out of the sanctuary and down a hallway in the opposite direction of the exit. She paused just outside the women's restroom and motioned for me to wait. A minute later, she reemerged, only to tug me inside the room.

Giada clicked the lock on the inside of the heavy wooden door, and I peered around, surprised to see two hideous floral armchairs, a full-length sofa, and several old-fashioned end tables. It was as if we'd been transported back in time.

"Why is there a full living room inside the women's bathroom?"

She bit back a laugh and shrugged. "Not sure. Maybe for funerals or weddings or something, in case you just need to get away?"

I nodded, still unsure why she'd dragged me into the bathroom, until she gripped the back of my neck and pulled my face down to hers. She kissed me like we were back in high school and had only a few minutes together before the next class bell rang. I still didn't know where she was headed with this, but I wasn't going to complain either.

Kissing Giada felt like drinking water after being trapped in the desert for weeks. I lost myself in the sensations, moaning into her mouth. She pulled back just enough to shush me, then reached for the fly of my pants.

My hand flew to hers, my eyes wide. Had she forgotten where we were?

"I locked the door," she whispered, knocking my hands to the side and unzipping my pants so fast she nearly pinched me.

I hesitated for half a second, then reached for her. I kissed and sucked at her neck while lifting her breasts up and out of her bra. I rubbed my thumbs across her nipples until they pebbled beneath my touch, forcing a breathy moan to slip between Giada's moist lips. I peered around us for options, but couldn't bring myself to make use of the creepy funeral couch. So instead, I lifted her onto the counter between the sinks.

I reached under her skirt, growling when I realized her already wet pussy was easily accessible beneath her flimsy thong. I yanked my pants down below my ass, then scooted closer. Dragging Giada's thong to the side, I thrust into her in one swift move before stilling, pausing so both of us a moment to adjust and appreciate the beautiful sensations.

After a moment, Giada shimmied against me, signaling her lack of patience with my antics. I gripped her ass in my hands to guide her hips closer to me, then commenced a delicious rhythm.

"Yes, Luca," Giada moaned, her head lolling back and knocking into the mirror behind her. Her hands drifted to her breasts, and watching her only amplified my arousal.

I could tell Giada was close when her breathing turned to a high-pitched whimper, and the second her pussy began to tighten and pulse around me, I stopped holding back. My orgasm swept over me like a burst damn, stealing my breath and nearly making my knees give out. I slowly lowered Giada to the counter, then grabbed a handful of tissues and cleaned myself up before buttoning my pants. I offered her a few tissues, but she merely groaned happily.

"I need a minute," she said.

I chuckled. "Okay, but we are still in the church bathroom," I reminded her.

"Shit," she mumbled. She dabbed at herself with the tissues while I tucked in my shirt and checked my hair. Giada's cheeks were flushed and her hair was wild, but I doubted anyone other than me could tell how thoroughly, well-fucked she'd just been.

I pressed another kiss to her pliant lips, then lifted her off the counter and back onto the ground.

"Alright, get out of here. I'll meet you in the hall in a minute," Giada said, smiling drunkenly at me.

I cracked the door an inch to peer out, then stepped into the hall once I confirmed it was empty. I checked my watch, then texted Lincoln to come grab Giada. He and Alessio, along with several of the other guys, were already in the neighborhood, scouting things out to ensure no one was setting a trap. I still had a bad feeling about the meeting, but at least now, I knew that whatever happened, I'd go out while on good terms with Giada.

She was still blushing when she joined me in the hall, but she'd touched up her makeup and smoothed her hair. Giada gazed at me, then covered her face in embarrassment.

I motioned her to me, then hugged her tightly. "I love you so much, baby. You know that, right?"

Giada nodded. "Love you too."

I kissed her forehead, then reached for her hand. "Alessio and I have that meeting in the neighborhood," I said casually, as if I'd already told her about it. "So Lincoln is going to drive you home, then I should be back early tonight, okay?"

She looked skeptical, but didn't protest. I walked her to the door, where Lincoln waited right outside. Then, I squeezed her hand one last time.

"Hey, you were right. Going to church did relax me after all," I said.

Giada's giggle burst out of her so abruptly that she moved her hand over her mouth.

I watched as Lincoln escorted her to the car then drove off. A few minutes later, Alessio joined me.

He immediately appeared suspicious. "Jesus," he mumbled. "Are you drunk?"

I shook my head.

"High?"

"No," I insisted.

"Then why do you look so relaxed?"

I wasn't about to tell him, but after a few seconds, his face crumpled into a grimace.

"Oh, God. Seriously? In a church?" He smacked his palm to his forehead. "You're an adult, Luca. And married. You own a fucking house where you can go fool around with your wife. You don't go to a…" he stopped short and shook his head.

I patted him on the back.

We tried to prep for the upcoming meeting as much as possible, then we both went out front to wait for Franco. I couldn't help but wonder if Father Ryan was still in the confessional, or if he'd retreated to his office. I only hoped he'd stay hidden until Franco and I had finished our business.

Mr. Gambino arrived with three other men, but after introductions, he motioned for us to head inside. I'd seen pictures of him before, so I recognized the sharp slant of his dark brows and his unfittingly warm smile, but I was surprised by his stature. The man couldn't have been more than 5'10, and while his belly was round, he wasn't a big guy by any means.

"Where would you feel most comfortable talking?" I asked, hoping he'd interpret my openness to signal that I hadn't planted any traps for him. Of course, he could've filled the place with wires or cameras for all I knew. Maybe he and his cronies had just enjoyed a free show courtesy of Giada and me.

"Let's just walk down the hall," he suggested. "What I have to say will only take a minute, and I'd hate to disturb the priest or any of the parishioners."

"Okay."

"We met once before," he said. "I wouldn't think you'd remember. You couldn't have been more than oh, five or six at the time. Your father and I had a falling out shortly after that.

He'd taken a fancy to my wife, you see, and…" He shook his head as if he hadn't meant to reveal as much. "Well, that's old history. I actually stayed in touch with your father-in-law a few years longer, right until he lost his own father. Obviously, I had nothing to do with that, but that's around the time that we both started focusing on building our own businesses."

He paused, and I decided to speak. "Mr. Gambino, can I ask you a question?" I waited until he nodded to continue. "What is it you want from me today?"

His smile widened. "Absolutely nothing. Well, actually, you could call me Franco. This 'Mr. Gambino' business makes me feel ancient, even though I am."

I smiled politely.

"Look, I'm not here to impress you with tales of how successful or far-reaching my business is, though I could. I'll be the first to admit that I'm too old for more enemies, and I certainly don't want to get on the wrong side of the Contis and the Marinos right off the bat. So I really just want to clear the air."

I stopped walking and turned to face him. "Okay. Let's hear it."

"I won't deny that, from time to time, Mr. Randazzo fed me information about your father's operations."

My breath caught in my throat, and I nearly gagged at the effort to not let my face betray my feelings. I only knew one Randazzo in town, and that was Elio Randazzo, the man we believed murdered my papà. Mr. Gambino seemed oblivious to the fact that this tidbit of Elio sharing info was news to me, and the last thing I wanted to do was to stifle his confession prematurely.

"I swear on my mother's grave that I had nothing to do with what he did to your father," Mr. Gambino continued.

I narrowed my gaze. "Why should I believe you?"

He pointed at me as if I'd just solved the riddle. "That's the rub, right? Why indeed?" He reached into his pocket and withdrew a small slip of paper. "You don't have any reason to believe me, except for what I've told you already. Shoot, you can ask Elio for yourself and maybe he'll tell you the truth, or maybe not." He leaned closer as if sharing a secret. "You know those dirty cops make unreliable narrators, so I'm not sure I'd trust a thing he said."

I wondered if he was under the impression that I already had Elio stowed away somewhere, in some private dungeon of sorts, but then he continued.

"It was in my best interests to let him keep doing what he was doing, drawing a paycheck from good old Uncle Sam to infiltrate my business while simultaneously staying on my payroll by spying on you all. I had nothing to gain from ending that arrangement, and I certainly didn't benefit from what happened to your father, not with you there to pick up where he left off."

I frowned at his crassness.

"I'm an opportunist, though, and I'll make friends where I can and avoid enemies when it suits me. So, here you go. My show of good faith."

Franco pressed the paper in my palm. I waited a moment, then unfolded it. A handful of addresses and names were scribbled on the paper.

"Those are all the names and addresses we've found affiliated with him. Hopefully you can use that info to track him down." Franco paused, waiting for the implication of his words to sink in. "I don't know what your father told you about me, but I'm no traitor. If Mr. Ragazzo were following my orders, I would never hand him over to you. But he went rogue. Seems he had an axe to bury. He wanted revenge after what happened to his buddy Mattia."

I stared down at the paper again, then up to Franco. His expression seemed kind, yet solemn. "Thank you," I said, unsure of what else to say. "I'll uhh...keep you posted?"

He patted my back and winked. "Please don't."

Right.

We smiled awkwardly at each other for a moment, then turned and walked back to the exit. Father Ryan poked his head out of his office, frowning to see me with someone other than my wife. I offered him a polite wave.

"Take care, Luca," Franco said, heading out the front door into the parking lot.

I paused, still reeling from his discoveries, and catching my breath. I realized the priest was still eying me warily as I moved towards the door.

"Giada left a few minutes ago. We'll see you Sunday," I said to the priest, following Franco out the door.

CHAPTER 6

Adrian

The next idyllic day, I left work early. The clear blue skies and warm sunshine looked too tempting to simply appreciate from a window. I planned to walk Scruffy to the dog park and soak in some vitamin D. Maybe I'd even text an old law school buddy about grabbing dinner at one of those bistros with all the outdoor tables.

The building's parking garage was emptier than usual, leaving me to guess that others who worked in the building had been smart enough to work from home on the gorgeous day. I caught myself whistling as I crossed the first row heading towards my assigned spot, and I reached into my pocket for my phone, deciding I should call my buddy and make dinner plans before my good mood waned.

No one had parked on either side of my Jaguar, but as I neared the vehicle, I saw a man crouched over on the passenger side. I frowned, thinking it was odd that he was walking so close, and then I realized the guy had broken the passenger window and was rooting around in my car.

I've always been a call-the-cops-and-wait-around type of guy, so I wasn't sure what possessed me to behave differently this time. But instead of backing away from my car and dialing 9-1-1 with the phone already clutched in my hand, I charged toward my car, shouting, "Hey you!"

The guy pivoted to face me as I reached him. I grabbed for the sleeve of his jacket right as he lifted his other hand, wielding a canister of mace, which he sprayed freely. I bobbed my head to the side, sparing my eyes, then held my breath as I wound back and punched the bastard squarely in his masked face, knocking him back against the side of my car.

I was gearing up to hit him again when something smashed into my back, nailing me right in that sensitive spot between the ribs and hips. I swirled around, coming face to face with two other masked guys.

All the breath whooshed out of me as I realized I was doomed. I poised my arms in front of my head, trying to shield myself from the barrage of punches and kicks slamming into me. I knew I needed to stay upright, that the second I fell to the ground, they could easily cause internal bleeding or worse.

But then something small, yet hard, cracked into the back of my skull. I heard a sickening crunch upon contact, and the last thought that crossed my mind was of Scruffy, frolicking in the park.

The world went black, and I felt the cold pavement meet my face.

Luca

I would've killed for ten minutes alone with Alessio, Thomas, and Giovanni so we could discuss what Franco had said before I had to pass the info along to my papà's guys. I'd probably still decide to go after Elio, but I couldn't say for certain if I actually wanted to find him. I'd already assumed he was responsible for my papà's death, and I figured it had something to do with Mattia's earlier death. Elio and Mattia had joined the family at the same time, and they'd always seemed close. When my papà had determined one of them was a rat, he asked Elio to take out Mattia. Conveniently, something had come up and kept Elio from following through with his orders, but Mattia still ended up dead from an apparent overdose. Elio hadn't seemed happy.

Now that we had confirmation of Elio's guilt—plus possible locations, I had no reason to delay the manhunt. Tony wouldn't care that the guy was a cop, albeit a dirty one, and he sure wouldn't care that he'd sought vengeance for his friend. I couldn't let the guys think I had any reservations about avenging my papà's murder. Especially since, for the most part, I didn't. I never could've let Elio get away with what he'd done. Even hinting that such a result might be acceptable would've put my life—and that of all my men—at risk, as we'd be seen as weak. But without an address for Elio, we could've spent ages hunting for him unsuccessfully.

"Start at the beginning," Tony instructed me the second Iacopo pulled away from the curb.

And so I did.

We drove straight to 4th and Main, meeting for over an hour at the club to discuss who should go look for Elio, and whether we believed that Franco hadn't ordered the hit. I, for one, actually did believe him, but I also wasn't sure it mattered. He hadn't pretended to have liked my papà or to be sad over his death, but maybe that was okay. He could still support me and the Marino family going forward.

Tony rattled off names of guys to send after Elio, and I agreed. He left Alessio, Thomas, and Giovanni off the list, which I appreciated. I wasn't sure if Tony sensed that I'd rather not involve them, or he just thought I needed them by my side, but I wasn't going to complain. We agreed the guys should leave right away, just in case Franco gave Elio a heads up that he'd tipped us off.

It was well past dinner by the time Alessio and I were heading home, so I stopped and bought a bouquet of flowers for Giada.

"This was a good day, Luca," Alessio said as we continued the drive after our pitstop. It was obvious from his tone that he knew I'd be resistant to the notion.

"And it's over," I said. No matter how I felt about the events of the day, I didn't have to field any more 'what ifs' with the Gambino family. I now knew why their boss wanted to meet me, and I'd survived.

"He's a killer, Luca. No matter why he did it, the fact is that Elio is a murderer."

I nodded. That was true. Maybe a court of law wouldn't deem execution an appropriate punishment for Elio, but they would agree with the label.

"We would've found him eventually, so this is better. We'll get it over with fast." Alessio paused. "And you're in charge now, so it's your call how you handle it. Or even who handles it."

I wondered if that was Alessio's way of volunteering to take care of Elio's punishment for me, but I didn't ask. I would have to be the one to carry out the sentence. There was no way around that. I was the boss. And I was the victim's son. I had no excuse to avoid the burden.

Adrian

I awoke to the smell of alcohol and a sharp sting on my forehead. I tried to protest, but my throat was dry and produced only a weak groan. I opened my eyes, blinking repeatedly until the blurry scene in front of me began to blur.

"It figures you sleep through an IV insertion but can't handle a little antiseptic," a familiar voice teased. I turned my head in her direction, seeing only a blurry face, brown hair, and a white coat.

"Melissa?" I asked, pretty sure I recognized my ex's voice.

A painfully bright light shone in my eyes, forcing them closed.

"Yes, it's me, Adrian. I'm going to hold your eyelid here for a moment. Just look straight ahead. Sorry about the light. You hit your head."

I tried to explain that I didn't hit my head so much as someone else hit me on the head, but I was too parched. "Water?" I asked.

I felt Melissa's fingers on one eyelid then the other.

"Alright, I want you to blink a few times. And Miss Angela, your amazing nurse, is holding your water cup, so just sip through that straw."

I squeezed my eyes shut and drank. The cool, crisp water reminded me of the mountains, and I made a note to schedule a ski trip for the winter.

"Adrian?"

I opened my eyes, obediently blinking. To my delight, I could now make out Melissa's face. And the face of another woman, I guess Angela, beside her. *Wow.* Angela was gorgeous. Her copper-colored hair fell in long waves over her shoulders, and her smile somehow reassured me.

"What happened?" I croaked.

"Someone found you in the parking garage and called the paramedics. It looks like you were attacked, and you seem to have a concussion, so I need to run a few more tests here, then Angela will wheel you over to CT."

"Angela," I repeated, smiling.

Melissa sighed. "We're going to act like this is part of the confusion from the concussion and that you're not seriously about to hit on the nurse in front of your ex-girlfriend. Okay, keep your eyes on the tip of my pen."

I watched as she moved it up, then down, and then to the side. I squeezed my eyes shut, dizzy, before letting her proceed with the other side.

They cleaned up a few more cuts and bruises on my body, then transferred me to CT. By the time I returned to a regular bed, my sister, Annie had arrived.

"We're still waiting on the results of your scans, so no eating or drinking until we see those. In the meantime, I'm fairly confident you have a concussion. You also needed some stitches on your arm. It looks like you fell on glass. Your ribs are bruised and your stomach is bruised, and we'll rule out any internal bleeding." She paused, then rattled off the symptoms I might feel from the concussion.

"We're keeping you overnight at least, but assuming your scans look good, you can head home tomorrow."

"Thanks."

Melissa nodded and started toward the door. "Oh, and the police want to talk to you."

I felt my eyes widen. "Police? Why?"

She frowned as if my question were stupid. "Because you were attacked, Adrian."

"Oh. Right," I said, trying to calm my nerves and steady my voice. "I guess, um, send them in."

Two cops I vaguely recognized from the courthouse filed into my room and introduced themselves. The female, Detective Rogers, spoke first.

"You're one lucky guy, Mr. Patras," she said, wincing at my appearance.

Annie had already told me I looked like shit, so I wasn't offended.

"I don't feel lucky. I had plans to take my dog to the park tonight."

Officer Wilkes quirked a brow. "Do you have any idea who did this to you, or why?"

I shook my head.

He frowned as if my response seemed implausible. Then he asked me to tell them everything I remembered.

"So, you didn't get a look at any of the guys? Didn't recognize their clothes? Their voices? Their build?" he asked when I finished.

"No. They wore masks."

"Right, but if it was someone you know…"

"Why would someone I know attack me?"

The Officer stared pointedly as if I'd just admitted something. I could see now why some of my acquaintances lacked confidence in the competence of our police force.

"Okay, Mr. Patras, my partner here doesn't mean to imply you had anything to do with this or that you are anything other than a victim. I assure you, we are doing everything we can to get to the bottom of this and find out who did this to you." The detective paused. "We've had your car towed to the police lot so we can check for fingerprints, but the evidence team will work fast so you can pick it up the moment you're released."

I cringed, picturing my poor car being manhandled by a tow truck, then possibly left outside overnight.

"There's just some things we can't make sense of," she finished.

"Such as?"

"You said your attackers had broken the window before you arrived, so it seems like they were trying to steal the car, right?"

I nodded.

"But when the paramedics and police arrived, your car keys were on the ground beside you. Why wouldn't they just grab the keys and take off with the car?"

"I guess they were interrupted before they had a chance to."

"Were your keys in your hand as you approached your car?"

I tried to remember, then realized. "No, I don't think they

would have been. The car unlocks and starts with the key in my pocket, so I usually leave the key in my pocket."

"Was your wallet in the same pocket?" Officer Wilkes asked.

"Shit. They took my wallet?"

He shook his head. "No. Your wallet was laying on top of you. We logged its contents for evidence, but you'll have to confirm if anything is missing."

Detective Rogers offered me a large Ziplock containing my car keys, cell phone, and wallet. I thumbed through my wallet, noting my license, health insurance card, attorney ID card, several credit cards, and my gym membership were still in place. There also appeared to be roughly two hundred dollars in cash. I couldn't recall exactly how much I'd left in there, but it seemed odd that a mugger hadn't at least taken the cash.

"We thought that was strange too," she said. "If they had time to remove your wallet from your pocket, why not just take it with them?"

Her question was rhetorical.

I tried to think back, and then it hit me. "Maybe they weren't trying to steal the car or mug me. They were looking for something!"

"Like what?"

I shrugged, wishing Melissa would return with the test results so I could be done with the interrogation. And so I could resume eating and drinking. I was famished.

"Did you keep anything of value or of interest in your vehicle?"

"No." There was probably some gum, backup gym clothes, and maybe a set of basic tools, but nothing anyone would want. "It's an expensive car, so maybe they just assumed..." I stopped midsentence when I remembered what was in my glove box. Thank God I only stored the gun legally registered to my name there and not the bonus weapon Angelo had tried to stick me with a while back.

"There's a firearm in my glove box," I told the officers. "I keep it locked, but—"

"The glove box was open when officers arrived on the scene," Officer Wilkes said. "And the gun was still there."

I breathed a sigh of relief, thankful the morons who attacked me didn't have even more firepower now.

"Assuming we find everything is in order with the weapon, it'll be returned to you once we verify registration."

I was about to thank them, when the officer aimed lower.

"Tell us about your relationship with the infamous mob boss who was recently murdered," he said.

My abs clenched, and pain shot through my torso. I struggled to keep my expression steady. "If you're asking about Salvatore Marino, I met him once. That's all I know."

"You attended his funeral."

"I dated his daughter-in-law for years. I wanted to see how she was holding up."

"So you're still close with Mrs. Marino?"

The question confused me. I barely knew Camilla Marino. Unless they meant Giada. "Giada Conti?"

"Her legal name is Marino."

I rolled my eyes. "I would not say we're close. I see her a couple times a year. Her husband hates me."

"Hates you enough to send someone to beat you up?"

I considered the possibility, not that I'd tell the cops if it was him. But I truly didn't think it was. Luca had no reason to be pissed at me, well, unless he didn't like me driving Giada home, but even then he wouldn't have done this. He owed me.

"No, I don't think so."

"What about the Conti family?"

"What about them?"

"You work for them, right?"

"No."

Officer Wilkes gazed back at me with an expression that told me he knew the exact nature of my relationship with the Conti family.

"Their family tends to get in a lot of trouble," he continued.

"I wouldn't know."

"Oh, you don't associate with them?"

"Like I said, I dated Giada for years. I still sometimes hang out with her brothers. I don't think I've ever seen them in trouble, though, and I'm not sure what this has to do with my attack."

The officers exchanged a look, then stood in tandem. "Thanks for your time, Mr. Patras. I hope you heal quickly. Give me a call if you remember anything else, and come by the station to pick up your firearm when you're better." Detective Rogers placed a business card on my tray table, then they both left.

I waited a minute, then tugged my cell phone from the Ziplock. As far as I could tell, they hadn't been able to unlock it. I dialed Angelo, and he answered quickly.

"I'm in the hospital," I said. "We should talk."

CHAPTER 7

Giada

I thought that Luca and I had turned a corner after our day together in the church. But he had promised he'd be home early that night, and he wasn't. Nor was he any more present or less stressed the next day.

I knew I needed to be patient. Luca was grieving. He was also transitioning into a new, hellish job. Literally every aspect of his life was changing.

Well, except me.

I was still the same old Giada, ready and willing to love him. I just wasn't sure Luca still wanted that.

I decided to push the envelope.

I crawled out of bed early the following morning, prepared to tell my husband I was headed to the gym before work if he woke. But the poor guy was so tired that he slept through my sneaking out.

I retrieved the muffins and pastries I'd bought the day before from my secret hiding spot inside the bottom oven, then I brewed a pot of coffee while attempting my Aunt Bianca's "no fail" frittata recipe. The poor woman had tried countless times to teach me the allegedly simple dish, and mine never turned out quite right—until recently. The last two times I'd followed the instructions, the finished product was not only edible, but delicious.

I set the table for two right as Alessio sauntered in. His eyes lit up, and he reached into the basket holding the pastries. I let him grab one, but when he went for a second, I swatted his hand.

"Ow," he complained, his gaze drifting to the table. "Oh, so this is *that* type of breakfast."

For a moment, I felt bad about excluding him. Then I remembered that he got Luca to himself way more than I did.

"Yes. And I want a solid hour with him before you interrupt for any reason."

Alessio eyed his watch. "Any particular reason you need to have this meeting?"

I didn't understand the question until I saw his eyes pause on my stomach. I blanched. "No. Definitely not that. I just haven't had any time with him lately. We're drifting apart. And he's always so stressed that—"

"Who's always stressed?" Luca asked, waltzing into the kitchen as if he didn't have a care in the world. He poured himself a cup of coffee and topped it off with a healthy dose of milk before pressing a kiss to my forehead. "Good morning, gorgeous."

This was not the distant, harried Luca I'd been worrying about. I wasn't sure what was happening. I exchanged a look with Alessio, but he merely shrugged.

"I'll leave you two lovebirds alone," he said, swiping a second muffin on his way back to his wing of the house.

Luca watched him go before turning to me. "What's all this? Did you cook?"

"Only the frittata," I admitted.

"Looks amazing."

I served us both a portion, and we moved to the table. Luca tasted his eggs and groaned with pleasure.

"Better than Bianca's," he lied.

I chewed my first bite and had to agree it was my best attempt by far.

"So, I hate to risk ending up in the doghouse, but is this a special occasion I forgot about?" Luca asked.

I smiled at his directness. "No, I just missed seeing you. You're so busy lately, and when I do see you, you're so stressed."

"I'm sorry."

"I don't want you to be sorry. I want to help you not feel so stressed. I'd like to be there for you."

At that, Luca became very engrossed in his food, so I waited a moment, then prodded further.

"Do you want to talk about your dad? I haven't lost someone that close to me, but I know the feeling. What they say is true, about how grief comes in waves. When I thought you were dead—"

"But I wasn't dead," Luca interrupted. "My papà is. So, not really the same thing."

I bit back a sigh. "No, you're right. I only meant that if you want to talk about it, I'm here."

"You never really liked him."

"Neither did you!" I blurted out, slapping both hands over my mouth the moment I let loose the words. I didn't breathe for a full minute, and then Luca chuckled.

"That's true." He wiped his mouth on his napkin and stood.

My stomach dropped as I assumed he was leaving, but instead he retrieved the coffee pot and refilled both of our mugs. "Thank you," I mumbled.

"I still don't really know what I feel about my papà. I'm sad sometimes, but it's not because he's not with me. It's more like regret that things weren't different with us." Luca paused. "And now they never could be."

I reached for his hand and squeezed it.

"Rationally, I know nothing would've changed with him anyway, so it's a moot point." He downed a long swig of his coffee. "I just figured I'd have another thirty or forty years to disappoint him."

"He was proud of you when he died."

Luca nodded. "That's the crazy part. And now, I feel like I'm supposed to miss him for things like holiday gatherings or the brilliant advice he gives me, but I just miss having him here to deal with his own guys. I don't like how they do things, but I'm younger and newer than most of them, so I'm going insane trying to prove myself."

"Do you think you'll get used to their way eventually?" I asked.

"I hope not. But I also don't even want to let on how uncomfortable I am with most of them."

Luca tapped his foot on the floor, and I realized his breathing was picking up now too. Clearly, this topic was raising his stress.

"You seemed happier this morning," I said, trying to get him to focus on whatever positives there may be.

"Yeah, because I sent all the guys I don't like on out-of-town errands."

"What kind of errands?"

Luca's expression changed, and for a moment, I was sure he was about to shut down. Instead, he set down his coffee. "I got a tip from a reliable source about the man who killed my papà."

My jaw dropped. "You know who it was?"

Luca nodded. "We had suspicions before, but this tip confirmed it. Crazy thing, it came from Franco Gambino. Remember him?"

I shrugged. "It sounds familiar."

"He's a boss of another family."

"Oh. So why would he give you a tip? Don't you worry it's a trap?"

"The guy we're looking for, he worked for Franco, and he was supposed to gather intel on our family business. My papà found out someone was spying, but he guessed the wrong guy was the rat. Franco swears he didn't order the hit on my papà and that Elio just went rogue."

"Wow," I said, unable to formulate any other response.

"Yeah," Luca agreed. "The even crazier part? Franco says the guy was actually an undercover cop. He was in deep cover, trying to get in good with the Gambino family, but by some weird twist of fate, the job Franco gave him was to spy on us instead."

"Franco knew he was a cop?"

Luca shook his head. "Not at first. Maybe not even until the end. I'm not sure on the details."

"Wow," I repeated. "Well, at least you have closure now. You know who it was, and there's no reason to think he'll come after you now, right?"

"No, baby. Zero chance of that. He's long gone anyway. He'd never willingly return to the tristate area, maybe not even New England."

"Good." I carried our plates to the kitchen, then caught a glimpse of the clock. Our hour was almost up, and we'd barely started talking. "What if you took a day off?" I suggested.

"Aren't you working today too?" Luca joined me in the kitchen.

"We could both play hooky."

Luca grinned, roping his arms around my waist from behind, kissing the side of my neck. "I have many good memories of playing hooky with you," he said, his hot breath sending shivers up my neck. "But I can't today."

I started to protest when my phone rang. "Angelo," I said aloud, planning to let the call go to voice mail.

"You should answer," Luca said. "I need to head out in a few."

I groaned but answered the call.

"Hey, have you heard about Adrian?" my brother asked.

"Hi sister dearest, how are you doing today? I hope I'm not interrupting, but I had a question," I parroted, wishing he were capable of learning basic manners.

My brother's sigh made static crackle across the connection. "Adrian is in the hospital, in case you didn't know."

His words took a moment to fully sink in. "Wait, what? Why? Which hospital? Is he okay? What happened?"

Luca zipped around the corner, apparently having heard the panic in my voice. I swiveled away from him, not wanting him to see my raw emotion as I processed this horrific update about my ex-boyfriend.

"He got jumped in the parking garage. They knocked him around pretty good, but he'll be fine."

"Who?" I repeated. "And why?" This didn't make sense. Adrian didn't get into fights. Adrian was the good guy. He kept his nose clean and didn't fraternize with the type of guys who jumped people in garages. It must have been a random attack.

"Not a carjacking and not a mugging," my brother said, as if reading my thoughts. "Cops wanted to blame it on him pissing off someone involved in organized crime. I sure don't know anything about it, though, but I told him I'd ask around."

"Well, I obviously don't know anything about it," I said. And then I stiffened. Did I?

"He should be getting discharged later today or tomorrow at the latest, but he can't be alone on account of the concussion so he'll be staying with his sister for a while."

"That's good," I said.

"Give him space, Giada. Don't visit him."

I rolled my eyes, but before I could respond, Angelo hung up. I groaned and muttered under my breath, "Good talking to you, too."

I needed a moment to process what I'd just learned, but Luca was right there, reaching for my arm, asking me what was wrong. My thoughts were flying in a million different directions, and I couldn't reign them in. If Angelo said he was looking into it, surely that was the truth. Besides, Adrian was one of the few people my brother seemed to like lately. Or at least trust. He'd never hurt Adrian.

Luca pulled me against his chest, smoothing my hair while repeating his questions about my call. Leaning against his firm torso, the steady thrum of his pulse against my ear, I remembered the moment I'd first learned that Luca was the one behind the violent beating of Enzo. At the time, I'd been terrified. Luca had found out that Enzo and I shared one little makeout session, and he'd gone ballistic.

But Luca wasn't that person anymore. He'd never hurt someone else, especially not out of jealousy. And besides, Adrian hadn't done anything wrong.

"Baby, you're scaring me. What happened?" Luca repeated, holding me at arm's length.

I gave him the brief version, then watched his reaction. Luca looked surprised, but then he asked, "But he'll be okay, right?"

Something about the tenor of his tone, the complete nonchalance behind his words, sent shivers up my spine. And then I remembered the week before, how angry Luca had been when Adrian drove me home. Sure, he'd apologized, but he'd also explained that he was mostly just embarrassed because the other guys saw and thought he was a pushover…the same other guys he just admitted to trying to impress.

"Tell me you didn't have anything to do with this," I said, my voice low and pleading.

Luca stared back at me for a beat, then dropped my arms, shaking his head. "How can you even ask me that, Giada?"

I hated the feeling in the pit of my stomach, but I had to know. "I need you to answer, Luca."

"No, Giada. Fuck no!" he swung his arm to the side, knocking the empty pan that held the remnants of the frittata onto the floor.

The resulting clammer was painfully loud, and it took all of my self-control not to scream.

Luca swiveled back to me, stepping right into my face. "I swore to you I'd never hurt him, no matter what. When I made that promise, I thought there might come a time when he'd rat me out to the cops or come between us, you know, something big, that actually matters. And I still made the fucking promise because I would do anything for you." His breathing came out raspy and uneven. "And now you think I broke my promise to you for what? Because he drove you home? Jesus, Giada. I'm glad he gave you a ride when you needed it."

"Okay," I murmured, fighting back tears.

"I can't even believe you'd ask me that," Luca repeated. "I thought you loved me." He started out of the room.

"Luca, I do love you!" I waited until he paused to continue. "I didn't really think you did, but I just had to ask. You're not... you're not..." I stammered.

"What?" he snapped.

"I feel like I don't know you anymore. You're not the same person lately."

"Yes, I am!" he shouted back.

"Really? Then show me. Spend the day with me and prove it."

Luca gazed back at me, his eyes filled with disappointment. "I can't make you see something when you won't open your eyes."

He stormed out of the house, leaving me alone with my tears.

Adrian

J'd been discharged late in the day, and I was exhausted by the time Annie and I returned to her apartment. She grabbed sheets for me while I rearranged her tiny living room to make space to extend the sleeper sofa. We made the bed together, then I collapsed onto it, already half asleep. Annie switched off the light, then I expected her to retreat to her own room. Instead, she sat on the edge of the couch.

"Why was Angelo Conti at the hospital?" she asked, her voice soft.

"I called him. I thought maybe he could find out something about what happened to me," I said. "He's got…connections."

Her uncomfortable swallow seemed too loud for the small space. "Do you think he was involved? Or someone else in his family?"

"No." That was the truth. The Contis had no reason to harm me. After talking with Angelo, his best guess was that someone was looking for something. With all the attention the Marinos had gotten since losing Sal, Angelo figured someone had been watching Giada the day I delivered those papers to Matteo and ran into Giada. The fact that someone out there thought I was now the Conti's errand boy was scary, especially since I didn't even know what was in the envelope I'd delivered to Matteo. Presumably, Matteo knew, but he was now in Italy. And if Angelo knew, he wasn't telling me.

I realized my sister was waiting for me to elaborate, so I did, desperate for her to leave and let me sleep. "The Contis are mixed up in some bad shit, but they have no reason to hurt me."

"As long as you stay on their good side, you mean," she added.

"I don't plan to piss them off, so it's fine." I shifted onto my side and yawned loudly. Thankfully, Annie took the hint and headed to her bedroom.

The next morning, I awoke to a pounding headache, instantly reminding me of my concussion. I swallowed some pills, thankful

I'd left them and a glass of water next to the bed, then rummaged through Annie's kitchen until I found a granola bar. I wolfed the snack, then crawled back under the covers, pressing a pillow over the side of my face to block the sunlight streaming in through the window adjacent to the couch.

When I next awoke, I was pleased to see I'd managed to sleep nearly another two hours. I gazed up to see Annie rush into the bathroom, and I chuckled, thinking she was probably trying to beat me. I made my way to the kitchen, where I found hazelnut flavored coffee pods, and prepared her cup first. The apartment walls were thin, and at first, I thought my sister was coughing.

But a moment later, I grimaced, positive that the sounds I heard were actually my sister puking her guts out on the other side of the bathroom door. I waited a moment until the retching sounds stopped, then tapped on the door.

"You okay, Annie?"

She groaned. "Go away."

I stifled a laugh, figuring she'd overindulged cocktails with her friends after putting me to bed the night before. I grabbed her a glass of water, then busied myself re-folding the sleeper sofa so there was space to maneuver through the living room.

I heard the toilet flush, then the sink running for several minutes, and then finally, Annie emerged. Her skin had a greenish hue, and she scowled at me.

"There's ice water on the counter," I said. "So I guess you had a fun night last night."

Annie sipped the water, frowning. "Huh? I went to bed after I tucked you in."

Instinctively, I held my breath, like the germs couldn't get me now even though I'd slept on her couch. "Stomach bug?"

My sister stared at me for what felt like an eternity, her expression unreadable. Finally, she blew out a sigh. "I guess I should tell you since you'll probably figure it out eventually even though you're apparently completely clueless."

"Figure out what?"

"I don't have a stomach bug, Adrian. And I'm not hungover."

"But you're…" I began, and then in a flash, *I* was the nauseous one. "Oh."

Annie nodded.

"I didn't even know you were dating anyone," I said, stumped.

"I'm not," she snapped.

I winced. "So…do you know who the father is?"

"Oh my God, yes, Adrian. Geez. Just because I'm not dating him doesn't mean I'm screwing a bunch of different men at once."

I bit back a laugh at her weird way of insisting she wasn't sleeping around. "Does he know?"

"Does he know we're not dating?"

"No, does he know you're…" I gestured at her midsection, still unable to say the word "pregnant."

She made a face. "I haven't told him yet."

"But you're going to?"

Annie's expression tightened. "I haven't decided." She paused. "I mean, I haven't decided if I'm keeping the baby, so…"

"Oh."

She stared back at me, almost as if awaiting my judgment.

"Look, I don't know your mystery man, but if it was me, I'd want to know if my one-night stand got knocked up. I'd want to be a part of the decision."

Annie blew out a sigh. "A, it's not a one-night stand. I just said we aren't dating. I don't like labels, but if I had to call it something, I'd say we're more like friends. And B, bullshit. If you're trying to claim you'd rather have some big, heavy, life-altering decision on your plate versus just never knowing and not having to stress about it all, I don't believe you for a minute."

Okay, she had a point. "Okay, so you're friends with the guy. Let's say you decide not to continue with the pregnancy. Then in this hypothetical scenario, what do you see that doing to the friendship?"

Annie dropped her head onto a pillow and groaned. "I don't think I could face him."

"Alright, well, let's say you tell him about it, but tell him you're not sure what you want to do. How would he react?"

My sister flung her hands in the air. "I don't know. But with my luck, he'd probably be a fucking saint about it and support me either way, or some shit like that."

"So, he's a nice guy?"

She made a frustrated face at me. "I said we were friends. Why would I be friends with a total dick?"

"Well, historically, you didn't have the best taste in guys, so…"

Another pillow smacked into me.

"Do you want me to talk to him?"

"God no."

We were both quiet for a few minutes. Then my sister turned to me, her expression soured, and she grimaced. "Are you wearing cologne?"

"Aftershave."

She gagged.

I stood and moved across the room. "Does the guy have money? I mean, if you had the baby, could he pay child support?"

Annie nodded.

"Is he married?"

"No."

"Just playing devil's advocate here, but if he's such a good guy, why don't you just want to have the baby? Seems like he could help take care of it. And you."

"Maybe I don't want a baby now, Adrian. Did you consider that?"

I shrugged. "Do you ever want kids?"

"Yes, of course."

"Just not now?"

"I don't know. The timing isn't ideal, but it's also not terrible."

I finished my coffee and went to make more. I nearly offered her one, but then I remembered her condition. I wasn't even sure if pregnant women could drink coffee. "Look, Annie, I'm trying to help you think all this through, but I'm not sure I get it. You know I'm on your side no matter what you want to do, but can you help me understand why you're so dead set on not telling him?

Tears brimmed in her eyes, and I almost felt bad for pushing her. But then she spoke. "If I tell him, he'll rush out and get me those stupid anti-nausea bands. He'll come to all the doctor appointments. God, he'll probably propose within a week. And even after I turn him down, he'll still wait on me hand and foot until the baby's born."

I tried to see what the bad side of that was. "You think he'll try to take the baby or something after?"

"No. He'd just pay for everything and continue to be the perfect gentleman."

Okay, I was definitely missing something. "Why would you turn him down if he proposed?"

"He is not the kind of man I would ever marry. And even if I didn't marry him, having a baby with him would mean I was forever shackled to him and his lifestyle and his…family."

"Does his family not like you?"

"They don't really know me, but I'm sure they'd love me," she replied, her smile suggesting she'd thought about it before.

I flung my hands in the air, officially giving up. Annie had never been the most rational person, and apparently the pregnancy hormones were making it even worse. "Okay, I'm butting out of it. Just please come talk to me before you decide anything permanent. Or else talk to the dad." I paused. "Where did you say he is?"

"Out of town."

I quirked a brow, unsure why she wouldn't tell me more specifics. It wasn't like I knew the guy anyway.

Annie shivered and tried to warm herself with her hands.

I gazed around the room for a blanket. Seeing none, I stood.

"There's one on the chair by the bed," she said, reading my mind.

I made my way into her room, wincing at the mess. Annie had never been a neat-freak, but this was bad. I spotted a fuzzy turquoise blanket on the floor beside the chair and grabbed it. I dropped it on my sister's lap before returning to her room, determined to at least pick up all the cups, plates, empty bottles of Sprite, and trash.

"You don't have to clean my room," she called from the living room.

I ignored her. I dropped one load of dishes into the sink, then went back for the rest of the trash. As I tried to sweep a pile of cracker crumbs into my hand, I accidentally knocked over the bowl containing the remaining crackers. I crouched down to pick up the crackers and poked my head under the bed to make sure none had fallen beneath the bed. I hated to think how long it would be before my sister would ever clean under her bed.

There weren't any crackers there, but something shimmery caught my eye. I reached for it, assuming it was an earring or other piece of jewelry. When I stood up, I saw that it was a silver cufflink.

The letter C filled the face of the cufflink.

My stomach dropped.

I recognized that cufflink, but there was only one person who owned it, and he had no reason to be in my sister's bedroom.

Unless…

I held my breath as all of her comments rushed over me. Not married, plenty of money, nice family, but a lifestyle she didn't like. It all fit. Well, except for the nice part, of course, but I supposed he could be nice to her while maintaining his asshole persona with the rest of the world.

I squeezed my eyes shut, suddenly worried I was going to be the one puking.

"Adrian?" Annie called.

I took a steadying breath, then stormed out to confront her. I gripped the cufflink tightly, marching straight to my sister.

"What is this?" I asked, depositing it in her hand.

She stared at it for a moment, then swore under her breath.

"Annie, is Angelo Conti the father of your baby?"

CHAPTER 8

Luca

I was in no mood for anything that week. I hadn't spoken more than two words to Giada since she'd accused me of beating up Adrian, but I also couldn't think about anything else. I knew I needed to get in a better headspace before I did something stupid and got myself killed, but I had no idea how to achieve that.

So instead, I kept busy. My mom and I met with papà's lawyer about the estate, and there were no surprises. Mom was on the title for both the Staten Island house and the Rome house, and the business assets were now mine. The property in Palermo was apparently already mine, and the lawyer recommended Mom add me to the title of the other properties as a precaution now anyway.

Papà had carefully arranged everything so as to avoid any estate taxes, but in the end, that also made the transition more seamless. For such a wealthy man, he technically owned virtually nothing at the time of his death. Even his fleet of luxury cars all bore someone else's name on the title.

Tomasso and Tony came out for drinks with Alessio and me after the meeting, and we finalized everyone's new roles in the organization. I had been careful to change as little as possible, not wanting to ruffle feathers by uprooting any of the power hierarchy the other guys in my papà's crew had enjoyed for so long. There was enough money in the coffers to give my guys the bigger slice of the pie they deserved in light of their new, enhanced roles, without diminishing the benefits any of the other guys had grown accustomed to.

My head was still spinning, but at least I'd figured out the basic stuff I'd been dreading for so long. Finally, I could focus on my personal life and salvaging my marriage before Giada stabbed me in my sleep.

Truth be told, I still firmly believed she was the one who needed to apologize, but I knew from experience that the easiest way to repair whatever was broken between us was for me to take the first step.

I was about to make dinner reservations for the two of us when my phone rang. It was Domenico. I sighed, then answered.

"We found him," he said.

My heart sunk. I knew exactly who they'd found, and what the discovery meant.

"Fantastic," I said, feeling anything but. "Good work." Domenico had headed to Virginia and D.C. with Alonzo, but Arturo and Dario were still following a lead in Pennsylvania. Finding Elio was the first step, but bringing him home might prove harder.

"Keep eyes on him until Arturo and Dario arrive to help. If you need more, I can send Lodovico and Iacopo too."

"No, Arty and D should be plenty. I think he's alone, so we might not even need backup."

"They can get there by tomorrow at the latest. Just wait," I encouraged.

I disconnected the call, then dialed my cousin Dario.

So much for date night.

Adrian

I was prepared to hold my sister's gaze until she answered. What I didn't expect was for her to laugh.

"You think I slept with Angelo?" she asked.

"I'm trying very hard *not* to think about it," I replied honestly.

Annie rolled her eyes and dropped the cufflink on the coffee table.

"Don't lie to me, Annie. I've seen that cufflink before. I know it's his."

"Angelo is not the only person with his initial on a cufflink. It wouldn't even need to be his last name initial. For all you know, I could be dating a guy named Craig."

I clenched my teeth and scowled at Annie.

I sank into the armchair closest to the couch. "God, Annie, you cannot have a baby with Angelo Conti." I paused, then thought further. "But if he knew I said that or even that I knew about the baby, he would kill me. Like, literally. Do you get that? Do you realize that's the kind of man you're sleeping with?" I rose to my feet again and began mumbling to myself while pacing the floor. There had to be a way out of this mess, but I sure didn't see it. I needed to concentrate.

"Adrian!" Annie snapped, interrupting my panic. "Chill out. I'm not sleeping with Angelo."

I held up my palm, not needing any more of her lies and really not needing any more visual images about her with Angelo.

"Adrian, I'm telling you the truth. And besides, didn't you just tell me last night how Angelo would never hurt a fly?"

"He has hurt thousands of flies, Annie! I said he wouldn't hurt *me*, and that was only true because I was on his good side. Now, who knows." My headache had returned with a vengeance, but I just rubbed my head while continuing to pace.

"Geez. It's not Angelo's baby, okay? Matteo is the father."

I stopped mid-step, swiveling to face her. "Matteo Conti?"

Annie nodded.

I shook my head, pointing to the cufflink. "But that's Angelo's…"

"Apparently, they both have the same set. It's not a stretch to think their dad might have gotten them both cufflinks with the family name."

"You're sure?" I asked. "I mean, that it's Matteo's?"

"He's the only guy I've been with for like a year, so yeah. I'm positive."

Relief coursed through my veins. If Annie had told me a half hour earlier that she was pregnant with Matteo Conti's baby, I probably would've considered it the worst-case scenario. But now, I realized her situation could be much, much worse.

I sat. I could barely think straight. My brain felt like a raft that had taken on too much water. I needed to let something filter out before trying to function.

"Say something," Annie pleaded.

I shook my head. I had no words.

"I can't believe you think I'd hook up with Angelo. Like, didn't you just finagle the guy out of murder charges less than a year ago?"

"I didn't finagle anything. Angelo was innocent."

"Sure, he was," she said, her tone contradicting her words.

"When did all of this start with you and Matteo?" I tried to recall the last time she'd been at their house with me, but the most recent thing I could remember was right after the Angelo and Julia stuff. Marco had invited her to one of his family dinners while essentially holding me captive at the house. I remembered Annie talking with Matteo, but didn't recall anything specific.

And surely they hadn't been dating—or not dating— for a whole year.

"Few months back," she answered, reaching for her glass of water again. "I was on a date actually and the guy was a total dick. Matteo was there randomly and stepped in, not realizing he knew me. Once my date left, we started talking. And drinking." She paused. "Lots of drinking. He walked me home and then, well…"

I cringed, glad she didn't offer any more details. "But you're not *that* pregnant. So it couldn't have happened that night."

"Do you really want to hear about every time?" Annie asked.

"Eww. No. Definitely not. I just, well, what makes you say you're not dating?"

She shrugged. "Because I told him we're not dating. Neither of us wanted our families to know, for obvious reasons. It was supposed to just be casual."

"He's in Italy now," I said.

"Yeah."

I ran my fingers through my hair, pressing them into my scalp as though jolting my brain to work harder. There had to be a logical way out of this, but the more I thought, the more guilt wracked me.

It was my fault that Annie had gotten mixed up with the Contis in the first place. I introduced them. I brought Matteo into her life. And now, thanks to my dumb decisions, my sister could be shackled to a mob family for life.

"You can't have Matteo's baby," I blurted out. "Yeah, he's no Angelo, but he's still a Conti." Jesus Annie, do you know what those men do for a living?"

"No, Adrian, why don't you tell me?" my sister challenged, staring me straight in the eye now. "Oh wait, you can't. Attorney-client confidentiality, right? Tell me again how I should live my life, Mr. Mob Lawyer."

I blew out a sigh and pushed to stand again, needing to pace.

"That's not the same and you know it, Annie. Everyone has a right to counsel. It's in the fucking Constitution. But not everyone has to sleep with a drug dealer."

"Matteo isn't a drug dealer. He doesn't even do drugs, let alone sell them."

I paced to one end of the room, then turned and made my way back. Technically, Annie was right. At least as far as I knew, none of the Contis were drug dealers. But that didn't make them good people. Definitely not good enough for my sister.

I did another lap, then another realization dawned on me. If my sister did have a baby with Matteo, then the Contis would be a part of my life forever, too, no matter what other choices I made.

"Shit, Annie."

"Like I said, I haven't made a decision yet. I could have an abortion, and he'd never know," she said, peering up at me. "Unless you told him."

I dropped to the couch beside her. "Annie, you really think I'd do that?" I shook my head. "You're my sister. You come first, no matter what my obligations are to the Conti family."

Annie watched me warily. "Okay, I believe you wouldn't tell anyone if I had an abortion. But what if I had the baby, would you tell him then?"

I frowned. "What do you mean?"

She shrugged, clearly frustrated. "Exactly what I said. Would you tell Matteo the truth if I don't ever tell him, if I have the baby and raise it all by myself?"

I couldn't help but cringe. If there were a ranking of ways to get yourself killed by a mobster, keeping him from his child was probably somewhere near the top of the list. But that still didn't change my answer. "Of course not, Annie. And you wouldn't be all by yourself, either. I'd help."

Before she replied, my mind returned to the logistics of it all. "You'd have to move away, back home, I guess. Otherwise,

Matteo would figure it out. And if he guessed it, well, technically he would have rights. So you'd have to hide the pregnancy and baby from him."

My sister didn't speak. I gazed at her, noticing the tiny scar above her right eyebrow. She'd gotten nine stitches in third or fourth grade and still had the scar to prove it. She'd fallen on a stick trying to chase after me and one of my friends when he'd stolen her baby doll and was threatening to toss it into the lake. Annie had been obsessed with dolls as a kid. She'd carried her favorite one, Shula, everywhere she went. I couldn't remember why she'd settled on such a dumb name, but I could remember how much she loved that damn doll.

Shit.

Even in elementary school, Annie had wanted to be a mom. And in high school, she babysat, rather than wait tables or work retail like her friends.

I rubbed my eyes and then turned to my sister. "You really want to keep this baby, don't you?"

Annie hesitated, then nodded.

"Just tell him," I urged. "Sooner than later."

She looked uncertain.

"He'll be a good dad. And you'll be a fantastic mom," I said.

My sister extended her arms, welcoming me in for a hug. We embraced for a full minute, and I tried to tell myself everything would be okay.

"Thank you," Annie said as we finally separated. "But you really need to shower and wash off that aftershave. It's making me gag."

Giada

*L*uca was avoiding me like the plague, still clearly pissed that I'd dared ask him if he hurt Adrian. I regretted my question, but at the same time, a part of me was glad I had asked. I meant what I'd said, that I felt like I didn't know him anymore. Luca had changed since his father's death, whether he acknowledged it or not.

All I could do was pray that the changes were temporary.

I went to the design firm two days in a row, an unusual occurrence for me. The first day, I went straight to church after work, hitting up confession, then staying for mass and private counseling with Father Ryan.

As always, the priest's words comforted me, especially since he wasn't Luca's biggest fan. He reassured me that everyone struggles with new grief, and that it's far too soon for me to panic that Luca's new personality traits will become permanent.

After work the next day, I met up with Gabriella for dinner and drinks. I predicted her advice would echo much of what Father Ryan had told me, but I was eager for the distraction anyway. I beat her to the restaurant, so I texted Adrian while I waited. My brother had told me to leave him alone, but I'd already taken it upon myself to send him a fruit basket from the entire Conti family.

"Hope your recovery is going well," I wrote. "Let me know if you need anything!"

Adrian replied just as Gabby sauntered through the doors of the restaurant. He said his sister was taking good care of him and thanked me for the basket.

"It was from my brothers and parents too," I replied.

"LOL. Sure, it was," he said.

I chuckled right as Gabby reached me. I stood to hug my best friend, then the waiter came to take our drink orders. We both selected a blueberry lemon martini, then turned our focus to the full menu. When our drinks arrived, Gabby offered some generic toast and we clinked our glasses together. She sipped hers, then stood to head to the bathroom before our food came.

I raised my glass to my lips, then paused, an unsettling sensation washing over me.

I'd sworn off alcohol the moment Luca and I decided to officially start trying for a baby, but then, since his father's death, I'd assumed we were pausing our plans to start a family and I'd started drinking again on occasion. We'd barely even been intimate since the funeral, so it wasn't like I could be pregnant anyway, and really, did anyone actually get knocked up the first month of trying?

I swallowed a tiny sip, and my stomach revolted. I motioned to the waiter.

"Something wrong with the drink?"

"No, it's fine, I just changed my mind. Could I have a soda water with lime instead?"

He nodded and scurried off with the rejected martini.

Gabby returned a minute later, just as the waiter brought my soda.

"Thirsty?" she taunted, quirking a brow.

"Let's just say it's been a rough week," I replied, not wanting to get into the possibility of a baby at the moment.

"Sorry," she said.

"How's work going?" I asked, eager to talk about anything but my chaotic life.

CHAPTER 9

Luca

I sat at my desk, alone in my office, swirling the amber liquid in my glass. Aside from the clink of the square ice cube as it knocked into the sides of the cup, the only noise was the rhythmic thumping of the bass from the dance floor.

I'd never liked this office, but this was the first time it had felt more like a coffin than a safe. There were no windows, and the solid wood door ran all the way to the ground. I supposed that design was intentional, lending a panic-room type benefit to the space. But I couldn't help but think how easy it would be to sit here at my desk and burn alive.

Two thumps on the door alerted me to a visitor. I downed the last swig of my whiskey then pressed the button under my desk to unlock the door, not caring who it was. A moment later, Alessio barged in. He took one look at me and winced.

"Jesus Christ, man, this is bad. What are you doing?" he paused, but not long enough for me to answer, then he stepped forward, squinting. "Are you crying?"

I pressed my fingers to my eyelids and rubbed. My eyes felt

like they were filled with sandpaper. I needed sleep. "Stronzo," I mumbled, calling my best friend the asshole that he was. "I wasn't crying. I'm fucking tired."

He sniffed my empty glass. "And maybe a little drunk?"

"Not nearly enough," I groaned. "Grab me a Manhattan, would you?"

"Yeah, not in my job description," he said, making himself comfortable in the chair facing my desk.

Apparently, I looked even more pathetic than I felt, because a moment later, Alessio pressed the intercom button on my phone to message our guys at the end of the hall. "Can you bring the boss a Manhattan, extra bitters, please? And a whiskey straight up for me." He released the button, then gazed at me. "I'll drink mine like a man."

We both chuckled at that, which I assume was his intention. "Only thing straight about you is your drink order."

We both laughed some more, then silence filled the small office. Alessio was the one to speak first.

"You thinking about your papà? Or about Elio?"

"Elio," I said softly, the answer feeling like a betrayal. "That's how shitty of a son I am."

A guy named Mike who worked up front brought our drinks, then closed the door behind him.

Alessio raised his glass in the air. "Cheers to the one man who kicked my ass more than my own father. Cheers to the man that gave me my best friend, a chance at a new life, and all the power I could ever want. And cheers to his son, the man who's going to build a bigger and better legacy than his papà ever could. It's an honor to stand by your side, mio fratello."

My heart clutched when Alessio called me his brother. He'd always been my best friend, but he had also always been more. He was my family, and his words were exactly what I needed at that moment.

I raised my glass to Alessio's, clinking gently. "Salute," I said, sipping my drink and letting the syrupy liquid sooth the back of my throat.

"I should get home," I said, certain Giada had returned from her dinner with Gabby by now. There was no reason for me to wait in my office. My men had confirmed that they had Elio. He was safely handcuffed, duct-taped and locked in the trunk of the car, traveling back towards New York. The earliest they could possibly reach the warehouse where we'd arranged to meet was noon tomorrow. I certainly didn't need to sit at my desk and stress until then.

"Luca." Alessio held me in place with his penetrating stare. "I meant what I said. You're a good man, and your legacy begins the moment we can put all this behind us."

"What if I can't put it behind me?" I asked, coming close to admitting the truth, that I was terrified my actions the next day would haunt me for the rest of my life. Was it even possible to already regret something before you've even done it?

Alessio frowned. "He's a murderer and a rat."

"He's a cop."

"He's a dirty cop."

"He signed on to fight the bad guys. Are we so sure that isn't what he did?"

Alessio said nothing for a full minute. Then, he spoke up. "I'll take care of him."

As exhilarating as the thought was, I couldn't let my second-in-command take on the burden of executing a traitor. Or torturing him. I wasn't entirely sure what all was expected of me yet, but I knew my papà's men were expecting blood. They thrived on the violence.

"It has to be me, and you know it," I said. Even if we made it seem like Alessio acted on his own accord and not as a favor to me, the guys would never respect me the same as if I handled the problem like the boss should. Like my papà would.

Alessio sighed, then thought for a moment. "Tell the guys

what you plan to do. You know, how you're going to rip out his toenails, break his knuckles and kneecaps, whatever. Then ask Elio to apologize. Or ask for an explanation. Whatever you do, get him talking, then lose your cool and shoot him point blank. It'll be over before it starts, and no one will be the wiser."

I considered that for a moment, then nodded. I felt a giant weight lifted off my chest and I almost smiled. I rose to my feet to pat Alessio on the shoulder then pack up my stuff, but I wobbled as I stood.

"I probably shouldn't drive," I said.

Alessio smiled. "This was my only drink, so I can take you. We are going to the same place."

I wrinkled my nose. I couldn't sleep next to Giada knowing what I was about to do the next day. "I'll stay at my mom's house tonight," I said, assuming he could guess why. "But you go home. I don't want Giada to be alone."

Giada

*L*uca didn't come home that night, and by the time I woke, Alessio was already gone. Not that I could've gotten any information from him that Luca didn't want me to have. Alessio was like a steel trap, and as much as he liked me, he liked Luca more.

I caught up on email while sipping my coffee and picking at my chia seed pudding. Usually, the concoction felt light and tasty, and with the mixed berries and pecans I mixed in, it was both filling and sweet. But this morning, the smell seemed off, and the texture was too thick and gloppy. I forced down a few bites, then dumped the rest of the bowl's contents into the sink.

Next, I attempted a short workout, but my energy was lagging and my stomach still felt weird. I couldn't be hungover, since I'd only drank a tiny fraction of a sip of alcohol, and I didn't feel bad enough for this to be food poisoning.

I pressed a hand to my stomach and my breath caught in my throat.

Surely I wasn't… I couldn't be. There was no way. We'd only done it twice. Maybe three times at most. I needed to get out of my head.

I made my way upstairs and showered, brushed my teeth, then did my makeup. I let my hair continue to air dry while I lathered lotion on my damp skin and then dressed. Finally, I dried my hair and then styled it into casual waves. I didn't have any set plans for the day, but I'd been putting off some errands for weeks. Besides, shopping always distracted me from my problems.

My mind wandered back to my earlier concerns as I stared at my reflection in the closet mirror. I clasped a bracelet around my wrist, then chose a necklace and rings. When I was all ready to go, I texted Lincoln.

"I need to run some errands. Are you free to drive me?"

"I'm parked in the drive. Ready whenever you are," he replied.

I rolled my eyes, torn between loving the convenience of his constant presence and resenting Luca's overprotectiveness. He told me the babysitter was only necessary until the press died down and we'd all settled into the new way of things. But it already felt like overkill.

A flash of purple in the corner of the room caught my eye as I was about to leave. I bent, retrieving my favorite rosary from behind the hamper. It had been missing since the day Luca accompanied me to the church, and I assumed I had lost it there, but apparently it had been in my own closet all along. My cheeks flushed at the still vivid memories of what we'd done that day.

I opened my calendar and counted how many days back that would've been. Then I tried to calculate when I'd get my period, but I had no idea. Since stopping birth control, my cycles hadn't returned to normal. I might have already been a few days late, or my period might not be due for a couple more days. I just wasn't sure.

I decided I didn't want to stress the unknown the whole time I was shopping, not when I didn't have to wonder. I flung open the linen closet in our bathroom and tore open the box. My heart began to race as I skimmed the instructions, confirming the rules hadn't changed since I last tested myself.

I had just finished washing my hands after recapping the test when my phone rang. I considered rejecting the call just so I could hurry and set my timer, but I didn't recognize the number, which usually meant it was one of Luca's guys. Well, or spam.

"Hello?" I answered through gritted teeth.

"Hey, Giada? This is Xavier Caruso. Luca is swamped but he really wanted to know if you could come meet up with him today."

I frowned, not sure why Luca had chosen some guy I'd met less than a handful of times to call me, but I could run the details by Lincoln to verify later. "Umm, I guess so. Where?"

He read me an address, and I texted it to Lincoln right away asking if he knew what was there.

"Could you get here by 12:30?" Xavier asked.

I stared at my phone, just as Lincoln replied. "One of Luca's warehouses," he wrote.

"Uhh sure," I said.

"Cool. Don't be late. And just come on in when you get here. Lincoln can come inside too, or whoever."

I agreed, and Xavier promised to tell Luca I was on my way. We hung up and I forced myself to count to one hundred before I peeked at the test stick. My stomach tightened at the bold blue dye answer to my question. There was definitely no misinterpreting the results. I chewed my lip, trying to process my feelings, and then my phone buzzed.

"We need to go now if you want to be there by 12:30," Lincoln said.

I groaned, chucked the test into the trash can, then hurried out the door.

Lincoln stood beside the car as I approached, holding my door open like a true chauffeur.

"Thanks," I said. "So, this is really a legit place? I don't know this Xavier guy well."

"Yeah, it's a warehouse by the docks. The guys store things there before they're ready to ship."

"And Luca is actually there?" With how strained things had been between us lately, I really didn't want to rush into something and get myself into some mess Luca would have to straighten out later. The last time I'd had a last-minute change of plans. Luca took three bullets for me. I definitely didn't want a repeat of that.

"I texted Alessio. He said everyone is there but that they're busy and not to bother them again unless it's an emergency."

I supposed that was good enough. I sat back and tried to guess what Luca might have planned. I hoped it involved food, because suddenly, I was starving. Maybe he'd staged some big romantic scene. I was picturing dozens of shimmering candles, rose petals covering the floor, and a scrumptious carb-heavy picnic.

I scrolled on my phone until the car slowed to a stop. I recognized seeing the warehouse before, and actually remembered the parking lot as the place Luca had taught me how to drive, back in high school. I smiled and started out of the car, spotting Xavier out front, smoking a cigarette.

He waved and stomped out his cigarette when he saw me. "Hey, glad you could make it. Luca's inside. I can show you where."

"Should I come inside or wait out here?" Lincoln asked.

Xavier shrugged. "Up to you. I think Luca wanted to be alone with his girl, but I'm sure he'd understand if you walked her in."

"You can wait here," I said to Lincoln, certain he wanted to get back to his studying. It was hard not to notice the stack of textbooks in the back seat. Business school did not look entertaining.

Xavier held open the door and I went inside. He led me across a massive, dimly lit room, lined with oversized shipping boxes. My heart thumped excitedly, and I hoped I wasn't under-dressed for whatever Luca had planned.

"He's right through there," Xavier said, motioning to a door. "Go on in."

His giddiness seemed weird, but I went to the door. I stepped inside, instantly realizing I was not alone with Luca. A handful of other men stood around, their backs to me. Everyone seemed focused on the front of the room. I heard Luca's voice, and I stepped around a bigger guy, eager to see Luca.

He stood at the front of the room, and another man was seated on a chair in front of him. The man looked sweaty and was hunched over, but he made no attempt to move. I wasn't sure what I was seeing, then all of a sudden Luca said something in Italian. The man answered, his voice too shaky and quiet for me to even tell if he spoke English or Italian.

Luca's arm raised, and an explosive boom rang out. For an instant, my heart stopped. If someone had shot Luca again, I'd never survive.

Then, the man on the chair slumped sideways, and Luca dropped his arm to his side.

A feral scream escaped my throat.

Then, every single person in the room—including my very much alive husband—turned to stare at me.

I froze for a second, then realized what I'd just witnessed. I sprinted out of the room, through the nearest exit I spotted, and I didn't stop running until I was several blocks away.

Still breathless and shaking, I pulled out my phone and requested an Uber.

Luca

*A*n uproar exploded in the room the second the gun went off. I'd expected some protests from my papà's guys. They'd been bloodthirsty for weeks and were banking on me drawing out the punishment longer than I did.

But what I hadn't expected was to hear a familiar, high pitched, distinctly feminine scream. One that I knew without even glancing up belonged to none other than my Giada.

I peered up, steeling my hand so no one could see the gun shaking in my grip. I caught a flash of Giada's dark hair as she burst through the door. Nausea churned in my stomach and I turned to Alessio.

"I'll go talk to her," he promised, motioning for Thomas and Giovanni to come to me.

Giovanni wrenched the gun out of my grip, wiping it thoroughly with a disinfectant wipe before dropping it into a cloth.

"It's over," Thomas said, quietly so only the three of us heard. Then, he turned to the other men, who were still bitching and moaning to each other, completely undisturbed by the dead man strapped to a chair on the floor. "Justice has been served!"

A couple guys cheered, but most grumbled. Tony made his way up to the front. I craned my neck to look past him, wondering if Alessio found Giada yet, but he stepped closer, preventing me from seeing anything but his ugly face.

"What the fuck, Luca? The guys were expecting a little more. We deserved more. Your father deserved more."

I forced down the bile threatening to rise in my throat. "My papà deserved justice, and that's what I did today. Could you not hear the things that traitor was saying, the way he disrespected my papà?" I paused, channeling all of my strength into my voice so all the men could hear me.

"Sorry if you expected fun and games today, but I came here for one purpose only, and that was to avenge my papà's senseless murder. I couldn't have stood here and listened to another word from that monster's mouth. If you didn't have an issue with it, maybe you need to reevaluate where your loyalties lie." I said, pausing just long enough to maintain momentum.

"My grandfather prepared the Marino family for a legacy of strength and power. My papà worked diligently to expand that influence across multiple continents. He didn't just build this very warehouse; he built the empire that all of us enjoy today. I, for one, have no regrets about not letting the rat who betrayed my papà soil this sacred land for another minute longer." I kicked his body for emphasis, then stormed out of the room as the men cheered.

"Jesus, that was impressive," Alessio mumbled, having listened from the door.

"Where is she?" I asked.

"She left before I got out here."

"Left? With who? Lincoln?"

Alessio made a face and shook his head.

"How the fuck did she get here if not Lincoln?" I roared, starting to the door.

"Hey, calm down," Alessio said, pressing a hand to my chest. "You've got gun residue all over your hand and shirt, and we need to oversee cleanup."

I glared.

"Lincoln drove her here, apparently Xavier called Giada and said you wanted her here, and then—"

"That son of a bitch! Where is Giada?"

"She ran out the back door of the building. She was already gone by the time I saw her, so Lincoln is looking for her now. I'm tracking her phone though and it looks like she's heading home."

"She can't walk home from here."

"I think she's in a car."

I muttered a string of expletives in my native tongue.

"I know, and I'm sorry. Lincoln and I will handle this, and you'll be able to talk to her later this afternoon, but right now we've got to clean this up and then deal with Xavier."

Every fiber of my being ached to run out the door and look for Giada myself, but I knew Alessio was right. She could calm down at home, and I could get my shit together here.

CHAPTER 10

Giada

I nearly hyperventilated four times during the ride back to my house. The driver kept staring at me in the rearview mirror, and then at one point asked if I needed to go to the hospital. I almost told him the police station would be a more fitting destination, but luckily, I snapped back to reality in time.

As he pulled into the circular drive leading to the house, nausea swept over me. What had I been thinking? I couldn't go home. Luca would find me in a matter of minutes, and I couldn't handle seeing him just yet.

But where else could I go? Thinking fast, I decided Gabriella could put me up for a day or two.

"Can you wait here for just five minutes? I need to grab some things, and then I'll be right back." I offered him two fifty-dollar bills, the largest I had in my wallet, then scrambled out of the car. I dashed up the stairs, grabbing my travel toiletry kit, a pair of pajamas, two outfits, and three sets of underwear.

Then I sprinted out the front door. It wasn't until I reached the car that I realized I'd left my phone upstairs on the bed. I debated returning for it, then decided not to mess with it. I knew where Gabby lived. I told the driver the street name, and we started off. After a few minutes though, it hit me. I couldn't go to Gabby now. She'd only recently begun supporting my relationship with Luca, and she'd be terrified all over again if I told her even a hint of what I'd just seen.

"Actually, can we change destinations?" I asked the driver, giving him the name of the church.

Adrian

J had just zipped my duffle and confirmed I'd picked up all my stuff when my phone rang. The caller ID showed that the church was calling me. I chuckled to myself about the countless jokes that could be made if I failed to answer the call of God, but I fully expected the caller to ask me for a donation.

"Hello?"

"Hi. Is this Adrian Patras?"

I hoisted the duffle higher on my shoulder as I locked the door to my sister's apartment. Finally, I was cleared to return to my own place, and thanks to Angelo getting my car repaired and delivered, I could drive myself home, too.

"Yeah," I replied.

"This is Father Ryan Wilson. I'm not sure if you remember me, but you were here with Giada Conti, err Marino, a few years back, and you gave me your number."

"Uh, yeah. I remember."

The man heaved a sigh of relief. "Listen, I apologize for interrupting your day, but I wasn't sure what else to do. Giada is here, and she seems quite distraught. I offered to call her husband, and she said no. She looks terrified, and she won't tell me anything."

I frowned, dropping my duffle into the passenger's seat before sitting behind the wheel.

"She said she left her phone at home and took an Uber here, so her husband doesn't know where she is. Normally I'd call the police in this sort of situation, but..."

"No, don't do that." I glanced at my watch, then sighed. I already had the day off work. "I'll come talk to her."

He thanked me then hung up. I texted the buddy who was watching my dog to let him know I'd be late, then headed to the church. When I arrived, Father Ryan greeted me at the door.

There were a few parishioners in the sanctuary, but I spotted Giada instantly. I made my way over to her, approaching slowly so as not to scare her. She reminded me of a lost puppy, panting and trembling, and she'd formed a protective barrier around herself with her massive purse and her overnight bag.

"Can I sit?" I asked.

Her eyes went wide, and she made no attempt to make space for me.

"Father Ryan called me," I told her.

She shot to her feet. "Who else knows I'm here?"

"No one!" I reached for her hand, surprised at how cold her skin felt. "Giada, come on. Let's go talk somewhere more private."

She shuffled out of the pew, and I grabbed her bag. Father Ryan flashed me an appreciative but concerned smile, then motioned for us to take his office.

"What happened?" I asked her once we were alone.

Giada shook her head, her teeth chattering.

The room wasn't cold, and for once, Giada's attire was appropriate for the weather, but still I shrugged out of my jacket and draped it over her shoulders.

"Giada, if you won't talk to me, can I call Luca?"

"No!"

Her shout was so loud that I jumped back in my seat a little.

"He's not going to hurt you," I said, praying I was right.

"You don't know that."

My stomach dropped. For Giada to admit her perfect husband, soulmate, love of her life, might not be as safe as she pretended, was huge. "What did you do?" I asked, my mind flitting to all sorts of doomsday scenarios.

"I didn't do anything. He…he…he…" She pressed her palms over her face and shuddered.

"Giada, you're scaring me. Can I drive you to your parents' house? They'll keep you safe."

She shook her head. "They'll just give me back to him."

I clenched my abs. "And you're afraid of Luca?"

Giada uncovered her face but still didn't look at me. "I saw something I shouldn't have. And I don't know all his new guys or his dad's guys or whoever they are, and I don't know what they'll do."

"They won't hurt you. That's one of their basic rules, as long as you're with Luca, you're untouchable."

She took her time answering, finally meeting my gaze. "What if I'm no longer with Luca?"

I had no idea how to respond to that, but I couldn't let myself get sucked in to her drama again. I was over Giada, no question about it. I wasn't suddenly oblivious to her beauty, but I'd finally realized she was not the woman for me, in any world.

"You're married, Giada, and last time I checked, you don't believe in divorce. And unless I've missed something huge, you're Luca's whole world. He's not going to let anything happen to you, no matter what you saw."

"I want to believe that," she said. "I wish I could just go back in time and never have seen anything. Because on some level, I know you're right. We could just pretend nothing happened and he'd probably convince his dad's men not to hurt me." Her eyes squeezed shut. "But I don't know if I can do that. I don't know if I can look at him, or touch him, or sleep in the same house as him, after what he did."

"You already knew he wasn't a saint, Giada."

"This is…different. I can't explain."

"What if I call him and have him meet us here? Father Ryan or I can stay in the room while you talk. We won't leave you alone till you feel safe."

She shook her head. "No, I need time. I just need to forget what happened before I see Luca again. I need to get away for a few days."

"Away," I repeated.

Just then, Father Ryan stepped into the room, carrying a mug of steaming liquid. He set it on an accent table by Giada. "Tea," he explained.

She nodded, her eyes still blank, and he started to the door.

"Wait!" she called. The priest turned. "I know you're working now, but could you do me a favor? Could you rent a car for me? Just for a couple days. If I rent it in my name, he'll be able to track me down, and—"

"Giada, this is crazy. You aren't seriously going to leave Luca."

"I just need a few days to think. I'll come back."

"You're in no condition to drive. You don't even have a cell phone on you."

Giada gazed at her purse then turned to the priest. "Can you buy me one of those disposable phones too? I have cash." She reached into her bag and pulled out a tidy stack of crisp bills.

I took a deep breath, certain I was about to sign my own death sentence.

"You're not going anywhere alone," I said. "I'll take you."

Luca

*C*leaning up the mess and disposing of the evidence took hours. Then, I had to confront Xavier. The asshole claimed he hadn't meant for Giada to see anything and that he'd only invited her because he thought her presence would soothe me after I dealt with Elio, but I didn't believe that for a second. As dumb as Xavier was, even he knew Giada was a good person, and that the worst thing he could do to me would be to remind my wife that I was evil.

"I realize you're still holding on to some resentment from a decade ago when I kicked your ass, but we're not kids anymore, and this shit stops here," I told him. "I'll let it slide this time because I trust you're smart enough to never cross me again. But if you so much breathe the wrong way from now on, you're out. I don't care how much my papà valued you; I do not tolerate disrespect," I said.

Xavier nodded, his eyes darting side to side from Tony to Tomasso, as if expecting one of them to start beating the shit out of him right there.

"Take him," I said to Tomasso, waving a hand dismissively.

A moment later, Tony and I were alone in the office. "The most important lesson your father ever taught me was that, in this line of business, when someone shows you who they are, believe them." He paused. "There's no second chances in this world. If Xavier comes at you again, you might lose more than your daily blow job from the princess."

My pulse raced at his disrespect of Giada. "I can read people, and he's not going to do anything else," I said. "He was pissed about something from the past, and he got his revenge. Now we're even."

"But you're not equals. You're the boss. He's a defiant underling. And if the others see Xavier get away with this shit, who knows what they'll try?"

I gritted my teeth. I hated to admit it, but Tony had a point. I hadn't fully won the loyalty of my papà's old crew, and now was not the time to show weakness.

"I'll take care of it," Tony said. "You can go talk with your wife. I just need your approval."

"Fine." I watched him leave, then pulled out my phone and clicked on the little dot showing me my wife's current location. By some miracle, Giada had gone straight home, and she hadn't left. I told Lincoln to park outside the house and not disturb Giada, but to stay alert. I hadn't decided yet if he was completely blameless for the day's unraveling, and if he let her sneak past him now, I'd have his fucking head on a platter.

Still, I wasn't exactly eager to get home. I was physically and emotionally drained, and in no condition to handle the fight I knew awaited me. Giada could be feisty and dramatic over little things, but this wasn't little. I'd betrayed her trust, broken direct promises to her, and I'd probably scarred her for life. This time, she was right to be pissed. I'd fucked up badly.

I drove myself home, sending Lincoln on his way and telling him I'd deal with him later. When I stepped through the door, the house was dark and quiet. I called Giada's name, but wasn't surprised when she ignored me. I checked the sunroom first, since that was her favorite spot in the house, then made my way up to our room. It, too, was empty.

I called her name louder, sprinting from room to room. "Giada, come on. I know you're hurting, but if you could just tell me where you are so we could talk…" I called through the empty hallway. Silence was the only answer. I reached for my phone, confirming Giada was still in the house, and chastising myself for not checking earlier. As angry as she might be, she'd never hide out in some corner of our McMansion without her cell phone. That device was practically glued to her hand.

I followed the blinking green beacon back to our bedroom, and then I saw it. On the corner of our bed, mostly covered by a decorative pillow sham, was Giada's phone. I grabbed it, unlocking the screen and seeing a slew of unread texts and even a voicemail from Gabby, sent hours ago. Giada hadn't just been ignoring my calls. She'd blocked everyone.

My heart raced as I considered the possibility that she'd been kidnapped. I re-checked the house, this time searching for any signs of struggle. But nothing seemed out of place. Then, I noticed Giada's purse was missing. I jogged back up the stairs and peered into our closet.

Giada's toiletry kit and overnight bag were missing too.

She hadn't been kidnapped. She fucking left me.

I swore at the top of my lungs, then began kicking and throwing anything and everything within my reach. When I'd finally depleted all of my energy, I sat on the edge of the bed and thrust my head between my hands.

As soon as my breathing calmed, I gazed at the mess around me. Pillows were now strewn across the room, the batteries had popped out of the television remote, and the decorative plants and other crap Giada adorned the room with were knocked over. Dirt spilled from the one real plant, and a few discarded items surrounded the waste basket I'd kicked over. Aside from the photo frame, it didn't appear that I'd broken anything. And honestly, I felt a little better now.

Giada hated my temper and would've been even angrier if she'd seen how I'd trashed the place. But, she wasn't here. She didn't get a fucking vote. Life got hard, and she ran off. She abandoned me when I needed her the most.

My phone buzzed in my hand, and I glanced down, noting yet another call from Alessio. I couldn't ignore him forever. Eventually, he'd come find me, and that was fine. I'd thrown my fit. The fury was out of my system. Now I just needed a plan. I needed to figure out where Giada went and bring her home soon.

"Giada isn't here. She left her phone. She must have taken off before Lincoln got here," I texted Alessio. "I'm going to check if she's at her parents' or Gabby's. Or maybe Enzo's." I cringed at the thought of that, but he was someone she trusted. And it would be easier to call him to ask about her whereabouts than to admit to her parents that she'd run away.

I stood slowly, collecting the pillows and tossing them all into a pile on the bed, unsure which adorned the chairs or bench anyway. I righted the potted plant, stepped over the dirt, then squatted to pick up the trash that had spilled from the wastebasket. There was a price tag, an empty envelope, and a few tissues, and a long white stick with a blue tip.

I reached for the stick first, my breath catching in my throat as I realized what it was. I'd seen one like this before, when Giada and I had eloped in secret right before I was arrested and she thought she was pregnant. This one was different, though. This stick had two bold blue lines, where the last one displayed a single horizontal blue line. The last test meant she wasn't pregnant. This one...

I stood, stumbling backwards until the edge of the bed hit the backs of my legs, causing my knees to buckle and drop me onto the bed. The room spun around me, and an uncomfortable warmth rushed over me as the contents of my stomach churned upwards. I made it to the bathroom in time, then sank to the tile floor beside the toilet, still clutching the test stick in my hand.

The room was pitch black when I heard a voice shouting my name. I must've fallen asleep. Surely, I couldn't have just been sitting there the whole evening.

"Jesus!" Alessio exclaimed, jogging into the bathroom. "I've looked for you everywhere, Luca. Would it kill you to answer your phone?"

I looked in my hand, quickly ascertaining that I was still holding the test stick and not my phone.

"Luca? Are you okay?" Alessio sounded more concerned now than when he'd arrived.

I was not okay, but that didn't seem like the right answer, so instead, I spoke another truth. "Giada just watched me murder a cop."

"Yeah, um. Look, I figured I'd give you some space, but..." Alessio crouched beside me. He paused, then placed his hand on my shoulder. "Amico, you're worrying me. What is that?"

I followed his gaze to my hand. "Giada's pregnant," I finally said, swallowing the lump in my throat.

"Oh shit," he mumbled, sinking to the ground beside me.

CHAPTER 11

Luca

*A*lessio forced me into the shower while he made some phone calls to track down Giada. A weird mixture of relief and dread filled me as I pondered my situation.

On the one hand, Giada was most likely safe. On the other hand, she'd never forgive me.

And for that, I didn't blame her one bit.

Time and time again, I'd fucked up, and Giada had forgiven me. As the hot water beat down on my sore shoulders, I realized I had always assumed I could never mess up so badly that Giada wouldn't eventually exonerate me.

But this was different. Forgiving me was different than letting me ruin our child's life. She could absolve me and still believe that our kid would be better off without me in his life. She wouldn't be wrong, either. Had my mother made the same choice decades ago, maybe I would've turned out to be a law-abiding human being, worthy of eternal salvation. Well, or at least worthy of a woman like Giada.

Instead, I was alone in the shower, trying to scrub the dried blood out of my nailbeds and wondering whether Tony had killed Xavier yet.

A loud knock on the door startled me from my thoughts, and I switched off the shower, grabbing a towel before walking to the counter.

"Do you want to deal with Lincoln or should I?" Alessio called through the door.

I assumed neither of us thought Lincoln's fuck up merited too tough of a punishment, but I also didn't want to take any chances. I had enough guilt to juggle already. "It's not his fault. She left before he got back here. I just want to find out where she went and make sure she's okay."

Alessio poked his head in the door, not entering fully until he confirmed a towel covered my lower half. "We'll find her, and you'll talk to her. But you need to eat something."

"Fine. Have Lincoln make dinner," I said.

"That's not what I meant," Alessio replied, even though we both knew that already. He leaned against the counter while I headed into the closet to find clean clothes. "I read through Gabby's texts, and there's a chance they were intentional."

"You think she's with Gabby and sending those so we assume Gabby doesn't know where she is?"

"Exactly. Yes."

Giada was definitely clever enough to do that, but I didn't think she had. She'd worked so hard to get Gabby to believe I wasn't a monster, and she wouldn't jeopardize the friendship by admitting she'd been wrong. "No. If she's not alone, my money's on Enzo. Or maybe her brothers."

Alessio frowned. "Have you called any of them?"

"And said what, exactly? I seem to have misplaced my wife after murdering a law enforcement officer. Have you happened to have seen her?"

Alessio moved into the closet, but kept his back turned in case I was still dressing. "Jesus, Luca. You need to stop saying that. The guy wasn't a cop. Not anymore. And who knows if he was ever a decent cop, or even a decent human?"

"That's not how Giada sees it."

"Then she's wrong. Because all you did was bring a cold-blooded killer to justice. And you did it as humanely as possible."

I zipped my pants, and Alessio turned to face me.

"You don't know exactly why Giada ran. I bet she's just scared. Once you talk to her, it'll be fine."

I rolled my eyes. "Call Enzo first. And tell Lincoln to hurry up with dinner."

Adrian

Giada was silent as I drove. She'd stopped crying, but still rolled the beads of her rosary between her thumb and forefinger as she peered out the window, her face completely void of emotion. Every so often, she peered at the burner phone resting between us.

"We can turn around if you want," I said.

"No!"

I gazed at her, unsettled by the fierceness of her tone. "We can't stay away forever," I said. "We only have enough cash for maybe a week at most, and if we use credit cards, they can track us."

"I'm sorry," she said after a lengthy silence. "Not just for dragging you into this now, but for getting you involved with my family in the first place. Normal people don't have to worry about being tracked, do they?" She forced an awkward laugh.

"I'm not trying to make you feel guilty," I clarified. "I'm only saying that if you've changed your mind and you want to start over or run away for good, we need to go back and get more money."

Giada reached into her purse and pulled out a roll of bills. If they were all hundreds, it had to be over five grand. "I grabbed this on my way out. You can use it for gas or food and lodging or whatever."

"That's um, a lot of gas money. But it still won't last forever."

"I just need a few days. It'll kill Luca if I'm gone for much longer."

"And you don't want that?" I wasn't trying to be difficult; I truly didn't know.

"No!" She scowled. "I still love him. I just wish I didn't."

I didn't even bother trying to make sense of that. "Are you going to tell me what he did that has you so freaked out?"

"No. They'd have to kill us both if we both knew."

"No one will hurt you, Giada," I said, praying that was the truth. Surely if she went back now, that would be the case. The longer she was gone, well, I didn't know. "And I've had a target on my back since the second I agreed to help you run away."

She pressed her hands to her face. "You don't really think that, do you?"

I didn't answer. Apparently, she didn't want the truth.

"Adrian, why would you help me if you thought they'd kill you for it?"

That was the million-dollar question.

"They don't even know I'm with you," she said. "Father Ryan rented the car, and no one saw us together."

"Luca is lacking many virtues, but intelligence isn't one of them," I replied. "If he doesn't already know who you're with, he will soon."

"So what are you going to do after I go back?"

I shrugged. To be honest, there was nothing special awaiting me back home. My job was shady, my friends were criminals, and I had no girlfriend. Maybe this was my sign to help Annie get away and start over somewhere else with her secret baby, too.

"Maybe I'll head back to stay with my parents until Luca forgives me."

"I won't let him hurt you," she said.

I suppressed an eye roll. The woman wasn't even sure her husband wouldn't hurt her, yet here she was, making promises about my safety.

"You really won't tell me what he did?" I asked.

Giada forced an exhale. "He shot the man who killed his father. In front of me."

I kept my eyes on the road, unsure of what to say. In the grand scheme of Luca's atrocities, this didn't seem so bad.

"It's not like it's the first time he's killed someone," I finally said.

Her brows furrowed together. "Well, he told me he'd never do that again. And this man was an undercover cop," she added.

I stayed quiet.

"He's been different since his dad died, like he has to be more like his dad just to impress the new guys. And the timing is terrible, because we'd just started trying for a baby, and I can't—"

"You're having a baby?" I interrupted, unable to conceal the horror in my tone.

"No. I mean, someday, hopefully, but I'm not pregnant yet, if that's what you mean."

"Thank God for that."

She flung her hands in the air.

"What does that mean?"

"Exactly what I said," I snapped. "It's a fucking miracle that you didn't get knocked up by Satan incarnate. You just finished telling me you're scared of Luca because he keeps doing horrible things. But now I'm supposed to be sad that you're not about to spawn even more evil Marino babies? Make up your mind."

Giada scowled. "When did you become this judgmental?"

"Maybe after the second time you dumped me for a sociopath."

She squeezed her eyes shut, then turned to the window. I wondered if she was trying to mask her tears from me, and a pang of guilt clutched my chest.

"I'm sorry," I said. "I'm still recovering from the concussion, and I think I'm tired. I probably can't drive much longer. We'll need to find a place to sleep for the night."

"No, we can't stop yet. We're barely out of town. Pull over, and I'll drive."

I was about to argue with Giada, but she was an adult. Her judgment sucked when it came to men, but surely she could manage to drive in a straight line on the highway for a few hours while I slept.

"Fine. I'll drive another hour, and then we'll stop for gas, and you can get some coffee. Then we'll trade."

Giada agreed, then turned back to the window for a few minutes. Just as I was settling into the silence, she spoke again. "Luca and I have been fighting a lot since his dad died. We don't have any time together, he's always stressed, and neither of us trusts his dad's guys. It's just been...hard."

I was about to tell her I didn't need to hear all about her relationship with the guy she left me for, but she continued.

"The most recent fight was about you."

"What did I do?"

She blew out a sigh, filling the car with the scent of her spearmint gum. "I asked if he had anything to do with what happened to you in the parking garage. He looked so sad that I'd even ask, like I'd done it just to hurt his feelings, but I really just wasn't sure."

I cringed. I could see why it might offend a guy to accuse him of senseless violence against an old friend.

"He never actually gave me a direct answer, now that I think about it, so maybe it *was* him."

"It wasn't," I said quickly, wondering later why I was so quick to defend the guy.

Giada turned to me, awaiting explanation.

I told her what Angelo had said, about the guys watching her probably saw me and realized I did some work for the family. Then I added, "whoever attacked me was hoping to find some information on me. Guess they thought I was a courier of sorts."

"Are you?"

"No." I paused. "I mean, I deliver stuff to your family from the office sometimes, but…"

"So you do work for my family?"

I sighed. If I was going to be on the Marino-family shit list, I might as well piss off the Contis too. "I'm not in the mafia, Giada. I've never taken any oath or anything like that. Yes, I do some work that sometimes benefits guys who are, but I'm on the outside."

Glowing lights from the looming exit ramp illuminated the interior of the car as Giada placed her hand on my thigh, just above the knee, and offered a mournful smile. "I'm not sure if I said it before, but I'm sorry I dragged you into all this."

For once, she looked sincere about the apology. "Giada, you didn't even know what your family was involved in back then."

"But I should have. There were so many signs, and I ignored them all because they didn't serve my personal narrative of my father being a saint."

"You were naïve, not willfully ignorant. There's a difference."

"Not one that matters." She spit her gum into the wrapper and wadded it into a tiny ball. "You were the most principled person I'd ever met when we started dating. You believed in right and wrong, and you wanted to make a difference in the world."

"I'm still that person."

"You were optimistic and happy, even excited about the world."

"I was boring. I just didn't know any better yet."

Giada snickered, but I continued. "You act like I have no control over who I become or how I act. I'll admit there was a time when I would've done anything for you, but I'm my own person, Giada. I made my own decisions. I still do."

Skepticism filled her expression.

"Your dad paid for my mom's cancer treatment. I have a healthy, living mom because of the mafia. I have a killer car and a job that doesn't demand eighty hours a week in the office like most new attorneys. I'm still able to sleep at night because while I might have helped some people bend the rules, I've never actually hurt anyone. I've definitely never killed anyone."

"Unlike my husband, you mean."

I didn't have an immediate answer for that. Silence filled the car again.

"You should've seen Luca in high school," she said after a few minutes. "He was much more laid back. Almost a jokester. Still protective, but high school Luca liked to have fun. He lived to make other people smile."

I tried to picture that, and failed miserably.

"But it's a slippery slope. The more his dad asked of him, the more withdrawn and jaded he became."

I remembered her telling me about this before, how she'd been completely infatuated with Luca and thought they'd be together forever, then he just dumped her after graduation.

"He didn't want that life for me, so he broke things off. I'm not sure if it was the realization that I was already doomed to the life anyway, or if he just really couldn't stay away that brought him back."

I sighed. "Yeah, I remember the rest of this story."

Giada snorted, and we were both quiet for another minute. "You and I would've never worked out, Adrian. You need a woman who reminds you of how much joy you used to find in the world. Someone filled with energy and life, like you."

"Yeah, well, let's just hope I'm still filled with life after your husband learns that I drove you across state lines."

Luca

I had just finished the scrambled eggs and toast Lincoln had prepared when Alessio joined us at the kitchen island. His calls had taken longer than I'd expected, but I already knew from his grim expression that he didn't have good news.

"Enzo hasn't heard from her, and Matteo is in Rome."

"So?"

"So, it's like three o'clock in the morning there, Luca. And I doubt he knows where she is if he's been sleeping on another continent since she disappeared."

I didn't need Alessio to finish the bad news. If Angelo had any useful info, Alessio would've started with that. "Fine. I'll call her coworkers before it gets too late."

Alessio nodded, but I could tell he was holding back something.

"What?" I snapped.

"Angelo said that Adrian isn't answering his calls."

I dialed Giada's oldest brother before Alessio even finished his sentence. "Where is he?" I demanded the moment the Conti heir answered the phone.

I probably would've calmed more if Angelo had lectured me on my manners or taunted me about my impatience. Instead, he just told me he was looking into it.

I huffed out a breath, feeling each moment like an eternity.

"The guy just checked out of the hospital, so he's probably sleeping, or…" Angelo's voice trailed off.

"What?"

"His car and phone are both at the same spot, looks like a rental car place. I'll text you the address."

I mumbled my gratitude then hung up, staring at my phone. By the time the text came through, Alessio already had his keys in his hand. Without any late-night traffic, we reached the shop in under twenty minutes. An oversized CLOSED sign greeted us on the door.

"Cazzo," Alessio swore under his breath.

I shielded my eyes from the street light and pressed my face to the door, peering in. A lone worker stood inside, his back to me as he tidied the counter. I pounded on the door, and the man turned.

"We're closed!" He shouted. "We open at seven am tomorrow."

"Guns or roses?" Alessio asked.

I didn't think shooting our way into the shop would encourage the guy to open up. So I reached for my wallet and pressed two crisp hundred-dollar bills against the glass. The man hesitated, then walked closer.

"We just have a question about the guy who rented a car earlier today," I said. "The one who left the jag."

The man hesitated, so I added a third bill to the stack. He opened the door, but only a crack. "I don't have any cash on the premises, and the cameras are on a live feed," he said, gesturing behind him.

Alessio motioned for me to head back to the car. I took a few steps back, but stayed within earshot.

"Look, we don't want any trouble. We think my friend's wife ran off with someone today, and we just want to confirm."

The guy hesitated. I handed the money to Alessio, who passed it along.

"Look, can you just tell us where they're headed?" he asked.

"We don't track our cars. That's a violation of privacy."

I peered up to the sky, completely out of patience.

"Look, you don't even have to let me in. I'll give you the money if you tell me the license plate of the car and confirm the name of the guy who rented it."

"We rented dozens of cars this evening," the man replied.

I sighed, and handed yet another bill to Alessio.

"We appreciate your time looking into this. The guy's name is Adrian Patras, although surely you must have remembered the man driving that onto the lot and leaving with…what, a Honda Accord?"

The man frowned. "I think it was a Civic. Hang on."

We waited while he returned to the office. Alessio watched through the window, and the man took so long that I started to worry he was calling the cops. But eventually, he returned.

"The guy's name was Ryan Wilson, not Adrian whatever," he said.

Alessio frowned, but the name rang a bell with me. I kept trying to think of where I recognized it from, as Alessio handed the man two of the bills, accepted a post-it note with a license plate number scribbled on it, then passed off the remaining bills.

Then, it hit me. The fucking priest rented the car. "Father Ryan," I said aloud, right as Alessio thanked the man.

Alessio blew out a sigh, then laughed. "God, that's brilliant," he mused.

We climbed into the car, and I turned to my friend, curious why he was so impressed with this turn of events.

"Think about it, they know you won't touch the priest."

I quirked a brow. "Why not? I have nothing left to lose."

"Stop being so dramatic. She's just pissed, not gone forever. But if you touch the priest, yeah, not sure she'd forgive that in this lifetime."

"My pregnant wife ran off with her ex-boyfriend, and you think I'm being dramatic?"

"She's just mad. It's not like they're back together. I mean, it's not *his* baby, right?"

My eyes grew wide, and my stomach churned again. That possibility hadn't even occurred to me.

We debated going to the priest's house, a small cottage adjacent to the church, then decided calling would be quicker and probably just as effective. His number was listed on the church website as his private, after-hours emergency number, and much to my surprise, the Father answered.

"It's Luca Marino," I said. "I believe you saw my wife today."

"Uhh," Father Ryan began.

"Look, I'm under a bit of a time crunch here. We already know she was with Adrian and that you rented a car for them. But I need to hear if she was okay."

The priest took his time answering. "She was distraught, but she didn't appear to have any injuries, if that's what you mean."

I squeezed my eyes shut, trying to steady my breathing. "Where were they going?"

"They didn't tell me."

I considered that. "I suppose you want me to believe you can't lie, since you're a priest?"

"I wouldn't hesitate to lie to you if I thought it would keep Giada safe," he replied. "But in this instance, I'm not. They didn't give me any hint of where they were going."

I hated that I believed him. "You said she seemed upset," I said. "Did you talk to her?"

"I tried to, but she wouldn't tell me anything. She was crying, and she prayed for a while. She seemed scared of something. When I offered to call you for her, it became apparent that you were what she was afraid of. I didn't want to involve the police, so I called Mr. Patras. He came to the church as a favor to me. Giada didn't know I called him until he arrived."

The priest's story painted Giada as a hapless victim in the story, not someone who left with her ex-boyfriend of her own accord. But that wasn't how it had actually happened. "But she left with him willingly?"

"Yes."

My stomach roiled.

"What are you going to do?" the priest asked.

"Find them."

"And then?"

"I'll bring her home."

"You won't hurt either of them?"

"No," I said without hesitation.

"Would you tell me the truth if you were going to hurt one or both of them?"

"No."

I disconnected the call and dialed Angelo. I put him on speaker, told him what we knew, and waited for him to tell us where Adrian might have taken Giada. But Angelo didn't have a clue.

"How do you lose one of your men?" I demanded.

"He's not one of my men," Angelo insisted. "He's not even… he just does odd jobs for the family on occasion. That's it. How do you lose your wife?"

Touché.

I blew out a sigh. "What about that old girlfriend of his, the doctor?"

"They're not together anymore. She wouldn't know anything. The only person who might know is…" Angelo abruptly stopped talking.

"Who?" I snapped.

"Adrian was staying with his sister Annie since he got out of the hospital. I bet he'll call her to check in, and she could find out where he is."

Relief flooded me. Finally, a decent lead.

"But Luca," Angelo continued. "You can't touch Annie."

"Jesus, I'm not going to hurt Adrian's sister."

"I'm serious. Don't threaten her, scare her, anything. Okay?"

"What?"

Angelo sighed. "I can't disclose anything else, but uhh, Annie is off limits, okay?"

"Yeah, fine."

"If she won't tell you anything, let me know. I might have another way to find out from her."

I hung up, prepared to brainstorm with Alessio about how to get Annie to tell us where her brother was without raising any red flags. Before we devised any sort of plan, though, my phone rang again. This time, it was Tony.

"Little busy here," I said into the phone.

"I'll be quick," he promised. "I know you're already stressed about Giada, but I have some bad news."

I winced. I couldn't handle anything else.

"Xavier and I went out for a drink after work today. He had two or three, but um, I don't think he'd eaten for a while, and maybe he has a lower tolerance than me. I offered him a ride home, but he insisted on driving himself."

"What happened?" I asked, wanting him to get to the point.

"I left ten minutes after him and saw his car wrapped around a tree off the side of the road. The paramedics were already there, but he, um, didn't make it."

My breath caught in my throat. Tony had promised to take care of it, but I didn't realize he meant this. Or maybe I had known, and I just didn't care.

"Where are you?" I asked.

"My car. Alone."

"Can you speak freely?" I asked.

He hung up, and a moment later, a call from an unknown number rang through.

"Pronto," I answered, assuming it was Tony. It was.

"Bartender saw him drink. If they test his blood alcohol, it'll confirm that. I stayed at the bar paying the bill till after it was done. If they run any tests on the car, they might see that his brakes were in need of maintenance."

Upon the confirmation of how they'd done it, I exchanged a glance with Alessio. I supposed I should feel relief and gratitude. My papà's men acted quickly and decisively, covering their tracks like the pros that they were. I didn't anticipate anyone to push for further investigation into the death of a young man with a history of petty crime and a drinking problem.

"Thanks for letting me know. Alessio and I may need to go out of town tomorrow. Can you manage everything for a day or two without us?"

"Of course, but why—"

"It's Giada," I said. "I just need a little time with her after…"

"Right." Tony cleared his throat, but not before I heard the judgment in his tone. My papà never would've let my mother or any other woman distract him from my work, and surely his men thought to do otherwise was a sign of weakness. Well, too bad.

"Grazie," I said, ending that call. I barely exhaled before calling my brother-in-law back. "Do whatever you need to for Annie to tell you where Adrian is. She'll never open up to me." I paused, then added, "Please."

He was quiet for a moment, then agreed. "I'll see what I can find out, but I probably won't hear anything until morning."

CHAPTER 12

Giada

I'd passed out while Adrian was still driving, and he powered through another two hours with his concussion headache before finally pulling over and waking me. He'd reiterated the offer to get some hotel rooms, but I'd declined.

We needed to be further away. I didn't trust myself not to run back to Luca if a mere half-day's drive separated us. Nor did I trust that Luca wouldn't find me before I had enough time to process everything, if I weren't further from home.

So we'd stopped for gas, I'd filled up on coffee, and then Adrian slept in the backseat while I drove for the next four hours. I'd never done much interstate driving, especially overnight or on such deserted roads, but the coffee and lack of any distractions proved to be the perfect combination for me to think.

I played out multiple scenarios in my head, but they all ended with real tears forming in the corners of my eyes. I knew in my heart I didn't want to leave Luca. But I also didn't want to stay and then someday have to say goodbye because he was in prison or worse, dead. The only solution that I felt okay with was the one where I turned back time, and Luca never pulled the trigger.

I couldn't reconcile my heart with my mind. I wanted so badly to be in this car running away from my problems with Luca. Yet I clearly wasn't willing to stay and fight by his side. So I kept driving, trusting that space and time would offer the clarity I so desperately needed.

Adrian woke shortly after sunrise, so I stopped at the next exit, desperate to relieve my bladder after all the overnight coffee consumption. He insisted we eat some food, then he took over driving while I slept.

When I awoke, I realized more than twenty-four hours had passed since I'd last seen Luca, and my heart still ached.

"I have to stop, Giada," Adrian said. "My head is pounding and my legs are cramping, and—"

"It's fine," I said, guilt hitting me like a wave when I thought about how much Adrian was suffering just to help me. "I should stretch my legs too. I'm sure we're far enough to stop for the night. Where are we?" I peered around, seeing nothing of note.

"Just outside of Jefferson City, Missouri."

I nodded, but I'd never actually been anywhere in that vast expanse between Chicago and California. The highway looked the same as it did in New England, but it was maybe a touch hotter. "Do you think it's too early to get a room somewhere? Then we could settle in before grabbing food."

Adrian shrugged. He drove a little longer until we reached a newer-looking motel chain at a busy exit. "I'll get us some rooms, and then I need to check in with Annie. I didn't tell her you were with me, but I did call her last night just to let her know I'd be out of town. She's been taking care of me since the hospital, and I didn't want to worry her."

"It's fine," I said. "I'll go get the room."

"Don't use any credit cards, and don't show them any ID," he said.

"I'm not an idiot," I replied, secretly glad for the reminder. The desk clerk did ask to see my license, but I said I'd lost it, and obviously I was over the minimum age to rent the room, so the guy reluctantly agreed. He might have been flirting a little, because he was visibly disappointed when Adrian came inside to join me.

I handed Adrian a key card. "Room 212," I said.

Adrian stopped abruptly. "I assumed you'd get two rooms."

"There's two beds. I didn't want to use all our money on one night."

Adrian's head drooped backwards as if he were cursing the gods for his bad luck at being trapped with me overnight. But he didn't insist on an extra room, so I counted it as a win.

We took turns showering, then I spent an inordinate amount of time doing my hair and makeup. I always felt better when I looked better, or rather, I felt worse when I looked bad. It wasn't as if I could forget the emotional turmoil wreaking havoc on my soul, but I also didn't need a reminder that I was falling apart every time I looked in the mirror.

I let Adrian pick the restaurant, then promptly vetoed his first choice of a buffet.

"Food poisoning is not going to make either of us feel better," I said, reluctantly agreeing to his second suggestion, of a low-priced steak and seafood chain.

"I forgot how big of a food snob you are," he said as we sipped our drinks.

"I'm better than Luca," I said, thinking about how he'd sooner die than eat in a place like this. I smiled, picturing his face if he saw the sticky menus, and a second later, tears welled in my eyes. I covered my face with my hands, determined not to ruin Adrian's meal with my bawling, but a moment later, he'd scooted to my side of the bench seat and wrapped his arm around me.

"It's going to be okay, Giada. You'll figure out what you want to do, and someday, you will be happy again. I promise."

I wished I believed him.

I calmed down by the time our food came, and we discussed innocuous topics while we ate. As we made the half-mile trek back to the hotel, the talk turned serious.

"You said the reason Luca left you in high school was to protect you from this life, right?" Adrian asked. "Well, it seems like that's what you need him to do now."

My heart raced at the thought, and I shook my head.

"I know he loves you, Giada. So surely he would do this, for you. Just tell him if he loves you, he has to respect your decision. If he knows you can't live like this—"

"But I can't live like that, either," I interrupted. "I don't want him to leave me. I want to be with him so badly. I just want him to not be..."

"A monster?" Adrian supplied.

"I was going to say his father."

Adrian shrugged.

"I wish it made sense, but..."

"You love him, despite the sociopathic tendencies."

I didn't disagree or even attempt to defend my husband.

"You do know you'll never be able to change him, right?" Adrian pressed.

I wanted to tell him he was wrong, that Luca had changed. But since his dad's death, well... "I just need a couple days and then I'll go back."

Luca

*A*nnie didn't know where her brother was headed, but he had told her which interstate he was on, so Alessio and I headed west. We took turns driving all night, and by the time Angelo called with an update, we were only a couple hours past

St. Louis, where Annie said Adrian had stopped at a Holiday Inn. There were dozens of nearby hotels in that chain, and all we really had to go by was the car they'd rented. So I didn't let myself get too excited.

Besides, I still wasn't sure what my plan was if I found Giada.

If she truly wanted to be with Adrian and not me, was I prepared to kill him and drag her back with me anyway?

No.

I'd promised her I wouldn't hurt the dick, and she'd never forgive me if I broke my word. Alessio thought it wasn't like that, though, that she'd simply used Adrian to help her escape. I agreed that was more likely, but again, I wasn't prepared to force her back with me or to punish him, so where did that leave me?

All I knew was that nothing mattered without Giada. I didn't care if my men perceived me as weak. I didn't care if the police dragged me to prison for my crimes. I didn't even care if someone took me out as revenge for killing Elio. My life was worthless without Giada.

"Hey," Alessio said, stopping and pointing.

I saw the car instantly, but didn't yet share his optimism. Metallic gray Honda Civics weren't exactly a rare breed. I pulled the post-it out of my pocket and checked the license plate with the one in front of us, but Alessio had already parked the car.

Damn him and his photographic memory.

He scanned the lot, peered up at the hotel, then started to the door. "I'll go find out which room. You stay put."

I rolled my eyes and followed Alessio into the lobby. He huffed a sigh of protest but made his way to the counter.

"Morning," he greeted the clerk, a young man whose name tag read JACK. "My partner and I are following up on leads of a possible human trafficking case. We found a car of interest parked in your lot out back and need to know what room the driver's in."

Jack opened his mouth to protest, but Alessio began rattling off the license plate numbers and some story about where the car had come from. "I don't know if they're using their real names to travel, but this is the man," he held up a clear photo of Adrian, then pulled back to his phone and swiped to a recent picture of Giada. "And this is the woman."

"I'd need to call my boss. I can't just tell you—"

"This girl's life may be in danger. Every minute here counts."

I assumed the boy would protest more, but instead he leaned forward and lowered his voice. "I can't tell you anything from our file, but I checked them in yesterday. He made the girl come in, and she paid in cash. She wouldn't show me ID or anything. I put them in Room 212."

"Thank you," Alessio replied.

He marched outside and started towards the stairs, but I stopped him. My chest felt tight, almost like I couldn't breathe.

"Come on, buddy. We drove all this way. Let's go get your girl."

I shook my head. "They just got one room," I said, unsure how Alessio didn't register the significance of that detail.

My friend rolled his eyes. "You don't know anything yet. Let's pay them a visit and stop guessing what's going on."

I started to protest further, but the loud clang of a heavy metal door shushed us both. We backed against a wall, an overflowing housekeeping cart blocking us from view, then watched as Giada and Adrian made their way down the stairs. Their backs were to us, and they were clearly headed to the car, but they didn't have any bags with them. I couldn't make out their words, but Giada's voice sounded light and cheerful.

Adrian's hand reached up and squeezed the dip between her collarbone and shoulder, and my stomach lurched. The two of them walked past the car and all the way across the parking lot towards a clump of restaurants in the distance.

"Guess they're going out for breakfast," Alessio said.

I watched until they were almost out of sight. At one point,

Giada turned, brushing her hair off her shoulder, and I got the slightest glimpse of her gorgeous, smiling face.

"She looks happy," I said.

"Yeah, well, she probably wasn't up all night driving like some of us were," Alessio replied.

Giada hadn't looked happy for weeks, not with me, anyway. And now she had, what, two nights with Adrian, and she was back to her carefree, joyful self? I sunk to my butt on the pavement, trying to level my breathing.

"Let's just go home," I said.

"No way. We drove all the way here. I'm not leaving until you at least talk to her."

"She deserves to be happy."

"And you are not thinking straight. Get out of your fucking head before you ruin the best thing to ever happen to you," he snapped. "Now look. They left the car, so they're clearly coming back. You go wait in the room to talk to her, and I'll babysit the car just to make sure they don't leave. Okay?"

I wanted to reiterate my demand to leave, but I also needed to see the room. I had to know if they'd shared a bed. "I don't have a key," I mumbled.

Alessio rolled his eyes, snatched a massive key ring off the housekeeping cart, and handed it to me. "If none of these work, just shoot the lock," he said, as if I were a complete moron. "Now go."

He yanked me back to my feet and nudged me towards the stairway. I stumbled to the room, unlocking it with the first key I tried, an oversized master key of sorts. I blinked, letting my eyes adjust to the dim room. Closest to the door was a bathroom and then a closet. The bathroom smelled of Giada's shampoo, and her makeup still rest on the counter. The closet was empty. There were two beds, and to my relief, both were unmade. Giada's overnight bag lay on the foot of one, and a black duffel sat beside the other.

At the far end of the room, there was a counter above a mini fridge, with a microwave on top. Residual steam still dropped from an individual-cup coffee maker, and a trace of Giada's lip gloss stained the side of a paper cup. I sunk into a chair at the small table at the end of the room and pressed my head into my hands, wondering how the fuck my life had gone so completely to shit.

Adrian

An inexplicable prickly sense hit me the moment we returned to the motel. I peered around, on high alert, as we approached our room, but saw nothing out of the ordinary.

Until we reached our room.

Giada swiped her keycard, but instead of the flashing light turning green with a little "click," nothing happened. Giada reached for the lever and found it was already open.

"Stop!" I said, shoving Giada behind me. I yanked the gun from the back of my jeans, as Giada tried to step around me. "I told you I'd keep you safe, so stay back," I said.

"This is my mess that I've dragged you into. I'm not waiting out here."

She pushed into the room, and I had no choice but to follow. I scanned the bathroom then the closet before gazing straight ahead.

Right as I did, Giada gasped.

"Luca!" she breathed.

The man gazed up at us, and I aimed my gun at him. He was seated at the table at the far end of the room, making no effort to move. Two guns were on the table in front of him, but his hands were hidden by the table. I kept my gun pointed at his head while stepping forward and searching the room more thoroughly.

"What are you doing here?" Giada asked.

"We don't know if he's alone," I cautioned her.

"I'm alone. Alessio's by your car," he said, as if we'd take his word for it. "I came for you. I've been looking for you."

Giada stepped closer.

"Giada! Stop. This could be a trap."

She moved like she was in a trance. I had no choice but to focus all my attention on Luca, as she was nearing him. I mentally kicked myself for never considering the possibility that I'd risk everything to help her escape, only for her to walk right into his web.

"I'm not armed," Luca said, glancing at his weapons on the table. He slowly raised his hands to show us.

I lunged forward and scooted his guns out of his reach. Luca made no attempt to stop me. I'd never before seen him look so apathetic and defeated. It was unsettling.

"Giada, go into the bedroom," I told her. She ignored me.

"I would never hurt her," he said.

"Oh? And how about me?"

Luca turned to me and cocked his head to the side, clearly enticed by the idea. Then he looked back at Giada. "May I speak with my wife?" he asked.

I assumed the question was directed at me, though his eyes were now locked on hers.

"I'm not leaving," I said.

His sigh was filled with annoyance. "I found you this morning, amore. I saw you then," he began. "You were with him." Luca paused, but none of us spoke. I, for one, was just shocked that he'd seen us and yet here I was, still breathing.

"You looked happy," he continued.

"I can't go back with you, Luca." Giada whispered.

"I know. And you shouldn't. I'll never change. I don't know how." He shook his head and slowly stood.

I tightened my grip on my pistol and held my breath.

"I decided to leave earlier, to just go back to Italy and never return to the States. I thought that would be for the best. But then I thought about all the times before that I'd tried to walk away, and every time, I find my way back to you." Luca paused and shook his head. "I can't keep doing that to you, and there's only one way to be sure."

Giada wrinkled her brow. "I don't understand what you're trying to say, Luca."

He walked towards her. In a flash, I envisioned him whipping her around to face me and using her as a human shield, forcing me to kill the only woman I'd ever really loved or let him walk away with her.

But that's not what he did.

Instead, before I could react or even process what was happening, Luca gripped Giada's hands, then dropped to his knees at her feet.

"I am so sorry, Giada. I don't expect you to ever truly forgive me, but I need you to know I love you. I've loved you since we were just kids, and I've loved you more every day. I wish I were the kind of man you deserved, the kind of man who could make you happy, but I'm not. I'll never be that man. And I'm so determined to stop hurting you."

"Luca, please," Giada said. She was crying now, much like she had nearly every hour since we'd run, except this time was even more painful to watch because he was here, touching her, and he was crying too.

It was the most infuriating, heartbreaking, and confusing thing I'd ever seen. Yet, I couldn't look away. Seeing this hardened monster literally on his knees begging for forgiveness…it was like watching a car crash.

I felt like I should give them privacy, like I was invading their private moment. Except it wasn't a private moment. Luca was a murderer, and I'd promised to keep her safe from him.

"I need to be sure I can never hurt you again, Giada, so you need to do a favor for me."

"She's not doing anything for you," I interrupted. "She owes you nothing."

Neither of them even turned to me.

"As long as we're both alive, we'll keep finding our way back to each other eventually. And if your inept bodyguard over there kills me, my men will have no choice but to avenge my death. The only way to end all of this nonsense is for *you* to do this."

"For me to do what?"

"I want you to kill me, Giada."

"What?" Giada and I both spoke at the same time, and with equal levels of confusion in our voices.

"It's the only way," Luca said. "As long as I'm alive, you won't be able to live a normal life."

For once, I agreed with the guy.

Giada shook her head. "Baby, no. I don't want to live in a world you're not a part of." She tugged him to his feet, and they just stared at each other for several seconds.

A throat cleared behind me, and a second later, the gun I'd forgotten I was holding was yanked out of my hand. I turned from the trainwreck in front of me to face Alessio, but I was still too confused by what I was watching to muster an appropriate level of terror.

Alessio emptied the bullets from my gun, then handed it back to me, a blank expression on his face. When I didn't immediately take it, he dropped it on the foot of the bed closest to us. Then, he picked up the weapons I'd knocked out of Luca's reach.

"Alright, we can chat about all this later. Time to go, guys," Alessio said, breaking the trance between Luca and Giada.

He grabbed Giada's bag and thrust it into her hand. "Get your stuff, Princess."

Giada gazed from Luca to Alessio then back to Luca. After a

moment, her feet moved, slowly carrying her to the bathroom. Alessio turned back to me.

"Giada," I began, keeping my eyes on Alessio. "If you don't want to leave with them, you don't have to."

"Are you trying to get yourself killed?" Alessio asked.

"Is there a chance you let me walk away as is?"

Alessio turned to Luca, but the man still stared blankly at the spot Giada had occupied a moment before.

Alessio sighed. "You don't work for us, so it's not our business what happens to you. Unless something happened with the princess."

I rolled my eyes. "I didn't touch her. She was scared and wanted some time to think, and she wasn't in any condition to drive herself. That's all."

Alessio turned to Giada, who had packed up her bathroom items and hoisted her bag over her shoulder.

"I just needed a break," she said. "Adrian didn't do anything wrong. You should thank him for helping me."

"Our sincerest gratitude," Alessio said, his tone clipped. "Next time you want a break, maybe ask your husband to arrange for you and Gabby to spend a few days in the Caribbean, okay? Luca didn't need this now. None of us did."

Giada squeezed her eyes shut, but I could see the tears slipping past. Alessio nudged her by the elbow towards the door.

"I'm sorry," she mouthed as she passed me. Then she turned to her husband. "Luca?"

After a beat, he stumbled after them. I watched from the second-story walkway as they made their way to the car. Luca and Giada climbed into the back seat, and Alessio sat in the front. They peeled out of the parking lot and I sank to the bed, realizing my heart was thudding irregularly.

Giada

Alessio ranted in Italian for the first several minutes of the drive. I couldn't tell if he was talking to Luca, or just muttering to himself. I couldn't remember ever before seeing Alessio so worked up.

Luca stared at me, as if he couldn't really believe I was there. I reached for him, but he flinched, and my heart ached. I'd been so focused on how much he had hurt me, but now I could see first-hand how much I'd hurt him.

Maybe Luca was right. Maybe we would keep torturing each other as long as we both lived.

"I'm sorry," I said, "I didn't—"

"No," Luca cut me off. "I just...let's get home." He turned to the window, and didn't so much as glance at me for the next hour. Alessio turned on the radio, and Luca shut his eyes. A moment later, his breathing slowed and his shoulders relaxed.

I'd never seen Luca fall asleep so quickly or sleep so soundly. Alessio tailed other cars, weaved through traffic, and shouted in

Italian at other drivers on more than one occasion. Still, Luca didn't wake.

"Did you give him something?" I asked, leaning forward.

Alessio startled at my voice, then briefly turned his head partway to face me. "What? No. He's just tired."

I caught his eyes in the rearview as he gazed at Luca.

"This is the first he's slept since you ran off. And he wasn't too well rested before that." He paused, then added, "You know, on account of his father being murdered and having the most horrific month of his life. He was in hell, and then, you just left."

The guilt hit me like a brick wall, as I was sure he'd intended. I'd abandoned Luca when he needed me most. That's what Alessio was saying. But there was more to it than that. There was...

"It's not that simple," I finally said, determined to defend myself.

"It really is. He needed you, and you took off. Your husband was suffering through the hardest and most traumatic time in his entire life, and you ran off with your old boyfriend."

"I didn't run off with—"

"Shh!" Alessio's eyes darted to Luca. "If you cared about him even a little, you'd let him sleep instead of pleading your case. It's pointless anyway."

I looked out the window and confirmed that we were on a clear, straight stretch of relatively empty highway. I unfastened my belt and began to crawl over the center console into the front seat.

"What are you..." Alessio began, but quickly guessed my plan and cleared the front seat. "Jesus, fasten your belt. If Luca saw you..." He shook his head. "You know, he worries about you all the time. When you left him, completely humiliating him, endangering his life—and mine—and dragging us across the country at the most critical time for him to be in New York, all he thought about was you. He worried nonstop about your safety, and all the while you couldn't care less about his."

"That's not even remotely true! I care so much. You know I do. But I can't live like that, constantly worrying about his safety. Not if he's going to off and…"

"He didn't have a choice. And besides, if he hadn't done it, someone else would've."

"You?"

"In a heartbeat."

I rolled my eyes. Alessio didn't need to work hard to convince me he was a heartless killing machine. I knew that. But Luca was different. He was trying to be better. He had a soul worth saving. I supposed, maybe, Alessio did too.

"If Luca hadn't taken care of it then, we would've faced attacks from all sides. He'd probably be dead now. At best, you would've lived your lives constantly worrying about people coming after him. That's what happens when guys like him are perceived as weak."

"I'm not stupid, Alessio. I know why he did what he did, and I still don't agree with it. There is always another way."

"Maybe for you. But in the real world, it isn't always flowers and butterflies. The rest of us don't have someone else waiting in the wings to sweep in and rescue us."

"You do, too," I said under my breath.

He scowled, then rolled his eyes when he understood what I meant. "Right, because Jesus will jump right in and save the mobster. Is that how it works?"

"Maybe."

Alessio laughed.

"I'm glad you're so confident in your assessment of the world. That must be nice," I said. "Have you ever even considered what happens if you're wrong, though? Maybe you stay alive an extra year or two, and for what, an eternity in hell?"

"At least I'd be in good company there," he said with a shrug.

I didn't have a response to that. It wasn't news to me that my faith was a complete joke to him.

"You know I'm headed there anyway, right? So what's the point for me, really?"

"That isn't how it works. You can ask for forgiveness, and as long as you stop…"

"Stop being gay?" he interrupted.

"Oh." I'd assumed he was talking about the killing people thing. "Well, no. That wasn't what I meant. If you want my opinion, though, God doesn't care about that. I don't see why he would anyway. I mean, none of us ever knows for sure whether we're doing enough until it's too late, but what matters is if you're trying to be a good person."

"That seems like a lot of unknowns. And the last time I checked, the majority view of the Catholic church has me headed straight to hell whether or not I kill people, so I might as well—"

"That's bullshit and you know it," I interrupted. "Can you imagine the world if everyone stopped hurting other people?"

"No."

"Well, it has to start with someone. Every person has to make the choice to be good. It's a domino effect. And whether or not you believe in something greater after this life, you have to acknowledge the potential to make things better here while you're still alive."

Alessio was quiet for several minutes. I gazed out the window, then turned to stare at my husband, still sleeping like a baby. Luca was almost unrecognizably calm when he slept. When I glanced back at Alessio, he was gnawing on his lip anxiously. I imagined the last few days had been hard on him, too.

After a moment, he realized I was watching him.

"It'll kill him, you know," he said. "If he knows you were… with Adrian."

That made no sense. "I was with Adrian. When he found me."

"I mean if he knows you were unfaithful."

"You think I slept with Adrian?"

"I don't want to know. What I'm saying is that you shouldn't tell Luca. He can't handle anything else right now."

"Nothing happened with Adrian. I would never…" I shook my head, dismissing the thought. "He was just helping me out. Everyone else was too afraid of Luca to help."

Alessio glanced at me again, frowning. "You really didn't sleep with Adrian?"

"No!" Geez, what kind of hypocrite did he think I was? "We slept in separate beds. We didn't even kiss. It wasn't like that at all."

"So, there's no chance the baby is his?"

I started to repeat my 'no,' then paused, letting his words sink in. "What baby?"

Alessio swore under his breath.

"What baby?" I repeated.

"Luca knows," he finally said. "He found the little test stick."

I shook my head. "What test stick? I'm not pregnant. Is that what Luca thinks?"

"You're saying it was someone else's test, in your bedroom?"

"No, but it was negative. I only took it because I was nauseous and…" I gazed back at Luca again, but he was still sound asleep. "I'm not pregnant."

"I saw the test, Giada. It had two bright blue lines on it. Luca showed me. That's not negative."

I considered the possibilities. I had set my phone timer and waited the appropriate amount of time. There hadn't been even a shadow of a second line when I'd looked. But what if… I glanced out the window and saw a sign announcing an exit in a half mile.

"Exit here," I said.

"Luca said to drive until we needed gas."

"Exit here!" I repeated.

Alessio flipped on his signal and scooted over. I pointed to a gas station near the exit and started to climb out of the car as soon as we stopped moving.

"Wait, I'm coming with you."

I rolled my eyes but waited. He locked the car behind us, apparently concerned someone would kidnap my sleeping husband, then walked me into the dilapidated building. I made my way to the health aisle, grabbed the only brand of pregnancy test they sold, and took it to the cash register. Alessio stared at the car as though he expected it to move on its own.

I declined a bag for my purchase and then walked towards the bathroom. "It'll take a few minutes," I told Alessio.

Alone in the bathroom, I winced at my reflection. My eyes had dark smudges and my hair was mussed. I ripped open the box, skimmed the instructions, then carefully perched over the disgusting toilet to pee on the stick. When I was done, I replaced the cap on the test stick and washed my hands before setting the timer. Then I rummaged around in my purse for some pressed powder, lip gloss, and a hairbrush.

When the timer went off, I looked a little better, and I'd successfully distracted myself from the possibility that I was pregnant. I picked up the stick, compared the single line to the picture of the negative result in the pamphlet, and nodded.

Not pregnant.

I shoved the instructions into my purse and carried the stick out with me where Alessio waited expectantly. From his apparent anxiety level, I wondered if he'd actually thought I was going to make a run for it.

"Not pregnant," I said, practically chucking the stick at him.

He eyed me warily.

"What? Do you want to come watch me pee on another?"

His expression changed instantly and he dropped the stick to the ground. "Eww! You peed on this?"

I grabbed the stick and stuck it in my purse, ignoring the overly interested expression from the cashier.

"I'm getting food. You want anything?"

I shook my head and started toward the car. Of course it was locked, so I waited outside until Alessio returned. I passed the time by trying to think what could've made the last pregnancy test, the one Luca saw, change. I'd heard it was possible to get a false positive if you read the results a long time after the testing window passed. I supposed that must have been what had happened. I explained as much to Alessio when he returned, but he seemed uninterested.

He polished off a snack-sized bag of chips before starting on a protein bar. He didn't speak for a good ten minutes, which was fine by me.

"What about euthanasia?" he said suddenly.

"What?"

"You know, like when someone has terminal cancer and the doctor gives them medicine to die painlessly. Is that wrong?"

"I don't know. You'd have to ask a priest."

"What's your personal view?"

I shrugged. "I suppose if the person is definitely dying, I'd consider it compassionate to help them do so with more dignity and less pain."

"Compassionate, huh." He shook his head like I'd said something ridiculous. "You ever heard of Alfred Ware?"

"No."

"He was the last snitch that tried to infiltrate your father-in-law's business."

"He was a cop?"

"Yeah, undercover. Didn't really discover anything that got anyone in trouble, certainly didn't get anyone killed, let alone the boss."

I rolled my eyes, certain there was a story here. "Okay, why are you telling me about him?"

"I thought you might want to know what happened to him."

"I probably don't."

"They cut out his tongue. Then cut off his fingers. When he started to lose consciousness from the pain, they woke him up. He was still awake when they cut off his ears. They watched him bleed to death, all the while talking about what they were going to do to his kids next."

My stomach contracted harshly and I raised a hand to my mouth.

"That's not very compassionate, is it?"

I didn't answer. I felt tears brimming in my eyes and knew once I started that I wouldn't be able to stop.

"That's what would've happened to Officer Randazzo, or whatever his real name was. It wasn't a possibility of him surviving after what he did, it was just a question of how he died." Alessio glanced at me for longer than he should've, given that he was driving. "Luca shot him once in the head. It was a clean shot. He died instantaneously. No pain. Seems pretty fucking compassionate to me."

I still didn't say anything.

"So while you're skipping off with your ex-boyfriend and thinking about what a monster your loyal husband is, maybe next time you should look at the facts first. He was a fucking saint to take Elio out like he did, especially after losing his own father."

I turned to Alessio, then sighed. I wedged my jacket against the car window and shut my eyes.

<hr>

Luca

When I awoke, Giada was no longer beside me. I sat up, panicked, then Alessio spoke.

"She's up here," he said, tipping his head to the side.

I saw her then, curled against her window. Her eyes were closed, but I couldn't tell if she was sleeping.

"Is she asleep?"

"I don't think so."

I pulled out my phone, checking the time. It was almost nine o'clock. I knew that wasn't really late, but we were still hours from home. Alessio needed sleep, as did I. When we returned home, we'd have to hit the ground running.

"We need a hotel," I said.

Alessio nodded. "There's probably several at the next exit that have a couple rooms open."

I considered that, but given that I'd just slept as though comatose for three hours in a car, I didn't trust myself to wake up if Giada left. But with Alessio and me both in the room, surely one of us would wake. "Can you just get one room?"

"Oh, we're gonna snuggle tonight?" he teased. "Yeah. That's fine."

I glanced down at my phone again, scrolling through the missed calls. Lorenzo had called twice.

"Giada and I talked some," Alessio said. "For what it's worth, I don't think she'll try to run."

"Not taking any chances," I said, dialing Enzo. He picked up quickly. "I already told Marco that we got her," I said. "We're driving back. Should be home around early afternoon tomorrow."

"Alright," he said. "And she's okay?"

"Yeah."

"And Adrian?"

I paused. "He didn't want to come back with us."

"Didn't want to or…" his voice trailed off.

I was still too groggy to fill in the blanks for him, so I waited for him to explain.

"Angelo wants to know if you killed him," Enzo finally said.

"No! I didn't touch him."

"Did Alessio?"

"Adrian is fine. No one hurt a hair on his precious little head. I don't really care what he does. If Angelo wants to deal with him, that's his prerogative."

"Wants to deal with who?" Giada asked, popping her head up and swiveling to face me. "You think my dad will hurt Adrian?"

I averted my eyes and waited for Enzo to respond.

"Alright, he might want me to go get him and bring him back."

I gave him the address where we'd last seen Adrian then hung up.

"We're stopping for the night soon," I told Giada. "And you should eat something."

"I lost my appetite," she said, glaring at Alessio.

I wasn't about to ask what that was about.

"What were you saying about my brother? Who was on the phone?"

I sighed loudly. "If one of my guys did what Adrian did, there would be consequences. But Adrian doesn't work for me, so I don't have any control over that."

"What kind of consequences? They won't hurt his fingers, right?"

"His fingers?"

Alessio made a face and shook his head. I was too exhausted to deal with any of this. We could talk tomorrow.

We checked into a hotel, then Alessio went to get sandwiches while Giada showered. I caught up on the rest of my calls, then once he was back, I took a quick shower. Then, it was Alessio's turn to shower. I sat at the worn table across the room and ate my sandwich while watching my wife. She'd already crawled under the covers but was sitting upright.

I had so many questions about her last couple days, but I didn't even know where to begin.

"I didn't sleep with Adrian," she said.

I nearly choked on the bite of sandwich I was chewing. I supposed I should've been happy about that, except it didn't seem like she deserved praise for not cheating on her spouse.

"I would never be unfaithful," she continued. "We didn't even kiss or anything. It wasn't like that, at all."

"Okay," I finally said.

"You believe me, right?"

I didn't know what to say. I wanted to believe her, but then I saw how angry she'd been. I could definitely see her breaking our marriage vows to teach me a lesson for what I'd done.

I wanted to ask why Adrian. Why not Enzo? Why not that damn priest she was so close to? Why not some random stranger? Or a girlfriend? Why did she pick the one person to run away with that would make me the most upset? The person would make me look the most pathetic?

But I was bone tired. Nothing good could come of talking now. Hopefully, Giada recognized that, too.

"Alessio told me you were compassionate, that you shot the guy in the head once, and that it was quick."

I winced.

"He said everyone else would've tortured the guy if you hadn't done that. He made it seem like you did him a favor."

I turned to the bathroom at the sound of the shower shutting off.

"I'm not the hero of this story," I finally said. I wadded up my sandwich wrapper and chucked it into the trash. Then I dragged the table in front of the door and perched the chairs on top of it.

"I'm not going anywhere," Giada said.

"Good."

When Alessio emerged from the bathroom, clad in his sweatpants and nothing else, he shook his head and laughed at the obstacle in front of the door.

He climbed into bed and switched off the lamp above his bed. "Nighty night, lovebirds," he said, rolling so his back was to Giada.

I tentatively approached my wife, pulled back the covers, then crawled into bed beside her. She flopped onto her back as I turned off the light. I gazed at her, wondering how we felt so distant now, when just a few weeks before, I'd felt closer to her than ever.

I'd hurt her. She'd hurt me. That was our cycle. Somehow, I'd have to learn to break it. I scooted closer, nudged her onto her side away from me, and wrapped my arm around her waist.

"Sleep now," I whispered. "We'll talk at home." I pressed a kiss to her the back of her head and then closed my eyes, focusing on the warmth of her flesh beneath the palm of my hand. A t-shirt was between my fingers and her skin, but I couldn't help but imagine what was just past that...a baby. Our baby. Our fresh start.

CHAPTER 14

Giada

A dingy, beige wall was less than a foot from my face when I awoke. I jerked back, disoriented, then stilled when I realized Luca was still wrapped around me. The room was no longer dark, so it must be morning, but with my back to the clock, I wasn't sure of the exact time. I slithered out from under Luca's hand, shocked when he didn't wake.

I stood slowly, then froze, suddenly aware of Alessio staring at me. He was perched on top of his bed, headphones in his ears and his phone propped on a pillow, so I assumed he had been watching a show.

"Morning," he mouthed.

Feeling painfully underdressed now, I grabbed my bag and went into the bathroom. I washed my face, brushed my teeth, tied my hair into a loose knot on top of my head and was just starting makeup when there was a knock on the door. Assuming it was Luca, I quickly opened the door, only to come face to face with Alessio.

I stumbled over my words. "Sorry. Did you need..."

He shook his head. "You need to tell him you're not pregnant," he said.

I blew out a sigh and turned back to the mirror, leaning forward so I didn't accidentally turn myself into a clown when applying eyeliner.

"There's a lot you two need to discuss, actually," he added.

"That's not really your business," I said, moving on to eyeshadow.

"I disagree. Luca's careless when he's worried about you. This isn't a good time for him to be distracted. And it's my business because if he loses focus now and gets himself killed, I won't fare so well either."

I swiped a second coat of mascara on my eyelashes then turned to face him. "Why is now so important? Are you worried he'll get caught?"

"Caught?" Alessio looked legitimately confused.

"He murdered someone in cold blood. Last I checked, police still frown on that."

"Oh, right." Alessio shook his head. "No, not even remotely concerned about that. What I meant was that this is basically the most critical time ever in Luca's career. With Salvatore out of the picture, Luca's it. He's the boss."

I shuddered involuntarily. "I'd like some privacy to change, please," I said.

Alessio shut the door.

By the time I was dressed and had finished my makeup, Luca was awake and Alessio was nowhere to be seen. Luca stared at me, his lips parted, a sad look in his eyes, for probably half a minute before turning away. It was unsettling, at best. I wasn't ready for a full heart-to-heart yet, but Alessio did have a point about the pregnancy part. Luca deserved to know the truth about that, at least.

"Where's Alessio?"

Luca nodded to the door. "On the phone," he mumbled. He switched out his shirt for a clean one before turning back to me.

"I'm not pregnant," I blurted out. "The test was negative, but I guess after it sits there a while, a false positive can show up."

His expression deepened. "Are you sure?"

"Yes. Your little sidekick made me take another test to be sure." The moment the words left my mouth, I panicked, realizing I'd just inadvertently told Luca that his friend knew before him. But apparently my concern was unwarranted.

"Okay," he said calmly, his face showing no expression. "We should head out."

Luca carried my bag out to the car, then climbed into the front by Alessio, so I figured we weren't talking during the drive at least. Whatever. I still didn't know what to say.

We'd driven for barely an hour when my stomach growled loudly.

Luca gazed up, and our eyes met in the rearview mirror. Then he turned to Alessio. "Let's stop for breakfast."

Alessio pulled off at the next stop, parking in front of a crowded diner. A waitress told us to sit anywhere, and the guys led me to a table in the back. Alessio sat on one side of the booth, so I sat across from him. Luca slid in beside me. The guys began talking in Italian, pausing only when the waitress came to bring us all coffee.

I focused on the menu, almost mournful when the waitress took our orders and walked off with my only distraction.

Something vibrated from Luca's pocket, and he reached in, pulling out my phone, not his. He frowned at the device, then set it on the table in front of him before reaching into his pocket for his own phone.

I reached for my phone, already relieved by the prospect of something to distract me from the painful awkwardness with Luca and Alessio.

Alessio tugged it right out of my reach, just as the waitress returned with a fresh pot of coffee.

"Give me my phone," I said.

"I think we can all agree you haven't demonstrated that you're trustworthy enough for a phone," he replied.

I turned to Luca in hopes of some sort of support, but he was staring at his own phone, ignoring us both.

The waitress caught my eye as she topped off my coffee. I felt my cheeks flush at the realization that a stranger had heard Alessio lecture me like a child.

I turned back to the window until our food came, and then I picked at my pancakes, struggling to swallow each bite around the lump forming in my throat. The guys returned to their discussion, and I sat in silence, ignored by everyone except the waitress, who returned twice to ask if everything was okay. I figured she was worried since I hadn't eaten much, but my appetite had vanished.

As the waitress came to refill Luca's mug, I again reached for my phone. I clicked on my messages, but before I could even read them all, Luca slid the device out of my hand and wedged it into his pocket.

I glared.

Luca thanked the waitress for his refill, and I scooted towards him. "I need to use the restroom," I said.

He didn't budge. "You need to eat more. Do you want me to order something else for you?"

"Not hungry," I replied.

Luca hesitated, then stood to let me pass.

I took my time in the bathroom, needing a moment alone. I was staring in the mirror, trying to garner the energy to leave, when the door swung open and our waitress came in. I smiled politely, then looked down. I began slowly tinkering with my hair, trying to look like I had a purpose to being in the bathroom and that I hadn't just come in there so I could breathe without Alessio and Luca glaring at me.

After a moment, I realized the waitress was staring at me. I turned to her, noting her nametag read Liz.

"I'm sorry to be so nosy, but are you okay?" she asked.

I briefly entertained that plethora of responses I could offer, then nodded. "It's been a long week is all."

She didn't seem to believe me. "Are you sure?"

I tried to smile reassuringly. Then I flipped on the faucet to wash my hands.

"Those men that you're with, um, one of them followed you," Liz said, lowering her voice. "It seemed like maybe they're worried you'll sneak out?"

That didn't surprise me, although I wasn't going to run. I shrugged. "There's not even an exit in here, is there?" I asked.

Liz shook her head. "But there's one directly off the kitchen. Two of our cooks are pretty big guys. They could handle…"

I shut off the faucet, wondering why I'd even asked about the exit. "Sorry, I don't…I mean, I'm not leaving. Without them, anyway. We drove together."

Now she looked even more alarmed. "So you know them?"

"My husband is the one next to me. His best friend was sitting across from us."

I saw her eyes flit down to my ring finger. I hadn't bothered to remove my rings when I skipped town with Adrian.

"I appreciate the concern, but I'm not like a kidnapping victim or anything. Promise."

"So you could leave alone right now if you wanted?"

I nearly laughed at that. "Yes," I said, my inner voice screaming the opposite.

"I saw them take your phone. Do you want to use mine to make a call?"

I shook my head. I'd love to tell Adrian I was okay, and to

check in with Enzo to make sure nothing was going to happen to Adrian, but I couldn't. I didn't have any numbers memorized.

"I could have the police here in three minutes," she said.

"No. Don't do that. Please," I shook my head furtively. "Honestly, I'm just tired. And stressed. I think you're misreading the situation."

"My ex-husband used to hurt me," she volunteered. "I made up all sorts of excuses for him, and then one day I realized I didn't have to live that way. No one deserves to live that way. If he loves you, he'll let you make your own decisions, go where you want, do what you want."

"Really, I appreciate your concern, but I'm fine. My husband would never touch me. My, um, father-in-law just passed and we've been on the road for a couple of days and we're all just..." I sighed.

Liz placed her hand on my wrist. "I'm sorry about your father-in-law."

I shrugged. "Don't be. He was an asshole."

There was a knock on the door. I knew without checking it had to be Luca.

"Giada," he called through the door, confirming my suspicions.

The waitress looked at me as though somehow this proved her right, but I could tell by Luca's tone that he was worried about me, not angry.

"Be right out, babe," I said loudly. Then I turned back to Liz. "Thanks. We really are fine, though. Promise. Sorry about your ex."

I pushed through the door and practically fell into Luca's arms.

"It's a women's bathroom, you know," I said.

"I was worried you weren't feeling well," he replied, right as our waitress stepped out behind me.

I glanced over at the table where Alessio was still drinking his milkshake.

"Can we talk outside?" Luca asked, following my gaze. "Alessio says he won't ride with us any further if we haven't worked things out."

I nodded and started outside, knowing he'd follow. There was a bench right outside, so I plopped down, certain based on the quantity of cigarette butts surrounding the bench that this was where the diner staff took their smoke breaks.

Luca shuffled his feet awkwardly. "The car would be more private."

I flung up my hands, gesturing to the complete absence of anyone nearby. "I don't know what we have to talk about anyway."

"Really?"

I shrugged.

"Okay, what about the fact that you ran off with your ex-boyfriend. Or that you stole a bunch of money from me. Or maybe we should talk about the pregnancy test."

"I'll pay you back," I mumbled, saving my retort about how he always claimed his money was mine too. We'd barely spent any money yet anyway.

"I don't want the money!" Luca snapped.

It was obvious he was upset. But I was, too. "If you want to talk, let's talk about what you did to that man. Or let's talk about how you asked me to kill you. Or maybe we should discuss how you're a completely different person now that you're the boss."

Luca paced tensely for a moment, then dropped onto the bench. His thigh brushed against mine as we sat. His eyes were shut, but I could tell from his breathing that he was thinking.

"I already told you the test was negative. I didn't really think I was pregnant. I know we'd talked about maybe starting to try soon, but then with your father..." I paused as a customer exited the diner and walked towards a Buick across the lot. "I realized the timing wasn't right. I felt weird, so I just wanted to make sure nothing had happened yet. If I had honestly thought I might be, I would've told you. I would've taken the test when you were around."

Lucas' eyes popped open, and he gazed at me. He didn't smile, but he definitely looked happier with that news. And he wasn't yelling or threatening suicide, so I was encouraged to continue.

"Nothing happened with Adrian. Nothing at all. He's still hung up on Melissa, and I'm not interested in him that way, either. He is just a friend, and it'll never be more than that between him and I."

Luca focused even more intently on my eyes now, as though he were searching for answers, or maybe administering his own lie detector test. Apparently, he found what he was looking for because after a moment, he nodded.

"I left because I was scared. I'm impulsive, you know? That's what I do. I get scared and I run," I said.

"That wasn't an impulse. You planned that. You left your phones, got new ones. You rented a car, left all of your stuff. There were a hundred things you had to do, a hundred steps you had to take to get away from me. And before each one, you could've changed your mind, could've come to me with your fears. But you didn't. At every turn you chose to keep running from me. You never intended to come back to me."

Luca's voice sounded so raw that I could barely swallow the lump in my throat. He was right, of course. I could've changed my mind at any point. But I hadn't wanted to. And yet, I'd never planned to go for good. I just needed time. I'd known that if I saw him, I'd go back to him. I couldn't resist him.

I tried to explain that to him, but he simply shook his head.

"No, Giada, you took vows. We took vows. Till death do us part, remember that?"

I gritted my teeth together. As if I could forget that. "But then you killed someone. In our vows…we really never specified whose death."

Luca turned abruptly as if I'd slapped him. Drawing in a sharp breath, stood again. "So that's it, then? You want a divorce?"

The way he said it actually made it seem like I had a choice, like there was some world where I could divorce him and not die inside.

"Is that what you want?" I asked.

Luca's expression crumbled, and he lowered himself back down to the bench, squeezing my hands. "How can you even ask that? I want you. I will always want you. I don't even want to think about a world where you aren't mine." Luca paused and shook his head. "But I also don't want to make you miserable. I want to be the man you love, a man you're proud of, not someone you're scared of."

"I'm not scared of you."

Luca raised an eyebrow.

"I was afraid you'd hurt Adrian, and then there would definitely be no chance of us making up."

"Well, I didn't," Luca said quietly.

I tried to explain what was going through my mind, why I'd done what I'd done, in a way he could understand. In a way that didn't make things worse than they already were. "I thought you had changed. I thought you were a man incapable of hurting an innocent person. But the fact that you didn't seem to think you even had a choice, well that scared me. That's why I left. I realized I couldn't stand by your side while you became your father. I can't."

"I'm not becoming my papà," Luca said, his voice filled with certainty now. "I did what I did in the most humane way I could think of, and while I wish it didn't come to that, it did. I can't go back and change it, but I can promise you that you weren't wrong about me. I can be the man you need me to be."

I considered his words, already feeling myself starting to be swayed. And I remembered what Alessio said, how Luca was doing Elio a favor by humanely killing him before anyone else could torture him. I didn't doubt that was intentional on Luca's part. But then I remembered what else had happened. "No. Luca, it was just yesterday that you asked me to kill you."

He gazed up at me solemnly. "I don't want to live without you, but I don't want to make you miserable, either. If you can't forgive me, if we can't move on..."

"Luca," I began.

But he interrupted me with a quick shake of his head. "When you left, I realized I couldn't do any of it without you. I can't get over my papà, I can't take care of my mother. And I sure as hell can't lead the family."

I knew without asking he didn't just mean the Marinos. "I'm not leading a crime family with you."

He actually cracked a smile at that, even though I hadn't meant the comment to be funny.

"I'm serious, Giada. If you can't forgive me, if you don't still love me, just put me out of my misery."

I squeezed my eyes shut as the pain of his words throbbed through my abdomen and moved upwards, causing a tightness in my chest. "That isn't fair," I said, without opening my eyes.

"Nobody ever said life would be fair," he said, his hand now resting lightly on my thigh. "But if you don't want me anymore..."

"Of course, I still want you," I said, opening my eyes despite the shame in my admission. The truth was Luca could probably kill a dozen people in cold blood, and I'd still love him. What did that say about me? About *my* chance at salvation? Maybe we were both past the point of redemption.

I gazed up, immediately greeted by the hopeful look in his eyes.

"I'm supposed to help make you a better person, not support you while you do horrible things," I said.

"You are making me better," he insisted. "I'm a work in progress."

He brushed his thumb across my cheekbone, wiping away tears I hadn't realized I'd wept. His eyes met mine, and a warmth spread through me. Staring into his deep, soft brown eyes turned my insides to mush. It was as if I could see into his soul, and the connection burned into mine.

"I love you," I whispered. "I will never stop loving you."

Luca raised a second hand to my other cheek, gently cupping both sides of my face as he leaned closer. His kiss barely brushed against my mouth, but then he lingered there, so close that the heat of his breath warmed my lips. He wanted more, but was waiting for permission. It pained me that he even felt like he needed to ask. He was my husband. My lips were his to kiss at will.

I leaned in, forcing the contact we both craved, not relaxing until his lips parted and his tongue swept forward to meet mine. His hands softly caressed my cheeks then moved down to my shoulders, waking every nerve ending in my body as he touched me.

How had I thought I could survive without this? Without him?

"I'm so sorry for running," I said, breaking off the kiss but staying close.

"I know." He wrapped his arms around me and pulled me close for a hug, pressing his lips into the top of my head.

He held me for a moment, then said, "I'll drive." His voice was louder, his tone so completely different, that I sat abruptly and opened my eyes. Alessio stood before us, and it was apparent Luca had been speaking to him. I blushed, wondering how long he'd been there, in light of the intimate kiss we'd shared mere minutes ago.

Alessio showed no indication that he'd seen anything private, though, simply nodding and tossing the keys to Luca. I gazed back to the restaurant and noticed the waitress watching us through the window as Luca opened the front passenger door for me. I hoped they'd left her a big tip.

CHAPTER 15

Luca

J offered to take the next driving shift, but Alessio clearly didn't trust my judgment just yet. Giada was tired and took the backseat, leaving me up front with Alessio. I scrolled through messages and emails from my guys, trying to stay abreast of as much business as possible while Alessio drove.

"Have you already decided what you'll tell everyone?" Alessio asked, interrupting my thoughts about a staffing issue at one of the clubs.

I peered into the backseat, assuming Giada was asleep since he'd spoken in English. Although, it wouldn't be the worst thing for her to overhear how difficult her little cross-country jaunt had made our lives. I was about to reply when Alessio spoke again.

"If I were you, I'd say you sent her away, for her own safety. You knew some shit was about to go down, so you had one of her dad's guys get her far away until you had everything under control."

I nodded, my eyes locked on the road. That was, really, the only explanation that let me save face. Except for one problem. "Marco knows the truth."

"Or does he? Angelo, yeah. Sure. But Marco? I don't know."

I shook my head. Nothing good could come from trying to trick anyone. "It doesn't matter anyway. From a business perspective, no one will think less of me if they think my wife ran off. It might even help keep her safer if they don't realize the lengths I'd go to for her."

Alessio shifted to gaze at my wife in the back seat. He waited a moment, then turned back to me before speaking. "She is safe, Luca. You got her back, and we'll keep her safe."

I squeezed my eyes shut for the briefest of seconds to clear them. "Yeah, you're right," I said with a nod. At least, he had better be.

I reached for my phone, ready to go into planning mode. By the time Giada awoke from her nap, we'd figured out her full protection detail for the week, as well as mine. When she stretched and lifted her head off the window, I was on the phone with Mr. Conti confirming he was on board with the little white lie about me sending Giada away. I was using a headset, and speaking in Italian as a precaution, but she seemed completely uninterested in the call until Marco asked to speak with his daughter.

I tugged out the earpiece and pressed the button on the car's control panel to divert the call through the car's audio system.

"Your father wants to talk to you," I said.

"Mine?" she asked, still groggy and confused.

"Giada?" his deep voice boomed through the stereo speaker, clearing up any confusion on her part.

"Hi dad," she mumbled.

"Are you okay?"

"Yes, I…"

"What were you thinking? You could've gotten yourself killed. You could have gotten Luca killed. Or me or your brothers, not to mention Adrian. And how do you think this makes us all look?"

"I didn't..."

"I have never been so disappointed, Giada," he interrupted. "You've always been reckless and selfish, but this takes it to a whole new level. When are you going to grow up?"

I glanced behind me to see Giada cradle her head in her hands. Without another thought, I turned down the speaker volume all the way, waited a few seconds, and then shouted, "Mr. Conti? There's static. Too much interference. We'll try you later."

Alessio chuckled as I clicked the button to disconnect the call.

I'd expected a thank you from my wife, but Giada was silent for so long that I assumed she'd fallen back asleep. When we exited the interstate, though, she spoke.

"Where am I going?" she asked.

"Home," I replied.

"Which home?"

"New York."

"Your father's or..."

"Our home," I said, cringing at the mention of my papà.

"What's going to happen to me?"

"What do you mean?"

"My father hates me. You hate me. I'm not naïve enough to think there won't be consequences for what I did."

I caught Alessio rolling his eyes at that, presumably because there were always consequences for Giada's actions, but never ones that seemed to affect her. And that was how it would be this time, as well.

"Nothing will happen to you, Giada. No one is going to hurt you ever. I won't let them."

"And Adrian?"

I took my time answering, cruelly wanting her to suffer

longer if she was going to worry about him so much. "Nothing will happen to him. If Enzo can find him, he'll bring him back."

"He's too smart for Enzo to find."

I refrained from pointing out we'd found him without much effort, and instead focused on the benefits to him. "He has no reason to evade Enzo. We've told everyone that your father asked Adrian to take care of you as a favor to me. You'll tell people it was my decision, not yours, to leave and that I thought it was safer for you to be out of town until things calmed down."

I gazed up at the mirror just in time to see her adorable brows wrinkle with confusion.

"Really?"

"Yes."

"Why would you say that?"

I blew out a sigh. "So Adrian doesn't have to die and so you don't look like a whore."

I didn't look at her reaction to my language, but I saw Alessio's eyes widen.

Giada was quiet for a moment. "So, I can just go about my normal life when we get home?"

Alessio snickered.

"Not what I said. The situation in New York is still very volatile. Until I'm sure there aren't any threats against any of us, I want you to stay home as much as possible. When you go out, one of my guys will go with you."

"If you give me my phone, I can call Adrian. I have the number for his burner phone," she said quietly.

I glanced at Alessio, who claimed he'd thoroughly searched her phone for any unfamiliar numbers. He shook his head.

"Tell me the number. I'll call," he said.

"He won't talk to you."

I shrugged, so Alessio handed her phone to her.

"Speaker phone," he said.

She dialed then switched to speaker so we could hear it ring. After two rings, someone answered, but said nothing.

"Adrian?"

"Giada! Are you alright? I didn't want to call your phone in case…"

"I'm fine," she interrupted. "We're almost home, actually. I…I owe you a huge apology, and I…"

"You don't owe me anything," he said.

I rolled my eyes, squeezing my own phone so hard I was surprised it didn't crumble between my fingers. I couldn't hear anything else Adrian said, though, because my wife switched her phone back to private. After a moment, Giada spoke.

"I can't do this now, Adrian. I just have a minute, and I wanted to tell you that you're not in any danger. Luca and my dad are telling everyone that they asked you to take me out of the city to keep me safe. Enzo is trying to track you down to tell you, but I figured you wouldn't take his calls."

She was quiet for a moment, so I assumed he didn't believe her. I wouldn't if I were him.

"Adrian, I really do appreciate everything you did for me," she said.

"Speaker phone!" Alessio snapped, waving his hand behind him as if he were going to snatch the phone right out of Giada's hands.

"You're on speaker with Luca and Alessio," Giada said.

"I'm driving to Chicago," Adrian said. "Going to visit my parents while I'm out here. But Giada tells me you're not planning to kill me when I come home?"

"For now," Alessio agreed. "But you stressed out my buddy, and that pisses me off. And our cover story only works if you don't go into extended hiding. So, get your ass back and tell everyone you were just doing us a favor."

"If I do that, no one gets hurt?"

"Correct."

"Fuck you," Adrian spit.

"Adrian, come on. He's serious!" Giada pleaded.

"Yeah, I know," he replied. "I can't stay away too long anyway. I have a dog, you know."

Alessio turned to me.

"Fine," I said. "Just stay in touch with Angelo or Marco."

The line went dead.

Giada

$\mathcal{W}$e made it home late that night, and I was so exhausted that I went immediately up to bed. Luca said he'd come upstairs later, after he caught up on some work. But when I woke the next morning, Luca was already gone for the day, and there was no sign that he'd ever slept in our bed.

I wasn't alone at any point the next day. Giovanni and Lincoln took turns babysitting me. In the evening, Alessio brought me dinner from the club.

"Where's Luca?" I asked.

"At the club still, working. He missed a few days and has to catch up," he said pointedly.

"How do I know he's not with another woman?" I countered, hating that a small part of me actually wondered if Luca was angry enough to be unfaithful.

"Not everyone forgets their marriage vows the second things get hard," he retorted.

The low blow made me lose my appetite.

Luca didn't join me in bed that night, either, and the next day, Lincoln was babysitting me. While I appreciated that he didn't appear to hate me as much at the moment as Alessio, Thomas, and Giovanni, he followed me around like a shadow.

"I'm not going to run away. You could give me some space," I finally snapped shortly after dinner. Every time I turned around to load a dish into the dishwasher, I smacked into Lincoln.

His eyes widened. "Are you fucking serious? Giada, I thought Luca was going to kill me after you ran away the last time. On my watch! No way that's happening again."

"Are you going to watch me in the shower?" I taunted.

"No, but I'll wait in the bedroom."

I lowered my eyes at his ridiculous response.

"You have a balcony. I'm not taking any chances."

I sighed. "This is ridiculous. I don't want to run away. I want to talk to my husband. In person. But he's avoiding me like the plague."

Lincoln frowned. "He's slept here every night this week."

"No, he hasn't."

"Yes, he has. Maybe he's in the guest room, or shoot, maybe he's shacking up with my cousin, but he's definitely been here every night."

That night, I set my alarm for two a.m., figuring there was no way Luca would stay out later than that. When I woke, I gazed around our bedroom, confirming there was no sign of Luca. It was possible Lincoln was right, though, and Luca was in the guest room. I opened the bedroom door, ready to creep down the hall to look for Luca, but the second I turned the corner, I smacked into a solid form.

I opened my mouth to scream, just as the figure reached around me and switched on a light.

It was Thomas.

"You scared me half to death!" I panted, breathless with terror.

"I heard you walking around in your room and wanted to make sure you weren't trying to leave." His eyes dropped down, then quickly raised back to my face.

I switched off the light, acutely aware that I was wearing nothing but a skimpy camisole and even skimpier shorts.

"Lincoln said Luca has been sleeping in the guest room. I

wanted to go see my husband. Is that allowed? Or am I forbidden from wandering my own house at night and seeing my own husband?"

Thomas frowned. "Don't you think Luca could use the sleep?"

I ignored his implication that I wasn't looking out for Luca's best interests and pushed past him. Thomas didn't try to stop me, so I slowly turned the guest room door knob. I was surprised that it was unlocked, but I tiptoed inside, shutting the door and locking it behind me. Luca was sprawled out on his back. I assumed he was still awake because it didn't look like a comfortable position. He didn't say anything, and now that I was here, I didn't know what I wanted to say, either. So I just crept closer, then sat on the bed. It wasn't until I scooted closer, resting my head on his chest, that I realized he hadn't been awake.

Luca startled the moment I touched him, every muscle in his torso tightening. After a moment, he gradually began to relax.

"I'm sorry," I whispered. "I didn't mean to wake you."

He didn't reply, but his arm stretched across my back, loosely holding me against him. Within a few minutes, I was asleep.

An intrusive thumping invaded my peaceful dream, and I opened my eyes to see Luca slip out of the bed. He whispered something at the door, then pulled on a pair of pants. I waited for him to offer an explanation of where he was going, or at least to brush my hair off my forehead and press his warm lips against my forehead. But, instead, he just turned and frowned.

"Sorry," he mumbled. He shoved his phone into his back pocket and left the room, still shirtless.

I rubbed my eyes and rolled over, determined to fall back asleep. I had no clothes in the guest room anyway, so I'd have to make the shameful trek back to my room in front of everyone wearing my skimpy pjs if I got up now.

I drifted in and out of sleep over the next hour before giving up and deciding to just go back to my own room. Luca had left his t-shirt draped over the armchair in the corner of the room, so

I held that over my chest and peered out the door. I no longer heard voices in the hall, but I knew I wasn't home alone. If I was lucky, I was alone with Luca. We desperately needed to talk. We'd been back for two days, and he'd barely glanced in my direction, let alone spoken to me.

I rounded the corner to the kitchen, my heart skipping when I saw a man's tanned forearm on top of a stack of papers on the table. With my next step, though, the rest of his body came into sight and I pouted. It was Thomas.

He swiveled to face me, his expression neutral, then he turned back to his papers.

I sighed. "Will he be gone all day again?"

"Probably." His voice sounded off, but I wasn't sure if he felt sorry for me or if he, too, hated me for what I'd done. Probably the latter. Or maybe he was just tired from me waking him twice.

"I'm sorry I woke you last night. I didn't realize…"

"It's fine," he cut in.

I waited another minute, then continued to my bedroom. I brushed my teeth and changed into compression leggings and a tank top, then tied my hair loosely behind my head. I returned to the kitchen for coffee, then went directly into the gym. No part of me felt like exercising, but after a half hour on the bike and a quick pilates routine, I was calmer. I walked back through the kitchen to refill both my coffee and my water bottle.

Thomas hadn't moved from the table, nor did he acknowledge me when I walked past him again. I was about to return to my room for a shower when I realized I had no further ideas for how to spend my day.

"Would you be able to drive me by my office later?" I asked, feeling more like a child than a grown woman in my own home.

"Luca wants you to stay home."

"I need to pick up some things. It won't take long."

Thomas gazed up. "Giovanni is coming in about an hour. He

can swing by on his way and pick up whatever you need." His expression told me he was intentionally calling my bluff.

"Nevermind. I'm going to call Luca and then take a shower."

"He's really busy today, Giada. The fewer distractions, the better. If you need something…"

"I don't," I snapped. "I'll just talk with him when he gets home." I stomped off to my shower, knowing that I wouldn't actually get to talk to Luca anytime soon.

CHAPTER 16

Adrian

My parents appreciated the surprise visit. I told them I'd needed to be in Missouri for work, which didn't feel nearly as dishonest as telling my father—also a lawyer—that the "work" was depositions, the only task I could think of that might require me to travel. That still didn't explain why I drove, versus flying, but they were just glad to see me.

Being at home felt safe, almost like I was in a time warp. As long as I remained under the cozy roof of my parents' 1960s bungalow, I didn't have to think about Giada, organized crime, or facing the wrath of Luca.

I couldn't avoid reality forever, though. I called Father Ryan on my second-to-last day in Chicago. He said that Giada had already checked on him and that he was fine and didn't anticipate any problems. He also said Luca and Alessio had called him earlier. I actually believed the priest when he said he wasn't worried about retaliation from either crime family. Maybe if I were godlier, I could enjoy that same level of confidence.

I spoke with Enzo as well, and he, too, assured me that no one was waiting to kill me. He, of all people, best understood my reasons for going the extra mile to protect Giada, but he was also annoyed that I hadn't reached out to him to do it.

The drive home from Chicago was long and boring without a passenger to distract me, and there was nothing to keep me from focusing squarely on my problems. If I'd had my usual phone, I would've passed the time calling old friends, but as it was, I could only contact people whose numbers I'd memorized.

I checked in on Annie, who was still firmly in the throes of morning sickness. She hadn't told our parents about the pregnancy yet—or Matteo—but she did seem firmly decided to go through with the pregnancy at least.

My last call of the trip was to Angelo, but he insisted I meet with him in person as soon as I made it back to town. I told him I wasn't due to arrive till after nine p.m., and he assured me that he was a night owl. Instantly, my heart began to race.

I wiped my palms on my jeans and reminded myself that I knew this was coming. I hadn't actually thought I could waltz back into town and never mention what I'd done, but I'd anticipated Luca, and not Angelo, being the bigger threat. I tried to think of anything I could say now, while safely ensconced in my car just outside of Allentown, Pennsylvania, that would help my case.

I went for the only path I could think of—my sister.

"Hey, uh, Matteo is still in Italy, right?"

"Yep." Angelo sounded almost bored.

"Do you know when he returns?"

"Next week."

"Huh," I said, having heard two weeks from my sister. "Okay, Annie was asking for some reason." I paused again. "Have you told him about what happened, I mean with Giada?"

There was a moment of silence and then a slow chuckle from Angelo. "I already know our siblings are fucking, if that's what you're hinting at," he said.

"He told you?"

"No. But my job and my ability to stay alive depend on me knowing everything about everyone involved in my life."

"Right. Okay, I'll see you in a few hours," I said, cringing as I hung up.

By the time I reached Angelo's house, my skin was ice cold from the air conditioning I'd blasted during the drive to try to offset my stress sweating. I popped three ibuprofen tablets in my mouth, as if that would temper the pain from a bunch of thugs breaking my knee caps or whatever their preferred punishment was these days, and I chugged a bottle of water to soothe my parched throat.

I rang the doorbell, surprised he hadn't sent Eddie or one of his other cronies out to drag me from my car. A moment later, Angelo answered the door. The first thing I noticed was his lack of shoes. Instantly, relief began to flood my veins. Surely the man would've worn more than a thin pair of argyle socks if he were about to torture me, right?

"Beer?" he offered, stifling a yawn.

"Yes!" If I could get completely drunk, that would absolutely make this easier. I should've thought of that in advance.

Angelo retrieved two beers from his fridge, then motioned for me to follow him to the living room. I peered around the house, surprised by the homey feel.

"Your place is nice," I said, omitting that it was nothing like I'd expect from him.

"Thanks. Giada decorated it."

"Ahh." That explained it.

Angelo popped the tops off of both beers and handed me one. He sat in an armchair, so I dropped onto the end of the sofa adjacent to it.

"You should've called Lorenzo," he said, skipping to the point.

"Yeah. He said the same thing. Honestly, I wish I had. I didn't mean to get mixed up in all of this, but the priest called me, and I was worried Giada was going to try to drive herself across the country."

"It was nice of you to help her," Angelo said, downing a swig of his drink before continuing. "Nice, but stupid. And reckless. And so disrespectful."

My abs tightened.

"Tell me honestly. Did even a little part of you enjoy knowing how this would make Luca feel? Or how it would make him look? Having his wife run off with her ex?"

I blew out a sigh, then focused on my beer while I gathered my thoughts. "To be honest, not at first. I just looked at the situation and thought helping Giada was the right thing to do. But later, while we were on the road, and I had time to think about it, yeah. I mean, I'd have to be an idiot to not realize the optics weren't great for him."

Angelo stared blankly at me, his unreadable expression pressing me to keep talking.

"Nothing happened with me and Giada," I added, cringing at the realization that I was talking about sex—or lack thereof—with his sister. "It's not like that with us now. Neither of us have any romantic interest in the other."

Angelo sighed and leaned forward to set his bottle on the coffee table. "Here's the thing, Adrian. You might find our rules antiquated or anti-feminist or whatnot, but you don't come between a man and his wife. That's a pretty basic rule in our culture. Especially when that man is a boss."

Angelo motioned for me to wait while he reached into his pocket. My heart fluttered as I noticed the gun at his hip, but his hand moved past that, sliding his phone out of his pocket. Angelo checked a text, then he placed his phone on the table next to his beer before continuing his thought. "The fact that Giada is, or was, a Conti does complicate things, because yeah, even though she's now a Marino, we're not going to let them mistreat one of our women. But that point doesn't really help you any for two reasons. One, you are not a Conti, and two, Giada was not in any danger."

Angelo checked his phone again, then gazed up at me. "I don't particularly like Luca, but I don't believe for one minute that he would hurt Giada. Honestly, I don't even think he'd cheat on her."

Angelo said this as if it were a shortcoming on Luca's part.

"Giada was scared. She wanted to get away. That was all," I said.

Angelo shrugged. "Right, but she didn't need to be scared. I understand she saw some things, but she's the boss's wife. None of Luca's men will ever touch her. And if you'd called Lorenzo, or me, or my father, we could have told you that. I expect Giada to rush into shit and make dumb, impulsive decisions, but honestly I expect more from you. You're a lawyer. You should use better judgment, think things through, you know?"

I nodded. Angelo wasn't wrong, but even if he had been, I wasn't about to tell him that.

"I can't change the fact that you made a shitty decision and stepped in where it wasn't your place and wasn't actually needed. If Luca wants to punish you for that, there's nothing I can do to stop him."

I opened my mouth to protest, but he continued.

"What I can do is offer you some protection for the future."

I raised my bottle to my lips, trying to decipher what he was saying.

"The difference between you and Enzo isn't just that you're a moron who got involved where you shouldn't have. Lorenzo is a Conti. So when he fucks up, we have his back."

Angelo crossed his arms as if he'd thoroughly explained everything. I supposed now was my time to ask questions.

"So, you're saying that because Enzo is…an official part of the family, Luca can't hurt him?"

"No. I'm saying he would've had a reason to step in and

protect Giada as a Conti, and that Luca would think twice before dishing out a punishment to a Conti."

"Okay, I guess that makes sense," I said. "But what does that have to do with me?"

Angelo chuckled. "And here I thought you were smart."

I ignored the insult, having felt far from intelligent as of late anyway.

"I'm offering to change that for you. I've always liked you, and you've proven yourself to be valuable and loyal to our family. I don't want to see you get killed."

"You think Luca's going to kill me?"

He shrugged again. "No. Giada would never stand for that. Plus, they've already spun their story to make it seem like you were doing them a favor. If they kill you now, it casts doubt on their version of events. I think you've essentially gotten away scot-free. This time."

I liked the sound of that, but still didn't understand what Angelo wanted. "So what exactly are you offering me?"

"You really don't think there will be a next time that you fuck up, Patras? And even if you don't, it seems like you could use a little more protection. Weren't you just in the hospital after getting jumped?"

"Not because of anything I did. You said that was probably something to do with your business."

"Oh, it was," he agreed. "But there's a dozen different guys that carry important papers around for the Conti's. There's a reason they went after you and not a made man. They figured you were more expendable to us. Which, at the moment, you are. And that means we're less likely to retaliate."

I set my beer on the table, trying to gather my thoughts. All of this was so far from the conversation I expected to have with Angelo that I was struggling to keep up. "I'm sorry, but I haven't slept much over the last week, and I'm not sure I understand. You're saying you'd offer me protection if I...joined the family?"

He nodded.

"Like, officially, joined…"

Angelo squeezed his eyes shut, quickly losing patience for my denseness. "You would be a Conti in every way but your legal name."

My heart thudded. "I…don't know what to say," I stammered after a painfully long silence.

"You can think about it. Obviously, you shouldn't tell anyone, and I wouldn't take too long to decide if I were you. This club is invitation only, and I can rescind the offer at any time."

"Yeah, understood." I scratched my head, trying to think of the ramifications of the decision. "I don't suppose there are any official club rules I could review, are there?"

Angelo flashed the Cheshire cat grin that used to terrify me. "No handbook for this club, I'm afraid. You could probably figure the big ones out, though. Obviously, you'd be pledging loyalty to me, my father, and everyone else who outranks you."

"Which is everyone," I guessed.

"Not exactly, but you're not privy to names and positions unless you're one of us."

I thought about my life, what I stood to gain or lose by officially aligning myself with the Contis. And then I thought of my sister. "So, if I say yes, does your protection extend to my family? You know my sister and your brother are involved, so…"

"Your sister is safe as long as she's with Matteo, anyway."

"And if they break up?"

Angelo shrugged. "Matteo's not going to kill your sister if she dumps him."

I phrased my question carefully, not wanting to reveal anything Angelo did not already know. I couldn't ask what the consequences would be if she birthed a Conti baby and never told them, so I tried to think of the next closest offense she could commit. "What if she cheats on him? Or steals his money?"

Angelo nearly spit out the sip of beer he'd just taken. "Are we talking about the same Annie? Because the one I've met doesn't seem the type to do any of that." He sighed. "I don't think Matteo or anyone else would do anything to your sister no matter how this fling ends. But if you're asking in general, then yeah, we protect our own. If you're a Conti, we take care of your biological family. If you ever find a woman dumb enough to marry you, we take care of her, too. As long as you play by the rules, you're set for life."

I inhaled slowly, then exhaled. "Okay."

"You're in?"

"No! I mean, maybe. I...I need time to think about it."

Angelo rose to his feet and stretched. "Don't take too long."

He walked me to the door. I shuffled to my car, started the engine, and somehow managed to pull around the block before I hyperventilated.

Luca

I stepped out of my papà's office and rubbed my neck. I'd been working there all day every day the past week, going home only to sleep, and still, the place felt just as cold as it had when my papà was alive.

I'd made contact with all the captains currently in the states, and we were going to meet later that night. I'd also checked in with guys from a few of the other heavy hitters in town just to see where the other families stood. For the most part, Alessio, Thomas, Giovanni, and Roberto were handling all of that, but it was still time-consuming and stressful, trying to piece together everything everyone said in an attempt to draw out what they really meant or intended.

Tomasso and two of my papà's other top guys had traveled to Italy with my mother, so I didn't have their support in person. I liked to think I could trust every one of my men in my home country, but I wasn't that naïve, and I didn't know them well enough to ensure their compliance. I needed to get overseas soon, but I wasn't sure how or when. Abandoning my post on the eastern seaboard a moment too soon could negate all our efforts over the past decade. But delaying too long before checking in on Sicily could prove fatal as well. I felt like I was fighting a war on two fronts, but I wasn't even sure who the enemy was.

Alessio sauntered through the room and dropped a paper-wrapped sandwich on the marble in front of me. "Eat," he commanded. He filled a glass of water and slid it across the counter to me as well before sitting beside me and unwrapping his own deli sandwich.

"You okay?" he asked.

I shook my head. I didn't know much, but I did know that.

My response didn't appear to surprise him. He bit into his sandwich and chewed casually.

"You'll feel better after tonight," he finally declared, pausing to down half his soda. "They all like you. Most of them more than your papà."

"And the others?"

Alessio shrugged. "The ones who liked him the most respect his plan. He chose you, so they'll follow you. You've done every-thing right so far."

"I left town for three days," I reminded him, even though he'd accompanied me on that rescue mission.

"So? That didn't affect anyone. It's fine."

"What about the other families?"

"What about them? We've got two continents of support. No one can orchestrate that attack. You already know Gambino likes you, so the other bosses will too. And besides, anyone would have to be a fool to go after you here. If they mess with you, they'd get the wrath of the Contis too."

The mere sound of the name made my blood pressure tic

upwards. I set down my half-eaten sandwich and grimaced. I already had heartburn.

"I'm not so sure about them," I said.

Alessio cocked his head to the side and frowned, almost as if he was disappointed in me. "You're being paranoid. Marco loves you like a son. More than either of his sons."

I shook my head. "That's how Marco operates. He doesn't threaten people to make them do what he wants. He befriends them, he makes them think it's their idea to do his bidding."

"So?"

"So what if he's not just a nice guy, trying to fill my papà's shoes right now? What if he actually cares more about his own family's success than mine?"

"Well of course he does, but it's not an either-or situation. We're partners, remember? His success is our success, and vice versa."

Alessio was right, but that didn't comfort me. There was still a possibility that Marco was simply buttering me up, tempting me to drop my defenses, all so he could take over the Marino family's U.S. operations. And even if he wasn't, there was a good chance that some of my papà's biggest supporters within the family would experience that same worry. They didn't share my connection to the Conti family and might not want to rely on an outside family as much as I would.

And then there was the other factor, weighing heavily on my mind even though I knew it shouldn't. Things between Giada and me had been strained since her little escapade. I got the impression she wanted everything to just go back to normal, but I wasn't there yet. I'd learned the very important lesson that my wife only stood by my side when I did what she wanted. I didn't feel that unconventional love she'd always promised, and yet I still couldn't bring myself to care any less about her. Giada remained my first thought every morning and my last thought at night, whether or not she loved me back.

"Giada's fine," Alessio said, reading my mind. "Giovanni just left to relieve Thomas. He said she worked out or something, and now she's just lounging around the house."

"She's not trying to leave?"

"Thomas said she asked about going to work, but that's all."

I forced another bite of sandwich into my mouth, even though I wasn't hungry.

"She asked about you. Thomas said she wanted to call you." He paused as though uncertain whether he should continue. "She sent me a text. She thinks you're ignoring her because you're mad."

"How did you respond?"

"I said you're busy." He held out his phone to show me, as if I wouldn't believe him.

I nodded, pleased with that response.

"But…like how long are you going to keep ignoring her, though? I mean, it's Giada. You can't stay mad forever. She seems sorry, and…"

My fist hit the counter so hard that the water sloshed out of my glass. "She ran off with Adrian. Adrian! It's been years since they were together. How long will I have to compete with him?"

"You don't. You're not. You won, Luca. Remember? You married her." Alessio paused and chuckled. "Twice. And the last I checked, she doesn't believe in divorce. So, she is yours until one of you kills the other."

"Not funny," I replied through clenched teeth.

He shrugged. "Do you really think she was unfaithful?"

I considered that, then answered honestly. It had crossed my mind, like a thousand times an hour, but I truly believed her when she told me nothing had happened, that it wasn't like that between them. "No. Maybe if we hadn't come when we had, but…"

"No harm, no foul then. So what's the problem?"

"Every time I do something she doesn't agree with, she runs

back to him, just to remind me that I'll never be that kind of man."

"Luca, she freaked out. She panicked. She didn't grow up in this shit the same way you did. It wasn't even a conscious choice. It's that reflex, you know? You stayed to fight, she chose the flight. It didn't mean anything."

"Anyone else but Adrian and I'd believe you. But it wasn't."

Alessio sighed, wadding up his sandwich wrapper and tossing it into the trash. He missed, ricocheting the garbage off the counter instead. He stood and disposed of it properly before rejoining me at the island. "If you want him gone, just say the word, and I'll do it. We could do, uh, car accident. Or slip and fall. I don't know. Carbon monoxide poisoning? Anyway, she'll never know it wasn't an accident."

I rubbed my aching head, pushing my fingers into the tender flesh along my temples. "No. I want to win fair and square. I want to get fifty years down the road and see the look on his face when he realizes she's still mine and that he'll never have her."

Alessio quirked an eyebrow. "Then I suggest you stop thinking about her and try to focus on the meeting tonight so you don't get killed in the next fifty hours."

"Not helpful," I replied through gritted teeth.

CHAPTER 17

Giada

I had managed to distract myself with work when a knock on the door interrupted me. I glanced at my watch, listened for the deep male voices speaking Italian in hushed tones, then refocused on the laptop screen. It was just the shift change of my babysitter. I didn't even look up when I heard footsteps approaching until Giovanni called my name.

Too lazy to stand and open the door, I just answered. "Yes?"

The door swung open an inch, then further once he concluded I was decent. "You have company. Luca has a meeting tonight, so he thought you could go eat at your house."

"This is my house," I said, keeping my voice clipped until he cringed.

"Your childhood home."

I had so many questions, but before I could ask anything, Lorenzo poked his head around the door behind Giovanni. His soft brown eyes and comforting smile were exactly what I needed to see.

"Princess!" he said, grinning widely. He held his arms out as I dove into them, hugging him until Giovanni cleared his throat.

Enzo stiffened and pulled back.

"I need to leave in twenty minutes to meet Luca, so can you be gone by then?" Giovanni asked. He directed his question to Enzo, but both of them turned to me. I glanced down at my outfit. I wore leggings and a long t-shirt, which was fine for a dinner with my family, but there was no way I was going to sit through a dinner full of people who hated me. I wasn't about to tell Giovanni that I planned to trick Enzo into taking me out alone, though.

"I just want to change tops. Maybe fix my hair. Give me ten minutes," I said.

"It'll be at least fifteen," Enzo said to Giovanni.

I rolled my eyes and shooed them both out of the room. I changed into a fitted cami, then tugged the scrunchie out of my hair and finger combed it before adding a dab of oil for shine. I touched up my makeup, reapplied deodorant, then paused in front of my jewelry armoire. I loved accessories, but they always made me think of Luca. He was the only man I'd ever been with who consistently noticed and appreciated my jewelry. If I were going out to dinner with Luca, I would choose my jewelry, eagerly anticipating his comments about the pieces I chose. Sometimes, we'd swap memories of previous times I'd worn the same accessories.

Tonight, though, it didn't matter. Enzo wouldn't notice anything I wore, and most likely, I wouldn't even see my husband.

"Giada? You ready?"

I frowned at the door, then slipped into ballet flats and opened the door. Then I froze. "You'll bring me home tonight, right? I don't have any of my stuff I'd need to stay out overnight."

Enzo nodded and led me to the door.

I wanted to ask Giovanni if my husband would even be

coming home that night, but I didn't. It's not like anything I said would matter.

Enzo walked alarmingly close to me as we sped to his car. He unlocked it and opened my door for me, then let himself in. I regretted not having dawdled so I could've appreciated the fresh air more.

"So how have you been?" I asked as he started the engine.

He gazed at me, then laughed. "Fine, but I feel like I should be asking you that question."

I blew out a sigh. "Well, let's see. That twelve-second walk was my first breath of fresh air since I returned home. I spend all day with my husband's friends, who hate me, or my husband's family, who hate me. My husband also hates me, and—"

"Luca could never," he interrupted.

"He hasn't spoken more than two words at a time to me since we got back. He won't even sleep in our room."

"Well, can you blame him?"

I flung my hands up. "Really, Enzo? Jesus. I knew my dad would be pissed at me, but I expected a little more from you."

"You skipped town with your ex-boyfriend. How did you think we'd all react?"

I turned to the window. Suddenly, I had no appetite. As eager as I'd been to leave my house a few minutes before, now I was done. "Just take me back home. I'm not hungry anyway."

"I can't do that. Luca isn't home, and he doesn't want you to be alone until everything's calmed down."

"I won't be alone. I'm never alone. He'll have Thomas come over or Roberto or someone."

"There's no one available tonight, Giada. They're all at a meeting. That's why they asked me to take you for the night."

"Well, I'm not going home. You could take me out to eat or we could just drive around, but I'm not setting foot into that house so even more people can glare at me and tell me what a fuck up I am."

"You're not a fuck up. It's more like the opposite. You're just too sweet and innocent. You make people want to help you, and then they get in trouble." Enzo paused. "Do you have any idea how it felt when Angelo told me to go after Adrian?"

"Nobody ever told you to hurt him. You were just supposed to find him and bring him home."

"Yeah, that was the plan. But at any moment, my orders could've changed. God, I like Adrian. I think he's a good guy. If I had to hurt him just because he ran off with you…" he shook his head. "You know, he was the one who found me after I got hurt over what happened between the two of us in the car that night."

Blood rushed to my cheeks and elsewhere as I vividly recalled the lengthy makeout session with Enzo that fateful night years ago. I had been the instigator of the makeout session, but Enzo was the one who got his ass kicked when Luca found out.

"I didn't make you do anything," I reminded him.

"I'm not saying you did. I was older, it was on me to put a stop to things."

"You did." Enzo had stopped things just before any clothes came off. In retrospect, I was so grateful that he had, as I couldn't imagine our friendship now if we'd seen each other naked.

"I should've done it earlier." He frowned and paused while starting to merge onto the highway. "My point is, you make men do things they shouldn't. None of us can think straight when you bat those long eyelashes and say please. But you're not twenty-two anymore, and you're not oblivious about the kind of world you live in. And you're married. To a boss. So, you need to grow up and stop asking people to do things that'll get them killed."

I couldn't remember Enzo ever being so harsh with me. Honestly, it was worse than the lecture from Alessio because I'd known Alessio was on Luca's side, but Enzo was supposed to be my friend.

I regretted applying mascara, as my tears were now likely smearing the black ink all over my cheeks.

Enzo swore under his breath. "Giada, I'm sorry. Don't cry."

"Don't cry? You're the only person I've seen in weeks who I thought might actually be nice to me, and now you just finished explaining how I'm a terrible person. God, you would've all been so much better off if I'd just stayed away!"

"Giada Francesca, don't ever say that!" His tone was harsh, and I'd never heard him use my middle name before. "Everyone was miserable without you. We were all worried and stressed. And you're not a terrible person. You're one of the best people I know. That's why everyone wants to please you."

I dabbed my finger under my eyes, but kept my face towards the window, not wanting him to see me cry. He let me enjoy the silence for less than a minute before pushing more.

"Why didn't you ask me, Giada? Why Adrian?"

"You would've said no."

"I wouldn't have snuck off without telling anyone, but I would've helped you. I will always help you, Giada. You know that, right?"

On some level, I did know that, but I was equally aware I couldn't ask him. He'd just finished telling me not to ask people for things.

"I remember what happened after our kiss. I didn't want to get you in trouble with Luca again, but I also didn't want to get you in trouble with my dad. You work for him. Adrian doesn't."

The mixture of emotions crossing Enzo's face was as clear as day.

I shook my head. "No. He doesn't work for my dad. He would've told me," I said. We'd spend countless hours together on our escape mission, so surely he could've mentioned that he joined the mafia."

"Giada, it's not my place to tell you anything, but…"

I shook my head. "No, Luca said he's just been doing odd jobs for my brother on occasion."

Enzo nodded.

"What, so you're saying my dad just forced him into…a life of crime?"

"Your dad didn't do anything. Adrian came to him ages ago. He asked. He hadn't finished the process, maybe he never would've, but…"

"But what?" Enzo's vagueness was infuriating.

"But he might not have a choice now. I don't know, but I could see that being the only way he could regain Angelo's trust."

"He doesn't need Angelo's trust."

"Giada, he might. Luca made it clear that no one is to hurt Adrian, but your brother doesn't answer to him. None of us do. And the fact remains that he broke some pretty serious rules when he didn't tell Angelo or your dad where he was going."

I bit my lip and tried to picture myself in a fantasy world, far away from this reality where I ruined everyone else's lives.

Adrian

I'd done my best to return to my normal life after my discussion with Angelo. I wasn't ignoring his offer, but I told myself I'd let it simmer for at least a week. Then I'd decide. I couldn't think clearly enough to make a life-altering choice when I was still reeling from the attack, my sister's secret baby news, and the shit with Giada.

In the meantime, I focused on normalcy and routine. I woke up and hit the gym. Then, I drove to work in the office, like a normal person. I walked the dog when I got home, then spent the evenings with friends or my sister or just hanging out with Scruffy and getting shit done around my condo. I liked my routine. It felt safe. I tried to imagine whether my routine would stay the same if I aligned myself with Angelo.

The more I thought about it, the more my blood pressure skyrocketed. And the more I pushed myself at the gym to offset the stress. And that, in turn, meant I was often running late by the time I left.

I jogged down the steps exiting the gym and rounded the corner, turning my gaze to my phone. After confirming the rain would hold off long enough for me to walk home, I shoved the phone into the side pocket of my gym bag. Right as I looked up, something slammed me against the brick wall behind me.

The impact jarred me, but even before opening my eyes, I was sure it was Alessio. I'd been waiting for this. His arm pressed across my jugular, so I couldn't tell if he had a weapon. I knew it was futile to resist, though. Best-case scenario, I'd fight him and win, only to die the next day. No, better to let him take me down now and hope his intention wasn't to kill me.

I leveled my eyes to his, trying to look braver than I felt.

"I thought you were heading to Italy for a funeral," I said.

"That's next week."

My eyes darted to the end of the alley. Maybe someone would walk by. Alessio didn't seem to care if anyone saw, though.

"Well? Get on with it," I said, leaning forward just until I felt cold metal against my throat.

He scowled. "Get on with what?"

"I assume you're here to kick my ass. Maybe break my knee caps? What's the current punishment for being a nice guy these days?"

"A nice guy? You think you're the hero in this scenario?"

I forced a laugh. "Well, I'm not a cop killer, and I'm not the hitman holding a switchblade to someone's neck in an alley, so I reckon I am."

Alessio pushed off of me, taking my bag with him. "Jesus Christ. Does Giada only go for narcissists?"

I was too busy focusing on my freedom to unpack all the shit in that statement. I rubbed my throat, afraid to take my eyes off of Alessio long enough to decide which direction was the best option for running.

"I'm not here to hurt you. I just want to talk," he said, taking another step backwards.

"Yeah, clearly."

He flipped the knife shut and slipped it into his belt loop, right next to a sleek metal handgun.

I crossed my arms in front of my chest. "If you want to talk, talk."

"Why'd you do it?"

"Because she needed my help."

"He'll never hurt her," Alessio replied.

I rolled my eyes. "Not in the physical sense, maybe, but he hurts her all the time. He admitted it, too. He said he'd never stop hurting her until he was dead. He asked her to kill him. Did you miss that part?"

Alessio flinched in a way that made me wonder if he really didn't know everything that had gone down in the motel. "He was hurt. Could you just step off your high horse for a minute and think about this from his perspective? He just lost his father, and then his wife took off with her ex-boyfriend. Without Giada, Luca has nothing to live for."

"That's no reason for *her* to suffer."

"How did you see this playing out, Adrian? Did you honestly think he wouldn't find her?"

I shrugged. "I figured he was busy with the funeral and taking over the family business. And once all that calmed down, I'd hoped he'd step back and realize she's better off without him."

"He can't live without her."

"Oh, please. I've seen him around women. He could find someone new by next week if he wanted."

Alessio shook his head. "You don't know him like I do. And

you didn't see the two of them together back in high school. They're like…magnets or something. They will always come back to each other."

I raised my hands. "Well, I guess everyone got their happy ending then. The lovebirds are back together, and now they can lead their evil empire as a team."

"You didn't answer the question. How did you see this working out? If Luca had given up looking, what would you have done then? Were you and Giada just going to settle down in some podunk town and start a new life together?"

"Maybe. I don't know."

Alessio dropped his gaze to his feet for a moment, looking less friendly by the time his eyes returned to mine. "I'm going to need you to be honest with me Adrian. If you're going to play games, I can't guarantee I'll play nice."

"I'm not playing with you. I don't know what you want me to say. I was happy before…everything. My life wasn't perfect, but I had no major complaints. So it's not like I was sitting around dreaming of running away with Giada. But she's a good person. And for all the times she's hurt me or screwed me over, I can't just write her off. So when she came to me, terrified, yeah, I saw a different option for her. Maybe for both of us. I had a chance to get her away from all this mafia shit for good, to just start over with a clean slate, so I took it."

"In this clean slate alternate reality of yours, were you and Giada together?"

I knew what he was asking, and I similarly knew the risks of answering honestly.

"I'm well aware of her stance on divorce, so…"

Alessio rolled his eyes. "If Giada had been willing to pursue something romantic with you, would you have agreed?"

In a heartbeat. Because I had zero sense of self-reservation, zero dignity, and zero capacity to remember the past. But I also meant what I told her, that I'd moved on and wasn't sitting around pining for her. "I don't know. Maybe?"

"Did she try anything with you?"

"No."

"She didn't try to kiss you?"

"No. Not since that time she had amnesia."

"Anything else?" His calm tone was unnerving.

"Like what?"

"Did you touch her?"

"Yes, of course. We were together for three days. But I never touched her in a way that I wouldn't touch my sister."

Alessio glared at me for a moment longer before changing subjects. "Have you talked to Melissa since you returned?"

"We aren't exactly friends anymore, but I checked on her at work one day to make sure you hadn't hurt her and she seemed fine."

"No one will hurt her. Luca wouldn't allow it."

"What a saint," I mused.

Alessio mimicked my posture, crossing his own arms, and neither of us spoke for a minute.

"Want some friendly advice?" he asked.

"Absolutely." I couldn't wait to hear what jerky thing Alessio had to say.

"Get your girl back. Then marry her, fast. No one is going to trust you until you're off the market."

I chortled. Like I hadn't tried to get her back. "Gee thanks. It hadn't occurred to me to try to piece my life back together." I shook my head. "Not everyone is so quick to forgive their partner as Luca."

Alessio's gaze narrowed. "Luca hasn't forgiven anything. He's got bigger priorities than marriage counseling at the moment."

"I saw a picture of them. At the church. They seemed fine."

"In public, sure. But they're not sleeping in the same room, and Luca won't talk to her."

That surprised me, given Luca's emotional plea back in Missouri. "Why would you tell me that?"

He shrugged. "So you'd know you have a choice. Giada or Melissa."

Alessio swiveled on his heel and walked off, leaving me alone in the alley with my gym bag a few feet away.

I shook my head, not liking either of those options. If I wanted a happy life, I needed option C—myself. I didn't particularly want to live the rest of my life celibate, but I sure as shit wasn't going to get involved with either of my ex-girlfriends again, either.

Giada

At the sound of the doorbell, I shut my laptop. Since I'd been under lock and key, no one bothered ringing the bell. When my new babysitter arrived, they simply let themselves in and traded shifts with the last.

I poked my head out of the room right as I heard Giovanni's voice.

"She's napping now, but I'll tell her you stopped by," he said.

As soon as I caught a glimpse of platinum blonde hair, I perked up. "Cami? Hey!" I scurried to the door, practically knocking Giovanni out of the way. "I couldn't fall asleep," I said, turning to glare at Giovanni so Cami couldn't see.

"Giada, since we're traveling soon, I think…" he began.

I reached past him and grabbed Cami's hand, dragging her into the house.

She held a large tote in one hand, which she offered to me. "I went in on some flowers with the rest of the office, but that seems lame and I've always been told you should bring food to someone when they're dealing with a death in the family."

"Thank you," I said. "Can you stay for a few minutes? Catch up?"

Cami nodded. "Absolutely."

"Giada, can I have a word in the kitchen?" Giovanni interrupted.

"Yep," I answered him before turning back to my friend. "Come on in here, and make yourself comfortable. I'll get us some drinks."

I led her into the great room then followed Giovanni into the kitchen.

"If you want Luca to forgive you, this isn't the way," he whispered.

"I've been playing by his rules all week, and he still hates me, so not sure I have anything to lose," I said, grabbing two lemon-flavored mineral waters and storming out of the room.

I plopped down in the armchair closest to Cami. "So how is everything at the office? I feel like I've been gone for ages."

"Um, you have! It's going fine, though. We all miss you, but we understand..." her voice drifted off at the end of the sentence. "I mean, are you okay though? I was just worried is all. I hadn't realized you and your father-in-law were so close..."

"We weren't," I said. "But Luca's an only child, and his mom has taken this really hard, so I'm just trying to be there for both of them. Luca's also trying to handle everything with his father's estate and take over the family business, and it's just been really chaotic. I'll come back to work as soon as I can."

"Oh yeah, that absolutely makes sense," she agreed. She still looked uneasy though. "Was that, umm one of your brothers?"

"No, it's Luca's," I said. "I mean, not his brother, obviously. His, like, I don't know. They're cousins or something. He's staying with us for a few days."

"Oh. Is Luca home?"

"No. He's been spending a lot of time at his parents' house."

We made small talk for a few minutes while sipping our

drinks, but then it became increasingly clear Cami was still uncomfortable about something.

"Your house is beautiful, by the way. You've added a lot of touches since the open house."

"Thank you. It's…a work in progress, but I'm definitely taking pride in all the decor."

"Obviously," she agreed with a smile. "Can I get a tour? I'd love to see what other changes you made since I last saw the house."

I hesitated, instantly picturing Luca's stuff all over the guest room. Except, she'd probably just assume those clothes belonged to Giovanni. "Sure. It's messier than usual, but…" I motioned for her to follow me. I started in the front of the house, sped past the kitchen where Giovanni was clearly straining to eavesdrop, then finished up in the back rooms.

When we were in the primary bathroom, in the furthest corner of the house from Giovanni, Cami shut the door and turned to me.

"Are you sure you're okay Giada? Something just rubbed me the wrong way about all the time you took off, and…"

I squeezed her hand and offered her my most reassuring smile. "I'm fine. I swear. It hasn't been an easy few weeks, but it's getting there. We're heading to Sicily for a memorial there soon, and then when we return, things should start going back to normal. I mean, maybe not the old normal, on account of Luca taking over the family business, but—"

"Giada, I read that your father-in-law was murdered," Cami interrupted, her voice quiet.

My jaw dropped. I supposed part of me had realized that was public knowledge, but I hadn't really expected people to know. Was I the only person who didn't read the newspaper every day?

"The papers called it a mob hit, actually."

My legs gave out, and I dropped to the bed. "Seriously?"

Cami sat beside me. "You didn't know?"

"What papers?" I asked in lieu of answering her question.

"All of them. Everything said that Salvatore Marino was the head of some big crime family, and that he was killed in some mob war."

"A mob war?" I repeated. "Jesus."

"I'm worried about you. You could come stay with me, or I'm sure you must have some information that the cops could use if you went to them. They could keep you safe."

"I am safe," I said, shaking my head. "Wow. Mafia, huh?"

Cami nodded.

"No wonder Luca is so stressed. I bet he read some of that garbage," I said, rising back to my feet and turning to the windows to collect my composure. "I didn't know every detail of my father-in-law's life, but I definitely would have known if he was a mob boss. He owned a shipping company, and that's what Luca is taking over. They do a lot of exports between here and Italy, and Salvatore worked a lot with my father, since he owns some docks. That's actually how Luca and I met. We've known each other almost our whole lives."

"Oh wow. I didn't realize that."

"Yeah. So really, I would know." I nodded my head to convey the seriousness. "Sal wasn't always a nice guy, and he had some enemies. And he ran some clubs, so things got hairy sometimes. But there's no mob war."

"Why would they say that if it isn't true?"

"I don't know, to sell papers? It seems like anytime an Italian man dies in a suspicious way, the press calls it a mafia thing. When I was a kid, my grandpa died in a mugging and the papers said that was a mob hit. It's just another form of racism."

Cami wrinkled her nose. She was about to say something else when Giovanni barged in.

He held up one of the peanut butter cookies Cami had brought. "Is it okay if I eat this? I'm starving."

I bit back a laugh. Giovanni detested peanut butter, so he must have really been desperate to continue eavesdropping.

"Go for it," I told him. "Maybe we should get some snacks too," I said, leading Cami back to the kitchen.

She stayed for another hour and a half, plenty of time for us to gossip and do our nails, then left right before Thomas arrived.

Luca

I glanced at my phone, then sighed. Even when we didn't let Giada leave the house, she still managed to make my life crazy.

Alessio knocked on the door, then frowned upon seeing my expression. "What happened?"

"Nothing." I shook my head. "Giovanni just wanted me to know that Giada's coworker came over and is trying to convince her my papà's death was a mob hit."

"Did he say how Giada responded?"

"She denied it, then he interrupted. And apparently, they made him eat peanut butter or something, so now I owe him big time."

Alessio snorted. "Well, I talked with Adrian."

I dropped my pen and scowled. "Why? I told you to leave it."

"I don't think you need to worry about him."

"I wasn't."

Alessio raised a brow.

"Okay, maybe I was, but nothing Adrian could say would make that better."

"I don't think he's interested anymore. I mean, I told him things were shit with you and the little woman right now, so if he's tempted, he'll make a move soon and then we'll know. But I really think he's moved on."

I exhaled slowly, trying not to envision stabbing my best friend. "Gee thanks. But as I've said, I don't really care if Adrian is interested in Giada. What does bother me is the possibility that my wife would rather be with someone else."

Alessio sunk into the chair across from my desk. I tried to think of a way to make him understand. I wanted her to want me the way I wanted her. I didn't want her to stay with me only because I physically trapped her in the house.

I wanted things to go back to how they were.

"Luca, you're missing my point. I'm trying to tell you that Adrian isn't the obstacle to your happy-ever-after with Giada. You are. Stop punishing her and at least act like you forgive her before it's too late."

I tried to explain why that wouldn't work, how she knew me too well to believe I'd moved past what happened when I hadn't, but he kept talking.

"At least make a fucking effort. Talk to her. Spend time with her."

"I went to church with her. She didn't say a single word to me," I reminded him.

"You only went with her so she wouldn't talk to the priest."

That was true.

"We're leaving for Italy in a matter of days. Do you really think it's wise to leave her alone when you're a whole ocean away and you haven't so much as talked in weeks?"

I sighed. I hated the idea of leaving Giada in the U.S. when I went to Italy, but I couldn't risk her safety. I'd met with the heads of the other families on the East Coast and that had gone well. We'd confirmed the status quo would continue, and everyone seemed willing to respect me as they had my papà.

But I had no guarantee of a similar welcome in Italy.

Back home, they viewed me as an outsider, an American. It didn't matter to the families still in Sicily that I was born there or that I'd spent more of my life on Italian soil than not. My English

was too smooth, my mannerisms too American, and my wife…
well, no one would mistake her for an Italian.

"She can join me in Italy once things are stable," I said.

"Does she know that?"

I cringed. Of course, I hadn't told Giada I wasn't bringing her
with me to Italy. I hadn't told her anything lately. Alessio was
right. The closest I'd gotten to her since I'd killed Elio was the
night she joined me in the guest room, and I'd snuggled her in my
sleep. I'd woken to find my arm around her and the longing had
about killed me. I'd spent a solid hour watching her sleep and
wishing she were still wholly mine, like she'd been before, and
then I'd gotten up to shower before I said or did something
stupid.

"I'll talk with her," I promised.

CHAPTER 18

Giada

My visit with Cami had been a good distraction, and somehow I managed to sleep well that night. But I woke early, plagued by what Enzo had suggested the previous day.

Why had I left town with Adrian and not him? I wanted to believe it was merely a matter of convenience. Adrian was by my side and willing to go when I needed him. But I couldn't pretend that I didn't think Enzo would've come if I'd asked. Maybe he was right. Maybe a part of my reasoning had been to hurt Luca.

I dressed quickly, then made my way downstairs to see which babysitter Luca had stuck me with for the day. Thomas sat at the kitchen table, dressed more casually than I usually saw him. He glanced up as I entered, nodded his head in acknowledgement of me, then watched as I marched over to the coffee maker.

I wondered how long he'd sit there, silently watching me, but I didn't test him. "I'd like to go to church this morning. Can you take me?"

A frown creased his brows.

"You can stay with me the whole time," I said, adding, "As long as you don't talk." I supposed that last part shouldn't be too hard for him. He wasn't exactly bursting with conversation ideas.

"I have things to do today. Is an hour long enough?"

"Yep."

We left ten minutes later. There was no mass until afternoon, but that was okay. I just needed to sit in the sanctuary and pray. Thomas sat a few rows behind me and, as promised, he kept quiet.

I'd just finished praying the rosary and was starting to let my mind wander when I noticed Father Ryan make his way towards the confessional. I stood, certain he saw me, then turned to Thomas.

"Do you mind if I…" I began, gesturing to the small booth in the hall beside the sanctuary.

Thomas rose to his feet. "That's fine, but I'm waiting right outside. Luca will kill me if you run off."

I didn't bother assuring him that I wouldn't, and instead I ducked into the confessional. I'd already spoken to Father Ryan since returning home, so I jumped right into my current dilemma.

"Luca's mad at me," I blurted out.

"Do you have something to confess?" the father asked, in a tone that reminded me I wasn't at the nail salon.

"Yes. I hurt my husband's feelings, and I think maybe I did it on purpose. But he hurt me first, and I'm still mad."

I could practically hear Father Ryan's smile through his words. "Forgiveness is a journey, not a destination."

"Uhh, I'm sort of in a time crunch. Could you translate?"

He chuckled. "You can regret hurting someone and can apologize for it without forgiving whatever wrongs you feel they've committed. But you still need to work towards forgiveness. Harboring anger or any other negativity isn't going to help either of you. At the end of the day, forgiving another is a gift to yourself, a way of allowing yourself to stop feeling bad."

I sighed. "You still sound like Yoda."

"Just talk with your husband, Giada. Tell him you're sorry and help him understand that you mean it. But be honest about any hurt you're still feeling, too. And keep praying on it until you feel better."

That made more sense, but I still felt unsettled. "Everything has been different since his dad died," I admitted. "And I realize that he can't help that, and that things are still going to be difficult for a while, but I'm really struggling because I don't feel connected to him like I used to. I want to feel like we're facing all these new challenges together. I want things between us to be like they used to be."

"So tell him."

"He won't believe me."

"Then show him, Giada."

"How?"

"If you want your relationship to be the way it used to be, you need to be the way you used to be, whatever that means for you. If you used to open your heart and tell him everything, do that. Be vulnerable."

"Be the change?" I interpreted.

"Uhh, sure. Something like that."

"Thank you," I said, starting to scoot out of the booth.

"Wait, do you need an actual confession?"

"Nope, I'm good." I grabbed Thomas and headed out. I insisted on a stop at the store and picked up all the ingredients for Luca's favorite Sicilian dish. Once we were home, I got to work on the rest of my plan.

Luca

*A*lessio had made a point of getting me home early, so I should've been suspicious, but I was still too stressed about everything with the business. The second I swung open the door, the sweet fragrance of Italian spices assaulted my senses. The lights were dimmed, and candles were everywhere.

My first thought was that Thomas was using my house for one of his internet dates. But then he rushed to the door, shook his head, and joined Alessio on the front porch.

"Good luck," Alessio said with a chuckle.

"Where are you both going? I need sleep tonight to get ready for Palermo. I can't…"

"Babysit your own wife?" Alessio completed. "Yeah, I think you can, man. But if you need one of us, we're just headed out for a bit, and then I'll crash in my room. So just call."

I turned and looked back at my house. With the candles, I hardly recognized it. Everything also looked oddly clean.

Giada stepped into view just as the front door closed.

"I made dinner for you. Pasta alla Norma," she said, her voice timid.

"You don't cook," I said, more out of confusion. Giada could prepare simple dishes, but nothing too complex. And she never cooked me Sicilian food. Pasta alla Norma was something I'd order at a restaurant in Italy, but likely had never eaten in the States. I didn't even think it was on the menu at most American Italian restaurants.

"Matteo helped via video chat. And I'm sure it's not as good as your mom's, but I tried. And I'm begging you, please just sit down with me for five minutes."

I'd planned to tell her I wasn't hungry, to excuse myself immediately so I could shower and change for bed. But she looked so desperate and so fragile, I couldn't say no. I nodded once, then gazed around the room, taking in all the details.

She returned to the kitchen to fill our plates, so I went to wash my hands.

"Who cleaned the house?" I asked. I hadn't wanted any extra people in the house until the business was more stable, so the usual cleaning crew had been on hiatus since my father's passing.

"I did," she said, adding, "Yesterday," as if wanting to remind me I hadn't come home the previous night.

"I know you've been busy. I'd like to help lighten your load," Giada continued, carrying our plates to the table.

A bottle of wine was already on the table, so I poured it into both glasses, filling mine nearly to the brim. I was already bone tired, but at least the alcohol would relax my frazzled nerves until I fell asleep.

"There's nothing you can do," I told her. I prayed she wasn't about to offer to help with some business crap.

"I can cook your favorite meals. I can keep the house clean. I can give you a massage or…other stuff. I can remind you that you are the most brilliant, hardworking, and amazing man I've ever met."

I exhaled slowly, sat, and began piercing the pasta with my fork.

"What I can't do is keep living here in silence. It's killing me to know you hate me."

"I don't hate you," I said, but I couldn't meet her eyes.

"Well, you sure don't like me lately."

"It's just going to take some time. I can't just forget that you—"

"Please don't say it," she interrupted.

I gazed up to meet her eyes, then reached for my wine.

"I can't do this now, Giada. I have too much on my mind, and I'm tired. I'll just say something that makes everything worse."

"I don't want you to say anything. Just eat and listen. Okay?"

I returned to the pasta in response.

"Do you remember autumn of my last year of college? We

were in Palermo. It was when I was just starting to learn about your family and your work, and I was terrified. I didn't think you actually wanted to be with me, so I was going out of my way to avoid you and ignore you as much as possible. And no matter how much I did that, you kept bringing me fresh pastries in bed and complimenting my hair and buying me dresses."

She paused for a breath. I didn't say anything, but of course I remembered that trip vividly. It was the first time I realized that the person I loved most in the world actually thought of me as a monster.

"I never realized how horrible that had to have been for you, trying to win me over when I was so desperate to reject you. And I get it now, because you're shutting me out in the same way." She raised her hand to signal for me not to interrupt. "And I don't blame you. What I did was awful and hurtful, and I did it at the worst possible time."

Giada paused again, but I still had nothing to say. I drained the rest of my wine and reached for the bottle, but she slid it out of reach. Our eyes met briefly, but I quickly looked away. I couldn't gaze into those big brown eyes of hers without feeling pangs of remorse and pain all over my chest. She reached for my hand and gripped it tightly. I focused on her perfectly manicured nails, wondering how she'd managed to do that without leaving the house, instead of dwelling on the feeling of the soft skin on her long, slender fingers.

"I wasn't thinking, Luca. I was scared, but also, I was angry. I felt like what you did somehow betrayed the narrative I'd set up for our lives. And I know now that wasn't true, but I need you to understand what I was feeling at the time. I need you to know it wasn't about Adrian. He never once crossed my mind until he showed up in that church after Ryan called him."

She squeezed my hand and continued. "I didn't call Adrian. I wouldn't call him for something like that. And I don't regret choosing you over him. I don't regret any second I've been with you and, if anything, I would regret the time I spent with him in college. Except I needed that time, needed to see what it was like to be in a relationship with someone else so that I saw how different things are with you. But I haven't needed that since then."

"Giada, stop. You don't have to—" I began, but she cut me off.

"And it is different with you. It always has been, and you know it, too. We've both dated other people, so I know you know what I'm talking about. No matter how much I felt like I cared for someone before you, it wasn't the same. That connection wasn't as strong. They might have been a part of my life, but they were never a part of my soul. And you are. You are woven into every fiber of my existence. Even if you left me now and I never saw you again, I could never forget who you are and the way you make me feel."

I swallowed the growing lump in my throat. She sounded sincere, and she was right. I did know what she meant. I'd thought I loved my ex, Chiara, when we were together, but it wasn't like this. I'd never experienced this all-encompassing visceral need with Chiara.

"I didn't run off with Adrian because I wanted another chance with him. I let Adrian drive because I was mad at you, and I knew me being with him would cause you the most pain. It had nothing to do with Adrian. It was all about you. I wanted to hurt you. And that's all."

I cleared my throat. "You succeeded," I said.

"I'm sorry."

I finally dared to gaze up as she spoke. Her eyes had glossed over with the same tears that coated her dark, thick lashes. She wore minimal makeup, which was just the way I preferred her. And her hair was mostly down, with just the front strands clipped back, also in my favorite style. I loved everything about her hair, the feel of the silky strands, the shine of it, and especially the way it fell across her shoulders, obscuring just enough of her upper body to leave some mystery. But I didn't like when it covered her face, since Giada had a face I could stare at for hours. And looking into her eyes was the one way I could tell exactly what she was thinking or feeling.

"Nothing happened with Adrian. We didn't touch, didn't kiss. I wasn't unfaithful. I didn't want to be unfaithful."

"I know," I said, breaking away from her stare. She released my hand and refilled my wine glass, but only partway.

"You think he's always in the back of my mind as some sort of runner up or back up plan, but he's not, Luca. It's only you. Not once since we've been married have I regretted choosing you over him. Not when I was scared, not when I was mad. Never."

She paused, inhaling slowly. "It's always been you, Luca."

I gazed up at her again, then refocused on my food. With newfound determination, I began eating like my goal in life was to clean that damn plate. I needed a distraction from her, from how she looked and what she was saying. I needed to just stay focused on work and the police investigation and the funeral, and all the things that I had to do. The second I let myself think about Giada, it would be too much. I wouldn't be able to handle everything. And I couldn't set myself up for failure. Not right now. Not when everyone was counting on me to step up to the plate.

"I want to be there for you now like I should have been right away, if you'll let me. I want to be the wife you need to get you through this. I want to be your best friend again. I want to be your lover." Giada breathed a laugh. "I honestly don't know how much longer I can survive if you won't touch me. It's like, I'll simultaneously combust from all the pent-up desire but also like I'm freezing up inside because I can barely remember what it felt like when you looked at me that way you always used to."

I dared to look up from my almost-empty plate, but only long enough to notice her dish was nearly full. "Eat," I commanded, praying for once she'd obey.

She did, except then I found my eyes drawn to her mouth. I watched the adorable way the tip of her tongue darted out to lick off her full lips between bites. I saw her cheeks redden as she noticed me eying the movement of her jaw and the subtle curve of her chin.

Giada raised her napkin to her lips, obscuring my view. I dropped my gaze, hoping the lack of attention would encourage her to eat. I'd tried not to pay her much attention the last couple of weeks, so I couldn't be sure, but she was probably losing weight. She always did when stressed.

"I'll eat more when you forgive me," she said, making me wonder if I'd said my thoughts out loud. "Food doesn't taste as good when things aren't right with us."

I agreed, although the pasta had turned out surprisingly well. It wasn't the most complicated Sicilian dish to prepare, but there were a lot of seasonings that had to be just right to achieve the traditional full-bodied flavor.

"Will you start cooking like this more if I forgive you?" I asked, daring to share a hint of a smile.

Her entire face lit up at the question, and I saw her dimples for the first time in weeks. "That depends."

"On?"

"On what sort of mood my cooking puts you in."

I wasn't sure what she meant by that. I watched her lips as they settled around the rim of her wine glass, then after her sip, she stood abruptly. She took my plate and hers to the sink, her back to me.

I gazed at her dress, trying to recall when she'd worn it last. Sometimes, she would do that—wear specific items to evoke a certain memory. This dress was navy blue, with large white hibiscus outlined throughout. It was loose in the back, not revealing any of her sumptuous curves, but it fell far above her knees, showing much of her thighs.

She rinsed the dishes then bent to load them into the dishwasher, and as she did, her long necklace swung down. I stepped closer, then laughed. It was the cheap pendant she'd bought herself in Palermo during the Thanksgiving trip she was just remembering. The chain was coated entirely in beads, and the pendant appeared to be some sort of odd metallic shell or tooth. In Palermo, she'd asserted her independence by paring that necklace with the Armani dress I'd bought her, likely for close to a thousand euros.

I stepped closer as she straightened, reaching my arm around to tug on the chain. "Well played, Giada. Did you think I wouldn't notice?"

"I'd hoped you would," she replied, holding unusually still.

I realized this was the closest I'd been to her in weeks. We'd barely made love since before my papà died, but it was more than that. Since she'd run off, we'd hardly even hugged. I'd told myself I could go without her touch, but now, I wasn't so sure. The fruity smell of her hair mixed with the sweet, floral tones of her lotion, and the heat from her body seemed to draw me closer.

I released the necklace, letting my hands both rest on the edge of the sink in front of my wife. With every breath, we seemed to inch closer, until finally I could feel the curve of her buttocks lightly against my pants. Her head tilted slightly to the side, causing her hair to cascade down her back and reveal the tender patch of skin along the length of her neck. Without thinking, my mouth drifted downwards, my lips settling against her neck without moving further.

Giada shivered and a soft sigh escaped her lips. Her body drifted backwards until she was pressing fully against my torso. I knew what she wanted, and God, did I ever want it too. But I was also scared. She said she'd left with Adrian only to hurt me, but the insecurities lingered.

Every time I touched her, I fell more under her spell. I wanted her more. I needed her more. I fell a bit more in love.

And if it wasn't mutual, if it wasn't forever, I wasn't sure I could handle it. If I let myself fall, I might not survive her leaving me again.

I shifted my head slightly, realizing only then that our faces were reflected clearly in the window above the sink. Giada's lips were parted slightly, her chest rising and falling dramatically with each tempered breath, and her eyes were locked squarely on mine.

"Please Luca," she said after a minute. "I need you to touch me. I can't breathe without your hands on me."

I hesitated, then shifted my hands from the sink to her hips. I watched in the reflection as her eyes fluttered shut momentarily. She sunk further against me, then spoke again. Her voice was raspy now, like she'd been exercising.

"The dreams I've been having lately," she began, with a breathy sigh. "The things you do to me in my sleep...and then I wake, and you're not even in the bed."

I kept my left hand on her hip, but ran the right one up her torso, firmly squeezing her breast as if testing a melon. It wasn't the way I usually touched her there, but she groaned nonetheless.

"I tried touching myself," she continued. "I'd close my eyes and pretend my hands were your hands, and it didn't work. It wasn't the same."

Working through the thin sundress, I tugged her bra down below her right breast, then her left. I then lightly stroked one then the other beneath the soft material.

Giada's breathing quickened and I could tell she was struggling to keep talking.

"I can't survive without you Luca," she finally said.

I worked my left hand beneath the hem of her dress, uttering my own satisfied groan when I found that Giada wore nothing beneath the dress. My lips closed around her neck right as my finger traced her slick epicenter. Her breathy sighs gave way to moans as I ran my tongue along her slightly salty skin just beneath her ear and stroked my fingers back and forth along her dampness.

I'd barely had time to savor the sweet, familiar sensation of this beautiful woman completely at my mercy, when she shuddered and groaned my name loudly.

An instant later, she'd swiveled to face me and my lips were on hers. Our kisses were deep and sloppy and full of naked need. Her teeth raked into my lips as my tongue thrashed around hers. Her hands found my belt, and within a moment, my pants fell to my ankles. My boxer briefs were tighter, and she could barely scoot them below my butt without breaking away from our kiss. I meant to help her, to finish undressing myself, but instead I hoisted her onto the counter beside the sink.

Her arm knocked into the soap dispenser, flinging it to the floor with a clank, but neither of us cared. I yanked her dress over her head then unclasped her bra with one hand, leaving her naked aside from the stupid necklace.

As I dragged her hips to mine, joining us as one, her legs wrapped around me. I felt her heels push against me, trying to work my boxer briefs down further, and I laughed against her lips. My senses were on fire, overwhelmed with the taste of her skin, the scent of her desire, and the breathy way she moaned my name over and over. Her arms and legs fully encompassed me, and I relished the sensation of being fully surrounded by my Giada while simultaneously moving inside her.

I cautioned myself that she might not climax again right away, especially since I'd never last long after going without her for weeks. I told myself I wouldn't let it bother me if she didn't, that I wouldn't read into it as some sign that she didn't actually want me as much as she claimed. But it was all lies. As her movements grew more frantic, it reassured me. And as her entire body tensed around me, I shattered into my own euphoric release.

We were both breathing heavily as I lowered her back to the counter, not having even realized I'd lifted her up at some point.

My arms felt weak and my legs were shaking, but I felt more at peace than I had in a long time. I rest my forehead against hers until the panting subsided. By the time I finally pulled out, we were both smiling, and I realized I'd needed that every bit as much as she did.

"I love you Luca," she said. "Ti amo."

I bit back a grin at her Italian. "I know baby. Me too."

CHAPTER 19

Giada

When Luca finally lifted me off of the counter, I couldn't help but giggle. I was completely naked in our kitchen, and he was still mostly clothed. I'd gotten his pants to his ankles, his shirt mostly unbuttoned, and his boxers lowered down to mid-thigh. He shrugged, pulling up his boxers while I finished the buttons on his shirt. He eyed me suspiciously until I put his shirt on myself, leaving my dress on the floor.

"I wanted to show you something else I've been working on," I explained, leading him into the living room. I'd found my photo book from high school, filled with dozens of pictures of Luca and me, and propped it on the coffee table along with the journal I'd begun keeping since my bout of amnesia.

He sat on the floor and pulled me onto his thigh. He flipped through the high school album first, with both of us laughing at the pictures.

"God, that haircut," he said with a cringe. "What was I thinking?"

"That was the peak of style," I said. "I can't believe how young I looked, though."

"You were young."

"So were you," I reminded him. Luca was less than two years my senior, but he definitely looked older than his years in high school. I wondered if it was the weight of everything he'd learned about the family business that had aged him so quickly.

"I wish you'd felt comfortable telling me everything you were dealing with back then," I said.

He raised an eyebrow. "I'm not sure you mean that. And besides, I don't. One of the things I loved most about you was your innocence. You weren't bogged down with all that crap. You reminded me that there were still pure things in the world."

I reached for my journal and thrust it into his hands without responding.

"I'm not reading your diary," he said.

"I want you to. I've marked all the pages where I mention you more than just in passing. You don't have to read them all, but I really want you to at least skim through a few."

He looked skeptical, so I begged, adding that it had taken me hours to mark the relevant pages.

He reluctantly flipped open the journal, clearing his throat before reading out loud. "I am exhausted today. Luca woke me up in the middle of the night doing this magical thing with his tongue. He said he was trying to see how long he could go before I woke up, but of course, I was wide awake the second he ducked under the covers. I never would've believed there'd be something I'd enjoy more than sleep, but wow, is he gifted with his mouth."

Luca scraped his teeth along his bottom lip and cringed, "You actually write that sort of thing in your diary? What if your mother finds this?"

Heat rushed to my face, but I stood by my entry. "My mother

would never read my journal. Eww. And the whole point of journaling is to record things I don't want to forget if I ever get amnesia again. I can't think of anything more tragic than me forgetting how much I enjoy *that*."

I could tell he was struggling not to laugh, but he jumped ahead another ten pages or so. "Luca came to church with me today. It's not his favorite place to spend his free time, so it always amazes me how often he'll go, just to make me happy. I think I concentrate on the sermon better when I'm alone, though. Today I started thinking about how grateful I am for Luca, and that made me wonder about the whole soul mate thing. I don't know if I believe that two people are ever halves of the same whole, but I definitely think Luca and I were made for each other. Like God just tinkered around until he got the exact model of man to challenge me and better me and complete me."

Luca fell silent, but I could tell he was skimming the rest of the page. When he finished, he gazed up at me. "Do you really believe that?"

I nodded.

He seemed to consider that for a moment. "Do you believe there's someone for everyone?"

I shrugged. "Maybe?"

He skipped ahead, nearly towards the end, stopping on the second-to-last entry I'd marked. This one was from less than a week before he lost his father.

"Today I was sitting on the steps with Cami at lunch, and this adorable couple walked by. The woman was like super pregnant, and they stopped right in front of us so the guy could tie her shoes. I can't wait to be pregnant so Luca will tie my shoes. Luca and I will make the most adorable babies. I hope we have at least one precocious little boy that looks just like him, right down to the determined scowl. I'm a little worried Luca will be insanely overprotective of our baby girls, but mostly I'm just excited. He's going to be such a great daddy, and I can't wait for him to see that, but I'm not sure I'm ready to share him yet. Hopefully I get a little sick of him soon so we can start having babies while I'm still young enough to lose the baby weight."

Luca laughed aloud at that entry too. "I'd tie your shoes for you now," he said through his smile, leaning forward and rubbing the tip of his nose against mine.

I inhaled slowly, relishing the moment of pure joy. As Luca pulled back, his expression changed. There was the slightest flicker of doubt, and then he turned to the clock.

"It's late. We both need sleep," he said, guiding me off of his lap.

I stood and offered my hand to help him up. "You forgot for a moment, didn't you?" I asked, hating that I sounded as disappointed as I felt.

He stared at me blankly, as though struggling to decipher my words. Finally, he nodded. "Yeah, I guess I did."

I sighed. "You can go back to hating me now. I deserve it." I started up to our bedroom, but he followed closely, stopping me before I reached the end of the hall.

"No, Giada, you misunderstood. I forgot my papà died, Giada. I forgot I was leaving for Palermo soon, that I was taking over his businesses, that I had to…" he shook his head, still unable to speak what he'd done to the traitor. "I could never hate you, and no one else could ever give me what you did just there."

"A sappy journal and ten-year-old photos?"

He smiled. "A break. I've had everything with my papà weighing on me twenty-four seven since it happened, and nothing has distracted me. But you did. You gave me a full hour of peace. Of joy."

I felt a tad selfish, since that hadn't been my intention. I'd only wanted to make him see that I still loved him, that I always had. Of course, I was glad I'd given him some respite from his grief too, but I regretted not planning to do that.

"Go start the shower. I need to blow out these candles so the house doesn't burn down."

I nodded, then remembered my bra somewhere in the kitchen. "Is anyone coming over tonight?"

"No, and Alessio will probably stay in his wing. We'll clean up the rest tomorrow."

I smiled and went to start the shower.

Luca

I knew I should sleep, but I couldn't. I kept replaying the words from Giada's journal in my head. I was half afraid of falling asleep only to wake and realize it was a dream, that she really had been interested in Adrian. Logically, it shouldn't have comforted me to know Giada only chose him to hurt me, but it did.

And as stupid as it was, I kept thinking about her journal entries, too. I'd never been too curious about what she wrote, but I would've guessed it was less flattering. Maybe the parts I didn't real were insulting. Still, I was reassured by what I read even if those were the only nice things.

Giada sighed and shifted in her sleep. She'd fallen asleep with her back to me but my arm was wrapped around her waist. As she shifted, my hand was closer to her breasts. I thought again about the first journal entry I'd read, and nearly laughed out loud at the notion of my sweet, church-going wife writing about oral sex in her diary. "Magical" oral sex, to be precise.

Giada needed her sleep, but so did I. And I was way too worked up to sleep now. In one quick movement, I ducked under the covers and buried my face between her thighs before she could stop me.

Her legs tensed as she woke, momentarily squishing my face, but then she relaxed and rolled onto her back, letting me spread her thighs to the side. Her soft laugh was muffled, but I heard her words clearly.

"I should've known you'd try this tonight."

"I guess I'll have to keep trying until you finally sleep through it," I said, lifting my head up.

She laughed harder. "If I sleep through it, you're not doing it right." Her fingers reached down to stroke my hair as I continued to show her how truly gifted I was. Within a minute, though, she tugged me upwards. I wanted to keep going, but I knew better than to fight Giada about what she wanted in the bedroom.

I kissed my way up her body, letting her hands guide me exactly where she wanted me. We both moved slowly, in part from sleep and in part because the urgency we'd felt earlier was now sated. My teeth scraped along her neck as I drove leisurely in and out of her warmth, feeling more connected to my wife with each thrust. Giada reached for my hand, clasping our fingers together right as she reached her climax. I followed suit shortly after, then rolled off of her onto my back, suddenly exhausted.

I handed her a tissue, then she snuggled over my chest. Within a moment, I was asleep.

I awoke too soon to the sensation of someone watching me. When I peeled open my eyes, I saw Giada's face inches from mine, smiling.

"It's too early for you to be that happy," I groaned, squeezing my eyes shut again.

"I forgot how much I like sleeping with you. Like, in the same bed," she clarified.

"I could be persuaded to wake fully if you wanted to 'sleep' with me again now," I said.

She squirmed against my thigh. "Tempting, but I might need an hour or so first. For some reason I'm sore."

I winced. "I'm sorry. Was I too rough?"

"No, it's just been a while since we did that, and twice in one night, plus some playtime before and again in the shower…"

"It hasn't been that long."

"Literally the longest we've ever gone, Luca. Not that I was counting," she said.

"Wow."

"Also, there's someone in the house. It sounds like they made coffee, so probably not a burglar, but I'm guessing you should maybe deal with them before starting on round three, or round five, or whatever we're calling it."

I rolled out of the bed, surprised to see it was after nine a.m. I spent a minute cleaning up in the bathroom, then slipped on some joggers and went out to chat with Alessio.

"Good morning," he said, a squirrely grin on his face.

"What?" I asked.

"I went to wake you up so we could talk, and you weren't in the guest room. And then I slipped on your belt, and the racket didn't wake you, so I wondered if maybe you were dead."

"Because of my belt?"

"Because you're usually a light sleeper," he explained. "But then I went to get water for the coffee, and I found this," he continued.

I followed his gaze to the sink, where Giada's bra was draped across the faucet. I snatched it and tried to shove as much of it in my pocket as would fit.

"I'm guessing dinner was good?"

"Dinner was very good."

"What did she make for you?"

"I have no idea," I replied.

We both laughed at that, and then I followed Alessio's gaze as he scanned the kitchen. Giada had actually cleaned up the dinner dishes, but there was a whole section of the counter where all of the items had been knocked onto the ground or off to the side.

"Remind me not to eat here again until the cleaning lady is back," Alessio mumbled.

I made myself a cappuccino while mentally reviewing everything on my list for the day. "So, no official meetings today, right?"

Alessio nodded. "You wanted to check in on the clubs and maybe check in with Big Dawg about the..." he began. His expression snapped out of work mode instantly, and a moment later, I felt Giada's arms around my waist, hugging me from behind.

"You could sleep longer," I said.

"It's no fun in the bed alone," she replied. Her words were barely a whisper, so I wasn't sure if Alessio heard until I saw his face.

He bit back a smile, then stared down at his cell phone.

I turned to face my wife. She'd thrown a sweatshirt over her nightgown, and hopefully she'd put on panties, or at least wouldn't reach above her head in front of Alessio. "Coffee?" I offered.

She leaned closer to sniff mine, then rose to her toes to kiss me. I meant for it to be a quick peck, but we maybe lingered a moment too long.

"Porca miseria," Alessio said. "I forgot how nauseating all this PDA is when you two aren't fighting. Sad part is that I almost missed it."

I grinned, then turned back to Giada. "Has it been an hour yet?"

She looked confused until I wiggled my eyebrows, and then she remembered her earlier comment. "I think by the time I've had my coffee it will be."

I forced my mug into her hands. "Take mine. I'll make myself more. Let me chat with Alessio here and then I need a shower, so…"

"Gotcha," she said, smiling. She turned on her heels and offered a dainty wave. "See you later, Alessio."

Alessio sighed. "You do have to actually do some work today. You know that, right?"

"Surely we can discuss some of this stuff on the flight tomorrow."

"Totally. Mafia shit is well suited to a crowded public flight."

I scowled and made myself a new cup of coffee, too impatient to even mess with the cappuccino maker this time. "I just need an hour. Or maybe two," I told him.

⁂

Giada

I curled up in bed, thinking I might have time for a catnap before Luca and Alessio finished whatever pressing business they faced. But I'd barely closed my eyes when I felt the bed dip beside me. I started to roll to face my husband, but his palm nudged me back down.

"Stay," he commanded, his voice as soft as it was deep.

I heard him rummaging in the drawer of the nightstand, then a moment later, he yanked the sheets down beneath the curve of my butt. I barely had time to register the cold air on my skin before his hands were there, coated in massage oil, kneading my tight back muscles.

I groaned loudly, shocked at how quickly the tension began seeping out of my body.

Luca chuckled, then leaned closer. "You might keep your voice down, amore. Alessio is probably still in the kitchen."

I replied with a softer moan, part in protest of his suggestion and part in delight. Luca straddled my hips and continued his work, massaging my shoulders before moving along my ribcage and settling on my lower back. He was liberal with the oil, keeping his hands well-lubed so they glided effortlessly across my skin. When he reached the swell of my butt, he kept massaging, releasing all the soreness in my glutes, then shifting his attention to my upper thighs.

I wanted to just relax and enjoy the massage, but every tug of his strong fingers along my thighs also spurred a twinge of pleasure deeper in my core. I wriggled against his hand, trying to force his hand where I needed the pressure most.

Luca chuckled. "I thought you were sore."

"That was before the massage. Now I just need help relaxing."

I expected he'd ask for clarification, or maybe protest my insinuation that his massage hadn't relaxed me. So I wiggled my hips in anticipation. But instead of words, Luca responded with a firm grip on my hip. A moment later, I felt the head of his cock prodding at my entrance. I shifted my legs slightly, making room for him, then moaned loudly when he thrust all the way in.

"Just remember this was your idea, not mine," he said, slowly dragging out an inch before pressing back in. "I would've happily finished the massage with zero strings."

"That wouldn't have been a full-service massage," I said, my voice already sounding raspy and desperate.

Luca bent his neck to whisper right at my ear, his breath sending shivers down my spine. "If this is what you expect from a massage, I'm never sending you to the spa again."

I barely had time to giggle before he rose up, steadied my hips, then began a relentless pace. I turned my face into the mattress, hoping the cushion would mute the sounds of my moans as Luca drove into me again and again. The angle this time was different, letting him stay shallower in my body while still hitting that sensitive spot again and again.

I felt the familiar tightening in my core sooner than I'd

expected, and I longed to hold back, to enjoy the delicious sensations a little longer. But then Luca whispered in my ear again.

"Come with me, Giada," he urged, a growl accenting his last word and signaling he, too, was dangerously close.

The sound of his voice along with the vision in my mind of Luca looming over me, moments away from filling me with his sweet release, was enough to push me over the edge. I dug my teeth into my lip as intense pleasure filled my core, then radiated out of my body, causing me to buck against him.

Luca held me tight, thrusting his hips twice more before moaning with his own climax. Warmth flooded me along with a slight sting of pain, and I decided I probably was still a tiny bit sore. Not that I cared. I needed all the intimacy with Luca I could get. And every time he filled me with his seed, I felt even closer to him. It was as if I needed him to mark me as his to make up for the rift I'd caused.

Luca dropped down above me, pressing me into the mattress, and I reveled in the security of the sensation. We both caught our breath, then Luca slid off of me and rolled me to face him. I flopped onto my back, limp with pleasure, and Luca rose to his elbow, running his free palm down my breasts to my abdomen. His eyes roamed lower, pausing on the small damp stain on the sheets at the apex of my thighs.

"I was thinking I should go back on birth control for a couple months," I said, lightly scraping my nails along his forearm as I spoke so he didn't jump to the wrong conclusion. "Not because I don't want a baby with you anymore. I do. But I just feel like the timing maybe isn't ideal."

"Yeah, I guess you're right," he agreed, but then he glanced down again. "But unless you're already on birth control, it might be a little late. I'm not an expert on this stuff, but I think we were supposed to use a condom the last few times if we didn't want—"

"I can't get pregnant now. I just had my period, like two days ago."

His eyes dropped to my groin again. "It started two days ago or ended two days ago?"

"Started, and it's already done. Blissfully short this month." I said, anticipating his next question.

"And you're not fertile until the middle of your cycle?"

"Yes. Theoretically, there's only a couple of days each month when you can conceive, but I don't think we should gamble that much. We probably have another day or two this month before we need to start using condoms just to be safe, and—"

"And by then I'll be in Italy," he interrupted.

I started to agree, then realized how he'd phrased it. "You mean, we will be in Italy," I corrected, my heart already racing because I knew that look on his face. He hadn't misspoken. He was leaving me.

Luca leaned over me, pinning me to the bed with his solid forearm. "Amore, I'm sorry, but I don't know if it's safe there. I need a little time there to get a read on the situation, and then you'll join me."

"How much time?"

"Two weeks."

My stomach dropped like I was on a rollercoaster. "I just got you back, Luca. I can't be apart from you for two whole weeks."

"Yes, you can. And it won't be like the past two weeks. We'll talk every day. Multiple times. I'll personally see that I keep making up for lost time and lost orgasms with as many video chats as it takes."

I giggled at that.

"You don't think I can make you come over the phone?" he asked.

"Oh, I know you can. I just prefer the real thing."

"Me too."

"Take me with you, and I promise to stay in the house. I don't need a babysitter. I won't leave without you," I assured him.

"I'm not risking your safety," he repeated.

I closed my eyes, unable to stand that sorrowful look in his beautiful brown eyes when he told me no.

"But it seems like if I'm gone for two weeks, you could wait on the birth control. I don't want to subject you to all those hormones and side effects when we aren't going to be together anyway. We can just use condoms when you come to Italy, and then we can figure out if we're ready to start trying again or if we need to postpone."

"Okay." It was easy to agree to that part. I hadn't noticed side effects from birth control when I'd been on it, but since I'd been off, I'd noticed clearer skin and fewer mood swings.

Luca was quiet for a moment, but he shifted to pull my body across his. "Write to me while I'm gone, will you?"

"Like my journal entries?"

"Yes."

"You're the one leaving me. Maybe you should write the love notes," I said, lifting my head to gaze at him.

"Oh, I'm planning on it."

CHAPTER 20

Luca

"*L*uca!"

A deep voice interrupted my dream, and I woke with a groan. After spending the majority of the flight hashing out work matters with Tony, I'd finally fallen asleep. I was reliving some of the highlights of my last forty-eight hours with Giada, namely a certain bubble bath we'd shared the night before my flight, when Tony rudely awakened me.

"We're home," he said with a smile that didn't match my mood.

I blew out a sigh and rubbed my temples. This was going to be a long two weeks.

After spending nearly every minute with Giada the past few days, I'd finally relented to one of Tony's earlier suggestions and asked Alessio to stay behind. At first, I'd bristled at the notion of leaving my second-in-command in New York while going to Italy to handle such important business matters. Tony had urged me to consider that I'd need someone trustworthy and capable to manage my business back home while I was abroad, but that wasn't what had sold me on the arrangement. Rather, I'd realized that with Alessio staying home, I could keep Giada safe without having to arrange for a babysitter at night.

Alessio enjoyed his own mother-in-law-suite type of space in the house, but he was still technically under the same roof as Giada. She was accustomed to sharing her space with him, so his presence wouldn't be an intrusion. Plus, Lincoln regularly drove Giada around during the day. So, her life wouldn't have to change while I was gone, and I wouldn't risk pissing her off so soon after wriggling back into her good graces.

Tony was far from my dream travel partner, but he was efficient and knew his way around the various families in Italy. I'd requested a meeting with leaders of all of the prominent families before we began the journey, but I wasn't surprised when a couple didn't respond. My papà had never built a relationship with the families in the north, so I hadn't expected to, either.

Tony spent the first week of in Italy showing me the ropes at all of my papà's businesses and making plans to visit with the guys who were open to at least discussing a relationship. Theoretically, I already knew what all my papà had been up to in Italy, but in reality, I'd been focused on my own endeavors the past few years and hadn't truly kept up with his clubs in Rome.

Ten days after we landed in Rome, I told Giada we needed to postpone her flight another week. I hated springing that on her, but I hated the knowledge that we'd be apart another week even more. But I was still going to be jetting around the country for at least another week, so even if she did fly to Italy, we wouldn't be together until I finished all the meetings.

The day after that, Giada didn't even answer when I called her. I cursed under my breath, then dialed Alessio.

"Tell me she didn't run off with Adrian," I said when he answered, only half joking.

"What?"

"Giada isn't taking my calls," I whined. "I think she hates me."

Alessio breathed a laugh under his breath. "What happened to you, amico? You used to be drowning in confidence and now, one missed call and you're about to shit your pants."

I rolled my eyes. "We just made up. I can't handle another fight with her yet. And the worst part is Tony telling me it'll actually be another two weeks before we can just settle down in Palermo."

Alessio groaned. "Okay, well, I wouldn't recommend telling Giada that just now, but honestly, I think you're overreacting."

"Did you miss the part where I said she rejected my call?"

He took his time answering. "She's not feeling well today. I don't think it has anything to do with her being mad."

"What?" In an instant, the tenor of my panic shifted entirely. "Is she sick? Did you take her to the doctor? Why didn't you tell me?"

"She's fine," Alessio said. "Tiny bout of food poisoning. Honestly, I think she just wore herself out. She's been trying to stay busy since you left. She's been going to work every day and then spending time with Gabby and her other friends when she's not working. She's also finalizing the plans for the basement and says she's starting on the guest house next."

I snorted at that.

"She thinks if she keeps busy, she won't miss you. But she's overworking herself and not sleeping enough. She's seemed really tired the past couple of days and today she got dressed to workout and then said she was taking a nap instead."

"Does she have a fever?"

"No."

"How do you know? Did you check?"

Alessio sighed. "She's not a toddler, Luca. She's a grown ass woman. If she's really sick, she can tell me or Linc, and we'll get her to the doctor. I promise. But I'm not going to hover over her like a Sicilian grandma just because she's exhausted and ate some iffy spinach."

I supposed he had a point.

"Tell me about the meetings," Alessio prompted.

And so I did.

Giada

*A*lessio eyed me warily as I made my way across the kitchen to the coffee maker. My two hour long late morning nap had vastly improved my energy level and mood, but now I was starving.

"I dumped the rest of the coffee," he said.

Right. Of course he had. Well, coffee actually didn't sound that good anyway, probably because it was already past lunch time. I grabbed a bagel and popped it in the toaster instead. I considered that maybe I'd have more energy if I abandoned my carb-heavy diet, but carbs were my comfort food.

"Luca called. He thinks you're ignoring him. I told him you were napping. Now he's worried you're sick." Alessio paused as I rummaged through the fridge to locate the cream cheese. "You're not, right?"

I blew out a sigh and stomped towards him, pressing his palm to my forehead. "Not sick," I clarified after a solid minute of confused silence. I plopped down beside him at the island, setting my lemon seltzer water on top of a few stray papers he seemed to be reading.

I debated how truthful to be. Since Luca left, I'd been mopey and sad. And my determination to make the time fly until we were reunited backfired, since I clearly overdid it. Now, I was constantly exhausted and dealing with a niggling headache that never fully went away. And I still missed my husband. When I thought about it, I realized I'd felt this way since my little road trip, with the exception of the couple of days where Luca and I had been happily inseparable. Obviously, it was stress.

"Honestly, I think I'm just depressed. Literally everyone who claims to love me has abandoned me."

Alessio quirked a brow and slid his paper out from under my drink. "I'm still here."

"We both know you're only here because Luca ditched you, too." I bit into my bagel, relishing the flood of familiar flavors mingling on my tongue.

"Wait, who else abandoned you? Isn't Gabby still here? And your parents come back in a couple days, right?"

"Gabby left for Bermuda with that new guy she's dating. Apparently his sister is a travel agent, and she got them some killer deal on a cruise. And my mom told me yesterday that they're staying in Italy another month. Apparently Angelo is dating someone there, and they figured they might as well stay since I was coming out soon anyway."

"I'm sure Luca would be okay with you going to stay with your parents."

"They didn't invite me. No one invited me," I reiterated. I shoved another bite of bagel into my mouth then, suddenly nauseous at the full realization of my solitude, I nudged the plate away. "No one even tells me what's going on anymore. Everyone hates me." I stood abruptly and stormed off towards the basement. If I was going to be trapped at home with no friends or family, I might as well make the house perfect, and I'd left my basement design plans on the stairs.

"Call your husband!" Alessio called after me.

I groaned and slammed the basement door.

Luca

I tapped my fingers on the table and winced at the sun peeking in through the side of my Bulgari Octo sunglasses. They were my favorite pair, both because Giada bought them for me and because the reflective lens kept prying eyes from observing where I was looking. But as stylish as they were, they weren't exactly effective at keeping the sun out of my eyes, at least not now, as the sun dipped just close enough to the horizon for its rays to burn directly into my retina.

"We could trade places," Giovanni offered, apparently fed up with my grimaces.

"Why isn't he here yet?" I snapped, ignoring his offer. "He picked the time. He's nearly forty-five minutes late."

It was a rhetorical question, and Giovanni knew it. I'd only met Cosimo a handful of times over the years, but one didn't have to know him well to peg him as a self-absorbed control freak who got his kicks off of making people wait. He was the same age as me, but he'd taken over the Ferrante empire nearly four years back, when his father was killed in prison.

Despite having an immature narcissist at its helm, the Ferrante family remained one of the biggest players in Naples, which meant I couldn't risk pissing him off. The Marinos had never managed a hold in Naples, and I didn't want to change that now, but with operations in Rome and Palermo, we didn't need any enemies in one of the biggest cities in between the two locales.

When I'd requested a meeting with Cosimo, I'd assumed that Tony and I would meet with him at one of the many establishments his family owned in Napoli. Instead, he'd chosen some touristy café near the coast. He'd also insisted that I not bring any of the "vecchi," or old men. Hence Giovanni's presence at my side. Tony had scoffed at the rejection, but predicted the meeting would be a waste of my time anyway.

Clearly, he had been right.

At exactly an hour after our scheduled meeting time, Giovanni nudged my foot. I gazed up to see Cosimo quickly approaching, with two men by his side.

"Let's walk," he said, barely pausing by the table where we'd been waiting.

I rolled my eyes, confident the sunglasses would cover up my insolence, then we followed him to a private boardwalk a block away.

"It's been a long time," Cosimo said, his English smooth but heavily accented.

I offered a polite smile. "This is my associate, Giovanni Costa."

Cosimo barely acknowledged Giovanni, but did turn to his own sidekicks. "This is my Luca," he began, pointing to the shorter one. "And this is Chadwick."

A choking sound escaped Giovanni, and I didn't have to look to know he was struggling not to laugh. For years, Cosimo had claimed I wasn't a true Italian because of the time I'd spent in America, but now he'd apparently trusted a full-blooded American enough to bring him into his inner circle? *Ridiculous.*

"Piacere," I said, echoing my sentiment in English as well. "Nice to meet you."

"We're on a tight schedule here," Cosimo said, eliciting another eye roll from me, "So let's get to the point. I assume you need my help?"

"No. I don't need anything from you. I just wanted to reach out now that I'm the official head of the Marino family. I realize our territories don't overlap, but it never hurts to have more friends."

"You need friends?"

I suppressed a sigh. "I have plenty of friends already. But I did want to make the offer to you. If you ever need anything, I'm happy to work with you. I know our fathers weren't close, but you and I could choose a different path."

"You expect me to work with an American?" he scoffed.

My eyes darted to Chad, then back to Cosimo. "I'm Italian-born and raised, but I do have an abundance of American contacts, which is very handy."

Cosimo frowned. "Listen, I don't know what game you're playing, but I'm not interested. Stay out of Naples, stay out of Rome, and we won't have any problems."

"I do a lot of business in Rome, and that's not about to change," I said, hoping my tone hid my shock at his words. This was the first I'd heard of Cosimo having any interest in Rome whatsoever.

Cosimo stepped closer to me. "No, your father did a lot of business in Rome. You're going to keep your work in Sicily or else we'll send you back to America."

I sighed. "Cosimo, you know the Marino family has a lot of contacts in Rome. We've been there for ages, unlike you. What makes you think I'd abandon my nightclubs, houses, and other businesses in Rome just because you want me to?"

"No one said anything about abandoning things. You can sell your properties and make a tidy profit. Build your empire back in America. But you're not staying in Rome because I have things on you."

"Oh? What things, exactly?" I pressed.

"Elio told us everything," Cosimo said.

My stomach tightened. I knew he was lying, just trying to goad me, but it was working. He'd managed to summon the name that carried the most emotional baggage for me. "Nice try, but Elio was working for the Gambinos, not you."

"Yeah, because Elio was such a loyal guy. He'd never be a double agent, is that what you're thinking?"

I swallowed. I already knew Elio was a double agent. He was an undercover cop, but he seemed to also be actually working for the Gambinos when he infiltrated our family business. If anyone but Cosimo was telling me this information, I'd have no issue believing Elio was also selling his information to a third party. But coming from Cosimo, I was skeptical.

"Well, I appreciate the heads up, but I don't know of any information Elio might share that could possibly hurt me," I finally said. "But if you see him, tell him I'd love to chat."

Cosimo scowled, likely aware that I'd already killed Elio.

"I don't know why you won't take me serious, Luca Marino. Mark my words. You stay in Rome, you will regret it."

And with that, Cosimo turned and marched back to the main road, Chadwick and little Luca tight on his heels.

"Cazzo," Giovanni swore under his breath the moment they were out of earshot.

I nodded. My thoughts exactly.

CHAPTER 21

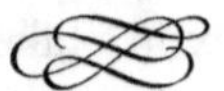

Giada

"*D*ear Diary," I wrote. "I'd love to say my mood has improved, but that would be a lie, and what's the point of keeping a journal just to fill it with lies? Luca extended our separation for another week. I'm pretty sure he never intends to see me again. He'll just keep delaying the reunion every single week until I take the hint. In other news, my parents and brothers are also in Italy. Oh, and like two days after Luca left, I got my period again. If this is what it's like without birth control, I'm done. I feel like shit."

I set down the pen, then an eerie feeling washed over me. I turned abruptly, and saw Alessio peered over my shoulder.

"What is wrong with you?" I snapped, chucking the pen at him. "This is private."

"I heard you let Luca read it," he replied.

"That's different."

The back door clicked open, and Lincoln came inside from

the patio where he'd been lounging the past hour. It was a gorgeous day, and I'd considered sitting outside too, but I already felt dizzy and lightheaded. I didn't think direct sunlight would help the situation.

"Back me up, Lincoln. Super creepy for your cousin to read my journal over my shoulder, right?" I asked, rubbing my temples.

"Absolutely," he said.

"Well, if she'd tell us what's going on, then I wouldn't have to snoop," Alessio said. "Luca's going to ask me how she's doing."

I squeezed my eyes shut, trying to clear my suddenly blurry vision. "You could just tell him to ask me," I said. "Although it'll have to wait, because I'm going to go take a nap." I rose to my feet and gripped my water glass, intending to refill it with the filtered water at the fridge.

I took a step, then frowned. Alessio was only a foot or two away, yet he looked blurry. Actually, the whole room seemed darker than a moment before, almost like the lights were on a dimmer switch. But it was mid-day, so that didn't make sense. I took another step, then cringed at the sound of glass shattering.

My gaze fell to my now-empty hand, and then I tried to look back at Alessio. A thick fog swirled around me and I felt my knees give out.

✦

Adrian

Scruffy started tugging on the leash the moment we turned the corner onto our block. "Buddy, heel!" I commanded, glancing side to side in case there was another dog approaching I'd missed. A moment later, I saw the cause for his excitement. I dropped the leash a few feet away from the steps to our building, letting Scruffy pounce on my sister, who was seated on the steps.

She gagged as Scruffy planted a big sloppy kiss just to the side of her mouth.

I tugged him back, then offered her a hand while she stood.

"His breath stinks," Annie mumbled, making her way into the building.

I was about to confess that he may have gotten into the trash earlier, but she'd already started talking about how bad she had to pee. I unlocked my apartment door to let her enter.

While my sister was in the bathroom, I kicked off my shoes, unleashed Scruffy, and braced myself for whatever bad news she had to share. Surely she hadn't just dropped by for a friendly visit.

When she emerged, I offered her a drink. She asked for hot water, then retrieved a Ziplock filled with teabags from her purse.

"Do I want to know?" I asked.

"Peppermint helps with the nausea," she said.

I blew out a sigh, and made her tea, grabbing a Summer Shandy for myself.

I was about to make small talk, when Annie jumped right into it.

"What were you doing with Giada a couple weeks back? And why did I have to hear about it from Matteo instead of you?"

I frowned. That was not what I expected we'd be discussing. "What exactly did he tell you?"

"He said you ran off with his sister. He said you could've gotten yourself killed."

"First of all, I didn't run off with Giada. And second of all, I'm fine."

"I thought you were over her," Annie said.

"I am. It wasn't like that. I was just doing a favor for an old friend."

"So you didn't sleep with her?"

"No!"

Annie narrowed her eyes at me. "Is there any chance you'll ever get back together with her?"

I considered the question for a full three seconds before answering truthfully. "No."

Annie sighed, then focused on her tea.

"I guess this means you spoke with Matteo?"

My sister nodded.

"Did you share any other news with him?"

She scowled. "I'm not telling him that over the phone."

"But you're going to?" I inferred.

Annie hesitated, then nodded. "Unless something changes, yes."

Relief flooded me. Thanks to Angelo's trip to Italy and some random new romantic relationship he was now pursuing, I'd bought myself more time on responding to his invitation into "the family." But he wouldn't wait for forever, and at least now I could decide based on what was best for me, and not what was required to keep my sister and her baby safe.

Unless…

"Wait, your decision doesn't have anything to do with me and Giada leaving town, right?"

"No. I just…well, I don't know. Matteo has called a few times from Italy, just to talk or whatever. And he really does seem like a good person. A nice guy. I know you don't like him, but—"

"I have nothing against Matteo."

Annie looked skeptical, but she continued. "I'm not going to like marry the guy or anything, but I think he'll be a decent co-parent. And if he doesn't want to be involved, well, the money would still be nice."

I nodded. "I think you're making the right decision, Annie."

We made small talk for a few minutes, and then I asked the other big question. "When are you going to tell mom and dad?"

She groaned and excused herself to go to the bathroom again in lieu of answering.

⁂

Giada

We were already on the way to the hospital when I came to. I was stretched out along the back seat—buckled in, but leaning against Alessio, and Lincoln was driving. I still felt weird, but not weird enough to justify a trip to the hospital. Lincoln said I made it one step away from the island before I'd toppled like a domino. Alessio credited the fact that my glass fell from my hand a moment before I fainted as the reason I didn't suffer injury during the fall. The second he saw the glass go, he knew something was off and apparently lunged forward, grabbing me before my head hit the ground.

Still, by the time we'd finished check in at the hospital and waited for my name to be called, I felt completely normal. If anything, I just needed a nap. Not a medical exam, and certainly not a hospital bill.

"This is ridiculous," I mumbled as a nurse led us to the room, Alessio and Lincoln flanking me on both sides. "I don't need to be here. I'm just tired."

Lincoln looked like he wanted to say something, but Alessio shook his head. They helped me onto the patient bed as the nurse eyed them warily.

"Okay, well you two don't need to be here. Pretty sure I can handle just sitting here all by myself."

Alessio nodded to his cousin. "Go to the waiting room."

We both watched Lincoln skulk off, then Alessio turned to me. "Better?"

"You could go with him. Do you think I'm going to run away or something?"

He dropped into a chair beside the bed and flipped open a magazine he'd snagged from the waiting room. "Pretend I'm not here."

I rolled my eyes, but smiled reassuringly at the nurse. Her cheeks had flushed and she looked exceedingly tense. She handed me a blue and white floral gown and promised to give me a few minutes to change. She stepped out, but Alessio remained in the room but stood and turned to face the wall. I shifted towards the opposite wall, removing my shirt and bra and then wrapping the robe around me. I loosely tied it shut in the front then slid off the bed to yank off my jeans. I pressed my hand against the paper sheet covering the bed, suddenly dizzy.

"Here," Alessio said, flying to my side and steadying me with his arm. Had I felt better, I would've snapped at him for peeking, but as it was, I appreciated the help balancing. I left my panties on, and once my jeans were to my ankles, Alessio instructed me to climb back on the bed. I did, and he then slid off my shoes and jeans.

The nurse returned right as Alessio folded my jeans and set them on the chair over my bra.

"So tell me what brought you into the Emergency Room today," the nurse said, reaching into a drawer for a blood pressure cuff.

"I fainted. I feel better now."

"Any chest pains or dizziness before?"

I shook my head. Alessio loudly slapped the magazine back onto his lap.

"She's been complaining about dizziness for weeks now," he said.

"Only off and on," I said.

"She's barely eating and she's always tired."

The nurse made some notes on her clipboard then wrapped the pressure cuff around my arm. We were all silent while she inflated the cuff and watched the dial move. "A little low, but nothing too worrisome. Have you eaten today?"

The mere mention of food made my stomach roll. "I had some toast this morning. I probably fainted because I missed lunch. Pretty sure it's not a major medical problem. Certainly nothing constituting an emergency," I said, glaring at Alessio and overemphasizing the last word.

"Has your appetite changed lately?"

I shrugged. I used to love food. I loved thinking about it, smelling it, seeing it, and most of all, consuming it. Now, all of those things made me pretty miserable. "I'm always hungry, but nothing sounds good," I finally said.

The nurse frowned. "Any chance you could be pregnant?"

Alessio's head swiveled to face us so quickly I almost laughed.

"No," I replied bitterly. I should've been pregnant. Without all the shit accompanying Sal's untimely demise, we should've been on our third month of trying. God, and if we couldn't even manage to find time to make the baby, how were we ever going to do all the fun new parent stuff I was envisioning? My life was a disaster.

The nurse flipped through my chart. "You didn't list any medications. You're not on any birth control?"

"No." I didn't dare make eye contact with Alessio as I said that. I figured Luca had told him the minute we decided I'd go off my shot, but I sure didn't need any confirmation.

"So…you're using condoms or…?" the nurse asked, her tone what I'd expect from someone lecturing a teen about birth control.

"Abstinence," I replied.

She cast a glance at Alessio as though expecting him to contradict me, and I realized her assumption.

"My husband has been out of the country for over a month," I said.

The nurse frowned and gestured to Alessio. "Oh. So he is a… relative?"

"No," I replied, at the same time Alessio said the opposite.

I rolled my eyes again.

"Alright, well, sit tight. I'm going to let the doctor know you're ready to see him." She left the room, pulling the door shut behind her.

We spent the next several minutes in silence, me staring at the ceiling, trying to decipher the random patterns in the plaster, and Alessio flipping through the women's gossip magazine. Then his phone rang.

"I gotta take this. You mind?" he asked.

"Nope." I assumed he intended to leave the room, which frankly I would've appreciated, but instead he just began chatting away in Italian in the room.

I flipped onto my side facing the opposite wall and groaned.

Alessio was still on the phone when the door opened again. This time it was a man, probably in his late forties, wearing a white coat. He smiled confidently as he sauntered in, leaving the door cracked behind him.

"Good afternoon. I'm Doctor Saunders. Can you confirm your name and date of birth for me?"

I did, right as Alessio disconnected his call.

Dr. Saunders turned immediately to him. "Sir, I need to ask you to head to the waiting room while I do the exam. Our hospital confidentiality policies require us to perform the exam in private."

"I'm not leaving you alone with her," he replied, as if it wasn't horribly offensive to both me and the doctor.

"Jesus Christ, Alessio. I'm not a child," I replied.

Dr. Saunders simply plastered a tight grin on his face. "I understand your concern for your…friend, and my nurse is actually going to join us in just a moment. She will remain in the room with us the entire time. If you'd like her to show you to the waiting room first though…" he began.

Alessio rolled his eyes and stormed out.

To my surprise, the nurse didn't join us right away. Instead, the doctor shut the door and sat on the round stool, rolling it closer.

"Nurse Anna will be right in, but I wanted to ask you some questions in private. Do you have any reason to fear for your safety?"

I shook my head.

"Has anyone hurt you, physically or mentally?"

"No."

"Is your visit today the result of an injury inflicted on you by another person, whether by accident or on purpose?"

"No. I just don't feel well."

"Do you feel that you are able to leave here alone and on your own free will?"

I laughed in lieu of answering honestly. I wasn't sure what it said about my life that everywhere I went people assumed I was a sex trafficking victim or something. "The two guys that brought me here today are friends. They both work for my husband, and he's in Italy now. He felt terrible for leaving me alone so long so he made them promise to take good care of me. That's all they're trying to do. They're worried something is wrong, and they know if something happens to me, my husband will blame them."

"I hear what you are saying, and I respect your choice. But I also want you to understand that *you* are my patient today. My job is to take care of you, no matter what the root cause of the problem may be. We can detain them, transfer you to a different hospital, and put you in contact with a shelter if you need those services."

"I don't," I repeated, my annoyance starting to rise. "I'm not here because someone hurt me. Look at me—do you see any bruises? Do you see anything in my medical record suggesting I have frequent injuries? I fainted, that's it."

The doctor didn't look away from my face or check my record. "Your symptoms are consistent with the sort of unspecified malaise we might see from someone who is experiencing abuse. Abuse isn't always physical, but it does leave its mark on your body regardless. I just want you to know we are here to help, not to judge. I can send in a social worker if you like. Her name is Krissie. I'll offer again to have her come see you at the end of your visit today, just in case you change your mind."

He stood without awaiting my response, then nodded and opened the door. Anna, the same nurse from earlier, joined us. The doctor asked me all the same questions she had, plus a bunch more. He did a full exam, from head to toe. He didn't comment on the fact that I hadn't stripped completely naked, and aside from pressing on my abdomen, including my lower belly, he hadn't even ventured near that whole region. He narrated everything he was doing and finding as he went, and the nurse was typing notes from across the room. That all took less than ten minutes, and then he stood, stripped off his gloves and helped himself to some hand sanitizer.

"I'd like to run your bloodwork and see if that gives us any answers," he said, returning to the stool beside me. "Everything on your physical exam appeared normal. Your labs will tell us if there's something going on with your thyroid or perhaps something like anemia that could explain the changes in your appetite and energy levels and the dizziness. Your symptoms are also consistent with stress, anxiety, or depression, though. Have you experienced any unusual stress lately?"

"Yes," I said, sounding more annoyed than I intended. "My husband is out of the country, and I'm worried about him, and lonely, and everything has been really tense. I don't like when we're apart."

I'd expected some follow up questions on that, but instead the doctor just smiled and stood. "Anna here will handle your blood draw, and I'll come back in to talk with you when the results are in."

I asked how long that might take, and he said they'd have the labs hurry but it could be an hour. I groaned. My entire day was now wasted, not that I'd had any big plans.

"Your friends are welcome to come back in while you wait," the doctor offered.

I actually would've preferred to be alone, but I figured asking for them would help convince him they weren't sex traffickers. "Yes, that would be great. Could you let them know?"

He nodded and left. I turned away while the nurse did the blood draw, and Alessio and Lincoln both returned before she was done.

"Do you want anything to eat or drink?" Alessio offered. "I can send Lincoln wherever if something sounds good."

Lincoln scowled, but the offer actually made me smile.

"I'd love some coffee."

Alessio's eyebrow shot up, reminding me that I hadn't been that great about drinking coffee lately. It was one of the few things that still sounded good, but then once it was in the vicinity, the smell gave me a headache.

"Fine. Maybe some ginger ale?"

"There's a cafeteria if you follow the signs," the nurse said.

"Get her a sandwich or something too," Alessio instructed.

"A bagel, if they have it," I said, surprised that something actually sounded good.

The nurse and Lincoln both left and Alessio handed me the TV remote. We watched trashy daytime shows until Lincoln returned, and then I found I actually managed to eat the bagel. After an eternity, the doctor returned.

I'd dozed off at some point, and Lincoln had left, so it was just Alessio and I in the room. I was exhausted, my head throbbed, and I had no energy left for anything by that point.

The doctor said my labs were back and asked Alessio to give us some privacy, I shook my head. He'd want to know what the doctor said so he could report back to Luca anyway, and I didn't trust myself to remember any details with how foggy my brain felt at the moment.

"Are you sure?" the doctor repeated, positioning his back to Alessio and locking his eyes on me like he was trying to send some telepathic message.

"Yep. Whatever it is, you can say it in front of him."

The doctor sat on the stool and pulled out his clipboard. "Well, your thyroid looks completely normal, so that's good. Your iron was a bit low, so we'd like you to start a supplement and that should help with your energy levels. You can discuss that with your primary care physician, though." He paused and inhaled deeply. "Your labs also revealed hCG in your blood."

I frowned, wishing he'd just spill it already. "So does that mean I'm dying?" I joked.

"No, it means you're pregnant."

I felt heat rush to my face, but I shook my head. "Umm, no."

Dr. Saunders nodded. "The blood test is very clear. We didn't do quantitative levels, and we can't say how far along you are based on the bloodwork alone, but you're definitely pregnant. Based on the dates of your last period you must be about four or five weeks along. And I couldn't feel the top of your uterus on the physical exam I did, so that lines up with those dates."

"So you're saying I got pregnant five weeks ago?"

"No." The doctor shook his head. "We date pregnancies to your last menstrual cycle, not conception."

"I don't understand. When would you think the baby was actually conceived?"

He shrugged. "We'd need an ultrasound to pinpoint it exactly, but roughly two or three weeks ago."

Alessio rose to his feet and dropped his head, clearly avoiding any possible eye contact with me.

Nausea washed over me. He must think I'd cheated on Luca. *Oh God.*

"I'll be in the waiting room," Alessio mumbled, brushing past the doctor.

Shit, shit, shit. "Alessio, I didn't…" I began, but he was already gone. He tugged the door shut behind him.

"Shit," I repeated, turning back to the doctor.

"I can give you a moment if you need it. We, um, also have a counselor on staff here if you'd like to talk with someone about your options if this pregnancy was unplanned."

I rolled my eyes. "Did you not hear the part about my husband being out of town the last month? This isn't an unplanned pregnancy. It's nonexistent. It's impossible."

He cast an uneasy gaze at the nurse.

She stepped forward with my chart. "Alright, these are the dates you gave me for your last period. Is that all correct?"

I listened as she went over it all, then reached for my phone to double check on the calendar. I'd only recently begun tracking it, because one of the best perks of the birth control shot had been the absence of any period. Even since going off of the shot, though, I'd only had spotty, light cycles, but they were way too frequent.

"Yes," I replied, my voice hoarse.

"So, when we date a pregnancy, we go by the first day of your last period. According to that, you'd be four and a half weeks along now. And that's pretty much when we'd expect to see you start feeling some of those early symptoms like fatigue and nausea. Ovulation happens in the midway point of your cycle, so that means conception did not actually happen until about a week or two after your period ended."

I appreciated the mini biology lesson, but my head was swimming.

"We paged OB and ultrasound, so someone will come by and do an internal exam shortly and then you can get a more accurate due date based on the ultrasound," the doctor said.

My phone buzzed with an incoming call. I sensed without looking that it would be Luca, and of course, I was right. I wondered how much Alessio had already told him. I pressed my fingers into my temples and tried to focus on my breath.

"Fuck," I said.

"We'll give you a minute," the doctor said uncomfortably. I watched as he and the nurse started to leave, then realized I needed to talk to Alessio. I had to convince him.

"Wait, can you get Alessio, um, the guy who was with me?"

The nurse's nod was a tad too perky.

For the next several minutes, I alternated between nearly hyperventilating and nearly puking. When I finally pulled it together and gazed up, I saw Alessio standing in the corner by the door. His arms were crossed in front of his chest and the expression on his face could only be described as disappointed.

"You didn't even let me explain," I said.

"You don't owe me any explanation," he replied. "But if you're wanting me to keep something from him, you know I can't. My loyalties are with Luca. You know that."

"Mine are too," I shot back, already starting to cry. "I didn't cheat on Luca. I swear. I haven't been with anyone else the entire time he's been gone. I haven't been with another man the entire time we've been married. I would never do that!"

Alessio's expression softened, and his arms dropped down to his sides as he pressed away from the wall. "I want to believe you Giada, but how do you explain getting pregnant? Do you have some immaculate conception theory?"

My phone buzzed again, reminding me of the voicemail from Luca that I still hadn't played. "You already told him?" I asked. An image flashed in my mind of my poor Luca hearing I was sleeping around while he was thousands of miles away working nonstop. It would kill him. My love meant everything to him.

I started to sob so hard I could barely catch my breath.

"Giada, come on," he urged, stepping closer and rubbing his palm on my back. "You have to calm down."

"It will break his heart if he thinks…" I began, barely able to even formulate words between the heaving sobs.

"Shh, it'll be okay."

"I did not cheat on Luca," I repeated. "I would rather die than hurt him."

Alessio dropped onto the bed beside me and pulled me into his arms. He clasped his hands around me and gradually tightened the embrace until I could barely breathe, let alone continue bawling. "Shh," he whispered. "Just breathe."

His grip loosened slightly as I calmed down.

"I can't explain any of it," I said, "But I did not cheat on Luca."

"Okay, I believe you."

I pulled back, needing to see his face to tell if he actually believed me or was just saying that to calm me down. He looked sincere.

"I know you love him," Alessio said, still holding me. "I just don't understand. Why would the labs—"

"I don't know." I paused. "Luca just called me. Does he know…?"

"No. I told him you weren't feeling well. I said you fainted, and we brought you here but that you were fine. I asked him to fly home tomorrow."

"Thank you," I breathed, relaxing against his firm chest. Alessio was the closest thing I had to Luca, and therefore my best shot at comfort. But knowing Luca would be home soon was huge. Whatever was going on, Luca and I would figure it out together.

"I didn't tell him about the pregnancy," he continued, smoothing his hand down the back of my hair.

That was a relief. Obviously, I wasn't going to keep anything from Luca, but nothing good could come of him knowing this information while he was stuck in Italy, especially when I didn't have any answers for him.

"God, he's going to kill me," I murmured.

"Uh, no, I'm the one he'll kill. And he'll make it hurt, too," Alessio replied.

Just as we went to separate, a throat cleared behind us. We jumped apart as if we'd been caught in some compromising position, then turned to see Nurse Anna.

"I apologize for interrupting, but Dr. Saunders wanted me to let you know that the OB resident on call is super backed up today. We can go ahead and discharge you and you can get in with your regular doctor hopefully on Monday for an ultrasound. Or, you're welcome to wait, but it might be a few hours."

Alessio and I both cringed at the thought of a lengthy wait.

"You can discharge me," I said.

The nurse smiled and ducked out.

"Are you okay now?" Alessio asked, dipping his head to meet my level.

I nodded.

"Alright. I need to make another call, but I'll be right back." He patted my hand. "We'll figure it out, alright?"

I was only alone a moment before the nurse returned, the doctor by her side. He plopped back onto his stool then scooted up closer to my head. "There's a few different options for paternity tests if you have any questions about who the father might be."

"I don't."

Dr. Saunders and Nurse Anna exchanged a pointed stare.

"I apologize, but I did overhear the tail end of your conversation with your, uh, friend," she said.

There wasn't a doubt in my mind what she thought had happened when I heard the way she pronounced the word 'friend.' "He was just comforting me," I said. "Just because a man hugs a woman doesn't mean they're having an affair."

She nodded but clearly wasn't convinced. "I just wanted to make sure you understood that if you are at all concerned about your safety, there are resources to help you."

"I'm not."

"Ms. Marino," the doctor said, lowering his voice and locking his eyes on mine. "Do you have any reason to believe your husband will harm you if he learns you are pregnant?"

"No," I said. "He really wanted a baby. We both did. Just not one magically conceived while he was out of the country."

"Do you have any reason to believe he will hurt your friend?"

I rolled my eyes at the nurse's consistent emphasis on the word 'friend.' "No, Alessio and Luca are best friends. No one is going to hurt anyone."

"Last question," the doctor promised. "Have you felt pressured to engage in any sexual behavior that you didn't want?"

"No. Can I get dressed now?"

The doctor snapped out of his somber mood, smiled, and stood. "Anna will get your discharge papers to you. Make sure you follow up with your regular doctor and get that ultrasound scheduled, and take it easy until the dizzy spells pass."

"Thanks," I mumbled.

As the nurse left, Alessio came back in. "Okay?" he asked.

I considered telling him to leave while I changed, but instead I just tugged the curtain between us. "Just peachy," I replied, adding, "The nurse thinks we are having an affair."

"We? Wait, like I'm involved now?"

I gritted my teeth at his obtuseness. "So it's okay for her to think I'm sleeping around but you're offended that she thinks you had something to do with it?"

"Well, yeah. I didn't do anything."

I tugged my shirt down over my still unbuttoned pants before yanking the curtain open. "Neither did I. Remember?" I glanced down at my phone. "I need to make an appointment with my regular doctor before they close."

"Alright. Lincoln is going to pull the car around to the front."

CHAPTER 22

Luca

I'd headed straight to the airport when I heard Giada had fainted, but by the time I actually got on a flight, I realized it would be Sunday afternoon before I made it to my wife. I'd expected to see Giada in the car with Alessio when he picked me up, so I tried to mask my disappointment when he was alone. He asked about my flight then reiterated his offer to fly to Italy and finish any tasks I hadn't finished.

Truth be told, I wasn't even completely sure what all still needed to be done. Yeah, I needed to figure out a solution to the Cosimo problem, but I had zero good ideas, so I supposed there wasn't a pressing need for me to rush back.

Since the moment I learned Giada was sick, I couldn't concentrate on anything except her. And the fact that she wasn't in the car told me I was right to be worried about her.

"How mad is she?" I asked, not realizing it was a non-sequitur until my friend turned to me with confusion.

"Giada?"

"Yes. She's angry at me for leaving her for so long, right?"

Alessio frowned. "Maybe, but right now, she's asleep. I thought you'd prefer she rest."

Another wave of guilt washed over me. "But you said she was okay."

He cast a sideways glance at me. "She'll be fine."

"So what all did the doctors say? I was already on the plane when she called me back."

He hesitated. "Giada could explain it all better. I'll let her tell you."

"I'm asking you," I said, my curiosity growing the more he protested.

"It's not my business. There's like…HIPAA and all that."

My entire body tensed. It had to be terrible if he wasn't saying it. "Jesus, is it cancer?"

Alessio turned to me. "No! She will be fine. I just think you should wait thirty fucking minutes and let her tell you herself."

"So help me God, if you don't tell me right away…" I began.

"She's pregnant, Luca." He turned to me as he spoke, then quickly returned his focus to the road.

I was actually speechless. I'd been so worried, but in reality, it was something good. Great, really. I mean, the timing wasn't exactly ideal, but I wasn't about to complain about that. "Are you serious?" I asked.

"Yep. They did bloodwork at the hospital. She has an appointment with her regular doc tomorrow. I guess they'll do an ultrasound or something?"

I thumped my fist on the dash, already thinking we should celebrate. Well, maybe not so much Alessio and me, as Giada and me. "I wish one of you had told me this sooner. I spent the entire flight worrying when I could have been excited."

He didn't say anything, and then it hit me. Alessio wasn't happy. He hadn't even smiled the slightest bit when he told me.

"What aren't you telling me?" I asked. "What's wrong? Is it Giada? Or the baby?"

The crease between his brows grew. "The doctor said she's like five weeks along."

I did the math in my head and that made sense. I'd left a little over a month prior. "Okay, so?"

He stared pointedly at the next light.

"What?"

Alessio sighed. "The way they date a pregnancy is weird. They said she got pregnant like three weeks ago. At most."

I must have looked confused, because he continued.

"Look it up online or something. They say the pregnancy is forty weeks, but they start that on the first day of the girl's period. So by the time the actual baby-making activities take place, she's already what they count as two weeks pregnant. By the time you can take a test, the first month is already done."

I rubbed my forehead, trying to get past the fact that my best friend and I were actually discussing the female menstrual cycle. But then it hit me.

"You're saying my wife got pregnant when I was in Italy," I said, my voice falling flat.

His silence spoke volumes.

I turned to the window. That explained why she hadn't told me. But it still didn't make any sense. Sure, the last month had been hard, but we'd been on good terms when I left. And besides, Giada wasn't like that. She wouldn't cheat on me no matter how hard life got.

Well, except she had run off with her ex-boyfriend recently.

"No," Alessio finally said, interrupting my thoughts. "That's what the doctors are saying, not me. Giada says she's not pregnant, but if she is, it's yours."

"And what do you think?"

"I mean, I'm no doctor, but I've researched the shit out of it since we left the hospital, and all of her symptoms match with pregnancy."

"Do you think she was… with someone else?"

He waited till the next light to answer, staring straight at me as he spoke. "No. I really don't." He turned back to the road as the light changed, but he kept talking. "She was genuinely shocked and upset at the hospital. And she's not that good of a liar. Plus, either Linc or I have been with her almost every minute of every day since you left."

I rubbed my forehead. "Giada would not cheat on me. Not now, anyway. Maybe a decade ago."

Alessio chuckled and then we were both silent until we'd nearly reached the house. "She's been pretty upset, and she's not feeling great. She's tired all the time and nauseous, and she gets these dizzy spells."

"Are you telling me to be nice to her?"

He shrugged. "You'll get answers at the doctor tomorrow."

The house was quiet when we got home. Linc was sprawled out on the couch, watching a basketball game with the volume painfully low, but Alessio must have sent him some telepathic signal because he instantly flipped off the tv and stood.

"I'll get out of your way," he said. "Good to see you, Luca."

Alessio shrugged again, then patted me on the back. "I'm heading out, too. Gotta check on the clubs."

I thanked them and then headed to the bedroom. I tried the knob, half expecting her to have locked me out. Historically, she hadn't been a fan of sleeping in an unlocked room when any of my guys were in the house. She must have been really tired. Or really trusting.

I paused, letting my eyes adjust to the darkness of the room, then crept over to the bed. I crouched beside her and gently stroked the side of her head.

She inhaled sharply, then shifted. Her eyes fluttered before opening fully. "Luca?"

"Si, amore."

"Oh, thank God," she murmured. "I missed you so much."

"I missed you more," I replied. I tugged off my shoes and crawled onto the bed beside her.

"I'm so glad you're back," she said, snuggling against me.

"I shouldn't have left you for so long."

She was silent for a moment, then bolted upright as though she'd just remembered. "Oh! Did Alessio already tell you?"

I hesitated. "He told me about the hospital. And he said you're still tired and you don't eat enough."

"I mean the other part."

"He did. But only because I made him." I paused. "I wish you'd told me when you left your message. I listened to it right before my flight took off. I sure would've liked something to be excited about on the plane instead of spending ten hours worrying you were sick."

"I'm sorry," she said. "I thought it might stress you out because of…well, did he tell you all of it?"

I took my time answering, not wanting to make any missteps. "Giada, if you're pregnant, it's our baby. You don't have to convince me of that."

"I would never cheat on you."

"I know that."

"The doctors seemed to think I was crazy. Or that I was raped."

My body stiffened. "Jesus! You weren't, right?"

"No! No. Sorry. Everyone was very nice to me in your absence."

"But not too nice," I added, teasing.

She sighed. "I really don't know how to explain it, though. At first, I was positive they were wrong, that I wasn't pregnant. But after everything I've read about it, well, I feel pregnant. My boobs hurt, and I'm nauseous and so, so tired. I don't understand how women do this multiple times when they feel this awful so early."

"I wish I could make you feel better."

She didn't answer, so I nudged her out of bed.

"Come on, you need to eat."

Giada groaned. "Isn't it bedtime?"

"It's six o'clock."

"Oh."

Giada

I slept so well with Luca back in bed beside me. He'd missed a full night's sleep already, so we both had gone to bed around eight o'clock, and I'd somehow managed to sleep till morning, waking only to pee. Luca woke before me, apparently tackling multiple hours of work before I eventually trudged out of bed to get ready for the appointment.

The waiting room at the OBGYN's office was packed, but a nurse called my name a few minutes after my appointment time. The nurse weighed me and checked my blood pressure, then asked me to leave a urine sample before the ultrasound. I clutched Luca's hand tightly as we followed her down the hallway. I changed into a thin gown, then the ultrasound tech came into the room.

She glanced down at the chart. "Usually we wait until closer to six weeks to do the first ultrasound, so I don't want you to get too excited. This early on, we probably won't see a heartbeat, but that's no reason for concern. I might be able to point out the yolk sac, and if we are very lucky, maybe the embryo."

I laid back on the exam table. Luca was already seated in a chair by my head, and he reached for my hand, bringing it to his lips.

His touch relaxed me instantly, even as the tech rolled a condom up some wand that resembled the one I used to curl my hair.

"At this stage, we do the ultrasound internally to get a better picture, and you can follow along up here." She tapped an oversized computer monitor angled towards us.

I tensed slightly as the wand pressed against me, but I focused my attention on the screen. A blurry grey and white picture appeared, resembling a black hole. As I felt the wand tilt, the picture changed. Now there was what appeared to be a short, stumpy creature inside the black hole.

"Oh my God," I said. "Is that…"

I turned to Luca, who was staring at the screen, his jaw dropped, and his eyes wide open.

The tech chuckled, turning away from the screen. "How confident were you in that five-week pregnant dating?"

"Not at all confident," Luca answered for us both.

"Is everything okay?"

She withdrew the wand and reached for some gel. "Everything is fine, but that is not a five-week embryo. I'll need to do some measurements, but I'm guessing you're closer to nine or ten weeks pregnant."

Luca laughed out loud, then dropped his head to mine. He pressed a soft kiss on my lips then simply rest his forehead against mine.

The tech asked me to lift my shirt, and she pressed a different device against my stomach. "At this point in pregnancy, we can get decent pictures this way," she said. A similar image as before appeared on the screen. She turned a dial and suddenly, the room filled with a staticky galloping sound.

"Is that our baby's heartbeat?" Luca asked, his face filled with awe.

"Yep, sure is. Sounds strong and healthy."

I clasped my hand over my mouth. It was all too unreal. "I don't even understand how this is possible. I had my period like a month ago. It was really short, but…"

The tech shrugged. "It's not uncommon for women to have some bleeding during pregnancy. After we do some measurements on the fetus, I'll check out everything else. Sometimes we see a subchorionic hematoma that usually resembles a darker area on the scan. Those are usually harmless and resolve on their own, but can cause some bleeding."

The tech went on to point out the head, arms, and legs, then said, "Okay, get one last look at your baby, and then I need to move on to the boring parts."

As she moved the wand away from the baby, I turned to Luca. His gaze was locked on me, and he was smiling. He bent to press a featherlight kiss to my forehead while the tech mumbled something about my cervix and the placenta. I kept my eyes on Luca until the tech gasped. I peered up at the screen and smiled, seeing the picture of the baby back on display.

"Did you say you could print some pictures for us to take?" I asked, hoping she hadn't forgotten.

"I, uh, yes," the tech said, frowning at her screen. She sighed loudly, then wiped off the wand and set it aside. "If you could wait here for just a moment, I'm going to grab the doctor. No need to worry, everything is fine, but I'd like her to look at the images while we're here."

She handed me a wad of paper towels to wipe the gel off my belly.

"Is something wrong?" Luca asked, his smile gone.

"No," the tech made eye contact and shook her head. "I don't see anything concerning. But I'm newer here and just have a question about something for the doctor. We'll be right back."

Luca swallowed audibly as she left, then squeezed my hand.

Luca

*A*fter the appointment, I'd planned to drop Giada back at the house then head to the club to check on everything since I'd been gone for so long. But by the time we finally left the doctor, I wanted nothing more than to celebrate with my wife.

"Figure out what sounds good," I told her, pulling her into a sideways hug. "I'm calling Alessio to let him know he's on his own for the day."

"I get you for a whole day?" she asked, mocking me with her eyes.

"We've got a month to make up for," I reminded her, dialing Alessio.

"Pronto," he answered promptly.

"Ciao. Listen, I'm going to spend the rest of the day with my girl. Can you keep tabs on everything again?" I braced myself for some hint of annoyance on his part since, after all, he had been essentially doing all of my work and his own for a full month now. But there was nothing.

"Yeah, of course. So, um, is everything okay?"

I realized I was grinning like a big dope, but I couldn't help it. "Yeah man, it is good. Very good."

Giada swatted my stomach, leaning in. "He deserves more than that. Give me the phone."

"You're on speaker," I told him, holding it towards her.

"We're perfectly healthy," she said. "And due in March."

"March?" he repeated.

"Turns out she's a little over two months pregnant, not one," I explained.

"Ahh, tanti auguri!" he said. "Congratulations."

"Thank you," Giada and I said in unison.

"Linc is here. Can I tell him?" Alessio asked.

I glanced at Giada, and she nodded. "Sure, but no one else."

"Got it. Ciao," he said.

I clicked to disconnect the call. "So what's for lunch?" I asked her.

She made a face. "Honestly, the only thing that sounds good now is…lemonade."

I considered that, then looked around. "There's a bagel shop about a block away. I bet they have lemonade, and we could also get you a bagel, in case that sounds good later."

She eyed me warily. "Alessio told you I've been craving bagels, didn't he?"

"He tells me everything."

"Clearly."

I turned to the bag of pregnancy information and free samples the doctor had given us. "I can't believe we nearly missed an entire trimester."

Giada nodded and nudged her bagel across the table. She'd taken a couple of bites, but mostly she'd just sipped her drink.

"Maybe it's best that you didn't know until now. You might have felt worse sooner."

She shrugged. "Looking back, I felt pretty icky since before you left. I just figured it was stress."

I nodded, then opened my phone calendar.

"Are you seriously working now?"

"No, I'm trying to figure out what we were doing nine or ten weeks ago," I said.

Giada giggled. "Well, I can think of one thing we apparently did."

"Clearly. But that was right after…" I paused still not able to casually refer to my papà's passing. "And there weren't as many times that you and I…" my voice trailed off again.

"Please tell me you don't track when we have sex in your calendar."

"No, but it's pretty memorable when we have a solid week where we don't, and I distinctly remember the week leading up to my meeting with Mr. Gambino was a nasty dry spell," I said, still scrolling through the vague references to events on my calendar and trying to piece together the past. Suddenly, I saw it.

I gazed up at Giada, smirking. "You, tesoro, got knocked up in the church bathroom."

The way her face instantly flushed confirmed my suspicions.

We both laughed. I finished my sandwich and tried to get Giada to take a couple more bites of her bagel, but she shook her head. She reached across the table for my hand, kissed it, then rest her head on it.

I waited a moment for her to pop back up, but she didn't. "Baby? You okay?"

She groaned and lifted her head slowly. "I'm sorry. I just want to lay down."

I bit back a smile and stood. I helped Giada to her feet. "Come on. I'll take you home. We will celebrate after your nap."

"I love you," she said, squeezing me tightly.

"I love you too, and I am so, so sorry."

"For what?" she asked, pulling back suddenly. "You said you believed me!"

"I did. I'm apologizing for leaving the country when you were pregnant. I never would've gone if I'd known."

"Do you really want to wait until we get to Italy to tell your parents the news?"

"Yes. Especially with what we learned today. A lot of couples wait until after the first trimester to tell people, so they won't be offended. Besides, I want to see their faces when we tell them."

CHAPTER 23

Giada

I rolled over in bed, reaching for Luca before I even opened my eyes. Instead of landing on his firm, warm, torso, my palm found a cold, fluffy pillow. I sighed and peered around the room. Definitely no Luca.

I snuggled deeper into the covers regardless, relishing the cozy warmth of the bed. Judging from how rested I felt, I'd probably slept hours later than my husband. I couldn't blame him for leaving me alone in the bed now, especially not after last night.

My skin tingled at the memory of all the less restful ways Luca and I had entertained ourselves over the last twelve hours. Despite having zero sex drive whatsoever since Luca had left town, my desire had flared back the moment I'd awakened from my nap the day before.

I'd woken to dozens of bouquets of flowers and a collection of all of the various crackers that didn't make me gag. Luca had massaged my feet while I nibbled on the food, then he'd drawn me a bath to help me relax. He'd even checked the temperature with a thermometer to make sure it was safe for pregnancy, since apparently I could no longer soak in water so hot my skin nearly boiled off. I'd insisted he join me, thinking his body would compensate for the lack of excess heat, and one thing had led to another, and we ended up making love in the tub.

After we dried off, Luca had insisted on giving me a full body massage, swapping out his tongue for his hands when he reached certain parts of my body. Then I'd insisted on returning the favor with my mouth and, after considerable reluctance, Luca relented. I was relieved to find I still enjoyed feeling of his hard flesh between my lips, and I didn't gag in the slightest at the salty taste of his warm release.

The rest of the day had been similarly dreamy, with us enjoying a leisurely stroll through the neighborhood together, a quiet dinner poolside, then another round of lovemaking in bed before snuggling together to watch a movie. If this was what the next six months would be like, I could handle it in a heartbeat.

Voices drifted up from the floor below, so I forced myself to sit up. I nibbled a couple of crackers Luca had left on my nightstand, then started the shower, tying my hair back so it wouldn't get wet. I was just finishing the shower, when I saw Luca, leaning against the vanity, staring at me through the steamy glass door, a contented smile on his face.

"You could join me," I said, my body already tingling in anticipation.

He shook his head slowly. I shut off the water and stepped out, letting my husband wrap a fluffy towel around me. He pressed a quick kiss to my lips, then let me dry myself.

"The guys are downstairs, but you need to eat. I can bring something up, or—"

"I'll come down in a minute," I said, gazing past him to the balcony doors. The sun was shining, and I figured it was already plenty warm outside, but I'd decided that I had more of an appetite when I wasn't indoors where all of the food smells assaulted me with every bite.

Luca nodded, then left.

By the time I'd dressed, my stomach was growling. I knew I had very little time between those first few hunger pangs and full-blown nausea, so I scurried down the stairs. Luca was seated at the kitchen table with Alessio, Thomas, Giovanni, and Roberto.

"We're dying to know, Giada. What did Luca do to warrant this many flowers?" Thomas asked, grinning.

I exchanged a look with my husband, who simply grinned.

"He won't tell us, but obviously there was some major fuck up," he said.

"He abandoned me to hang out with you guys for a month," I replied. I opened the fridge to see what looked good, then slammed it quickly, already grimacing from the smells.

Luca was at my side in an instant.

"I'm fine," I said, feeling anything but. If I puked all over my own kitchen in front of the guys, they'd surely all figure it out real fast. Our backs were to them, though, so hopefully they couldn't see my face.

"What sounds good?" he asked.

I tried to think of anything I'd kept down without effort the past week, but only one thing came to mind. I giggled despite my icky feeling.

"What?" A confused look filled Luca's handsome face.

"I was just remembering one thing I didn't have trouble swallowing yesterday," I said with a seductive eyebrow wiggle.

Unfortunately, Alessio stepped up behind me right then. "Jesus, now I'm going to be sick," he said, shaking his head. "Try oatmeal. And a vanilla protein shake," he suggested.

Luca gazed at me for confirmation, and I nodded, grateful that Alessio had apparently paid attention to what I'd been able to eat lately. I trudged outside to the patio. When Luca brought my food, he sat next to me for only a minute before Alessio came out and called him back in. Still, I stayed by the pool until I finished, proud that I actually downed every single sip of the protein shake and nearly every bite of the oatmeal.

When I entered the kitchen, the guys immediately quieted, but I could tell I'd interrupted a lively discussion. I dropped my dishes on the counter, then turned to Luca for an explanation. His grave expression made my chest fall.

"I'm so sorry, amore, but something's happened, and I need to be back in Italy right away."

I opened my mouth to protest, to remind him that he promised me he'd stay for at least a week and that we'd fly back together, but he continued before I could.

"How fast can you get packed?"

My lips curled into a smile despite the awareness that there was still something bad happening.

"One hour," I said.

Luca

We managed to get three seats on the last flight leaving New York for Rome that evening, which was a miracle. Business class was sold out, which meant we were crammed into the very center of the jet, Alessio and Giada on either side of me. I felt terrible about making my pregnant wife take the red-eye and not even giving her a window to nap against, but less than a half hour after take-off, she'd passed out.

Alessio and I tried to talk business, but on a crowded flight to Italy, we couldn't assume that most people wouldn't understand us like we did in New York. We substituted code for what we could, then took a break. Alessio walked the aisles for several minutes, then I stepped out as he returned. Giada woke with three hours of the flight remaining.

She sipped ginger ale, then asked what was going on with Cosimo.

I shook my head. "Not here."

"That's what you said at the airport," she reminded me.

I said the only thing I could think of to distract her. "Let's talk baby names."

Giada's face lit up. "Girls or boys?"

"Both."

"What are your favorite girls' names?"

I considered the question. I'd never actually given any thought to what I'd name my future daughter, but I knew I wanted an Italian name. "What about Valeria? Or Rina?" I paused, thinking of others. "Matilde, Ariana, Cara, Bellina…"

"That sounds too much like Bellini. I like Valeria. Annabella is Italian though, right?"

I nodded.

"Elisabette or Isabella?"

"Those are beautiful too."

"Name some other Italian ones," she said.

I tried to think in alphabetical order. "Brigida, Carina, Caterina, Claudia, Elena, Emma, Flora…"

"I like Caterina, Elena, or Emma," she said. "What about Sofia?"

"That's pretty. Umm, there's Giuliana, Mariana, Rosina, Violeta…" my voice trailed off as I tried to picture a miniature version of Giada and think of the perfect name.

"Should we switch over to boys now?" Giada asked.

"We've hardly narrowed it down. Shouldn't we pick our two favorites first?"

Giada started a new note on her phone, and we listed all the ones we'd come up with so far. I told her the meanings of the ones I knew, then Alessio chimed in on some.

"All of my favorites end with an A," Giada said. "And none of them sound good together."

"You just need one name, you know," Alessio chimed in. "It's not like you need to name all of your kids right now."

Giada exchanged a glance with me, then gazed at her phone again. "I guess you're right. I'm just overwhelmed."

"We have time," I reminded her, squeezing her hand.

I managed a short nap, but was still far from refreshed by the time we'd landed in Rome. Lodovico picked us up at the airport, then drove us straight to my parents' house. Tomasso had assured me it was the safest place for Giada and me, but I remained skeptical. I still hadn't given her the details of why we needed to get back to Italy so quickly, and I wasn't sure how much to tell her.

The truth was that Tony had convinced me Cosimo was just a dumb kid, posturing and trying to scare me off. He'd insisted Cosimo wouldn't do anything even if I expanded our operations in Rome.

He'd been wrong.

Within a day of my departure from Italy, Cosimo had set a fire in the bathroom at Oro, one of our clubs. I'd been irked that security hadn't stopped him at the door, and even more pissed that they let him in with a lighter. The fire hadn't caused any damage, but I didn't get the impression he meant for it to. What was most concerning was the material he'd used to start the fire —photos of my mom at home. Some of the photos had been taken around town, and others in front of her home.

The message was clear. Cosimo wasn't messing around, and he wouldn't play by the rules.

Tomasso swore not to leave my mom's side until we figured out a solution. The house already had top-notch security, so there really wasn't a safer place for Giada to stay. But still, I hated placing my pregnant wife potentially in danger.

Giada

*L*uca's mom greeted us with an Italian-style breakfast when we arrived. The buffet was loaded with jam-filled croissants, biscotti, and brioche, along with yogurt and a variety of fruits—both dried and fresh, nuts, and granola. I loaded my plate with carbs, suddenly ravenous. When the house-keeper offered each of us a cappuccino, I eagerly accepted mine.

Luca's brow rose, his face questioning.

"I'm allowed one coffee a day," I whispered under my breath.

"I'm just glad it sounds good again," he replied.

We'd planned to settle into the house and relax for a little while before taking an early afternoon nap. I assumed I'd end up sleeping till dinner, since I'd been napping most days even without the time change, but I guessed Luca would struggle to sleep more than an hour or two, even though he'd basically pulled an all-nighter on the flight.

I knew Luca had to meet with the guys about whatever catastrophe had caused us to hop on the first flight out of town, so I figured I'd be on my own unpacking. One of the guys had carried our luggage to a guestroom, and Luca's mom led me up the stairs to the room, inviting me to "freshen up" in a tone that implied I stunk. Still, I'd resigned myself to remaining on my best behavior around Camilla. No matter how rude she was to me, I was going to be kind. She was still struggling with grief, so I would give her grace.

I popped air pods in my ears and began unpacking, shim-mying along to my music while I hung my dresses. I nearly screamed when arms wrapped around my waist. I turned to see Luca grinning.

"What are you so happy about?" I asked, his smile contagious.

"You ate food!"

I nearly snorted at the ridiculousness of him being so happy over something so basic. "I promise I haven't been starving myself."

"Alessio made it seem like you were," he retorted.

I made a mental note to lecture him later about ratting me out. "Well, Alessio didn't offer me a buffet of cornetto and brioche."

Luca's grin widened. "Maybe being in Italy will be good for you. I'd been so convinced travel was risky now, but maybe this is just what you need. All of you," he added, rubbing his palms over my belly.

I swiveled to the side, gazing at my profile in the mirror. I nudged Luca's hands to the side and lifted my shirt, tucking it into the underside of my bra. I had lost weight lately, and even with the croissants and coffee filling my belly, it still appeared a bit flatter than usual. I extended my abdomen as much as I could, then sucked it back in, trying to note the difference.

"I think the belly comes later," Luca said, his warm breath tickling my earlobe.

I tried to picture it, but just couldn't. "I don't understand where everything will go. How am I ever going to fit two babies in here?"

A loud thunk made us both turn to the door. Alessio stood in the entryway to the bedroom, his eyes wide. He gazed from Luca to me to my stomach, still on full display.

I tugged my shirt down quickly, already realizing it was too late.

"What did you just say?" Alessio asked. He waited a fraction of a second, then turned to Luca. "What did she just say?"

Luca turned to me, then motioned Alessio into the room, shutting the door behind him.

"The doctor sort of saw two babies on the ultrasound," I said once the three of us were alone.

"Two babies," he repeated, "Like twins?"

Luca nodded.

Alessio opened his mouth to speak, just as my phone rang loudly. He bent to retrieve it from the floor and handed it to me. "Sorry for dropping your phone. Your brother called twice, and I thought it might be important, but then you said…" his voice trailed off as I clicked to answer Matteo's call.

Once Matteo confirmed that everything was okay, I gave Luca a thumbs up, and he and Alessio headed over to Alessio's room, probably to keep discussing the whole twin thing.

"I know you just arrived and are settling in, but mom is desperate to find out your availability," Matteo said.

I turned back to my suitcase, grabbing a stack of t-shirts to place in a drawer. "I definitely want to see you guys too," I said, tempted to add that I had news to share. I refrained, only because I worried it was too obvious. I didn't want them guessing my news before I could show them the adorable ultrasound photo. "We'll be in Rome for at least two weeks though, so—"

"Good. Mom was asking about next week. Are you and Luca free then?"

"I'd have to confirm he doesn't have some work thing, but I know I don't have any plans. Does she want to do dinner, or what?"

Matteo exhaled so loudly that my whole body tensed.

"What's wrong? What aren't you telling me?"

"Nothing. I mean, nothing bad. It's just, uh, well, Angelo is getting married. In a week," Matteo said.

I shrieked. Nothing could've possibly prepared me for that news.

Luca

The look of shock on Alessio's face reflected everything I'd been feeling every minute since Giada and I learned the news. I sat on the foot of the bed beside him, neither of us saying anything. I covered my face in my hands. When I finally looked back at Alessio, he just shook his head and raised two fingers, as if confirming.

I nodded, and Alessio said, "wow."

We sat in stunned silence a minute longer, and then Alessio reached into his duffel bag. "I got this at the airport gift shop while you were waiting for Giada to finish in the bathroom. I guess now that you have double the naming to figure out, you could use the help."

I opened the paper sack he handed me, smiling as I saw an Italian baby name book. "Grazie," I mumbled, flipping through the pages. "It's not just double the work naming them, though. It's double everything."

Alessio shrugged. "Any chance they're wrong?"

"No." I sighed. "We were so excited to see that the dates made sense for when we'd been together, and the tech showed us all these cool pictures of a baby. Then she said she was going to scan the rest of Giada's uterus and do some measurements or something, so she started moving the little ultrasound wand around, and the baby appeared again. We didn't even realize it was a different baby until she freaked out and went to get the doctor."

"Wow. And they're both girls?"

"We don't know. Apparently they have some blood tests they can do to tell you the gender early on, but they're not as accurate for twins, so we'll find out in another month or two. All we know so far is that they're each in their own sac, which apparently means it's not as high risk."

"Okay, so, on the plus side, it's clear that you don't like seeing Giada feeling sick, so now you guys can get two kids with her only having to go through this all once."

"Yeah," I said, only feeling a microscopic bit better. "But I wasn't exactly ready for one kid, let alone two. This pregnancy is the worst possible timing with all the fallout from my papà and taking over the businesses. And Giada and I nearly broke up like a month ago. I would've liked to get our relationship back on solid ground before we add more complications. And now this shit with Cosimo? I don't know what to do about any of it. I'm not sure I can even take care of my wife, let alone two kids."

Alessio grabbed the book and flipped open to the boy's section. He pointed to his own name.

"I'm not naming a kid after you. Do you know how confusing that would be?"

He chuckled. "Read the meaning. Defender or helper. That's my destiny. So you don't have to worry about it all because I'll be right here, helping and defending, just like I've always done."

"Yeah," I said. "Thank you."

We were quiet for another minute, then Alessio spoke again. "You've always dreaded this day," he reminded me. "Not the baby part, but losing your father. Even in high school, you talked about the burden of being the only son and the pressure of knowing you'd have to someday follow in his footsteps and take on everything, all alone. And when you and Giada first started talking about having kids, you told me you hated knowing you'd be putting the same burden on your own firstborn son."

He wasn't wrong. I still juggled guilt over the life my poor kids would be born into. Yeah, they'd have money and power, but they'd be trapped in the same life of obligation. I hadn't figured a way out, nor did I see a different path for my offspring.

"Luca, think about it. Your kids will never have to shoulder that burden alone. From birth, they'll have each other. They will always be a team."

"We might have two girls."

Alessio shrugged. "So? They'll still have each other. And you know damn well that even if you wait until you have a son and let him inherit the throne, any daughter of Giada is still going to be poking her nose in her brother's business and helping out where she can." He paused. "Your whole life would've been different if you'd had a brother to share it all with."

"At least I have one now," I said.

I leaned in, intending to hug Alessio, but just then, Giada shrieked. Alessio and I both shot out of the room in an instant.

CHAPTER 24

Giada

I couldn't wrap my head around the fact that Angelo was getting married in a week. Nor had I fully processed the hurt of learning that my brother hadn't even bothered to tell me he was seeing someone new. Sure, we hadn't been close for most of our lives, but for over a year now, ever since he literally saved me, I thought we'd been friends.

Luca confirmed our availability for the last-minute wedding, then convinced me to nap. Thanks to jetlag and pregnancy fatigue, I had no trouble falling asleep, but I woke up still pissed off. And hungry.

Luckily, Luca's family had gathered for a big, traditional dinner.

I suppressed a groan as I savored the last bite of my pasta al forno. I glanced up to see Camilla eying me. She had her typical scowl on her face, but her eyes narrowed in a way that told me she was currently judging me for something. Normally, I had little patience for her heavy-handed criticism. But throughout this visit, I'd been reminding myself over and over that the woman just lost her husband. She was entitled, for now, to be a bitch. No matter what she said, I was determined not to engage.

"Giada, dear, how is your old friend Adrian doing?" my mother-in-law asked, smiling sweetly.

I cast Luca an alarmed look, but he quickly turned to his mother, probably glaring at her even though we both knew she'd never back down based on silent cues.

"I don't really know. We don't keep in touch regularly," I replied, successfully keeping my voice calm and level.

Camilla's brows dipped closer together, so I suspected she was trying to frown but couldn't actually produce lines along her forehead thanks to an excess of cosmetic procedures. "But I heard you just took a cross-country trip with him, did you not?"

I dropped my hand onto Luca's thigh and squeezed gently. I could handle this line of questioning. I did not need him jumping to my defense against his grieving widowed mother, no matter how much she deserved to be yelled at.

"Well, sort of. Luca was really worried about everything happening in New York, so he thought I'd be safer out of town. It didn't really make sense for anyone working with him to take time off, so he asked Adrian. We haven't actually spoken since we got back, so..."

Camilla smiled sweetly then dabbed her lips with her napkin. "Hmm. That's not what I thought. I heard you just took off with him and then changed your mind or something and came back. It seemed weird, but I don't pretend to understand how things work with you young couples these days. I saw a documentary on swingers the other day." She paused and gazed around the table, nodding enthusiastically. "Do you know what that is? These couples, they find other couples who I suppose are bored too, and—"

"Mamma, basta!" Luca scolded, his voice firm but his expression soft.

A mischievous grin crossed her lips. "Well, anyway. I wouldn't expect Luca to partake in that sort of arrangement, but these days, everything is a surprise to me. I tell you, though, when Salvatore…" she paused to draw the symbol of the cross on her chest, "When he and I met up with you two that first time you got engaged…or, maybe it was the second? Not the third. Well, regardless, I remember I told Salvatore then and there that it concerned me, things with that other boyfriend of yours. You just couldn't make up your mind then, but he assured me, once you were married—"

"Mamma!" Luca repeated.

I squeezed his thigh so hard I worried my nails would puncture his suit pants.

"I remember that brunch we had too," I said, forcing a smile through gritted teeth. "And I tell you, I'm just so glad I chose the right man to marry the first time. Maybe if I'd ended up with someone else I would've still been unsure, but with Luca by my side, I can't imagine ever having any doubts. You raised a great son." I loosened my hand on his thigh and patted it gently, signaling that I was done. His fingers found mine, and he flashed me a brief appreciative grin.

"Well, that's a relief. How is your Italian coming along?"

Luca flung both of his hands in the air and launched into an animated rant in Italian. His mother replied, also in Italian, and while there were enough gestures for me to follow the gist of the discussion, I reached for my water glass and tuned them out instead.

"Giada, perhaps you would be interested in a walk?"

I looked up to see Tomasso smiling politely at me. I didn't know him well, but Luca seemed to trust him. He worked for Salvatore, but was a part of the inner circle that was treated more like close family than an employee.

A walk did sound pleasant. Even if I weren't currently the topic of a very heated discussion I couldn't understand, I could've enjoyed a break from the stuffy house. I gazed at Luca, who dipped his head in a slight nod to grant permission.

"That would be nice," I said to Tomasso. I stood, which prompted Luca to stand as well. He pressed a kiss against my cheek, and I whispered, "Be nice." He winked, and I left.

The outside air had cooled considerably now that it was dark, but the temperature felt refreshing. Tomasso gestured for me to head to the right, then thrust his hands into his pockets as we walked side by side.

We were both quiet for the first minute, but then Tomasso addressed the tension head on.

"I hope you don't take it personally. She's going through a stressful time, and besides, no one would be good enough for her son in her mind."

"I get it. I just wish Luca would let it drop. I don't need him lecturing her on my account."

"He is very protective of you," Tomasso said.

I nodded in agreement, then noticed an odd smile on Tomasso's face. He tilted his head to gesture several yards behind us, where Giorgio followed. Somehow, I hadn't noticed we had a tail.

"Luca usually has someone accompany me here in Italy. I get lost easily, and as you know, I don't speak Italian." I smiled at the last part so he would know I wasn't bothered.

"I would've thought he'd trust me to ensure you returned safely," he added.

I wrinkled my nose. I could see how that might feel offensive to him. "The more stressed he feels, the more paranoid Luca is about me. Knowing I'm safe is just one less thing for him to worry about. I'm sure Salvatore was that way with Camilla."

Tomasso chuckled. "No."

"I'm sorry for your loss, by the way. You and Salvatore were very close, right?"

"We go back over thirty years. It will be strange not seeing him every day."

"Are you close to Camilla?"

He tensed for a moment, but then nodded. "I live at the house, so we've gotten very close over the years."

"Luca worries about her, too."

"She'll be fine. She was a good, good woman to Salvatore. But she will move on and get through this next chapter of her life with the same grace as the last."

That seemed an odd way to describe Camilla, as I'd never associated her with grace, but I supposed at least it was nice to hear she wouldn't die from grief. "I honestly think I'd die without Luca."

Tomasso frowned. "Luca's family, his associates, they'd never let anything happen to you, even in his absence."

It amused me that he thought my concern was my own lack of independence. I chuckled, then explained. "No, I mean, I'd miss him too much. I thought I'd lost him once and..." I stopped myself before I dwelled too much on those emotions. I still felt the raw terror of watching him die like it was yesterday. Thinking about it was still too intense. "I just don't think I could live without him."

Tomasso's expression changed. "I'm glad you two have each other," he said.

We fell quiet again for a few minutes.

"How is he handling everything?"

I wasn't sure exactly what he meant by everything, so I addressed it all. "He and his father had their differences over the years, so that's complicated everything for Luca, emotionally, I mean. And it was so sudden. But if you're asking in terms of work, I think he'll be fine. From what I can tell, Luca has a different management style from Salvatore, but he's very capable."

"Different management style," Tomasso repeated with a chuckle. "That's an interesting way to put it. How much does he share with you about his work?"

"Not much," I answered. Even if it wasn't the truth, that was the only acceptable answer to the question.

Tomasso seemed satisfied by that. "I knew Luca as a child. I remember when you two started dating. You made him happy even then."

I smiled right as my phone buzzed. I read the message from Luca. "So sorry. Bomb diffused now. Mamma safely sequestered in her room for the night with a cocktail. I'll make it up to you. Twice."

As soon as I realized Tomasso was watching me read, I blushed.

"Does he want you to return?" he asked.

I nodded, and we headed back to the house.

⁂

Luca

"I think we should wait until everyone is back in Connecticut before we tell them about the babies," Giada said, opening the empty fridge and wrinkling her nose. "Although does that make me just as bad as Angelo, keeping secrets just to hurt people?"

I opened my mouth to answer, but she kept going. Alessio and I exchanged a look. We'd left the house over a half hour before, and Giada hadn't stopped talking. I wasn't sure if she was excited or nervous or just overly caffeinated.

"Not that we're waiting because we want to hurt him. It's the opposite actually. I don't want to steal his thunder. You know, let him enjoy all the attention for his wedding before the world's cutest babies steal his thunder. But still, he obviously is trying to hurt me, and I don't even—"

I swiveled Giada to face me and planted a firm kiss on her lips. She kissed me back for half a second before pushing me away and gagging.

"Were you eating yogurt earlier?" she asked, sprinting to the bathroom.

Alessio made no attempt to hold in his laughter. He handed me a stick of peppermint gum, and I accepted, begrudgingly.

After my mom's outburst at dinner the night before, we'd decided Giada and I should stay at my apartment until we left town. I'd been concerned about security, but there was no way we could keep the pregnancy secret if we spent the next two weeks living with my mom. Alessio was heading to Palermo the next day, but Giorgio promised to stay with Giada at the apartment whenever I couldn't be there.

"False alarm," Giada said, returning to the room. "We really need to head to the grocery, though. There is no food here."

In truth, the cupboards were well-stocked, since I'd only been gone for roughly a week. But we did need perishables. "Make a list and I'll have someone get it," I said.

"I could go," she said.

"I'll tell Giorgio to drive you," I replied, not even bothering to try to ask her to stay in. "I'm fine with waiting to tell your parents as long as you want. And as for your brother, I don't think he's trying to hurt you. My guess is that your parents pressured him to start dating again, and he accidentally knocked her up. But either way, you should be happy. You've always wanted a sister, and now you'll have one."

Giada worked her bottom lip between her teeth, clearly considering that possible perk.

"Alessio and I have some errands to run, and then I'm taking him to the airport. I'll be back by dinner time, and in the meantime, Georgio will be right outside. Text him when you want to go to the market."

My wife pulled Alessio into a hug and wished him safe travels. Then I leaned in to hug her before turning towards the door.

"Seriously?" she snapped. "You're just going to leave without kissing me goodbye?"

Alessio let himself out of the apartment before she heard him laughing. I turned back to my wife and bowed my head apologetically.

"I always want to kiss you. I just didn't want to make you sick again," I said.

Giada rolled her eyes then kissed me like I was headed off to war.

Alessio and I started off on our errands, but had just finished our second stop when Tony called.

"Cosimo just left his shop. Gian thinks he's headed back to his apartment. How far are you?"

I swore under my breath and glanced at Alessio, who was driving.

"Ten minutes," he said, revving the engine.

I relayed the message to Tony, then prayed we actually made it in time. Lodovico and Iacopo had been watching Cosimo's apartment all day, and Tony and Roberto had joined them already. But for the full effect, I wanted to be there, too.

I called Tony as we pulled to the curb on the side of Cosimo's building. "We're here," I said.

"Perfect. Gian said they're still five minutes out. It's number 312. Take the stairs."

Alessio and I jogged up to the unit, then greeted our guys.

"The moron has zero security here," Tony said. "I've seen kittens who were more threatening."

"He's alone?" Alessio asked.

"Naa, two guys with him. Both equally dumb."

I assumed that meant he was still with Chad and his guy, Luca. I gazed around the apartment, then plopped down on the couch. He'd see me the moment he walked in, but first, the guys flanking both sides of the entry would disarm him and his sidekicks. After what felt like an eternity, we heard voices approaching.

I sucked in a deep breath, feeling a moment of anxiety as Cosimo worked his key in the lock. If something went wrong and I died now, I'd never meet my twins. Giada would be all alone. A pang of regret hit me. Why had I brought Alessio along? I should at least keep him safe so Giada still had someone if I got killed.

The door swung open, and in an instant, Tony trained a gun on Cosimo. Lodovico and Iacopo restrained Chad and Luca, and Roberto held the door while they walked them back into the hall. Cosimo hadn't even noticed me yet, his gaze still locked on Tony. Alessio patted down Cosimo, unloading the gun from his ankle holster before setting it on the floor.

"Have a seat," I said, drawing Cosimo's gaze to me as I motioned to the seat beside me. "I mean, it is your apartment."

Cosimo's eyes darted around his apartment, and I suspected he was debating the likelihood of making it to one of his weapons before one of us shot him. After a moment, he sat.

"I'm not here to hurt you, just for a chat. Normally I would've knocked and waited till you invited me in, but I thought this was what you and I were doing now, just breaking into each other's property," I said.

Cosimo said nothing, but kept glaring.

"This isn't your city," I continued. "The Marinos run this city, and if you try to shove us out, we'll double our business here. If you back the fuck off, there's room for both of us here. But you've got to stay in your lane. Do you understand?"

Cosimo didn't answer.

"I'm going to need a yes or a no," I said. "Can you play nicely? No more visiting any of my clubs or businesses. Don't go near anyone even loosely connected to the Marino family. And if you can handle that, we'll let you live. We'll even let you keep doing business here. But if you can't, I'll have to pay you another visit, and next time, we'll do a lot less talking."

"Fine," Cosimo said.

I rose to my feet. "Glad to hear it, and good to see you again."

I strode out of the apartment, Tony and Alessio watching my back. The three of us left the apartment, pausing at the door as our other guys nudged Chad and Luca into the apartment, then we started down the hall. My nerves didn't settle until we were safely back inside my Maserati, headed towards the airport.

Giorgio texted that he'd already driven Giada back to my parents' for dinner by the time I finished working, so I headed there. I greeted Giada, then wolfed my dinner. The rest of the family had already eaten, and my aunt was attempting to teach Giada to bake a crostata. I didn't anticipate Giada ever successfully recreating any of my aunt's dishes, but I wasn't about to complain about tasting the samples.

I was about to sit down and relax when Tomasso caught my eye. "While Giada is occupied, Luca, would it be possible for me to have a word with you in private?"

My mother glanced up from what she was doing, her eyes tense.

"Sure," I said, suppressing a groan. I was starting to understand that being the boss meant never having a day off, but it didn't seem like too much to ask to have a full hour in my own home without some pressing business concern being brought to my attention.

Tomasso gestured to the office. I tensed. No part of that office felt like mine, not yet anyway. I didn't want to literally take my papà's seat.

"Let's go to the courtyard. I could use the fresh air," I said.

He nodded and followed. It was colder than I'd expected, but not unbearable. The plants were mostly dormant, but the courtyard still looked vibrant with all of the greenery outlasting the winter. I sat on one of the stone benches by the fountain. It had been drained for cleaning, so now it was just two frogs frozen in time with their mouths open. For some reason, it amused me to think that the stone creatures would be waiting for the gardener to return for their next squirt of water.

Tomasso sat across from me and smiled.

"So, what's up?" I asked, intentionally speaking in English. I wasn't sure how soundproof the courtyard was, and I didn't want to risk any of the lower-ranking house staff overhearing anything they shouldn't.

"I wanted to ask your permission to date your mother," he said, his voice completely level.

I spit the coffee I'd just sipped all over the damn frog statues.

He offered me a handkerchief, which I waved away.

"You want...my mother?" I asked, pained to even hear the words aloud.

I'd prayed I misunderstood, but he nodded.

"I hope this doesn't seem too soon to ask. I wanted to be respectful of your father and allow Camille time to begin the grieving process, but..." he sighed and shook his head.

I scratched my head, wondering how I had actually thought a business matter would be the most painful thing to discuss. "I appreciate that, but it's not nineteen-thirty. You don't need my permission. I would suggest you talk to her, and go from there. I really don't need to be involved in my mother's...social life."

Tomasso smiled. "I apologize if I made it seem like I was trying to treat your mother like a possession. I actually, well," he sighed. "Your father was my capo. I did not always agree with his decisions or actions, but I respected him. And I was always loyal. It was his wish that you seceded him as the boss, and I respect that. I want you to understand you have my complete respect and loyalty. I don't seek to replace your father or oust you from anything to which you are entitled. What I mean is, I don't want you to see me as your competition. If anything, it's the opposite. I want to support you and help you in your journey, the way a father would."

I chugged the rest of my coffee, welcoming the slight burn

from its heat as a distraction from the weirdly awkward conversation.

"Right, well, I appreciate that, and um, like I said. It's up to her. Good luck." I shifted to stand, but Tomasso motioned for me to wait.

"I'm sorry. I'm…bungling this whole discussion," he said, now seeming as flustered as I felt. "Your mother already knows what I'm talking to you about. We've already…"

I cringed, praying he wasn't about to say they'd already hooked up or anything similar that I absolutely did not need to picture my mother doing.

"Your mother and I have been involved for years, Luca," he said.

The implication of his words hit me like a wall of bricks. Tomasso wasn't asking for permission, but for forgiveness. And it was a forgiveness that wasn't mine to give. I rose to my feet and turned, ruffling my hair with my hand and then thrusting them both into my pockets for a moment to stop myself from lashing out or hitting something.

"I'm sorry if…" he began.

I raised my hand to shush him. "I need a minute, Tomasso. You just finished telling me how loyal you were to my papà. I think you're confused though, because my definition of loyalty doesn't include adultery. You weren't loyal. You didn't respect him. You betrayed him."

Tomasso clasped his hands in his lap and nodded, which only infuriated me more.

"You say you're now loyal to me, but what does that even mean? You obviously have no idea what true loyalty entails."

"Luca, I'm not going to touch Giada," he said with a chuckle. "I assure you I only have eyes for your mother."

I lunged forward then stopped myself, taking a deep breath and then lowering myself back onto my bench. I clutched the sharp stone edge until I felt the jagged stone press into my skin. The hint of pain both grounded me and distracted me.

"I would never in a million years worry about Giada getting involved with someone like you," I finally said. "The issue is I don't know how to trust someone who just told me his idea of loyalty to the boss includes sneaking around with his wife."

Tomasso nodded. "I know. I agree. And I…I wish I had some valid excuse, but I don't really, except, well, your father never loved your mother."

I flung my hands in the air. "Jesus, seriously? Do you hear yourself? So now it's his fault?"

"He was unfaithful to her. You know that. He made no attempt to hide it."

"That's different," I said.

"Why? Because he's a man, and she's supposed to be this pure, innocent woman?"

"No! Because he didn't sleep with the spouse of someone he'd pledged loyalty to. He didn't destroy his boss's marriage."

"Nor did I. We were discrete, Luca. You never knew. No one did."

"Hiding a betrayal doesn't make it any less of a betrayal."

"Do you honestly think he would've cared if he knew?"

I stood abruptly, wiping the trace of blood off my fingers. I needed to pace. "My papà would have killed you if he'd known," I finally said. I was certain we both knew that was true, but I also realized it didn't answer the question he'd actually posed. My papà cared about his reputation. He would have cared deeply if other people knew his wife was unfaithful. But would it have hurt him to know other she had feelings for another man? Probably not.

"I wish you hadn't told me any of this," I finally said aloud, swiveling back to face him. "I don't know what you expect me to do with this information."

"Do you want your mother to be happy?"

"Of course I do. But I can't pretend I don't know what you've done. I can't pretend to trust you. So what do I do with that?" I shook my head. If I cast him out, his life would be in danger. If I continued to let him work inside my innermost circles, my life was in danger. If he'd betray my papà, the man he knew well and pledged his loyalty to, there was nothing stopping him from betraying me. Sure, he wouldn't do the same type of betrayal, but disloyal was disloyal. People didn't change.

"Why did you fucking tell me?" I spit.

"I told you because I respect you. I think you are a good, honorable man. I'm confessing my sins and asking for forgiveness."

"I'm not a fucking priest. And it's not me that has to forgive you."

"But you do have to trust me."

"Exactly. And now I can't," I shook my head. "You aren't a fool. You had to know that would be the end result of this conversation."

He frowned. "So your answer is no?"

It took me a moment to even recall what the original question was. "Do what you want with my mother. I am not now nor will I ever get involved in her love life. But as for the rest...I don't know. I can't trust you. There is nothing you could say or do to regain my trust after years of lies to my papà."

His lips pressed together in a firm line and I actually saw a tear forming.

"Luca, please. Sit," he begged.

Against my better judgment, I did.

"I understand where you're coming from, but please under-stand. By making your mother happy, by loving her and treating her with respect, I'm also honoring you. I will care for her the way you would want her to be cared for. I'll care for her the way your father should have. And I am telling you now, I will never do anything to hurt you. I will never let anyone else hurt you. I have looked out for you your entire life, and you would see that if you looked back."

I hadn't seen much of Tomasso in my early childhood, but then when he'd reappeared in my teen years, he had always been kind to me.

"Luca, I would give my life in a heartbeat if it would save yours."

"Why would I believe that?"

Tomasso didn't break eye contact, but he sure took his time answering. From the raspy way he was breathing, I half expected him to keel over. But finally, he spoke. "Because your mother and I haven't just been involved the last several years. We dated ages ago, when she was in college. We were also together nine months before you were born."

I started to reply that the longevity of his betrayal certainly didn't help his case, but then I stopped. I realized the significance of what he was telling me. But I had to say it aloud to be sure.

"Are you telling me you think you're my father?"

His lips parted slowly. Everything seemed to be moving in slow motion. "We never had a test done. We were worried what might happen to you if anyone found out," he finally said. "But I'm telling you I might be."

I stared at his damp eyes for a full minute, trying to decipher whether there was any familiarity whatsoever, and then I pushed off the bench and walked into the house. Keeping my head down, I stormed straight through the center of the house, dodging the kitchen where my mother and Giada both stood. I went right out the front door. I climbed in my car, hit the ignition button, and took off.

CHAPTER 25

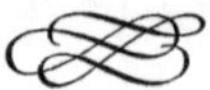

Giada

I heard the side door of the house slam and made my way to the window just in time to see Luca speed off in his Maserati. My pulse shot up. Obviously, something big had happened to require him to leave without saying anything, and I knew from experience he probably wouldn't be able to tell me what right away.

I turned, nearly slamming into Luca's mom as she was standing behind me looking out the same window. Her horrified expression increased my own panic tenfold. She abruptly took off and went towards the courtyard, where Tomasso had been talking with Luca before he stormed off. Tomasso was still there, which seemed odd.

He and Camilla exchanged an unsettling look, and then he shook his head sadly. Camilla pressed her palm to her forehead, sighed dramatically, then scurried out of the room without saying anything. I heard her bedroom door close, leaving Tomasso and me staring at each other.

"Where did Luca go?" I asked.

"He didn't say," he replied with a frown.

"Is everything okay?"

The lines on his forehead bulged further. "I, uh…"

"What were you guys discussing before he left?"

"It was a personal matter, not business," he replied.

"So did he get a phone call or something? I don't understand why he just left."

Tomasso sighed. "I am sorry. I don't know. I think he was upset about what we discussed."

"Do you know when he'll be back?"

His blank stare infuriated me. I pulled out my phone and called Georgio to request he come take me to the apartment.

I tried Luca's cell phone a few times while I waited for Georgio, but it went to voice mail. My words came out calmer than I felt, and I just told him I was worried and asked him to call me.

Georgio arrived quickly, but was just as clueless as I was when it came to Luca's whereabouts.

"He's not answering my calls," I said as he pulled away. "Can you try him?"

He did, but Luca didn't answer.

An hour later, still with no sign of Luca, I made myself a sandwich for dinner and tried to distract myself with television, but I couldn't find any decent shows in English. So I grabbed a book instead and filled the tub. It was a gorgeous oversized clawfoot tub that Luca swore he'd never used before I first stayed with him. Luckily, the bath left me tired, so I changed into pajamas and climbed into bed. I tried Luca's phone one last time, but it went straight to voice mail. It didn't even ring once, which told me he'd turned it off. I interpreted that as a good sign, that he was doing something where he didn't want to be distracted, not that he'd been kidnapped or was lying in a ditch somewhere.

I switched off the lamp and reassured myself that when I woke, Luca would be stretched out beside me.

Except, he wasn't. It was just after midnight when my bladder woke me. I praised myself for sleeping as long as I had under the circumstances, but then tried his phone again. When Luca still didn't answer, I considered my options. I could call Georgio again, except it was the middle of the night. And if he hadn't known where Luca was or wasn't willing to tell me before bed, he certainly wouldn't now.

I called Alessio, hoping his flight had already landed.

"Oh, thank God. Have you heard from Luca?" I asked when he answered.

Alessio silenced music in the background before answering. "Not since he dropped me at the airport. Why?"

Shit. "Well, whatever errand he rushed off to this evening is apparently taking a long time. He's still not home and his phone goes straight to voice mail."

"Where are you?"

"Our apartment."

"And when did he leave?"

I sighed, then told him the whole story starting with his weird private conversation with Tomasso.

"Alright, can you put Georgio on for a minute?" his voice was clipped, and I never heard Alessio stressed.

"He's not here."

"Where is he?"

"I don't know. I told him I was staying in for the night and that he could leave."

Alessio groaned loudly. "Giada, when Luca isn't there, Georgio should be."

"I barely know Georgio. I can't sleep when he's here. Why couldn't you or Lincoln have come?"

"Linc doesn't speak Italian and I'm…busy taking care of more important shit."

"Gee thanks."

"I'm calling Georgio, and he'll come back. If you want him to stay in his car, fine. But he'll be there if you need him. And I'll track down Luca, so don't worry."

"How are you going to track him down? His phone is off."

"Giada, don't worry. I'll talk to Tomasso, check in with all of our guys in Rome, and I'll make sure someone swings by my place and the clubs to look for him. I'm sure he just lost track of time."

Luca

I glanced up from what I swore would be my last drink just as Roberto strolled into the bar, his cell phone pressed tightly to his ear. I spotted him first, but before I could decide whether I wanted to hide or wave, his gaze locked on me.

He crossed the room in three giant strides, thrusting the phone into my face before I could even greet him.

"Jesus, Luca. We've been looking all over for you. Alessio wants to speak to you."

I wrinkled my nose. Clearly, they'd all forgotten about how that whole pyramid of authority went if they thought I had to answer to Alessio. Or anyone else. Nope, that was the benefit of having a dead father. No one to answer to.

Well, except maybe the backup dad.

"What happened?" Alessio shouted in my ear, ratcheting my headache straight into hangover zone.

"I needed some air," I said.

"Air?" he repeated. "What prompted this need?"

"It's personal stuff, with my mom."

"Is everything okay?"

"Not really, but there's nothing you can do anyway, so call off the search team and let me finish my damn drink."

"Yeah, veto. First off, you sound too drunk to walk, let alone drive yourself home. And second, do you have any idea how worried Giada is?"

I cringed. I'd meant to text her and let her know I was ok and wouldn't be back, but then Tomasso had kept fucking calling. I had to turn my phone off. And then it got late. I figured she was asleep.

"She's pregnant, Luca, and it's now the middle of the night; but she's wide awake crying about your drunk ass. So whatever is going on, you either need to tell me so I can work on it or let Roberto drive you back to my place to sober up."

I blew out a sigh, then chose option B. I couldn't go home to Giada now, not like this, and I sure wasn't heading back to the house with Mom and her lover.

"Will you call her back and tell her something came up?"

"What if she asks questions?" Alessio replied.

We both knew she would. Giada was nothing if not inquisitive. "Make something up. You're a creative guy."

"I'm not lying to your wife. Especially without any idea what's really going on."

I tipped the glass backwards, letting the amber liquid glide down my throat as the ice clinked against my teeth. I wondered if my papà ever asked Tomasso to cover for him with my mom. If he had, Tomasso probably fucking did what he was told. I bet Tomasso never openly challenged his authority.

I slammed the glass against the bar a tad harder than I'd intended. "Alessio, I told you to make something up," I repeated, saturating my tone so he'd get the message.

"Not my job."

"No? Because I'm pretty sure your job is to do whatever the fuck I tell you to do, no questions asked."

Alessio spewed out a string of expletives in Italian, leaving me to wonder whether he thought I couldn't hear him or simply forgot it was my native tongue, too. "Fine. Whatever you say,

Boss. Anything else? Want me to send some girls to the apartment to meet you? Or perhaps some dinner?"

I did not have the energy for his attitude. "Just fucking take care of things with Giada, okay? Thanks." I hung up before he could answer.

I moved to shove the phone into my pocket and then realized it was Roberto's phone. I gazed up, seeing him staring at me. "Take me to Alessio's," I instructed.

He nodded, then offered me an arm like I was an elderly invalid. The room tilted and spun as I stood, but I swatted his hand away. I didn't need to look any weaker than I felt. We made it to the car, and I leaned my head back against the leather seat, pressing my fingers against my forehead to dull the dizzying headache. Roberto wisely kept quiet, though I noticed him cast several glances in my direction.

I shut my eyes, determined to ignore the judgment. I'd hoped that I might get a few minutes rest in, since I knew I wouldn't actually fall asleep. How could I sleep after that bomb Tomasso dropped?

I peeled my eyes open and swore. I needed to be with Giada. That was my only hope of sleeping ever again.

"Capo?" Roberto turned to me questioningly.

"Drop me at my own apartment instead," I said.

He nodded his agreement, then calmly turned the car at the next light. When we reached the villa, Roberto parked the car and walked around to my side, opening the door for me. I started to say I didn't need a hand, except I did. My last drink had hit me— hard—and I could barely stand unassisted. Roberto swung a hand around my waist and helped me towards the door. As we reached the door, Georgio appeared.

"What are you doing here?" I asked.

"Alessio told me not to leave Giada until you were home." He paused, then added. "I've been in my car."

I tried to nod in acknowledgement of his words, but the

gesture nearly toppled me over. I managed to get the door open, then paused, letting my eyes adjust before dismissing my men. I had barely gotten the door shut and locked when Giada appeared.

"Tesoro," I whispered, right before passing out.

Giada

Under usual circumstances, I never would've fallen back asleep. Pregnancy had rendered me in a constant state of utter exhaustion though, so I could pretty much sleep through any trauma. Luca had passed out on the floor, then woken a few hours later and moved to the bathroom, where he spent the rest of the night crouched by the toilet.

I awoke with an unsettling mixture of concern and fury. As I sat, feeling my bladder contract painfully, the latter emotion won out. I made my way to the bathroom, finding no trace of Luca or the mess he must have made the night before. Normally, I would've gone to confirm he was okay before doing anything else, but pregnant me had to pee first, and ask questions later.

I washed my hands and shook them dry while moving towards the living room. Luca was asleep on the couch, a blanket pulled nearly to his chin. I stared at him for a moment, my emotions again vacillating between anger and sympathy. I wanted to be the bigger person, the type of wife who would let her exhausted husband sleep and find out what had set him off the night before later, when he was well rested.

But patience had never been my strong suit.

"Luca," I said, nudging his arm.

He groaned and pulled the covers up. I repeated his name one more time, and he mumbled something disgruntled in Italian before slowly sitting upright, rubbing his head.

"Coffee?" he asked. He at least had the decency to look sheepish while voicing his request. Not surprisingly, my expression made him rethink his ask.

"Amore, I'm sorry. It was a rough night, and I didn't mean to worry you. I thought you would've gone to bed already and I planned to sleep at Alessio's, but…"

"We are having a baby, Luca," I interrupted. "Two, actually. You can't just stay out all night. You can't drink like a college kid. You can't—"

"Giada, he said he was my father," Luca said, peering up at me between thick dark lashes.

I dropped to the sofa beside him. "What?"

"When Tomasso asked to speak with me alone, he wanted permission to date my mother."

"That's stupid, why would he need your permission?"

Luca rubbed his eyebrow. "Because she's my mother, and because I'm the boss now." He patted my thigh then stood and made his way to the kitchen, busying himself with coffee preparation. "It's a sign of respect."

"So if you said no, he just would find a different girlfriend?" I practically laughed at the terminology. His mom was well into her fifties, so hardly a girl anymore.

He took so long to answer that I moved on to my next question.

"Wait, did you say no? Are you actually trying to tell your own mother who she can date?"

Luca scowled. "First off, it's not like a completely ridiculous notion for me to have some say in the matter. My papà hasn't even been gone that long. But second of all, that isn't even the point. Tomasso said…well, he told me he's loved her for years. Decades, to be precise."

"Aww." I came to join him in the kitchen.

His scowl deepened. "She was married all that time! How is that sweet?"

Hmm, I supposed when he put it that way... "Well, it's romantic that he waited so long."

Luca poured two small cups of coffee and handed the first to me. I waited as he switched off the stove, whisked the milk he'd been warming, then divvied it between our mugs. It never ceased to amuse me that Luca refused coffee with milk after noon, when he was so diligent about adding frothy milk to his first cup of the day.

"He didn't wait," he finally said. "My mother was unfaithful to my papà."

"Oh. When?"

"For their entire marriage. Maybe before."

"Why didn't she just leave your father if she loved Tomasso?"

Luca quirked an eyebrow and shot me a look that quickly answered my question.

"You really think he would've hurt her if she left?"

I could see Luca debating the answer in his head for a moment before he shrugged. "Tomasso worked for him. He wouldn't have had a choice. He couldn't let one of his guys steal his girl and..." Luca stopped midsentence like a deer in headlights.

Until I saw his panic, it never even occurred to me to question the parallels. "Wait, if I were to hook up with Alessio, what would you do?"

Luca laughed so abruptly he nearly spit out the frothy milk.

"Okay, Roberto?"

"I'd cut off his coglioni."

I wasn't totally sure what that meant, but I could guess. It didn't exactly answer the question fully though. "But..."

"Amore, stop interrupting. We are not my parents. You are not going to start an affair with one of my guys, and I would never hurt you. And that isn't the point. The point is Tomasso said they've been together since before I was born. He said he might be my father."

My jaw dropped, even though I should've known that was where this discussion was headed. Pregnancy brain had hit me hard, apparently.

Within a matter of seconds, I'd thought up multiple perks to this revelation. "So you don't have to worry about becoming like your father. I mean, like Salvatore. And you don't have to be in charge anymore, and…"

Luca held up his hand to stop me. "Giada, Tomasso is not my father. He can't be. And even if he were, it changes nothing. We could never tell anyone."

"It changes everything. Luca, you're free," I began.

"Jacob," he said. "Remember him? My half-brother? We had the paternity test done. If Salvatore Marino were not truly my biological father, then the paternity test for Jacob wouldn't have been positive."

"Unless you're actually Jacob's dad and not his brother," I suggested.

Luca glared. "I'm not."

I shrugged. I did believe Luca, and the fact that I was so eager to assume he'd cheated rather than actually be related to Salvatore Marino was probably pretty offensive.

He sat at the bar beside me and sipped his coffee.

"Wait, so if you know he isn't your father, why were you so upset last night?"

"Because I didn't remember that right away," he said, flinging his hands up. "And even if it isn't the truth, it's a big bombshell that Tomasso thinks he could be my father."

I considered that, dropping my hands to my belly. To the outside world, I probably just looked like I'd overindulged in salty foods the night before, but I was already starting to notice a difference, especially now that my appetite was back. "Yeah. I couldn't imagine looking at my child every day and wondering who her father was."

A smile briefly crossed Luca's face, just like it did any time I suggested our child was a girl. But he quickly turned serious again.

"I don't know. It's pretty messed up. How did they go my whole life just wondering, what if? God, and when I look back at things, there were so many times during my adolescence when Tomasso would step in and try to help me. He kept trying to help me avoid getting beaten by my papà and it never made sense."

I tightened my hands against my stomach. I hated when Luca talked about his teen years. I'd known him then, but I'd been utterly clueless. I had no idea all of the shit his father had done to him. And whenever I thought about it now, it made me nauseous. It also made me want to hurt someone. It was a marvel Luca turned out as well as he had.

"She named me after him, Giada. My middle name—Tomás. That has to be because of Tomasso." He shook his head. "Talk about betrayal. Naming your kid after your…lover?"

Secretly, I agreed. But just to play devil's advocate… "It's also sweet. A way to honor your roots without destroying your stable home life."

"He worked for my papà, Giada. Tomasso pledged his loyalty to my papà—all the while sleeping with his wife. How am I to trust a man like that?"

Luca paused, but not long enough for me to speak. "And I can't tell him how I know he isn't my father, because I don't want anyone to know about Jacob."

"So just tell him you had a paternity test done. Say it was your dad's idea if you want." I stopped myself before pointing out he could just tell him about Jacob too. Now that Salvatore was gone, I didn't see the benefit in keeping that secret longer anyway. But that was a stressful discussion to save for another day.

Luca drained the last of his coffee then stared at me, still scowling. "My mother is a whore."

"Luca!"

"What? She is. My whole life, I've thought of her as a victim.

Some innocent bystander trapped in my papà's web while he cheats. But I've had the story wrong the whole time. Maybe if she hadn't cheated on him, maybe he would've been faithful. Maybe he only became a monster because the woman he loved treated him like dirt."

I rose to my feet and placed a hand on Luca's back, rubbing gently. "Just tell them you need some time to process it all. You don't have to figure out everything right away." I paused. "And you don't need to rewrite your whole life script."

CHAPTER 26

Luca

I couldn't believe how quickly Giada forgave me for staying out half the night, but I made a mental note to buy her something pretty later anyway. I enjoyed spoiling Giada just as much as she enjoyed being spoiling, so there was no reason not to err on the side of caution after screwing up.

I would have loved to lounge around the apartment and nap that afternoon, but Giada had made plans to meet her brothers at a nearby bar. My head throbbed and my stomach churned as we walked into the bar, but I downed some Ibuprofen and hoped an afternoon drink would cure my hangover. I ordered a cranberry and seltzer for Giada, certain that would resemble one of her usual drink orders enough to throw off any suspicions from her brothers.

I'd hoped to garner some dirt on Angelo, but he remained elusive about the reason for the rush, repeating only the vague details we already knew. His fiancée hadn't joined him, which seemed odd. He claimed she was an old friend of the family with whom he'd recently rekindled his romance. I made a crack about an unexpected pregnancy, watching Angelo's face for any signs of truth behind my joke, but the guy actually replied—with a straight face—that they were waiting until the wedding night.

Giada rolled her eyes as if he was kidding, but I wasn't so sure.

Unfortunately, I didn't have the time or mental energy to dissect the mystery of my wife's brother's love life. I had to go balance the accounts at the clubs with Tony.

"Georgio is outside," I told Giada as I left. She'd been planning on shopping at a couple of maternity boutiques and claimed she'd outgrow her other clothes any day now, but she still hadn't gained an ounce. Her stomach was still flat, though perhaps not as much as it had been when I first returned from Italy. If anything, she'd only regained the weight she'd lost from being sick.

"If you still want to shop, he'll go with you. He'll be discreet. But if you want to go back to the apartment and nap, that's okay too."

"You're the one who needs a nap today," she said, smoothing her palm across my cheek. "Have fun with Tony." She kissed me, then watched me leave.

Giada

$\mathcal{I}$ told Giorgio the name of the maternity shop I'd wanted to visit, then added that I was shopping "for a friend." Not that he looked like he cared either way. He asked if I wanted him to come inside to translate, and when I said no, he promised to stay in the car if I needed anything. I started towards the boutique, then paused, noticing a men's shop next door.

"I might check out that one too," I said, pointing.

Georgio nodded. "I'll be here if you want to drop off bags in between stores."

I smiled and made my way into the boutique. Georgio was so much more laidback than Luca's guys back home. Clearly, he understood there was no real danger to me while shopping and he was just old enough to not be quite so concerned with Luca's paranoia about my safety.

Two clerks flocked to me and began tittering in Italian. I waited for a pause, then said hopefully, "English?"

Thankfully, one of them switched to English. She still seemed confused why I was shopping for maternity items, but when I told her I was expecting twins, she acquiesced and showed me a few more forgiving items. I ended up with a new pair of shorts with an elastic waistband and a cute skirt. Neither item looked particularly "maternity," and it occurred to me that I could just purchase a few more loose-fitting dresses to get through the rest of summer and early fall.

I definitely needed a new bra or two, since somehow, my breasts had grown before my stomach. The saleslady assured me there was a lingerie shop just past the butcher's and I planned to stop there before heading back to the apartment. First, I meandered next door, to the men's shop. I wanted to buy Luca something special to commemorate becoming a dad, but for now, I was just gathering ideas. I did find a pair of swim trunks and a tee-shirt I thought he'd love. It wasn't exactly Armani, but surely an independent Italian boutique was Italian enough for my fashion-snob husband.

I stopped off at the car to hand my bags to Georgio, then pointed down the street towards the lingerie shop. He said he'd pull the car closer, but I insisted on walking there and asked him to just stay put. The shop was less than a block away, and the weather was idyllic. I hadn't been paying much attention to my surroundings, but as I neared the lingerie shop, I happened to glance up right as I passed the butcher's next door.

The sign bore the name FERRANTE in bold, blue letters. I paused, trying to recall why that name sounded familiar.

An eager sales lady was already measuring me for a bra when I remembered. Ferrante's was the butcher shop owned by the family of the guy who'd been tormenting Luca. I groaned, hating that the place had appeared bustling and successful when I'd walked past. If the guy was going to make my husband's life stressful, at least his business could fail.

The saleslady spoke virtually no English, and since I didn't speak Italian, it took forever to make sure she understood that I was pregnant and wanted a bra with a tiny bit of room to grow. I also still wanted something sexy though. She brought me bra after bra to try, and with each one I fastened, I found myself growing more and more annoyed with Cosimo.

Luca hadn't told me all the details of course, but he'd made it clear that the guy was a moron just trying to posture and scare him off. Normally, I didn't think Luca would struggle in the slightest to deal with such a jerk, but now, Luca was a mess. He'd already been grappling with the loss of his dad and the new business and then the stress of the pregnancy…and now learning about his mom's torrid love affair. Well, I didn't blame Luca for drinking himself into a stupor. He had too much shit to think about.

I texted Georgio that the lingerie shop was taking forever, and he replied with a thumbs up. I laughed out loud, not having pictured that being the emoji of choice for a late-thirties Italian mobster. Maybe the criminals here were just a tad more chill than back home.

I bought three new bras and decided to stop into the butcher's shop, just to see what it was like. The line of people had dwindled somewhat, so I was able to walk right in. I grabbed a number, then stood in the back, trying to ignore the cuts of meat on blatant display in every corner. A door swung open off to one side behind the counter, offering a glimpse of another room, with dead animals hanging from the ceiling.

I gagged and was about to leave when I heard my number called. I pressed on the space between my nose and lip, desperate to quell the nausea, then approached the counter. "Parli Inglese?" I asked.

The man frowned, wiped his hands on a dirty rag, then nodded.

"I'll take a pound of prosciutto," I said. "And um, can you tell me if Cosimo is here today?"

The guy behind him perked up. "Cosimo?" he repeated.

I nodded.

Both men turned and seemed to appraise me anew. After a moment, the one who'd claimed to speak English said, "Come ti chiami?"

I hesitated, familiar with the phrase, but struggling to translate for a moment.

He pointed at me, then said, "Name?"

"Giada Conti," I said. I was about to correct my mistake when the man turned abruptly. He whispered something to the other guy, then nodded for me to wait. The guy in the back disappeared for a moment, then returned. Just as he did, the door to the creepy room swung open again and a fresh wave of smells washed over me. I gagged again.

The guy eyed me warily.

"Sorry," I mumbled, not sure how much he'd understand. "I'm pregnant, and the smells make me nauseous." I gestured to my belly and cringed, hoping he'd figure it out. He motioned for me to follow him and, thankfully, led my down a short hallway in the opposite direction of the meat locker.

A man about my age sat at a desk in a junky-looking office. Presumably, this was Cosimo. Up close, it was hard to see how anyone found this short, unkempt man intimidating.

"Giada," he said, rising to his feet and running his eyes up and down my body, not once, but twice. "Marco's daughter all grown up."

I swallowed uncomfortably.

"We met when we were children. Do you remember?" He didn't wait for me to answer. "Have a seat. We were just planning my birthday party, but I can always spare a minute for an old friend."

"Thank you."

"It's the big three-oh," he said. "September twelfth."

"Happy birthday?" I said, still a tad confused.

"Thank you. I'll be sure you and your dad get an invitation. He's in town now, right?"

I nodded. "My oldest brother is getting married, so—"

"Oh, wow. That's exciting. So what's new with you?"

"I was actually here about some business you have with my husband," I began. "I figured we could talk, and—"

"You're married too? Damn, missed my chance."

I cleared my throat. "Luca Marino is my husband."

I waited while the weight of my words sunk in.

His face reddened and he rose to his feet. "You tell him to leave me alone. I didn't break into his house. I don't know who he thinks he is, busting into my country and threatening me, but I won't stand for it. He can bully me all he wants, but as long as I have dirt on him, I'm on top."

"What kind of dirt?"

His face contorted. "What does that matter? Old-school blackmail never fails." He paused, then cast a glance to a side table, where a small safe sat in plain sight. "Luca may have more foot soldiers and weapons than me, but I have the intel."

"I don't—" I began, but just then, a man poked his head in the door.

They spoke in hushed tones, not that I could understand the language anyway, and then Cosimo motioned for me to wait.

"I'll be right back," he said to me, before saying something to the other guy in Italian. I assumed he asked him to watch me, since the man stood guard right at my back.

I sighed, then gazed at the safe again. I guessed that whatever intel Cosimo had was stored in that safe. It had a simple locker-style combination lock, which presumably wouldn't be too hard to open, if one had experience with safes. Sadly, I had no such knowledge or experience. And I had a babysitter.

If I could guess the combination, then maybe I'd have a chance. I'd assume a basic guy like Cosimo would choose something obvious, like the building's address or his birthday.

With the door open, the pungent odor of raw meat wafted into the office. I gagged again, and the man at the door cringed, his expression a mixture of disgust and horror.

An idea came to me, and even as I decided to try it, I realized there was no chance it would work. Even if I managed to snag a moment alone, I'd never have time to try more than one combination on the safe. And if the guy returned while I was opening it, there was no telling what they'd do.

I reached into my purse and texted Georgio, "Stepped into butcher's shop but will be back at the car in one minute." That way, if anything happened, at least he'd know where to find me.

Then, I stood up. "Can you close that door? The smell is making me nauseous," I said to the guy guarding me, clutching my stomach for effect.

He hesitated, then closed the door—but remained on the inside.

Damn.

"I'm pregnant," I said. "Morning sickness is rough. Do you have kids?"

He nodded, then held up two fingers. Ahh, so he did speak English.

"Any idea how much longer Cosimo is going to be? I really wanted to finish talking to him about my brother's wedding and hear about his big birthday party, but my stomach is a mess. I did some shopping and I..." I paused to gag dramatically. "I'm pretty sure I'm going to throw up if I don't eat a cracker or something real soon."

The man frowned at me, and I waited a moment, then forced a more dramatic dry-heave.

"I'll bring you a wafer," he said, scurrying out. He left the door open, but the door faced a wall in the narrow hall, so no one could see in until they reached the door. And thanks to the ceramic tile floor, hopefully I'd hear anyone approaching before they reached me.

I flew out of the chair and immediately tried Cosimo's birthday on the combination lock. I did some quick mental math to calculate the year of his birth since I knew he was turning thirty, then started to turn the dial to nine then twelve, for September twelfth. Despite the rational part of my brain knowing this was unlikely to work, a flicker of disappointment still wound its way through me when the lock failed to release.

I sighed and plopped back in my seat, only to pop up a second later. Cosimo was Italian. He wouldn't enter his birthday as nine then twelve. Italians wrote dates with the day, then month then the year. I craned my head out the door, confirmed no one was coming, then swiveled the lock again, my hands trembling with excitement.

As I slid the dial to the last number, the tension changed beneath my hand and my breath caught in my throat. I tugged on the small latch and the safe swung open.

Inside, I saw a large stack of money, two handguns, and what appeared to be a grenade. *Yikes.* Two manilla envelopes were beneath the weapons and money. Gingerly, I shimmied the envelopes out. I'd barely opened the first one when I heard footsteps. I wadded half the contents of the first envelope into my purse, then crammed the envelopes back into the safe. I made a loud puking noise to cover the clink of the safe as I shut it.

The man entered the room while I was still standing, but I

quickly grabbed a tissue and held it over my mouth in a way that hopefully made it appear that I'd just retched. I glanced over at the man and reached for another tissue.

"I'm sorry," I said. "I don't want to vomit everywhere. I need to go. Just tell Cosimo we'll catch up later." I scurried past the guy and into the main lobby of the shop. I half expected someone to stop me as I pushed out the door, the mundane chime seeming to mock the seriousness of my business. I took two more steps before slamming into a large man.

I grunted and gazed up in terror.

It was Georgio.

"Oh, thank God," I mumbled. "We need to go. Now."

He scowled at me, but grabbed me by the wrist and led me back to the car.

I didn't relax until we were back onto the main freeway to the apartment. I tuned out the lecture from Georgio and prayed I'd grabbed something useful.

CHAPTER 27

Luca

I rushed home the minute I read Georgio's text, telling me my darling wife had wandered into the butcher shop owned and operated by my current arch-nemesis. Georgio stepped out of his car as I arrived, and in a flash, I had him backed against the hood of his car, my hand at his throat. It took all the self-restraint I could muster to pull my arm back to my side rather than snuff the life out of him, so once I'd released him, I stepped back, worried I'd be tempted to attack again if I stayed closer.

"I'm sorry," he croaked. "She said she was headed into a lingerie shop, and—"

"Do I look like I'm in the mood for any of your excuses?" I asked, pausing for only the second it took him to shut the fuck up. "If anyone had hurt a single hair on her head, the authorities would be looking for pieces of your body in the Tiber. Do you understand?"

He nodded.

"Get out of my sight. I don't want to see you, or hear you, or even think about you until the next time I'm in Italy. Go see Tony for a new assignment, and tell Roberto he's driving Giada from now on."

I turned and jogged into the apartment, ignoring his feeble "grazie."

I tried to calm my temper as I turned the knob to the apartment, but the adrenaline coursing through my veins made the task hard. I stepped inside to find Giada on the floor, a slew of papers spread out around her, and an Italian-English dictionary on her lap. She winced when she saw me and raised a hand.

"Okay, before you start yelling—"

But I cut her off, tugging her to her feet and kissing her. Surprised, she didn't respond for a moment, but then she kissed me back. I held her until my pulse slowed and my muscles relaxed. Giada was okay, and she was in my arms.

When I finally broke off the kiss, I held her at arm's length. "You're not hurt?"

"I'm fine, Luca," she said, as if she'd just stubbed her toe and not willingly secluded herself with a rival mob boss.

"What were you thinking?" I asked, not pausing long enough for her to reply. I continued my lecture until I'd listed every possible thing that could've gone wrong, including the things that could still come to pass. Then, I caught my breath and gazed back down at the papers. "What is all this?"

Giada clapped her hands together like an excited child. "I guessed the code to Cosimo's safe, broke in, and stole all his secrets!"

My lips parted, but no words came out. After a moment, I sat, then asked her to tell me the story from the beginning, and she did. I had to admit that she'd executed a brilliant—if slightly haphazard—plan, and that it was one only she could've pulled off. Yes, there was a good chance she'd stolen nothing of value, and an equally good chance that Cosimo would now be even angrier that we stole his papers. But on the other hand, if we got anything even remotely useful, we could blackmail him right back if he ever figured out who had robbed him.

"I've been trying to translate to see what everything means, but I'm not getting very far," she admitted.

I tugged Giada's legs across my lap, needing as much contact with her as possible after fearing the worse earlier. "Let me see." I spent the next few minutes reviewing the papers. With each document I skimmed, my heart beat faster.

I must have been grinning, because Giada asked, "Did I get whatever he was blackmailing you about?"

"No," I said, not bothering to tell her that such information wouldn't have actually been that useful since he could still have another copy, or at least remember whatever was in it. Her lips formed a pout right as I continued. "But this is better. I'm pretty sure this is information we could use to prove he committed tax fraud," I said, holding up most of the documents. "And this," I continued, waving a separate paper, "Is dirt he was using to blackmail the Gambino family."

"So I did good?" she asked, tentatively happy.

"No, you were very, very, very bad, and you are never to do anything like that ever again for any reason," I said. "But you did walk out with enough info to get Cosimo off our backs for good."

Giada squealed and I kissed her again.

"I'm going to call Tony and have him and the guys meet me here," I said. "So we only have twenty minutes tops to celebrate."

Tony confirmed what I'd suspected, that the information we now held was valuable. But we also decided not to tell Cosimo we had it, at least not for a little while. Hopefully, he'd be too focused on his dumb party to even realize he'd been robbed until Giada and I were back in the U.S., and by that point, he'd probably have had dozens of other potential thieves in his office and would never think to blame Giada.

I was desperate for a day off, but that wasn't in the cards. The next day, we were holding a memorial service for my papà. Most of the family had come to the U.S. for his actual funeral, but Mamma felt it was important to honor him here on his homeland, too. I agreed, and I hoped the event would offer us all some much-needed closure.

Giada was feeling good most of the day and stayed by my side, squeezing my hand in between each guest we greeted, and squeezing my butt whenever no one was looking.

I'd stayed up most of the night stressing about the speech to give, and in the end, I went with the truth. I talked about my papà, his values, and the way he recognized that the people by his side would always be his most valuable resource.

"That's probably the most important lesson he ever taught me, that at the end of the day, who you choose to surround yourself with will determine the life you lead and the legacy you leave." I paused, swallowing the lump in my throat at the realization that the one time my papà had screwed up, and accidentally brought the wrong person into his inner circle, he'd paid for his mistake with his life.

"I'm proud to be a Marino, and I'm eager to continue the legacy built by my papà," I concluded.

The audience clapped, then Giada rushed to my side, kissing me as if no one was watching. Well-wishers trickled into my parents' old house until well past dinner time. I socialized as long as I could stand it, then spotted Tomasso and my mother.

I led them into my papà's old office and, for the first time, I sunk into the worn leather chair. I rested my hands on the edge of the polished mahogany desk and inhaled slowly. Sitting at his old chair, in his favorite room of the house, I could almost smell my papà. I could still picture him perfectly, and his voice echoed through my mind almost nonstop. But this was different. This memory was softer, more loving. And for the first time, it occurred to me that my papà may not have been so terrible after all.

Well, to be sure, he wasn't a stellar human, good husband, or loving father. But he had lived his life according to the morals he'd believed to matter. And in so doing, he'd inadvertently shown me a different way. I didn't have to run the business like he would, treat my wife like he would, or raise my kids like he would. I could continue my papà's legacy without following directly in his footsteps.

I cleared my throat and gazed up to my mom and her apparent lover. "You have my blessing to date, marry, or whatever it is you want," I said, registering my mother's complete shock at my words. "And Tomasso, I understand what you were trying to tell me about the questions you both have about my DNA, but I'm not taking any tests. Salvatore Marino was my papà in every way that matters. I'm not going to disrespect his memory by questioning that now." I turned to Tomasso. I sensed a hint of sadness in his eyes, but he remained still and stoic.

"Tomasso, I appreciate everything you did for me growing up, and I'm open to building a relationship with you now. You're welcome to keep working for the Marino family as long as you want, and if you'd like, my children will call you nonno."

I paused, letting them both struggle with a moment of confusion at my offer for Tomasso to be a grandfather. Then I continued. "Giada and I wanted to share some news with you."

I called into the hall for my wife, then waited until she joined us in the office, smiling nervously. She handed my mom and Tomasso each a different ultrasound photo.

"We're having twins," I explained. "In early March."

They both flew from their seats, overflowing with excitement. They each hugged me, then Giada, and then I remembered the other important bit.

"Please keep this news to yourself. We decided to wait until after Angelo is back from his honeymoon to tell the Contis."

My mother smirked even more at the realization that she was the first to know.

We spent a few more minutes celebrating, then decided we

should rejoin the rest of the gathering, since we were technically hosting.

Tomasso reached for my arm, holding me back as we stepped out of the office. "For what it's worth, I think your papà would be proud of you. And I am, too. You've grown into a better man than either of us could have ever hoped, and you're going to be a great father."

I inhaled sharply at his words, then nodded my thanks. "I'll be out in a minute," I said, returning to the desk the moment he shut the door.

Alone in the office, the memory of my papà was even stronger. I wondered if somehow, he was there, watching me from whatever version of the afterlife held him now. I reached into the drawer where he'd always kept his secret stash of bourbon and poured a few sips into a crystal glass. I raised the glass to the ceiling. "Cheers, papà. Saluti."

And as I swallowed the syrupy liquid, I wiped a solitary tear from the corner of my eye.

Giada

The next three weeks flew by in a blur. The day after the celebration of life for Salvatore Marino, Luca attended some top-secret meeting with all the Marino family guys based in Italy so they could officially swear their loyalty to him.

One day later, we attended my brother's wedding. I still knew next-to-nothing about his bride, Catalina, but she was pretty and seemed nice. Both Angelo and Catalina appeared uncomfortable and stiff the entire wedding day, which Matteo insisted was just wedding jitters. Luca remained convinced that something else entirely was going on, but I supposed we'd have to wait and see what exactly that was.

Two days after the wedding, Luca and I flew down to Palermo, reunited with Alessio, then repeated the whole loyalty ceremony there. Luca figured he needed ten days in Palermo to organize all of his business matters before flying home with me. Feeling generous and eager to lounge on the beach in the sunshine, I agreed to a solid two weeks.

When he and Alessio couldn't be with me, Luca asked Roberto to keep an eye on me. That fact amused me to no end, since Roberto had been my babysitter on my very first trip to Palermo with Luca, back before we were truly a couple again. At the time, I hadn't known anyone was watching me, which led to a few awkward moments involving me sunbathing topless. I reminded Roberto of the incident and he merely blushed.

Oh well.

As long as I stayed hydrated, I felt pretty good lounging on the beach. Over the past week, I'd found I could go longer in between bouts of nausea, and there were fewer days where I needed a long nap just to make it through dinner.

A week into our time in Palermo, Matteo called. After a few minutes of small talk, his tone changed.

"Listen, I was calling to tell you some news, actually. I was going to wait until you were home to tell you in person, but I didn't want to piss you off again by springing it on you like we did with Angelo's wedding news."

My skin prickled with unease as I tried to decipher what he was saying. The words "news" and "Angelo" repeated in my head, and then it hit me.

"Angelo's having a baby!" I guessed, already confident in my conclusion.

Luca gazed up from his laptop, and nodded, his expression clearly conveying the "I told you so" he was refraining from speaking aloud.

Matteo was silent.

"Matteo? That's it, right? You're calling to tell me about the newest Conti baby."

An awkward chuckle escaped his lips. "Well, yes, but—"

"I knew it! You guys are all such terrible liars. That was the only explanation for the shotgun wedding." I pictured the bride's unease throughout the ceremony. "Oh my God, and that's why Catalina seemed so uncomfortable. Morning sickness is a bitch!"

Luca cringed, and I realized my mistake, quickly adding, "I mean, I've heard."

Matteo didn't seem to pick up on my slipup. "No, Giada, listen. Catalina isn't pregnant. Trust me."

"What?"

"Yeah, um, Annie Patras is though."

Stunned, I had nothing to say for a solid minute. I knew Angelo had made questionable decisions in the past, but this was extreme, even for him.

"Wait, so you're saying Angelo married someone else knowing Adrian's sister was pregnant?"

"I…well, I mean Angelo didn't know," Matteo said.

"God, he's such a sleaze. Does Catalina know?"

"No, Giada, you misunderstood. Annie isn't pregnant with Angelo's baby. She's pregnant with mine."

I fell silent for a second time in as many minutes.

"Giada?"

"How did Annie get pregnant with your baby?" I asked, dumbstruck.

Luca's eyes widened.

"Well, I mean in the usual way…" my brother said.

"Wait, you're dating Annie?"

"It was casual."

"Clearly," I replied sarcastically.

"She didn't want to tell anyone."

I blew out a sigh. Then, I realized this meant my babies would have cousins. "What's her due date?"

"Uhh January"

"Aww. Well, congratulations, I guess."

He laughed. "Thanks. I just found out when we got back home, so it's all still new to me. Adrian's known for weeks, though."

I wondered if he'd known sooner, like when he drove me to Missouri. I supposed it didn't matter.

I congratulated him again, and he thanked me. Just as I was about to hang up, he added, "Giada? It's a girl."

I squealed so loud that Luca covered his ears.

I couldn't wait to get home to tell everyone our news. Our ultrasound was scheduled for our second full day back, and the doctor thought we'd be able to learn the sex of the babies then. I was so excited.

CHAPTER 28

Luca

I buried myself in work our first day back in the States, planning to spend every second of the next day with my wife and our beautiful babies.

The ultrasound appointment was at ten am, and I was every bit as nervous as Giada was excited. The nurse ran some labs on Giada then checked her blood pressure and weight. After happily announcing that Giada was nearly back to her pre-pregnancy weight thanks to the morning sickness finally dissipating for the most part, she and Giada chatted about the weather and the upcoming holidays.

As Giada lay back on the ultrasound table, I squeezed her hand, wondering how she remained so calm while I felt like my heart might burst from running so fast. Giada turned to face me, then giggled at the loud crinkling sounds of the paper sheet beneath her. Somehow, that quick look from her calmed me, just like she probably knew it would.

An hour later, I felt even more relaxed. The ultrasound had revealed two healthy babies and absolutely nothing of concern.

We'd met with the doctor after, and she too assured us that everything looked great. So, we'd headed to Giada's favorite restaurant to celebrate. We ordered our food, and then Giada pulled out an oversized notebook stuffed with colorful tabs and stickers.

"What is that monstrosity?"

"It's a pregnancy planner," she replied, as if that were the most mundane thing in the world. Thankfully, she read the confusion on my face and elaborated further. "There's a countdown of all the important things we need to do before the babies are born, and then of course there's a tracker for all the stuff we need. I figured we could start on the registry today."

"In Italy, it's considered bad luck to buy things for the baby before he's born."

"Well, in our family, it's bad luck to make your wife wait to start shopping until she's a sleep-deprived, hormonal mess, stuck at home with two babies."

I nodded. "We can buy everything today."

Giada smiled, then explained the concept of a registry to me. I supposed it made sense, although I doubted my close relatives would appreciate being told exactly what they could and couldn't buy for the babies. But I kept that to myself.

"I figure the boys should share a nursery at first, but then I'd like them to have their own rooms by the time they're…" Giada's voice trailed off as she gazed up at me. "What?"

I shook my head, still grinning widely. "Boys," I repeated. "You just said it so casually."

Giada bit her lip, and a moment later, a tear slipped out of her eye. I slid out of the booth and scooted in beside her, wrapping my arms around her and pressing a kiss to her head.

"Were you hoping for girls?" I asked. "Or one of each?"

Giada hesitated before answering. "I would've been happy either way, but I was so relieved when they said they're both boys. We could have a girl next time, but—"

My laughter cut her off. "You swore you'd never do this again," I reminded her.

She shrugged. "I was exaggerating. Morning sickness wasn't that bad."

I suppressed a chuckle, amazed at how quickly she'd forgotten the misery she'd endured for weeks on end.

"Can you imagine how different your childhood would have been if you had a brother by your side the whole time? Even now, if you had someone else to bear the burden with the business?" Giada continued.

I nodded. "Yeah. Alessio said the same thing when he found out it was twins. They'll always have each other."

I returned to my side of the table as the waiter delivered our meals, then happily planned an afternoon of shopping.

"So what about names?" Giada asked as we pulled into the driveway that evening. She had to be exhausted, but she'd shown no signs of slowing down since the ultrasound.

"You didn't like the list we made on the plane?"

"We didn't narrow it down very much. Now that we need at least four solid boy names—"

"Four?"

"Yes, a first and middle name for each boy. Plus maybe an extra in case we decide his name doesn't suit him when he's born."

I considered that. "But if we don't decide on the actual name before they're born, the doctors and nurses will keep calling them Baby A and Baby B," I reminded her.

She sighed. "True. Okay, we should name them both. Ooh! We could tell my parents the names when we see them tomorrow!"

I chuckled at her enthusiasm but shook my head. "Nope. That is one Italian tradition we should follow. No one but us gets to know the name until the boys are born."

Giada considered that for a moment, then smiled. "Our little secret. I like it."

We started into the house and she squealed loudly, causing me to jump.

"I'm so excited to start decorating the nursery. Oh my gosh, and getting maternity clothes! I'm going to need a whole new wardrobe."

Giada's excitement was contagious, and we were both still in such a good mood the next day, that I decided to knock out one potentially unpleasant task before the dinner at the Conti manor.

"You don't have to come," I told Giada, for the thousandth time.

"I haven't seen Jacob in months," she reminded me. "Besides, I can hang out with him while you chat with Carla."

I sighed, and conceded. Jacob was my half-brother, and an all-around cool kid, despite his mom, Carla, being a lying tramp who tried to scam me by telling me he was my kid. Since learning the truth, I'd been giving Carla money for Jacob's care because I agreed that it was best if my papà not find out about his love child. In exchange for the money, I got to spend time with Jacob on occasion and make sure Carla was taking good care of him.

By all accounts, she was. Carla may have been a crappy human in all other respects, but she seemed to be a good mom. She loved Jacob, and I sensed she was genuinely trying to do her best with him.

I'd half expected her to make a grab for money when I told her my papà had passed, but she hadn't. Legally, I suspected Jacob might be entitled to something, even though my papà had specified his personal items were all to go to my mother and his businesses went fully to me, his successor, regardless of the existence of any other children. I had asked the lawyer about that language, wondering if my papà had known he had other kids, but the lawyer said it was standard in such situations, where a parent has specifically trained one kid to take over the business.

Anyway, even without the residential properties that my mom kept, I was now a very wealthy man. And while part of me reasoned I'd earned my wealth by virtue of all the shit I'd had to endure growing up—and all the shit I'd have to keep doing on my papà's behalf, I also realized I had money just because I was born a Marino. And even though he didn't have the official name, Jacob was a Marino, too.

We met Carla and Jacob at an indoor gym. Giada took Jacob by the hand and entertained him with a haphazard game of basketball, while I spoke with Carla. I told her about the pregnancy, but not that we were expecting twins, or their gender. And then I told her I'd set up a trust for Jacob. He'd receive quarterly payments throughout childhood, then a lump sum on his eighteenth birthday and twenty-first birthday. He'd receive the remainder of the trust when he turned twenty-five.

I hoped the money would be enough for him to go to college and then someday to have a down payment for a house or something. I wanted Jacob to have a normal childhood and to ease into adulthood without the burdens poor kids face—but also without the unique burdens I faced. Really, I wanted Jacob to have the opportunities I wished I'd had…enough money to be comfortable but not to fully support him without him working, and no obligation to join an all-consuming family business.

"So now that you're having your own kids, you just don't want to see him anymore? Real nice, Luca. You're like an uncle to him," Carla snapped.

I handed her an envelope. "There's a letter from the lawyer that explains all the terms of the trust, but one of those terms is that I still get to hang out with him a few times each year."

She appeared contrite, but didn't apologize. "What if I let it slip who his father was?"

I bristled at the casual way she referred to my papà in the past tense, but played it off with a shrug. "It won't hurt me, and Jacob won't lose the money. But if I were you, I wouldn't tell anyone. The Marino family still has enemies, and the best way you can protect Jacob is by keeping quiet."

Carla sighed, then turned to watch Giada with Jacob. By the time we were ready to leave, she actually thanked me and congratulated us on the pregnancy.

Small miracles, I supposed.

Giada

*D*inner at my childhood home was not exactly the cozy family affair we'd anticipated.

"Just your parents and brothers, huh?" Luca said, maneuvering his new Alfa Romeo in between a Ferrari and a Porsche. His gaze narrowed as he spotted Adrian's Jag.

"He probably drove Annie," I said.

Luca nodded stiffly, and I reached over and squeezed his thigh. "If you don't want to see him…" I began.

"It's fine. Let's go share our news." Luca lifted my hand to his lips and kissed softly. Then he smoothed his hand over my abdomen and beamed.

The front door swung open before we started up the steps. My aunt Bianca grinned widely and held open her arms for a hug. She greeted both Luca and me, then shooed us into the house, where my other aunts, uncles, and a few cousins, all similarly greeted us like they hadn't seen us in years.

I spotted my mom and made a beeline to her.

"Hi sweetheart!" she said, shoving a serving spoon into a massive casserole dish of baked pasta. "Do you want red? Mia, pour Giada a glass of red," she ordered my cousin, without waiting for my response.

"No, mom it's fine. I don't need wine. I just…well I thought this was going to be just the six of us." I caught a glimpse of Angelo's wife out the corner of my eye and corrected myself. "Err, seven."

Mom flung her hot-pad-clad hand in the air. "Well, the family here hadn't yet met Catalina, so we thought it was a good time for that. Here, carry this to the table please." She thrust an over-sized salad bowl into my hands.

I barely made it out of the kitchen before Luca snatched the bowl from me. "You don't need to be carrying heavy things," he scolded.

"It's lettuce," I said, although to be fair, it was enough lettuce for like thirty people, in a thick crystal bowl. And as I gazed across the room, I happened to notice Annie was just sitting in a chair, relaxing. I started over to her, but had barely said anything more than congratulations when my mom called everyone to the table.

I eyed Annie enviously as she rose to her feet. She looked unmistakably, yet adorably, pregnant. As far as I could tell, she hadn't put on weight anywhere other than her belly and breasts, but the curve of her abdomen was distinctly baby and not merely bloat, like mine seemed to be at the moment.

I took my seat at the table by Luca, and devoured the deli-cious, Italian meal. Like during most big family gatherings, it was near-impossible to get a word in, and a collection of smaller side-conversations dominated the table. Everyone appeared enamored with Catalina, including Angelo, which I supposed made sense since he'd married her. But any doubts I'd had after watching them throughout their actual wedding were now erased.

I turned my attention to my other brother, who was grinning at whatever Annie had just said. I wasn't sure what would end up happening with the two of them, but based on how happy they both seemed, I wouldn't be surprised if they walked down the aisle next.

Luca's hand rubbed soothing circles on my upper back, drawing my gaze back to him. He raised his wine glass to his lips, wiggled his eyebrows, then sipped. I bit back a giggle, not because anything was particularly funny, but just because I felt so much emotion that it seemed close to bubbling over. Here I was, surrounded by all these people, and as loud and crazy as they all seemed at time, they all loved me, and they all made me happy in their own ways.

My mom stood, signaling that the ladies would begin clearing the table. I shot to my feet, casting a nervous glance to Luca as if to signal that it was now or never. He gave an imperceptible nod, and I spoke.

"Actually, Mom, if we could hold off on dessert for just a minute, I um…" I paused, and exchanged an uneasy look with Luca. "Well, Luca and I wanted to share some news with you all."

My mother shrieked and clutched her chest like she was having a heart attack. Bianca screeched. My cousin Giulia cheered. I hadn't even actually said the news out loud, and already everyone was congratulating us. Luca stood, accepting the praise and congratulations from everyone, along with an oddly sloppy kiss from my aunt Sofia.

In the midst of the chaos, I caught Adrian's eye. He was staring at me, a sincere smile on his face. He mouthed the word "congrats," and I mouthed back my gratitude.

"Do you know yet if you're having a boy or a girl?" Annie asked when the noise level finally dropped to a tolerable level.

Luca cleared his throat and grinned. "You tell them, amore," he said to me.

I squeezed his hand. "We're actually having twins. And they're both boys," I said, tempted to cover my ears to ward off any permanent hearing damage from the excited cheers and shrieks from the entire family.

After a solid hour of celebratory hugs from the family, a delicious dessert that I could barely chew in between dozens of questions about the pregnancy, my mom launched into an Oscar-worthy tear-filled speech, lamenting how happy she was to see all of her kids settling down. Then, all the ladies—except for me and Annie—started clearing the table while the men headed off to the den to gossip and drink whiskey. My dad grabbed Luca by the shoulder, signaling that he, too, would be joining in this family tradition.

"And I've got to pee again," Annie said with a laugh as she walked past me.

I smiled, not minding the silence one bit. I leaned back in the chair, closed my eyes, and pressed my palms over my abdomen. I'd been feeling tiny flutters, almost like the sensation of butterfly wings flapping against me, for a couple weeks now. And I was convinced that any day now, I'd be able to feel the movement from the outside, too. I couldn't wait for Luca to be able to enjoy our boys' kicks too.

"You look happy," a voice said, snapping me from my thoughts.

I gazed up to see Adrian. He sat beside me, smiling.

"I am," I said. "We both are."

"I'm glad," he replied. And I didn't doubt for one minute that he meant it. "You know, maybe you should name one of them after me. We are basically going to be family, what with my sister having your brother's baby and all."

I giggled. "Luca would never agree to use a Greek name for our boys," I teased.

Adrian

I was exhausted by the time "dinner" finally concluded, although I hadn't exactly exerted myself. Mostly, I'd just observed.

I'd watched Annie with Matteo, trying to predict what the future held for them. Whatever their next step ended up being, I wasn't worried. I could tell Matteo loved my sister, and I figured he'd probably take good care of her even if she never agreed to settle down with him.

I'd also observed Angelo and Catalina. Admittedly, their relationship had fascinated me from the moment I heard they were getting married—days after Angelo lamented the pathetic state of his dating life. Now that I knew what had actually led to their union, and how their relationship had transformed since then, I was even more intrigued. Unfortunately, I couldn't divulge the secrets I'd learned. That was Angelo and Catalina's story to share.

And of course, I'd also watched Luca with Giada, even before they shared their news, but more after. Honestly, I should've figured it out sooner. The signs were all there. Not with Luca, of course. That man had no tells. I'd often heard that men became more protective when their partners were pregnant, but Luca had always treated Giada like a precious, yet fragile treasure.

Giada was the one who had changed. Seemingly overnight, the naïve, indulgent and impulsive girl I'd once dated had matured. She hadn't become jaded or any less generous or joyful, but now there was a peacefulness about her that had been missing when she was younger. The Giada I'd met back in college had been so full of love, and I truly couldn't think of anyone better equipped to love two babies at once.

I'd even watched Marco throughout the meal as he calmly surveyed the kingdom he'd built. He'd surrounded himself with a family, both of blood and by his own choosing. He'd spent his life teetering on the line between right and wrong, gambling on the gray area just past morality. One thing was for sure. Marco's bets had paid off.

Gazing around, seeing the opulent room filled with people bursting with happiness and love, I couldn't say I disagreed with Marco's choices. Nor could I remember why I had so many reservations about my own.

Matteo offered to drive my sister back to her place, so I asked Angelo if he had a minute to chat before he headed out.

Angelo glanced at his new wife, but she was cheerfully chatting with Giada like the two of them had been best friends for ages.

"Sure, Patras. Out back?"

I nodded and led the way to the patio. We sat in the corner, at one of the oversized dining tables that would probably be moved to storage for the winter any day now.

"What's up?" he asked.

"I'll only take a minute of your time," I began, suddenly nervous. "I just wanted to tell you that I've been thinking about your offer from a while back."

"You have?" Angelo quirked a brow. "I figured you'd forgot all about that."

I shook my head. "No, there's just been a lot going on."

Angelo chuckled. "Ain't that the truth."

"Anyway, if the offer's still on the table…"

"It is."

"Well, then I accept," I said. "I want in."

Angelo's dark eyes peered back at me for a solid minute before his lips parted in a wide smile. "Good decision. Welcome to the family, Patras."

The End

EPILOGUE

Four Months Later

Luca

I started towards the front door, already bracing myself
for the chaos about to ensue.

Alessio skidded to a stop between me and the front door,
shaking his head. "Go sit by your wife. I'll get the door."

"Grazie," I murmured, turning back to the living room. I
rounded the corner and stopped in my tracks at the sight of my
wife.

Giada sat in the massive armchair, one boy in each arm and a
huge grin on her face as she peered down at them both. She'd
purchased the oversized chair specifically so she'd have some-
place comfy to lounge on this level of the house while she fed the
babies, but we'd jokingly called it the "throne" since it was so
grand.

Now, more than ever, Giada resembled a princess. Her dark

hair tumbled in loose waves over her shoulders and her eyes sparkled in a way that defied the sleep deprivation she'd experienced.

Giada was so perfectly suited for motherhood. So far, I wasn't so bad as a father, either. I didn't think I'd end up winning any parenting awards, but hey, who knew? Life was crazy like that. For instance, I wouldn't have thought it possible to ever love Giada more than I did a couple of months ago, but now, seeing her loving our boys, I swear my heart grew even more.

Giada gazed up and met my eye right before our families rushed in. We'd only been home from the hospital for about five hours, but that was apparently the longest we could hold off the masses.

After a surprisingly uneventful pregnancy, she'd gone into labor at exactly thirty-six weeks. We were nervous about complications from the early delivery, even though the doctor had warned us Giada was unlikely to make it to forty weeks with twins. Thankfully, the boys were both perfectly healthy and a decent weight for their gestational age.

Delivery had gone smoothly, but the doctors kept both Giada and the boys for a full week due to their mild prematurity. Our parents and siblings had seen the boys in the hospital, but Giada was eager for the rest of the family to meet them.

"Ohh," a feminine voice cooed behind me.

I turned to greet Annie, who rushed forward with her daughter in her hands, Matteo following behind.

Giada's smile widened, and she shifted to stand.

"Don't get up!" Annie and I both shouted at the same time.

Giada flashed us a playful grin, but stayed seated. Annie knelt in front of her, holding her daughter right in front of the boys.

"They're beautiful," Annie said. "Absolutely perfect."

Giada beamed proudly, then turned to her niece. "Miss Elena Olivia, I'd like to introduce you to your cousins. This is Gian Renzo and Benito Samuele."

"Or Benny and John, if your Italian is rusty," I said, smirking at my wife. We'd both wanted traditional names, but it was important to us that the boys could fit in on either continent.

"I'm learning Italian now," Annie said, standing up and handing Elena to Matteo so she could hold Gian.

"What? It's possible for an American woman to learn Italian?" I said in exaggerated teasing tone.

Giada wrinkled her nose and stuck out her tongue. God, she was adorable.

"Samuele after your uncle?" Angelo asked.

I nodded, loving that every time I heard the name, I'd think of the uncle who gave me the quaint cabin in the woods where Giada and I created some of my favorite core memories. Renzo was a nod to Lorenzo, but of course I'd never admit that to his face.

My mother-in-law reached for Benito, then handed him off to Angelo, arranging the child in his arms and then snapping a few photos of the duo. Finding herself with both hands free for once, Giada moved to stand, but this time, it was my mother who rushed forward and encouraged her to relax. She pressed a mug of tea into Giada's hands, then nodded approvingly when Giada sipped.

I stood beside Giada and watched as she gazed around the room, surveying her kingdom with a peaceful grace. Her hand flitted to her chest, as if she needed some physical reminder of how deeply intwined in her own heart each of these people were. That was where Giada's legacy would be, in the lives she'd nurtured, and the people she'd loved.

"What'cha looking at?" Alessio asked, sidling up to me.

"Just admiring my beautiful principessa on her throne," I replied, winking at Giada. She scowled, never having loved when we referred to her as the princess, in any language.

Alessio shook his head, then addressed Giada directly. "Oh

sweetheart, you are not the princess anymore. You are the queen."

She smiled at that, as did I.

"My queen," I added, scooting into the chair beside her. "And my tesoro."

Giada rest her head against my chest. "Ti amo Luca Marino."

My chest swelled like it always did when she spoke the one Italian phrase she knew well. Not that I didn't also enjoy hearing that the most beautiful woman loved me in English, too.

Her eyes drifted shut, and I let my own do the same. Even though we'd been in the hospital, with round the clock nursing help, we were both exhausted. We weren't naïve enough to think that would improve any time soon, but it was a good type of fatigue, almost like being too full after a delicious meal.

Around us, sounds of the adults' laughter and joyful chattering mixed with Elena's babbling and the coos from the twins, creating a beautiful symphony. I heard my mother singing an Italian nursery rhyme, and my smile widened. She'd truly blossomed in the past few months, transforming into a happier, more relaxed version of herself than I'd ever remembered as a child. Tomasso was good for her, I supposed.

I pictured my papà here, imagined Benito in his arms and not Angelo's. I tensed. Nothing about this scene felt right for Papà. Maybe he'd lived and died on the exact timeline he was supposed to. Maybe everything had happened for a reason after all.

Giada sighed and curled her fingers into my biceps, prompting me to open my eyes. She gazed up at me, her brown eyes twinkling mischievously. "I love that the boys have a cousin so close in age," she said. "We should time our next baby to be close in age to Angelo's first."

I nearly choked on my own breath. "Let's just see how we do with this batch first, okay baby?" I pressed my lips against her hair, inhaling the delicious scent of her strawberry shampoo, and confident that I would agree to a dozen babies back-to-back if that was what my angelic wife wanted.

ACKNOWLEDGMENTS

Phew- what an adventure this series has been! I've had the time of my life with these characters, and I can only hope you've enjoyed getting to know them.

Much thanks to my editor, Sarah, and my cover designer, Jeremy. Kim, thanks for always helping with my book summaries, and Lisa, for your input on all the covers.

If you haven't already checked out the prequels, I recommend you indulge yourself with Mafiosa Princess Beginnings and Becoming the Prince next. If you're all caught up, be sure to check out the spin-offs and novellas.

I always welcome emails from readers, and I try to reply to as many as I can. If you have friends who enjoy spicy reads, I'd appreciate you recommending Mafiosa Princess or any of my other works. But if you really want to help me or any of your other favorite indy authors, reviews make SUCH a difference.

And now, on to the next adventure!

ABOUT THE AUTHOR

Liza Malloy writes contemporary romance and women's fiction. She's a sucker for alpha males, bad boys, dimples, and muscles, and she can't resist a man in uniform. Liza loves creating worlds where her heroine discovers her own strength and finds her Happily Ever After. When Liza isn't reading or writing torrid love stories, she's a practicing attorney. Her other passions include gummy bears, jelly beans, and the occasional marathon. She lives in the Midwest with her four daughters and her own Prince Charming.

Visit her website at https://authorlizamalloy.wixsite.com/lizamalloy

Join her email list at http://eepurl.com/gnuROD

* 9 7 8 1 9 5 0 4 7 8 4 8 4 *